THE AFTERMATH OF DEVASTATION

The continuing voyages of HMS SURPRISE

ALAN LAWRENCE

I've sweltered in the Sargasso, mired with ne'er a breeze,
Voyaged o'er all the oceans, crossed the Seven Seas;
Shivered in South Atlantic waters, fighting fear and chill,
'midst towering bergs of ice; the memory lingers still;
I've sailed thru' hurricane and tempest, aboard the Dear Surprise,
Rushed in haste to quarters, when'er battle might arise;
In warm Greek waters, in the summer of 'twenty-four,
The Turk came out to fight us, four score of sail and more;
The prodigious fleet o' the world before us had appeared,
Close-hauled and closing, so slowly they neared;

Fire! The order at last, the readied guns roared;
From abeam all ships, fiery flame and shot poured;
'twas a long day we fought; firing shrapnel, grape and shell;
Carnage come upon us, the guns soon hot as hell;
Amidst the bloody fallen, the ship nigh on a wreck,
Men dying all about me, death stalked the deck;
The Turk raked by our broadside, at last he turned away;
Wounded, I feared I would ne'er see the end o' that day;
My eyes fixed upon the red horizon, the setting sun a'fire,
The barky shipping water, her prospects fearfully dire;

Long hours I lay in blood, water the sole consolation;
Dozens with the surgeons, all in fear and consternation;
To my maker, I was minded it was time to confess;
I strived for solace in sleep, before came welcome darkness;
I gazed at glowing heavens, lighting up the stormy night;
Marvelled at the skies, glorious infinity sparkling bright;
The full moon a friend above us, we struggled on for port;
Will we make it - grave uncertainty the constant thought;
And through all, I ne'er failed to thank the Good Lord above,
For bringing me safe home to Falmouth, the blessed place I love.

Making home
by Alan Lawrence

THE AFTERMATH OF DEVASTATION
The continuing voyages of HMS SURPRISE

Through many nations and many seas have I come;
To carry out these wretched funeral rites, brother;
That at last I may give you this final gift in death,
And that I might speak in vain to silent ashes,
Since fortune has borne you, yourself, away from me.
Oh, poor brother... snatched unfairly away from me;
Now, though, even these, which from antiquity and
in the custom of our parents, have been handed down,
a gift of sadness in the rites;
Accept them, flowing with many brotherly tears;
And for eternity, my brother, hail and farewell.

                      Gaius Valerius Catullus
                      84-54 BC

A tale of the struggle for Greek independence by
ALAN LAWRENCE

Mainsail Voyages Press Ltd, Publishers,
Bideford, Devonshire

www.mainsailvoyagespress.com

THE AFTERMATH OF DEVASTATION
The continuing voyages of HMS SURPRISE

This first edition is copyright (c) Alan Lawrence 2017. Published by Mainsail Voyages Press Ltd, Hartland Forest, Bideford, Devon, EX39 5RA. Alan Lawrence asserts the right to be identified as the author of this work in accordance with the Copyright, Designs and Patents Act 1988. The reader may note that this book is written by Alan Lawrence. It is not authorised, licensed or endorsed by Patrick O'Brian's family, agent or publishers. There is no association with any of those parties.

ISBN-13 978-1545136768

ISBN-10 1545136769

Typeset in Palatino Linotype 11 point.

All rights reserved. No part of this publication may be reproduced, stored in a retrieval system, or transmitted, in any form or by any means, electronic, mechanical, photocopying, recording or otherwise, without the prior permission of the publishers. Specifically, the author and publishers DO NOT consent to the scanning and/or digitalisation of this book in part or in whole by AMAZON or GOOGLE or any of their subsidiaries or associates, nor by any other entity or individual, which this author and publisher consider would be a flagrant breach of the copyright attaching to this book. This book is sold subject to the condition that it will not, by way of trade or otherwise, be lent, re-sold, hired out or otherwise circulated without the publisher's prior consent in any form of binding or cover other than that in which it is published and without a similar condition being imposed on the subsequent purchaser. A CIP catalogue record for this title is available from the British Library.

Cover painting by Ivan Aivazovsky: 'Sailing off the coast of Crimea in the moonlit night';
Photograph courtesy of www.russianpaintings.net;
Cover comment by Ilene Bennett, Pennsylvania;
The Reef Knot graphic in this book is courtesy of and copyright (c) United States Power Squadrons 2006

The continuing voyages of HMS SURPRISE,
the series:

The Massacre of Innocents (first edition 2014,
second edition 2017)

Freedom or Death (2017)
was originally published split within the lengthy first editions of the preceding and succeeding titles, both of which have been abridged for the second editions

The Fireships of Gerontas (first edition 2016,
second edition 2017)

The Aftermath of Devastation (2017)

THE AFTERMATH OF DEVASTATION
The continuing voyages of HMS SURPRISE
A FOREWORD BY THE AUTHOR

In this, the fourth book of my series, I have continued the story of both actual historical events and the fictional adventures of my characters directly following on from the end of my prior book. That one concluded with the near miraculous survival of *HMS Surprise* after enduring the very real hurricane of the night of 22nd/23rd December 1824 as she returned home from Greece across Biscay and came into the home waters of the Western Approaches. This story describes the aftermath, in terms of both the severe damage to the ship and the insidious mental corrosion inflicted upon its tired men.

I would like to express warm thanks again to my own, now veteran crew of helpers: to Elaine Vallianou for her encouragement, Geoff Fisher for the cover finalisation, Ivan Gorshkov for the Ivan Aivazovsky cover photograph, Don Fiander for permission to use the reef knot graphic, Don Seltzer for general sailing advice, Peter Collett for particular technical advice on entering the Carrick Roads in adverse weather conditions, David Hayes (webmaster at *www.historicnavalfiction.com*), and my Sally for her unstinting support; all of the above have stayed aboard with the enthusiasm and technical help they provided for earlier stories. My enduring thanks are offered to a generous bunch of shipmates once again. Last but not least, thanks are due to George Loukas for invaluable help with research and translation of Greek texts on the subjects of the Egyptian landing on Sphacteria and the escape of the brig "*Aris*" from the bay of Navarino.

There are a great many books about historical conflicts, of both factual record and fictional story. The former are generally written with the emphasis on the detail of historical accuracy, of particular events, whilst the latter are essentially stories of the fertile imagination, with fictional participants for the most part. In my own work I have kept close to historical events, shaped my stories around them with much factual detail, whilst striving all the time to offer brief political perceptions of those times, but never forgetting that in fiction the interest, the value lies with the warmth and credibility of the characters on the page.

The poem on page 168 was written by Edward Capern who was known as "the Rural Postman of Bideford".

Several of Mark Twain's memorable and witty quips are uttered, generally with minor amendment, by Lieutenant Pickering, ship's wag.

At the end of this book is a glossary of contemporary words occurring within the story with which the reader new to the naval historical world may be unfamiliar.

This book is dedicated to the serving men and women of the Royal Navy.

'Give you joy, shipmate! Come aboard! Voyage with HMS Surprise! Share her crew's reminiscences in familiar old haunts and revel too in their exciting new adventures. Come aboard! Swiftly now, there is not a moment to be lost!'

Alan Lawrence   *April 2017*

THE AFTERMATH OF DEVASTATION
The continuing voyages of HMS SURPRISE
HISTORICAL NOTE

The great Bay of Navarino is famous in history for being the place where the destruction of the Ottoman fleet in 1827 by Allied squadrons from Britain, France and Russia occurred. However, it is less well known for a much earlier conflict, in 425 BC when the Athenians invaded the island of Sphacteria (which forms the west side of the bay) to defeat the Spartans, a very influential battle in the Greek Peloponnesian wars.

Much less well known than either of the above two battles is the invasion of Sphacteria by Egyptian troops in 1825 (the subject of the closing chapters of this book) when Ibrahim, their general, determined that the island was the key to capturing the bay, the town of Pylos on its eastern side having endured his land siege whilst being resupplied by sea.

The miraculous escape of the Greek brig "*Aris*" from the Bay of Navarino on the 8th May* 1825 is something of a legend in Greek revolutionary history. It is commemorated by the celebrated Greek artist Konstantinos Volanakis with his famous painting "The Sortie of *Aris*".

That the brig did escape from dozens of Ottoman ships blockading the bay exit and that she did so in a near total lack of wind whilst being bombarded for four hours or more by many of those enemy ships must count as something of a minor miracle, but it was also a feat of naval tenacity and courage that must surely be one of the greatest in military history, the odds against her, against surviving being simply staggering.

* All dates referred to within this book are of the Gregorian calendar.

* * *

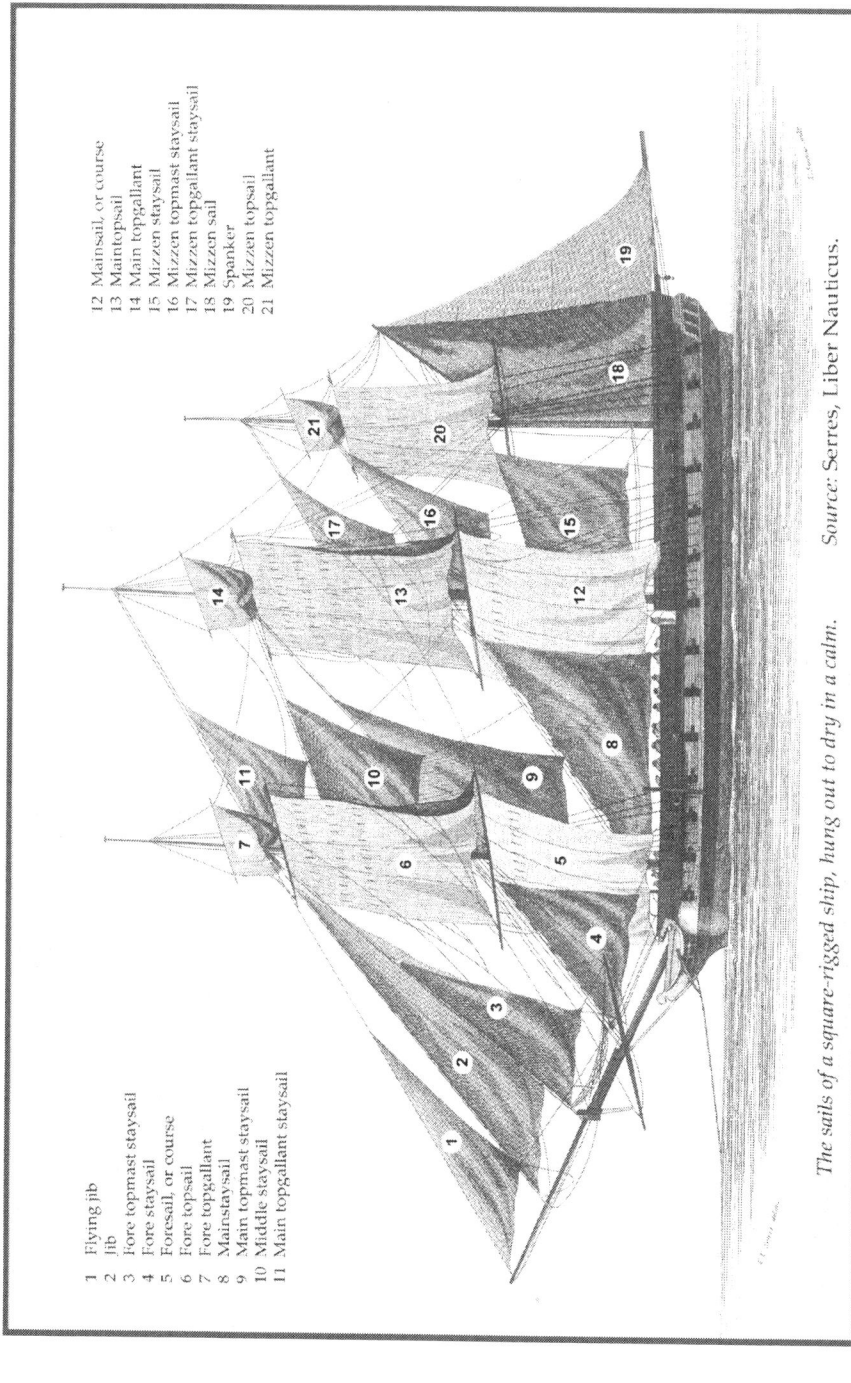

The sails of a square-rigged ship, hung out to dry in a calm.   *Source: Serres, Liber Nauticus.*

1 Flying jib
2 Jib
3 Fore topmast staysail
4 Fore staysail
5 Foresail, or course
6 Fore topsail
7 Fore topgallant
8 Mainstaysail
9 Main topmast staysail
10 Middle staysail
11 Main topgallant staysail
12 Mainsail, or course
13 Maintopsail
14 Main topgallant
15 Mizzen staysail
16 Mizzen topmast staysail
17 Mizzen topgallant staysail
18 Mizzen sail
19 Spanker
20 Mizzen topsail
21 Mizzen topgallant

Chapter One

Tuesday 23rd November 1824   14:30   *Falmouth*

The distant frigate was exceedingly slow-moving, close-hauled whilst striving to sail north off the Cornish coast and, as was plain to any watcher on the land with the least familiarity with wind and tide, she was struggling to make the most modest of progress in the weak north-westerly, now faded to little more than an impudent breeze after the stupendous ferocity of the prior night's destructive tempest. She had first been sighted an hour after the low noon zenith by a cold and shivering observer atop Pendennis Castle, the youngster gazing with excited eyes through a borrowed glass, his chilled hands near numbed to all feeling, his racing thoughts filled with anticipation, with precious hopes and anxious expectations, an obscure glimpse of what were conceivably topgallants on the far horizon first registering as the ship approached Manacle Point and its treacherous rock outliers from the south. Small and indistinct in the faint, flickering, grey light of overcast skies, illuminated by a weak winter sun and almost surreal within a hazy and shifting definition, her wavering image to the fanciful mind appeared more akin to some ghostly apparition emerging as if from the timeless mists of legend and ancient folklore. The enduring uncertainty of the large gathering of anxious local watchers, growing in number every minute, many visibly fretting and all anxious as to her identity, persisted uncomfortably, worrying many. The vessel's image was confusing, all certainty obscured by her having only two masts: for her mizzen, it had been remarked, was seemingly entirely absent; but then came the pleasure of clarity, rising conviction slowly crystallising to sublimely satisfying certainty, overwhelming relief clawing its way to the fore of apprehensive minds as her topsails, courses and finally her hull emerged in a rare shaft of bright sunlight from the murky confluence of cloudy sky and dark grey water: a frigate it surely was; the barky was returning. The dear *Surprise* was coming home!

The excitement in Falmouth consequently had become general and was rising by the hour, a veritable turmoil of conflicting feelings abounding throughout the small town, the thoughts of many being suffused with tremulous and conflicting feelings of joy, trepidation, exultation, fear, jubilation and anxiety: every variety of emotional fire burning in minds plunged into excitement and confusion, every family blessed by surging hope and taunted by bilious foreboding; both sentiments raging through the thoughts of all in the most extreme of measures. All afternoon, the constant flow of reports of the ship's painstakingly slow progress across Falmouth Bay had reached the townsfolk from the fascinated spectators on the heights of Pendennis Castle; since then the town had ceased to do anything at all in practical terms, had simply downed tools, its populace wholly seized by, focussed upon and determined to await the sensational arrival. Thousands of Falmouth folk were now praying with rapidly beating hearts and racing minds for her safe passage to port within the dwindling few hours of wintry daylight.

On her quarterdeck, although it was Lieutenant Pickering's watch, all her officers had gathered about the port side, the so welcome sense of relief, of homecoming rising within every one of them; for in the violence and horror of the prior night's hurricane all had doubted they would see this joyful day. Indeed, the ship had escaped catastrophe by a hair's breadth: blasted so far over by the titanic wind force of the hurricane as she weared away from perilous beam seas that her yard tips were in the raging waters; only the desperate and superhuman efforts of the few on the quarterdeck manically cutting away the drag of the mizzen to enable her to complete her turn downwind and thus allowing the ship to right herself had saved her. The unmitigated fear and horror of those terrifying minutes was indelibly engraved within the hearts and minds of every man aboard, and doubtless would never be forgotten for as long as they drew breath.

The master, Jeremiah Prosser, a Falmouth man, gazed all about him from near the helm where he was standing with the officers, studiously placing his understanding of position in the context of the many and familiar landmarks of the coast: Porthoustock strand left astern, Pencra Head off the port quarter, Porthallow abeam, Nare Point and Rosemullion Head off the port bow and Pendennis Point seven miles fine on the bow; and thence, as they all knew well, it was a little less than two final miles to her intended anchorage and undoubtedly very many happy and joyful reunions. 'The wind a north-westerly, 'tis a cussed, wildering passage into the Roads, sir,' offered the master, 'Thankfully 'tis weak.'

'We have precious little choice, Mr Prosser; she is taking ever more water and will not long endure out here in seas stronger than a millpond,' replied Captain Patrick O'Connor, the steel edge of his own enduring trepidation evident in his voice. He shivered, pulled tighter his griego, no warmth in the low sun of the frigid afternoon, the fine rain returning and the biting, raw wind gusting a very little, the air chill, piercing.

'Well, sir, 'tis a mixed blessing...' the master resumed, anxious that his captain should understand his dilemma, 'the wind so weak, the barky so slow, 'tis a devil to be sure she will tack. The Lizard is a plentifully dangerous shore, sir. Thankfully we'se east of it, and the north-westerly is a blessing, no doubt, but after we clear the Manacles, 'tis the Shark's Fin reef and its outliers next - look there, sir - fine on the larboard bow, the white water, 'tis Gwinges, Mean Garah and Morah rocks.'

'I see them, Mr Prosser.' The shortest of pause, 'Mr Macleod, helm a point to starboard if you will.'

'I venture an hour and a half, sir, and we will approach the Roads,' declared the master.

'No doubt,' murmured Pat O'Connor, most uncomfortable in his understanding. 'Doubtless you will take her in through the western passage?'

'Aye sir, and keep her as far off the wind as we can until we are half the way to Saint Mawes. I venture she may make one tack... just the one without she falls in irons... and so we must bear past Castle Point and some way into the Roads afore she makes her turn.'

'Mr Prosser, she is all yours,' Pat murmured to the master, anxiety coursing through every fibre of his being and so plain in his voice, 'You will do me... that is to say *all of us*... the greatest favour if you will bring her home whilst we have light enough remaining to reach the quays.'

'Aye aye, sir. I believe you may count on that. Helm, starboard two points, Barton,' remarked Prosser, and after a minute, 'There it is, steady as she goes.'

'Call the line, Mr Macleod,' said Pat to his First.

'Aye aye, sir.' Duncan Macleod echoed the command to Timmins at the rail.

'By the mark three knots,' came back the shouted reply, Timmins' great pleasure resonating in his report, a wholly unconstrained smile broad across his face, not the least doubt within his own mind of Prosser's abilities.

'A trifle more than an hour, Simon,' declared Pat, striving for a tone of reassurance, to his silent, deathly pale companion standing alongside him and gazing over the rail. He was a man of modest stature, his clothing shabby, dried red-brown stains evident on his collar, all over his smock and down his breeches. 'The tide is with us... an hour and a half, no more, and I am persuaded we may step ashore in Falmouth town.'

'I rejoice to hear it, my dear; I do so,' murmured Doctor Simon Ferguson, ship's surgeon and O'Connor's longstanding close friend of many years, staring intently at the far land, unmoving, his thoughts relapsing into a tolerable meld of private contemplation and small hope.

The frigate had been keenly expected long before: her appearance had been awaited throughout every hour of the prior evening and all day since the brightening of the dawn, the emerging winter sun's welcome rays a harbinger of the collective hope soaring throughout the town, though with too its accompanying and unwelcome fellows of angst and agitation. The startling news of the frigate's unexpected return, believed likely to be on the 23rd or thereabouts, had reached Falmouth during the prior day, delivered by the elated crew of a mercurial messenger: *Surprise's* swift tender, *Eleanor*, a Garmouth-built schooner; and the stupendous tidings had spread like wildfire throughout the town, the Eleanors reporting that *Surprise* had last been sighted off Gibraltar when *Eleanor* separated from her; and so all the town was informed that she was homeward bound and had, presumably, been in the Western Approaches to the Channel during the calm and quietude preceding the great storm of the prior night and the morning. That Falmouth, exceptionally, had escaped the severe and widespread destruction inflicted upon numerous Cornish and Channel towns and villages generally, ports and small seafront harbours particularly, save for many a toppled chimney and thousands of lost roof slates, was because it had been protected from the wind's worst ravages by the low hill behind the town which, together with its adjacent promontory, was the fundamental safeguard of the inner harbour, a sure haven from the combined furies of Biscay's customarily south-westerly winds and long fetch seas at their ferocious worst. The catastrophe, as it had been described to be all along the Channel coast - for a tempest of such violence had never happened before in living memory - had left the port largely unscathed. That the storm had been the most extreme weather event ever recorded, phenomenal and utterly destructive, its violence unprecedented, not a single person in the town had the slightest doubt. The full force of the hurricane had been reached in the early hours, well before the dawn of the 23rd, but since noon, as if in heavenly apology, hardly a breeze had stirred the placid waters of the Channel, and every pilchard seiner and long liner persisting since the fishery had become so considerably diminished had ventured out in the opportune hours since.

'Simon,' asked Pat gently and with mellifluent affection, staring at his companion's rigid immobility, his introspective silence, his thoughts plainly a thousand miles away, 'how do you fare, old friend?'

A long minute passed before the reply was uttered, 'Tolerably relieved to be in contemplation of blissful *terra firma*.' The words were spoken very quietly, in a tone of deep dismay, his thoughts dwelling on the dreadful experience of the hurricane and the agonies of his wounded and injured patients, hurled about below deck with little constraint offered by flimsy hammocks, no man able to assist his fellow in the violence and frenzy of the sea, the diminishing hopes of all, the shouts, the fear, screams, the descent into panic, and at the end a numbed resignation, waiting... waiting for the ferocity of watery engulfment. 'I am minded that there never was a more frightening day, Pat...' a long pause, 'and so greatly debilitating,' Simon's voice tailed off to silence, his face unmoving, his vacant eyes staring into the distance, wholly bereft of focus, of seeing.

'Be not so dismayed, brother. There is not a man aboard the barky who felt any less terrified... I include myself, I do. It was a close run thing, so it was.'

'I am still mindful of that... of those dreadful hours... horrifying. I cannot shake it... and... and I have been turning it over in my mind since joyous tranquility came upon us.'

'Rest assured, we will never see its like again.'

'I am very sensible of your kindness,' Simon shivered.

'Will I bring you a jacket?'

'Thank you, no; the tremulation is wholly within.'

'That will be the Castle,' declared Prosser with satisfaction, pointing towards the high point on the coastline off the port bow. 'Helm to starboard... handsomely it is on the helm there,' and *Surprise* shifted near imperceptibly to shave a trifle more from the line of her passage, every man's eyes on the Black Rock ahead. Prosser murmured again, 'Steady as she goes.' He nodded his visible contentment to the helmsman, Barton, Pat's cox'n, the makings of a tired smile on his deeply tanned and lined face, tiny dribbles of moisture clinging to his eyebrows and running through the grey profusion of unshaven stubble.

'I do so hope we may enjoy a prodigious fine supper ashore together, Simon... eh?' offered Pat, striving to cheer his friend.

'That would make me very happy.' The words, uttered by rote and without the least tone of conviction, betrayed Simon's indifference to any thoughts of food, on which subject he had no opinion to offer, being wholly consumed with a persevering introspection with recent events, the near disaster. The unprecedented strain remained, etched deep into his mind, and he was wholly unable to shake it: conscious endeavours towards contemplation of other matters registered indistinctly, momentarily, and rapidly faded as the recollections of horror forced themselves upon him once more.

All about the ship, many men stared west towards the coast, most of them superfluous to the ship handling, two score standing on the foc'sle, two dozen more striving but failing to remain unnoticed or at least to appear innocuous in their captain's gaze just forward of the quarterdeck, and four score or more thronged all along the port side, spirits everywhere rising and conversational chatter rampant. They were nearly home, home after eighteen bloody months away, twenty-two dead and forty-seven wounded; almost home - bar one day - and then they had endured the hurricane of the past twenty-four hours, desperately fighting for their lives. Their captain, Patrick O'Connor, had brought the barky through the very worst of hell's fury, for so it had seemed, and they had - "thank God" the thought foremost in all their minds - survived. That was reckoned by everyone to be the nearest thing to a miracle that any of them would ever experience, and every man in all the hours since had constantly reiterated his heartfelt and personal thanks to the Almighty - and to their captain, for it had surely been his unrelenting determination to save them which had been the decisive factor. That was certain without the least doubt, and it was something which would not leave their minds even whilst praying for a swift arrival and a happy reunion with their wives, their children, their sweethearts; for there was not a man who had expected to endure the terrifying maelstrom of the night, so severe had it been; even now the pumps, constantly working, struggled to hold back the rising water in the bilges, the depth inexorably rising, and no headway could they make against it.

'I am minded to return home, Pat... to Tobermory. That is to say if you are agreeable to my absence,' Simon paused momentarily in reflection, '... and when the wounded are suitably accommodated... with all the necessary care they will doubtless require for some considerable months.' Simon turned to look his friend square in the face, 'I have been turning it over these past weeks... during these testing tribulations... a minor consolation in my nightmares... so many... so many men lost.' His voice dropped, 'It may be that my seafaring time is done.'

'I beg you to cast aside such uncommon silly notions,' declared Pat, his head throbbing as if bound by a tight cord, utterly shattered by the extreme demands imposed upon him by the hurricane, the exceedingly long, crushing spells on deck in the tempest's full force.

'I am with longing to be once again in the Isles, the sea a mere vision... an innocuous background, my feet firmly planted on and striding o'er the machair. That is my most earnest wish, brother.' The supplication made, Simon stared at his friend, awaiting the so significant reply.

Greatly taken aback, Pat resorted to jest, 'Why, doubtless Sinéad will be pressing me to return to Ireland, to Claddaghduff and the farm, where we possess of five cows, a mule, a half-dozen of swine and a score of fowl.' No reaction from Simon he pressed on, 'My presence is demanded, necessary - so she says. I am required there... doubtless to inspire the potatoes. Of course, the year so late, the damnable potatoes likely will have rotted... and cutting the turf off the bog before the winter proper will demand all our attentions, no doubt. We have already put a little by... if the neighbours ain't stolen it in our absence.' He groaned, 'But I must not bore you with such domestic tedium.' Simon visibly unimpressed, Pat tried again, 'Come, Simon, a month or two ashore will doubtless answer the case, and then I venture you may care to return to the barky,' and to himself with a rising feeling of apprehension, *if she floats still.*

From the men, untroubled by such thoughts, banter - loud and unconstrained - resounded throughout all the ship, reaching the officers on the quarterdeck, but none gave it any mind. 'Saint Anthony Head to starboard, Pennance Point on the larboard beam, sir,' the master declared, coming over from the helm to the side to make plain his observation over the scores of jubilant crew voices, the Pendennis headland almost within touching distance, or so it seemed after the uncertainties of the night. Pat broke off from his own thoughts, those of Galway and his ship's future already forgotten; he nodded, pleased and relieved to hear the pronouncement, for no further words could he find in that abrupt moment of departure from his own concentration; his own mind after Simon's remarks had returned to reflection on the near catastrophe during the recent hours of darkness, and plainly Simon too was much affected by it. He shivered, wiped the countless rain droplets from his face and stared all about him, the familiar working sounds of the ship and the sea slapping gently along her side a comfort, the inquisitive circling gulls swooping and arcing all about the ship, calling as if in aerial welcome, the steady white wake creaming behind her a reassurance to a mind shattered by the ferocity of the night.

The last sure knowledge of their position during the prior day had been whilst in Biscay, within the great Bay: an indistinct and weak sun sighting before the onslaught that had near destroyed them. It had been a night of horror, the most frightening experience of a lifetime, one which Pat and doubtless every other man aboard would never forget until their dying day, and he silently thanked God again for their arrival in familiar waters, their home port less than an hour away. Black Rock now looming fine on the starboard bow, they would shave Pendennis Point, the tide still on the flow, and then bear west into the Penryn River, keeping clear of the Bar, and then on into the King's Road, to double anchor, to sanctuary, safety, relief, to grateful rest and the congenial arms of waiting families.

'Will 'ee care for coffee, sorr?' another reminder of Galway, Pat's steward, Murphy, started his thoughts, his thoughts returning to the present, to small immediacies and looming necessities.

'Thankee, I should like it of all things. What do you say, Simon?'

'I am in contemplation of that delicious nectar, thank you.'

'Light along, Murphy, and fetch it up here, if you please.'

'So we are sure to reach blessed Falmouth this day, Pat?'

'I dare say, but before I swear to such... the wind is a trifle troubling... of concern. Do you see, this wind is not kind to us, a little stronger and it would quite bar our way into the Roads. We are ever in dread of a north-westerly as we approach the Black Rock.'

The last hour of the afternoon was slipping by, the sun sinking inexorably lower, the weakening late afternoon light signalling its relinquishment of a tenuous hold on the day, and hundreds more of spectators had gathered to stare from the heights whilst *Surprise* continued to toil north-east. Now a quarter-mile beyond Pendennis Head and the feeble wind gusting directly on her port beam, from all over the bay as she closed home the drift-netting and long-lining pilchard fishing boats had swiftly coalesced all around her, their net-shotting hastily set aside. First one, two and three, quickly becoming a dozen in joyful escort, their numbers rising all the time as she was sighted by fishermen seining further afield within the estuary, until eventually a score or more were close alongside her; their crews - all of whom being men of Falmouth and well known to the Surprises – continually shouting loud exhortations of welcome and friendly greetings whilst striving to make personal enquiry of the scores of *Surprise's* jubilant crew all along her sides, men everywhere leaning against the hammock netting, Royal Navy protocol wholly abandoned.

Finally she passed the Black Rock off her starboard beam to enter the Carrick Roads, distant St Mawes Castle three-quarters of a mile ahead as eight bells rang out, the attention of all on deck turning to considerations of the wind and the necessary manouevres to attain her intended anchorage.

'She is yours, Mr Prosser,' declared Pat, the master entirely familiar with his home port and its approaches.

'Thankee, sir.'

Another five languorous minutes, Trefusis Point in sight, and Prosser ordered a course adjustment: two points to larboard, and *Surprise* was as close to the wind as she could go. The shore of St Mawes headland off the starboard bow, *Surprise* was steadily and inexorably closing on its jagged shore, a mere half mile ahead.

'Would we be in peril, so... the rocks in such near proximity?' asked Simon nervously, turning to his friend, no little anxiety in his voice.

'There ain't the wind to make short boards in here... in the Roads,' declared Pat. 'Close-hauled and so little room to manoeuvre, she would slow, lose way with each tack and likely fall in irons... when we will be here for the night, not the smallest prospect of reaching Falmouth town. Mr Prosser knows that, no doubt. The barky will shave the rocks to starboard and has way enough for just the one tack, no more, else we will be anchored until the morrow.' Pat did not care to mention the other more greatly worrying uncertainty of every seaman aboard: if the tack failed and the ship fell off, there was precious little searoom to let slip anchors before the north-westerly would put her on the rocks.

The attention of every man on deck was gripped by the looming necessity for the single tack *Surprise* would strive to make and the prospects of it succeeding; indeed, some men held a lingering doubt which they could not dispel. All were mindful that the rocky coastline of the St Mawes headland was so close in their lee, a danger looming large, very large; only Pat's confidence in Prosser prevented his own order to turn away, small anxiety rising again within his own mind: would she pass by and complete her turn with so little way in the feeble wind? It was an echo of the unwelcome feelings which had beset him all day, anxieties which he had thought he had left behind with the dawn, and he did his utmost to dispel his fretting, but with little success.

A silent Prosser held her firm on her course, calculating, computing, weighing the northing she was making, would have to make so as to gain a near beam wind for her run into Falmouth port - if, that is, she succeeded in her turn. A few minutes, no more, and the moment of decision was near upon them: she must come about or she would fall off to likely smash herself to assured destruction, precious little of sea room available to her. The officers exchanged nervous glances and Pat bit hard on his lip, suppressed his rising anxiety and his unuttered words, not wishing to overrule the master. He nervously forced himself to finish his coffee. Another minute and *Surprise* had passed by the immediate peril of the closest stretch of the headland, still bearing north-north-east, shifting a little further into the broadening Carrick Roads, a trifle more of leeway available to her, but moving further away from Falmouth town, the north-westerly wind not helpful at all in bringing *Surprise* to her intended anchorage.

Little of the day remained to bring her round, time fast diminishing to take her into Falmouth's outer harbour before the end of all daylight. Doubtless Prosser had weighed all the variables: tide, wind strength and direction, depth of water, currents, the barky's response to the helm and the diminishing scope - space and time - to make the intended single short board without which she would be unable to make the sanctum of the inner anchorage and must stay in the Roads for the night - a most unwelcome prospect indeed for everyone. 'Hands to the braces, Mr Macleod,' he could only murmur, anticipating the master's imminent call. 'She has precious little way enough to tack,' the nawing concern left unspoken.

'Hands to the braces,' bawled an anxious Macleod, in a voice that might have been heard on the Falmouth quays, as if such might prompt the master.

'Hard a-starboard,' bellowed Prosser at last in the firmest of voice, long familiarity with the approach bestowing conviction and certainty in his order. Near imperceptibly *Surprise* answered her helm, two score of men hauling hard on the braces, and she began her vital turn to the west. Slowly, so very slowly she turned, adopting a northbound course, then north-west, coming directly into the wind, progress slowing, way falling off, all eyes on the sails, their edges shivering as she turned through the wind, making the most graceful, the perfect of long, looping turns. Her men raced like demons to haul round her yards; all were quickly braced tight and tied off once more. Still close-hauled she inched onwards, turning, gaining a little more way, westwards now - nearly home - the gentle wind off her starboard beam, the worrying imminence of the St Mawes rocks receding. Pat and all his men breathed a long sigh of relief; he marvelled in the master's confidence, in his abilities; it was exceedingly impressive how well these old Falmouth hands, Prosser particularly, knew their home port and its approach waters, its currents and tides.

Ahead, off the port bow, all along the waterfront, on Falmouth's several quays and strands, for the first time the people became visible; great multitudes of them thronged in their thousands. To their near companions standing alongside them in the excited crush it was plain that many of them were left profoundly emotionally overcome by the electrifying news, news which left them burdened with a desperation to greet their returning close kith and precious kin aboard the approaching ship, closing home at last. Shouting children, scores upon scores of them, a hundred, two hundred or even more rushed repeatedly and manically all about the town, running up to the castle and back down to the Town quay whilst others ran furiously from the Fish strand to the Market strand and back again without the least pause, the youngsters wildly frenetic in the enthusiasm of youth and seeking any fresh crumb of news or, in the absence of such, the most speculative morsel of gossip. It was an energised, exhilarated multitude, amongst all of whom the loud and vociferous mental tumult of those inconstant twins, capricious excitement and pernicious anxiety, had risen to intolerable heights; particularly so amongst waiting wives and mothers, all of whom longed so dearly to hold tight in their arms their own husbands and sons: for *Surprise* had been gone since distant June of the prior year and communications had been few and tardy, no news at all having been received in the two months since September. Hence no one could know whether their particular loved one had survived that faraway conflict, the enduring and bitter struggle for Greek freedom from the Ottoman empire. Many a tearful soul strived to hide their fear and trepidation whilst they waited; indeed, whilst they shivered with nauseating apprehension on the waterfront, for they could not dispel that most sickening of feelings: profound uncertainty. Would their most precious person in all the world be aboard this ship? Was their own beloved really coming home? Could they allow themselves to believe it? The alternative was too painful by far to contemplate.

On she came, now a hundred yards abreast of the Bar; the observers on shore noted the near imperceptible shifting of her yards, the striking of her topgallants; her bow turning she fell off a little, now bearing south-west, the weak wind abeam; orders were shouted, acknowledged, course yards hauled round, braces slackened; she was slowing noticeably, turning further, distant Trefusis Point and the Kiln quay astern, her bow pointing south towards the Fish strand, her men hauling hard on the braces, her topsails shivering, the ship losing way, her topsail yards slackened, slowing more, until - at the master's determination, all her sails fluttering and no depth of water available to her closer to the quay on the ebb tide - she let go both her anchors in the King's Road, all her fishing boat companions in her lee. On the waterfront an explosion of noise erupted: shouting, cheering, screaming, clapping; the crowd was ecstatic; arms everywhere along the waterfront were waving frantically in sublime euphoria.

'Well done, Mr Prosser,' declared Pat with heartfelt feeling, seizing and shaking the master's hand with conviction.

On the frigate's quarterdeck her officers were gathered near the helm, their tired attention frequently alternating between the activities aboard ship and the huge crowds in welcome on the shore, for they had never before seen suchlike in any homecoming. Aloft on the yards, men were clewing up her sails; at her waist, foc'sle and rails all along her port side were scores more of her men, a hundred or more; another dozen perched at her tops; everywhere relieved, homesick sailors stared with animated curiosity towards the quays and strands, a mere two cables off. Tense minutes passed swiftly, and in the dying of the late afternoon light, nigh on the approach of sunset, the weak and diffuse sun's radiance diminishing as it began its descent behind the hill, the several thousand people in the press of the crowd were moved to new heights of animated excitement, continuing to wave vigorously and to hail across to the ship in joyous greeting.

Captain O'Connor gazed through his glass; although so close, from aboard *Surprise* individuals within the great throng were not readily discernible with any degree of certainty to eyes staring into the low winter sun. Its radiant, red glow was fast fading as it inexorably sank further behind the low hillside at the back of the town, orange reflections rippling all across the water, and within a very few minutes ultimately disappearing to leave a farewell pink haze lingering in the western sky with lengthening black shadows the length of the waterfront; the more subtle, muted light of dusk settling upon the scene and bestowing a tranquility, an ambience of greater quietude to complement the ship's collective sense of relief, of blessed arrival; and so the crew, holding back their natural exuberance with great difficulty and checking their considerable impatience to be ashore as fast as could be, chattered amongst themselves in joyful, elated high spirits and unconcealed excitement.

'Well, we'se here,' boomed Murphy's satisfied and loud declaration, cutting through the vibrant hubbub to the ears of all on the quarterdeck and as far forward as the waist. Captain Patrick O'Connor, a man of modest build and greying red hair, his attention diverted from his ship by his steward's exultant and definitive pronouncement, looked all about him to his closest companions, friends all: to an affable Commander Duncan Macleod, his First, a rather stout man in an ill-fitting uniform; to Doctor Simon Ferguson, ship's doctor, a shabbily dressed, thin man, his clothes filthy with dried blood, his ashen face a frozen picture of concern and apprehension. He looked further afield: to Lieutenant Pickering, his Second and the ship's wag, chattering animatedly to Lieutenant Mower, Third and a proficient poet, who had been seriously wounded in the August battles and who even now looked pale and fragile, for weak as he still was he generally struggled to endure even half a day on his feet. Pat looked to a deeply tired Michael Marston, ship's chaplain and assistant surgeon, who had consoled him in his private despair when Simon had been captured by the Turks; and to Abel Jason, long time purser in their former years aboard *Tenedos* before *Surprise* and recently pressed to help as assistant when the surgeons were overwhelmed with the wounded and the dying: so many horrors brought before them in two days immersed within a tide of blood. All these men were much more than his longstanding officers, every one of them had become the most valued of friend, for the bonds between them had been forged in the furnace of fierce fighting and the deeply distressing aftermath of despond as losses had mounted throughout the summer campaign. What was now to become of them all? Would the barky be paid off? He pondered these and more questions of such ilk with some discomfit, for *Surprise* was plainly unfit for further service: six feet of water in the hold and the pumps, worked constantly by an oft-changing rota of fatigued men, could not hold back its insidious gain. He stared momentarily at the master, Jeremiah Prosser, a legend in the seafaring community of Falmouth, a former whaler, a lay preacher in the Wesleyan community of the town and long a non-commissioned officer and comrade aboard *Tenedos* before *Surprise*.

Pat's head turned about and he gazed intently at his cox'n at the helm, George Barton, a Portsmouth man; although Barton had served for only the present voyage aboard *Surprise* with Pat and never before, he was the identical twin of Pat's former cox'n, Brannan Barton, who had been killed fighting alongside Pat whilst boarding *Chesapeake* in the year '13; his brother George had presented himself at Plymouth Dock after being summoned by Prosser whilst *Surprise* was being refitted for her Greek expedition. In the many months since, Barton had exhibited all the same reliable characteristics of his fondly-remembered brother, becoming a dependable stalwart of the crew. Was that finally the end of all service together with these magnificent men? The question was bearing heavy on Pat's mind.

Macleod broke into his thoughts, 'I venture those are our lads from *Eleanor* in the cutter coming across, sir, out from the quay; aye, there's Codrington... and Reeve.' Pat nodded to signify his understanding, for of words he could find none in the profound moment of realisation that his task was done, finished; home for this tired frigate and all her weary men had finally been reached. It was not too soon, he thought with considerable relief. He presumed the schooner, which no one had observed in the excitement of arrival, all eyes on the nearer quays and strands, was moored somewhere further north-west along the waterfront, perhaps near the Green Bank quay, but in the lengthening black shadows he could not make her out.

'Brother, will we begin and set the sick ashore whilst we have light enough?' asked Simon Ferguson quietly, looking to his friend, Pat's uncertainty plain in his face, a conflicting amalgam of wavering resignation, a heartfelt sense of deliverance and a rising satisfaction.

Pat started, blinked to clear moist eyes, to remedy momentary melancholy, the low sun bright in his gaze, his mind jolted back to his reply, 'Of course, of course; indeed, we will.' He patted Simon's shoulder encouragingly and called loudly over the rising babble of raucous greetings, questions and acknowledgments, his crew's customary restraint in protocol cast wholly to the winds in their joy of arrival, 'Mr Pickering, hail those men if you please.' All *Surprise's* boats had been pulverised to complete destruction in the full force of the hurricane, the large remnants violently wrested away in the tempest's fury, smashing against the ship's side and crashing overboard, tearing away great lengths of the rail and much of the hammock netting, the fragments and remnants carried off, flying high on the wind. Pat shouted again to his Second, nodding towards the pilchard fishermen, their boats all in close proximity to the frigate, 'Mr Pickering, perhaps those men will aid the disembarkation of our lads, the wounded particularly?' The request was relayed and granted immediately, without the slightest of hesitation, the seiners tying alongside the frigate; lines were hastily thrown and tied.

'Mr Macleod, all hands aft, if you please,' cried Pat, Duncan's shouts of 'Silence, fore and aft!' from just abaft the main mast having not the least effect, the jubilation general and so overpowering. Pat paced forward to the waist, frantically ringing the bell himself in passing. He bawled over the loud and endemic babble of all his men down to the gun deck, 'Hear me, hear me!' A brief pause for the gabble to subside, 'Welcome home, lads!' A huge cheer erupted, replaced by a hundred echoing acknowledgements before it subsided slowly to a low murmur, the men awaiting Pat's resumption. 'The sick and wounded will be set ashore directly. Bring 'em up now from below... and lads...' Pat lowered his voice, 'have a care with your shipmates... gently does it, act not in haste.' A further uproar of exuberant chatter returned, and the men bent to their tasks once more with boundless enthusiasm.

With exceptional caution, with infinite patience, amidst joyful banter abounding everywhere, the Surprises assisted their injured comrades up from the lower deck. Many of the weakest, the more severely wounded and the pitifully fragile were coming up from below for the first time in weeks; they struggled physically, their legs unsteady, many carried by their fellows. All waited patiently, in good cheer, readying themselves to be lowered in the bosun's chair to the pilchard boats for the short row to shore, to the awaiting welcome of warm words and the grasp of the myriad of hands.

'Smithwick Creek, Mr Pickering; the Market strand for our lads,' shouted Pat, 'Tell the boatmen plain, set them ashore there; this ain't the time to be damned by Doctor Fox's infernal quarantine on the Custom House quay.'

'Aye aye, sir,' Pickering nodded and reiterated the order, shouting down to the fishermen alongside, Falmouth men all and every man well known to the Surprises.

The small warmth of the dwindling day had cooled off completely and the last vestiges of the sunset's ethereal light had further dimmed into the soft, diffuse illumination of a faintly orange twilight as *Eleanor's* officers, Codrington and Reeve, scrambled up the nets to come aboard, anxious faces showing grave concern for what they might find.

'Good evening, gentlemen,' said Pat with a weary smile.

'Welcome home, sir,' declared Codrington affably, great warmth in his voice, Reeve smiling broadly.

It was obvious to any observer with the least maritime experience that *Surprise* was noticeably much too low in the water, the absent mizzen also so stark a clue to what horrors had surely been inflicted upon the frigate and her men, and the unceasing torrent stream from the pumps cast over both sides was another striking indicator of what they both knew without the least doubt would be substantial deteriorations. All of the accompanying eight Eleanors swiftly followed their officers, the schooner's men engaging with keen interest with the Surprises, customary pleasantries rapidly exchanged but swiftly forgotten, to press for news of their shipmates, of the Biscay crossing, before helping to lower the casualties, the exceptionally weak and sick, down to the patiently waiting fishermen. Near fifty men were recuperating from grievous wounds and required such assistance; the battles of the summer in Greek waters, the most recent in September - two particularly damaging and costly engagements - had seen a score of the crew killed; indeed, it was the singular concern pressing painfully on Pat's mind in that moment: how to break the despairing tidings to those mothers, fathers and wives waiting on the quay for sons and husbands who were not aboard, who were not returning: men who would never be seen again. He determined to set the grim thought aside as a wave of sadness swept through him, and his stomach turned with a rising flood of bilious nausea. Striving with difficulty to ignore it, he consciously applied his mind to the disembarkation of the last of his wounded men. Mr Boswell, the gunner, bereft of a left arm taken off by a cannon shot, seemed to be in good cheer. His wife, by old convention the only woman allowed to serve aboard, clung fiercely to his right arm even as he wrested it away and offered his hand to Pat in farewell.

'Goodbye Mr Boswell, Mrs Boswell; take care, both of 'ee,' offered Pat quietly, seizing the gunner's hand in a vice-like grip and pumping it for an interminable ten seconds, neither man wishing to relinquish the connection, the bond which had long existed between them since the *Tenedos* days of long years ago and which now seemed infinitely tenuous, fragile, its perpetuation so uncertain. 'I will see you ashore in the coming days, there is no doubt.'

'Aye, sir; thankee,' mumbled Boswell, nodding, his wife plainly emotional and greatly distressed in her moment of profound relief in the realisation that it really was the end of the voyage, the homecoming was upon them; she blinked frantically, quite overcome, all the time mopping her face with a cloth whilst striving unsuccessfully to obscure the flood of salt tears until the crying came, without constraint, open, loud, her small frame shaking, wracked by sobs, Pat and all nearby moved to murmurings of consolation, and the gunner seizing her close with his good arm.

A half-hour more passed by, the crew melting away, many fewer men remaining aboard *Surprise*, and the much dimmed twilight was fast fading as Falmouth embraced the night. Pat stared towards the shore, total darkness fast approaching. He wondered where his wife might be, his children. The emerging moon's soft illumination was something of a small consolation; it was complemented by scores of distant flaming torches held aloft on the Town quay, upon which many hundreds were gathered, all talking at once, the excitement and joy of families engrossed with their returned loved ones wholly endemic, the many and loud discussions carrying across the placid water to *Surprise* as a coalescing low murmur with frequent spikes of shouting, of excited greetings. He turned away and looked about his ship; the ambience on deck was greatly quieter, many fewer men visible: all the casualties had disembarked, a hundred and more of the fit men of the crew gone ashore with them; yet still boats were returning to tie alongside all the time, and the last remaining handful of men were scrambling down to board them in robust good humour, bidding their farewells to the dismayed and grumbling half-dozen of hands reluctantly held back to attend the pumps, still requiring of constant attention; for there were insufficient Eleanors to endure all night with the laborious task. A brace of lanterns lit the quarterdeck with a muted yellow glow, almost all the boats departed at last, and the ship become near deserted except for her officers: silence abounding save for the rhythmical squealing and gushing of the pumps constantly working. Vapours were beginning to rise off the still waters, a mist developing as the chill settled into the air all about them. Pat's thoughts flickered between the final disembarkation of his men to a concern for his own wife and children, likely somewhere within the far crowds; as had Duncan's keen mind, his wife and daughter too surely awaiting him on the quay. What was to be done? Both men gazed long and wistfully at the distant multitude; in the gloaming it was difficult to discern even the shapes of individuals amongst the crowds and quite impossible to make out their families, the lingering remnants of twilight near gone.

'Pat, dear,' Simon interrupted his contemplations, the chaplain and purser standing behind the surgeon, 'Marston, Jason and I are going ashore, to attend the wounded; that is, with your permission.'

'Of course, make it so; do not tarry for even a moment. Should you see Sinéad ashore, please to say I will be there on the morrow; the barky cannot be left whilst she ails so. In the morning there will be time to settle matters here; the pumps...' Pat's voice tailed off, his mournful gaze shifting towards the shore, the depressing realisation firming within him that he would not be greeting his wife or his children this evening. He shivered again in the cold air of the breeze.

'Of course, brother; we are away.'

The trio departed for the rope ladder, an uncomfortable feeling of loneliness settling upon Pat with the rising awareness that near everyone had departed, the warming cheer of homecoming fading to disappointment, to melancholia. The former excited babble of his happy men had been succeeded by the disquieting, unsettling silence, save for the distant hubbub still carrying across the mirror of black water from the quay, hundreds of voices audible though indistinct. Supper this evening in a cold cabin, in an empty ship, utterly bereft of the customary routines and all his shipmates absent would surely be a sombre and wretched occasion. He stared in bleak resignation towards Duncan, his friend looking equally forlorn. 'Duncan, I am at a stand. I beg you will go ashore with the men; lose not a moment before the last boat is away.'

Duncan shook his head emphatically, 'I should like it of all things, but I am nae here as your First now, Pat, but as your friend. I am staying 'til the morrow; I beg ye will say nae a word more about it.'

A silent Pat nodded at Duncan, gratitude welling up within him. He stepped towards the companionway as his attention was caught by unfamiliar voices to see a dozen of Falmouth men climbing aboard the gun deck, a greatly unexpected surprise at this late hour. The group assembled, stepped up the companionway and paced aft to his quarterdeck. They were plainly fishermen; Pickering and Prosser were engrossed in talking animatedly to them. Indeed, one or two of the men, the more elderly ones, looked vaguely familiar to him.

'Sir,' the master approached and touched his forehead, 'here are men from the Chapel... all are long known to me...'

'Yes, Mr Prosser?' asked a curious Pat, deep fatigue settling upon his mind and his body in recognition of the momentous day - longer, it had been thirty-six hours without rest save for the briefest of catnaps. Thankfully it was coming to its toilworn end at last. He stared hard at the master in puzzled enquiry. That his own tired and struggling brain was in desperate need of sleep was obvious to him; he wondered almost absently in his mental exhaustion what on earth all these men were doing coming aboard, his own men departed.

'Some are *Tenedos* old hands... as you may collect,' continued Prosser, seeing plain his captain's fatigue. He turned back to the newcomers, beckoning, his voice raised, loud, emphatic, 'Lads...' The men approached, closing around Pat.

Pat directed his enquiring gaze towards the men in scrutiny; he rubbed sore eyes, strived to dispel the deep fatigue which had overtaken him, a few seconds passing before his exclamation, 'Why, 'tis Tregenza... and Opie, if I ain't mistaken... and Spargo... 'tis grand to see you... so it is, but what are ye doing here, lads?'

'Sir, these men have volunteered,' Prosser interjected, 'to stand by, to help the Eleanors... to pump... that is to say, by your leave.' Pat being visibly struck dumb by the unsolicited gesture, the master continued, 'It was remarked on the quay that the barky is down in the water, sir... and... and 'tis plain to all the pumps is workin' mighty hard.' Pat patently struggling for words, Prosser continued, 'Beg pardon, sir; ye may care to go ashore... d'reckly.' The Falmouth fishermen, all staring at Pat, concern in their faces, nodded heads; a few - *Tenedos* veterans - muttered firm "ayes" of encouragement.

Pat's confusion of tired thoughts was further interrupted when at that moment Codrington spoke up, 'I am staying aboard, sir, as is Mr Reeve; we will remain with the ship; there is nothing pressing you to linger here that we cannot attend; please... I beg you will go ashore if you will, Mr Macleod too. Your wives will be waiting... and doubtless fretting.'

The surging wave of relief, of gratitude was overwhelming; the greatly dimmed spark of pleasure in his homecoming flickered brightly to rekindled life, and Pat's burning, tired eyes opened from the squint of their deep black recesses, 'Why, thank you kindly, Mr Codrington... Mr Reeve... lads,' he muttered, still in enduring realisation of the benevolent purpose of *Eleanor's* officers and the fishermen. He was more than a little taken aback by the generosity of men he had not seen for several years. His mouth dried up, his throat constricted, a flood of blessed liberation quenching his raging anxieties in a bountiful surge of release, and it was all he could do to add in a near whisper, 'That is uncommon friendly of you... all of you... thankee lads.... thankee.' He beamed at all in the gathering, seizing each of the hands of those immediate men he had recognised in turn, shaking them emphatically in a fierce grip as if his gratitude might flow strong through the physical bond, no more words could he find in the whir of his fatigued confusion, in the deep flush of his pleasure, cold despond falling away.

'Hallelujah and praise the Lord,' exclaimed Jason, leaping out of the boat and landing with great satisfaction on the wet sand and shingle of the Market strand at the mouth of Smithwick Creek, the crunching sound and physical sensation of his boots settling firm within it delivering a joyful relief from the still lingering recollection of his deep despair during the interminable ordeal of *Surprise* fighting for her survival. 'Terra Firma and both my feet upon it at last, *at last!* Give you joy, colleagues!'

'I could not countenance any contrary perspective,' replied Simon, emphatically and with deep approval, clambering over the gunwhale with some difficulty whilst clutching his surgeon's bag and striving to avoid toppling into the water, his belt caught up on the rowlocks. 'Thank you, friend,' he murmured to an obliging seaman extricating him from his predicament. He leaned back to retrieve an old and well worn cloak from the boat, one loaned to him by Pickering, and he threw it about his shoulders, shivered and looked all about him in mild astonishment. Hundreds of animated Falmouth folk stood close by on the strand, the crowds so many that they were standing a mere few yards above the rippling water, the illumination of many torches lighting joyful faces all about him, scores talking loudly within a vibrant hubbub of happy reunion.

'Praise the Lord, indeed,' Marston was wholly in accord with his friend, 'and let us be thankful for his benevolence.' The words went unheard in the background cacophony of so many loud voices. He hauled his own bag from the boat and stood staring in some little bewilderment, gazing all about him at the sizeable gathering, water lapping at his boots, soaking his feet until he became aware of the wet and extremely cold sensation. He briskly stepped forward up the gentle slope and out of the water to join his companions who were now surrounded and hard pressed with multiple questions, Simon having been identified by one of the Surprises present as the ship's surgeon.

'... will he keep the leg?' Marston could see plain Simon's confusion, besieged by concurrent concerns coming thick and fast. '... Doctor, his breathing... he is labouring so...' from another, great anxiety plain in her voice, trembling, frightened.

'My dear Mrs... Mrs Goodridge is it? Stay your fears, I beg you; I will attend your husband on the morrow.' A distressed Mrs Goodridge plainly had great fears, could not stay them for the world. Her shoulders, her whole body slumped; her words failing her she was reduced to sobbing, desperately staring hard at Simon in bewildering anxiety. He set down his bag and took both her hands in his own, squeezing them gently, 'Take courage, my dear; I have given him a draught; it is the laudanum that will keep him comfortable this night, and you are to remember that he is to be given nothing more than caudle to eat this evening.' Mrs Goodridge nodded earnestly, digesting the words of such momentous relief. Simon swiftly turned his head from one supplicant to the other, 'Yes, Mrs... Mrs Currie? So it is; you are concerned of your son, the *younger* brother, is that not so?' Mrs Currie nodded vigorously. 'And a brave soul he is too.' He seized Mrs Currie's shaking hands, her body visibly trembling, her face awash with streaming tears of concern, 'Gather your strength, my dear.' A few seconds pause and he resumed, 'I believe, with the blessing, we may be confident he will retain the leg...' Simon smiled encouragingly, 'I should like to clean the wound and dress it again in the morning. It calls for the most delicate of hand. Would you care to be with me? Perhaps I may show you the procedure, how it is done?'

'Oh yes, sir; I would be most obliged,' croaked an infinitely grateful Mrs Currie, wiping the tears from her face, 'most kind of 'ee, sir, most kind; thankee sir, thankee.' Simon turned to face two more insistents, the press of people pushing him back towards the water.

'Ladies,' Marston's voice boomed out, 'Gentlemen...' He pushed in resolutely, ahead of Simon, to interpose himself between his besieged friend and the crowd, 'Ladies, Gentlemen, if you please!' The immediate crowd quieted, heads everywhere turning to stare at this last arrival. 'If you please,' he shouted again; near silence descended, the majority of the gathering and all nearby brought to an attentive interest. 'I am the Reverend Michael Marston, chaplain and assistant surgeon aboard this gallant vessel. I beg you all, I ask your forbearance...' Letting slip his own bag Marston raised both his arms as if in appeal, 'My colleagues are greatly fatigued... it has been a tumultuous few days... the night particularly, and we are thankful to our Lord to be here...' He halted for a brief few seconds to assess the effect of his plea; the crowd substantially quieted he pressed on, 'For there were times when, I confess... in the extremes of the tempest... when my own thoughts were bleak indeed...' He paused again. A general low murmur of accord signified general understanding, and Marston promptly resumed, 'I beg you will allow Doctor Ferguson a necessary recuperation... to rest this night... and we will both attend all of our patients early on the morrow.' The hum of consensus in reply was louder, growing, could be detected from within the many of the crowd. Marston raised his arms again, and the murmurings died away once more, 'Please, everyone... set aside your worries, your anxieties this night... and place your confidence in Doctor Ferguson... and our Lord.'

Prosser, appearing alongside Marston in that instant, shouted loud to the multitude whose voices were rising again, 'Hear me, hear me! It is arranged that the wounded, the sick and the injured will be accommodated this night in the Chapel... in the Market. Whilst there all may readily be seen by the doctors in the morning and in the coming days.' Ignoring the babble of query, Prosser without pause pressed on, shouting at the top of his voice, 'Bring blankets, fetch food; away now ye go. Cut along and lose not a moment!' With this the crowd resumed their loud and voluble discussion, fortunately leaving a fatigued Simon undisturbed, their attentions shifted to Prosser's declaration of arrangements.

'Allow me to thank you, Mr Marston, Mr Prosser,' whispered Simon, patently exhausted, visibly no vestige of strength left to him.

'Will I take your bags, Doctor, Mr Marston?' asked the master, 'There are rooms arranged for you at Wynn's Hotel, for Mr Jason too; 'tis but a short walk, a minute or so.'

'I am uncommonly obliged to you, Mr Prosser,' uttered Simon with considerable relief, enfeeblement plainly overtaking him.

'God bless you,' added Marston with feeling.

'I believe I may make my attempt upon a beefsteak for supper,' pronounced Jason, his spirits rising. '... and a claret too will answer admirably well. What do you say to that, Doctor? Will that accord with you, eh?'

'It might, Jason.' Simon's apprehension was lifting a very little. He offered a wan smile, 'Indeed, I rather think it will do all that is required... or almost all. I would not wish to look singular... and I confess the beefsteak offers a particular appeal at this moment; yes, indeed it does.'

Without further ado, Prosser seized up both bags and swiftly strode forth, up to the cobbles beyond the Market strand, Simon, Marston and Jason stumbling behind, legs tired, following as best they could to keep up. They were pressed at every step by effusive words of thanks from men of *Surprise* and their grateful relatives, frequently halted by the proffered hands of many smiling strangers pressed insistently to be shaken until, with no little relief, they turned left to step along Market Street, the crowd thinning with each weary step, and relief, blessed relief overtaking them with every yard.

'Well, 'tis time to go, sorr,' said Murphy, with Pickering and Young Pennington standing by him at the rail, ready to assist their captain over.

'I am minded you had best set us ashore at the Town quay, lads,' Pat declared to the fishermen as he settled in their boat. 'Doubtless there will be someone awaiting there my declarations... for Customs and quarantine.' He continued in a subdued tone, 'and I venture it will be remarked that many of the men have been set down on the Market strand.'

Duncan descended the rope net and caught the bags thrown by Murphy. The steward clambered down, muttering oaths, indistinct and for his own ears. 'What a cross-grained, snappish gaberlunzie ye is, Murphy,' declared Macleod, the steward taking absolutely no notice but settling at the bow, scowling, all other spaces on the thwarts taken.

The steady row took all of ten minutes across the calmest of water, through the veneer of chilly mist with not the least of adverse wave nor any wind to hold them back until, the boat's crew clutching the line cast from the Custom House quay and tying the boat alongside, Pat, Duncan and Murphy ascended swiftly up the steps, Murphy continuing his incessant grumbling as he hauled up the baggage. At the top they stopped, all stunned; every man gazed about them in astonishment: from the windows of all the buildings about the quay spectators looked down upon the swarming great throng of townsfolk, a thousand or even more, all souls enjoying the festive ambience of general jubilation, a celebration reinforced by the very visible and plentiful ale clutched by many more people pouring out from the Marine Hotel on the North quay. Hundreds of people were milling about, clutching glasses of ale and tin cups of gin and other liquors: it was Falmouth's party of the century.

'Give ye joy of your homecoming, sir,' declared Duncan joyfully, his pleasure so obviously unrestrained.

'Prodigious fine welcome it is, to be sure,' Pat smiled in the dawning and deeply gratifying realisation settling upon him that he had finally brought his men home. They were here all about him, with their families: scores of his men and hundreds of their people, wives and sweethearts, parents and children, many of whom he recognised and greeted in passing as he and his companions struggled to make headway through the exuberant, joyful crush.

Murphy's spirits too soared visibly, a rare and toothless grin emanating from him, his so rarely exhibited pleasure radiant in the overwhelming realisation of dry land finally reached, precious sanctuary gained and, not least, alcohol aplenty evident in the general celebration and therefore, to his mind, in close proximity. 'Well,' he cried, 'will ye be a'wishin' for a whet, sorrs?' Pat merely nodded, the still rising sense of relief all-enveloping him. Murphy started for the North quay, towards the Marine Hotel, the dunnage suddenly no weight at all. Pat and Duncan looked to each other, shrugged shoulders and set off in his train, no further thought given to the Customs office above the quay.

Murphy ploughed a determined path through the crowds who, for the most part, separated before his vigorous elbows and shoulders pushed them aside. Ignoring all calls, shouts and greetings from those Surprises mingled with the welcoming crowds, he pressed on until, hundreds of persons in a jabbering phalanx all about him, many in solid and unmoving embrace, in deep conversation, no thought for anything else at all in the intensity of reunion, he admitted defeat, stopped with infinite reluctance, cast down the baggage and glowered at all persons surrounding him, the press of people so heavy but the oasis of the hotel still a distant forty yards off. Pat and Duncan had gratefully followed in his turbulent wake, exchanging hearty congratulations along the way with several of their men who, whilst they could not wholly be described as worse for wear, undoubtedly faced the prospect of such on the morrow. They too were stopped in their tracks, subsumed within the immobility of the crowd.

A familiar voice cut through the hubbub to reach Pat's ears, shrill, near shrieking, a hint of desperation, of anxiety within it; and then from the crowd burst Sinéad, breathless, gasping, words quite beyond her as she threw herself into Pat's hastily receptive arms, both of them hugging each other tightly in determined embrace, no words sufficient, no other gesture adequate in the tide of joyous relief, euphoria surging through the heart of the wife who had feared her husband lost. Immediately following was Kathleen who was simply scooped up in Duncan's arms and raised aloft as if akin to a prize won, and then set down again with infinite gentleness from the big man, her tongue wagging, setting to with frenetic express, the words all a'jumble, unceasing, the radiant joy in her eyes apparent to all standing near; and then came the youngsters: Duncan's Brodie, Pat's Fergal and Caitlin, all equally anxious to greet their fathers, to cling tenaciously to arms already clasped firm around beloved wives. Murphy, standing by Pat, his eyes wavering between the joyful reunions and the distant Marine Hotel, somehow, miraculously, still managed to hold the very thinnest of smiles.

Chapter Two

Sunday 28th November 1824   12:00   *Falmouth*

The visitors' room in the Customs House at Falmouth Port, a gloomy place in the most clement of times, north facing and which saw nothing of the sun at any time in the short winter day, was filled with the conversation of the distinguished visitors: the guests of Samuel Pellew, the Excise Collector. The men were arrayed around the large table and against the walls of the rather small room in some little discomfort, for the hard wooden chairs, more customarily used by the clerks during the day, were pressed to serve for this social occasion: a dinner for which the ensemble had gathered from all about the English southwest counties. During the agreeable, sociable preamble, exceedingly generous measures of drinks flowing and the amicable chatter verging on garrulous, the animated conversation was the subject of a particular interest, one which had been debated with excited anticipation: the recent arrival of the long-awaited frigate in its home port, a mere five days beforehand, had been met with huge delight within the local population, and the senior officers of said ship were keenly expected at any moment. Indeed, their exploits, seemingly substantially exaggerated in the telling - as had already been remarked over the table - were the talk of the Cornish town.

Seated with his back to the window, one of the mariners present was himself expounding on the most extreme of past ship manoeuvres with flowing, tactile intensity. Another former Royal Navy officer, though not in uniform, sat to his left, whilst to his right was a rather small and wiry man of more uncertain background, garbed in somewhat distressed not to say rather shabby attire. The officer in full spate at the window end of the room was a man of between sixty and seventy, his generous frame overflowing his seat, his elbows and body leaning over the table. He was wearing his best uniform - the white-lapelled blue coat, white waistcoat, breeches and stockings of an admiral in the Royal

Navy, with the Knight Grand Cross of the Bath on his breast. He was enjoying a generous glass of whisky - doubtless duty-paid - whilst his still bright blue eyes, staring intensely from a deeply bronzed face - energetic and enthusiastic despite the lines evidencing the encroachment of advancing age - gazed fixedly at the civilian at the other end of the table: Samuel Pellew, the Excise Collector, sitting in silence and utterly absorbed in the discourse. The conclusion of the speaker's hugely entertaining reflections upon past service at sea - for they had been warmly appreciated by the other guests as such - had arrived, the definitive ending delivered with evident satisfaction to all in the room, vigorous clapping abounding from all present; and with his final word the admiral's fist thumped resoundingly down upon the table, shaking the cutlery and rattling the wine glasses. He leaned back in his chair, grasped and drained his own glass entirely, sighed happily, and he turned towards his neighbour to his right with a beatific smile. The words 'What d'ye have to say to that, eh?' were formed in his mind but had not quite escaped his lips when his ear caught the resonant, loud double-tap upon the door. Slightly piqued by the interruption, he heard with a rising tide of satisfaction the announcement delivered by the incoming clerk, 'Please to be upstanding, gentlemen. Allow me to introduce - and will you welcome - the officers of *His Majesty's Ship Surprise!*' The ship's name was announced with emphasis, with ringing and unqualified proud endorsement, the clerk swiftly shifting aside as the three late guests entered the small room.

    The admiral's thoughts had already switched from his own recollections of former days in command of frigates, *Nymphe* and *Arethusa* the two he had commanded himself in earlier times, and he now burned with a veritable avalanche of curiosity, of eager anticipation of what tales these new arrivals - now famed mariners - would bring with them; and this before any details at all, the slightest thing, had reached the Admiralty. Indeed, it was the First Lord himself who had sent him to meet the arrivals after the briefest of news of *Surprise's* return had recently reached Plymouth by post-chaise and subsequently London by semaphore, the packets and all coastal shipping still being hugely disrupted by the recent hurricane. He stood and squeezed his bulk around the edge of the table, struggling somewhat as he stepped behind the still-sitting gentleman to his right, and with some difficulty he arrived near the door, his outstretched hand half an arms length behind those of the other two persons present. In the few moments before any introductions, he studied the entrants discreetly: the first was a man of small stature, younger than himself by perhaps twenty or even more years, once red of hair but which was now greying, and dressed in His Majesty's uniform, oddly bar any rank insignia or decorations. The second was a man of similar build to himself - rather large, he grudgingly conceded - who also wore a uniform bereft of anything other than buttons; several of which, he noticed, were missing. The third man, he was rather intrigued to note, in many respects resembled the guest still seated to his right at the table; he was in civilian dress, though considerable attention to it would be necessary before he could ever conceivably aspire to appear within fashionable London circles. He wore a greatly creased black coat over an obviously deeply brown-stained shirt and breeches, both of which had plainly seen better days, and the man - waiting for his own introduction - hung back a little and gazed all about the room with an unassuming but demonstrable air of intelligence.

'Gentlemen,' declared the Excise Collector, 'allow me to introduce Captain Patrick O'Connor and Commander Duncan Macleod of *HMS Surprise*, with their surgeon, Doctor Simon Ferguson.' The Excise Collector turned back to the visitors, 'Gentlemen, may I introduce Admiral Edward Pellew... and Doctor Cornelius Tripe of Devonport...'

For only the merest instant the room was silent, all within it staring with the most eager anticipation at their fellow guests, several of them whose reputations preceded them, and every one a person of the highest repute - the admiral particularly was a legend within the Royal Navy - and then came babel. 'Captain O'Connor,' roared Edward Pellew, a rapturous smile on his ruddy face, seizing the first newcomer's hand with the most vice-like of grip and pumping it for excruciating seconds, 'I hope I see you well, sir.'

'... and may I introduce my other brother,' Samuel Pellew strived but failed to interject with the least conviction, 'Admiral Israel Pellew.' The latter introduction rather fell flat, not the slightest of headway gained, Edward Pellew and Patrick O'Connor already wholly engaged in assessment of each other, the two surgeons immediately exchanging the most cordial of greetings. Only Macleod seemed to retain his sense of the customary proprieties in this momentous occasion, shaking hands vigorously with Israel and Samuel Pellew in turn.

Five minutes elapsed, the introductions were long satisfied and cordiality was general; the customary pleasantries had swiftly been abandoned to immediate and vigorous discussion, everyone engrossed in passionate conversation: the retired Royal Navy veterans, Edward and Israel Pellew keenly questioning the newcomers whilst both the physicians, firm friends and past colleagues at Devonport, were exceedingly pleased to engage with each other again. A loud knock and the servant entered once more, prompting a small pause as he murmured to the host. In the hiatus Edward Pellew inclined towards O'Connor standing with him at the window. 'Captain O'Connor, I hope you will allow me to speak briefly of a singularly pressing matter before we dine,' he said discreetly in a half-whisper, 'though is is hardly decent in me to do so before we have raised a glass.' Pat nodded, curious. 'The First Lord has asked me to attend your ship... in the light of her being at sea in the worst of the tempest,' Pellew coughed, 'to provide some preliminary assessment of repairs and such restorations that she may require... or... or whether... that is to say...'

O'Connor grimaced, nodded, his mind now racing; "or whether *what?*" being his unspoken thought, words failing him in that anxious moment of fundamental uncertainty. Was this an indication, a portent that *Surprise*, so badly damaged as she was, might be sent to the breaker's yard, the decision made with all despatch? The war against Bonaparte was becoming a mere memory, and the navy no longer had want of so many ships. It was not beyond possibility that his own would be relegated to a prison hulk or even scrapped, such a sorry state was she in, though he could not, did not say anything.

'I shall be writing to London later this week,' Edward Pellew continued, the implication being urgency. O'Connor, still silent, nodded again, and the admiral waited patiently, sensing Pat's discomfit.

At that moment the door opened, a welcome distraction to both officers, the servant bringing a tray with more glasses, with bottles of wine. Striving to keep the tray and its contents balanced he edged through the compact throng to set it down on the table, the room still buzzing with spirited conversation, all reticence due to rank wholly discarded, noisy minutes passing, all the commissioned officers debating the respective virtues of frigates, *Surprise* and others, both past and present; the surgeons too were engrossed in discussion, Simon's intricate descriptions of medical observations of wounds recorded and their healing progress during the recent Mediterranean voyage were reported in the most graphic detail and with particular reference to the present wounded, all of whom were ashore and accommodated within the Wesleyan Chapel, presently tended by Marston and Jason.

Edward Pellew stared all about him, enjoying the enthusiastic exchanges between fellow seafarers, albeit the loud and simultaneous voices were quite alien to his customary way of things. His brother Samuel being seemingly wholly absorbed in the discourse, the admiral, after a decent interval, rapped his knuckles upon the table, a hush resulting. 'Gentlemen, please, will you be seated,' he prompted, gratified by the silence and smiling very kindly to the guests. Chairs scraped on the wooden floor, and the ensemble settled at the table, the servant hovering anxiously, pouring the wine on Samuel's nod. 'It falls to me - and a happy duty it is indeed, allow me to say - to welcome you all to Falmouth; Captain O'Connor, Lieutenant Macleod and Doctor Ferguson... welcome back, *welcome home*.' The admiral smiled encouragingly, 'You are become heroes in this town, your ship celebrated; indeed, such is so... for there is no other within His Majesty's fleet which has experienced so many engagements in so short a time.' Polite murmurings of objection from O'Connor were brushed aside by Pellew, and he continued in full spate, 'The packets for many a month have returned from Argostoli and thence from Malta with but the briefest reports of your encounters... at Psara... at Kasos... and recently at Samos. Truly it was the prodigious battle of all time...' The servant, returned, lingered at the table with interest, listening attentively; slowly he refilled the glasses. 'Not once but twice the Turk defeated. Outstanding, O'Connor... truly outstanding... admirable; indeed, it truly was.' Pellew turned to Macleod, 'And your reports, *Commander*...' the rank expressed with great emphasis, the promotion from lieutenant so very recent, '... Macleod, were received with particular interest by the First Lord, and though I am these three years retired, I am pleased to say His Lordship shares some of his confidences with me on the occasion that there may be some connection, however trifling, with His Majesty's south-western interests, Devonport and Falmouth particularly.' Edward Pellew ignored the servant's tentative gesticular attempts to bring something to his attention from the other end of the table and pressed on, 'However... gentlemen... however... setting present political matters aside for one moment... I must say... we are also greatly favoured today by the presence of a truly esteemed physician.' Pellew nodded to the man on his right, 'Doctor Tripe has been for many a year an outstanding servant of the navy at Plymouth Dock...' general applause around the table, '... and I am exceedingly pleased, gentlemen, to make the acquaintance of Doctor Ferguson of the *Surprise*,' Edward Pellew smiled, '... and... and allow me to mention, if you will, another HMS *Surprise*... yes, the most delightful of frigates she was too, a veritable joy to behold whenever she came into my gaze.' Pellew was beaming broadly now, '*HMS Surprise*... twenty-eight... Indeed, she was modelled on the French *Unité* - did you know, gentlemen? A sweet little ship... she was so, and taken off Ireland in the year '96. My squadron it was too... aahh,' Pellew exclaimed. 'Oh to be at sea again, eh... eh?' The admiral turned to his brother on his left, 'What d'ye say, Israel?'

Admiral Israel Pellew, however, had no opportunity to say anything, the servant edging around the table with difficulty and pressing his attention on Edward Pellew to whisper in his ear. 'Dinner, gentlemen, is about to be served,' announced Pellew eventually, and the servant exited, visibly relieved. The stares of every man had lingered on Israel Pellew before the announcement, and all now returned to him, his face retaining an amalgam of envy, of rueful regret, of suppressed longing, wishful wonderment, a roving imagination and the cravings for something lost much evident in his flickering eyes amidst a face otherwise immobile, subsumed in deep reflection. A long second and he replied, nodding, his few words significant and very softly spoken, 'I should like it of all things.'

'Hear hear,' declared Edward Pellew, banging his fist on the table. 'Commander Macleod, let me tell you this before we eat: the First Lord telegraphed to the Yard yesterday, and a rider here this very morning has brought his message: hence I must presume it is of some import. He has asked me to request you to attend him - at your earliest convenience - to apprise him of matters in Greece generally and the islands particularly. You will leave for London on the morrow.'

Macleod coughed up a mouthful of wine, 'Of course, sir,' he spluttered, nodded, greatly taken aback, the order utterly unexpected, his anticipated pleasure in spending time with his family deflated, utterly swept away in the bleakest of instants.

'Mr Jason is to accompany you,' the admiral pressed on, 'and you are to depart on the morning tide aboard *Eleanor*... with, of course, Captain O'Connor's consent.'

Pat, similarly shocked, simply nodded, his thoughts flailing without conclusion, wondering what such an unexpected order was about, his own presence not requested: how odd was that?

'I hope you will allow me the honour to come aboard, Captain O'Connor,' Edward Pellew resumed discreetly, adding, almost as an afterthought, 'at your convenience.' The words were uttered in a voice which resonated with warmth, but with too an undisguised intention of express investigation.

Pat's heart sank, his greatly pleasurable anticipation - and it surely was after months of poor food - in the promised dinner evaporating. He turned to face the admiral. 'Perhaps you would be so kind as to do so on the morrow, sir?' he murmured, his mind now burning with curiosity as to Pellew's keen interest and real purpose, Duncan's summons also a mystery, and then his thoughts returned involuntarily to the many and varied damages to his ship, almost all her men ashore, and the lamentable paucity of provisions aboard - likely nothing to offer his esteemed guest - and his spirits sank further.

'I should be very happy,' replied Pellew, smiling. 'If you are so minded, may we appoint eleven o'clock?'

'Then I will await you at that hour, sir,' murmured Pat without enthusiasm.

'Cornelius, dear colleague,' said Simon in a hushed voice, resuming his conversation with his neighbour at the table, 'How are you? Tolerably well, I trust? I have of late been contemplating on the recovery of our men, the wounded, and re-reading much of your published works; indeed, I oft refer to your *Observations on the Preservation of Health in the Navy at Plymouth Dock* with considerable interest.'

'That is gratifying, colleague, to be sure,' replied Tripe with a civil inclination of his head. 'I hope it was of some little use.'

'Of course, there is no doubt... of immense use... thank you.' Simon brightened a little, his mind striving to engage with a fellow philosopher, to allow some tiny gesture of relief from his preoccupation with his patients and his grave pertubations, his face shifting from the rigid mask of long-engraved strain.

'Allow me to refill your glass,' offered Tripe pleasantly, striving to change the conversation to more pleasurable matters, Simon plainly discomfited. 'I have myself recently been reading a paper by a Doctor Stephen Maturin... I was in London, attending the Royal. It is about the discovery of *Testudo Aubreii* - a tortoise it is - I was engaged with a particular fascination... such a giant.'

'Indeed he is, and a most interesting paper it is too. I collect the day of my own reading of it with an absolute recall. It came to Cephalonia on the packet... from the Society. I can imagine the beast, I see him in my mind... eating the shoots of *Ficus Religiosa*.'

'The sacred fig.'

'Indeed it is. You are familiar with the flora of the Indies?'

'Oh yes; you collect I share your passionate interest in the flora as well as the fauna of all the continents; yes, most certainly, very much so.'

'Let us behold dinner this moment,' boomed Edward Pellew's authoritative voice, cutting through the room. 'Capital, capital,' he remarked as three servants entered bearing plates, covered silver serving trays of several sizes, six more wine bottles, condiments and napkins. The stewards busied about the table to set everything down, removing the tray lids, the largest one revealing the most exquisite side of roast beef that Pat, Simon and Duncan had ever seen: piping hot, the delightful scent of its vapours filling the room, tantalising; gastronomic heaven was before them. Duncan's eyes lit up in happy anticipation of food the likes of which he had only dreamed of for many a month.

A customary pause, the toast was awaited, the attention of *Surprise's* officers wavering between the glorious banquet and their senior colleague. The stewards refilled the glasses. 'Gentlemen,' declared Edward Pellew, raising his own glass, 'I give you... ABSENT FRIENDS!' The words, the customary toast on Sundays within the Royal Navy, were declared with resonating conviction, and received with poignant significance by O'Connor, Macleod and Ferguson. There was not the least hesitation before the thundering reply from all present, 'ABSENT FRIENDS!' Every glass was drained in one and clunked down with emphatic and resounding confirmation.

'Allow me to carve this delectable beef,' announced Samuel Pellew, smiling, the host seizing his opportunity to take some small part in the exalted gathering, swiftly slicing thick cuts off the joint, crisp on the outside and pink within, passing on plates piled high to his brother Israel on their way round the table, the Surprises drooling over the divine delicacy; nothing like this beef could they recall eating since a year or longer. Not evan a momentary hesitation and several hands extended to the serving spoons and the steaming trays of familiar vegetables: roasted potatoes, boiled potatoes swimming in expensive, melted butter; to fresh peas and several other, unfamilar, vegetables - at least to mariners: Dutch carrots and broad beans, the trays filled to overflowing, the sight beatific to men long tired of unfamiliar and short rations; rotten, weevil-infested ship's biscuit latterly becoming an unavoidable necessity at their shipboard table.

'Gentlemen,' pronounced Edward Pellew, gazing all about the table with satisfaction at the beatific anticipation evident on delighted faces, 'Our acquaintances are made - eh - and now to dinner... without the loss of a moment!'

The wine glasses were replenished once more by the attentive stewards and the eating of the glorious meal - for that was the measure of it for the Surprises - began without delay, a pleasurable hiatus of silence descending on the table as the guests attacked their meal without the briefest of moments lost. Admiral Pellew's dinner was quite splendid, far exceeding the aspirations of even the greediest of souls, and Duncan came close to that definition even by his own reckoning. It was better than anything that anyone could rightfully expect even from the flagship of any fleet, but for the Surprises, long deprived of everything that might be termed proper food, it was far, far beyond their most enthusiastic expectations and so they gorged with an intensity of application which amazed the hosts all through the soup to the main course, the Pellews striving vainly with intermittent interjections of enquiry, all of which passed largely ignored save for the occasional platitude murmured by their brothers or Cornelius Tripe, all maintaining a modicum of polite interest which the three Surprises, after heroic but the briefest of endeavours, could not long sustain. Ultimately the conversation faltered save for pleasantries and polite murmurs of 'Allow me to help you to another slice,' and 'Most kind, if you will,' or 'Well, perhaps I will take just the one more potato,' or 'May I pour you another glass of wine?' and suchlike.

'Tell, did you find occasion to indulge your naturalist interests during these past months at sea?' asked Tripe, persisting, an awareness within him that things were not well with his friend.

'Precious little, I regret to say...' Simon replied. His friend nodded his understanding, such was no surprise to him. 'It pains me greatly now as it did then, but it seems that I was rarely out of the cockpit, no time left to me to undertake any explorations of such nature...' Simon set down his glass, his tentative smile fading, his countenance betraying the obvious distress radiating from his very being. In a low voice, his reservations set aside in the presence of a medical colleague of such standing, he continued, 'Such a ghastly profusion of casualties: near two dozen killed and four dozen wounded; why, without the help of Marston - you may meet him in the Chapel attending the men, he is a treasure - and dear Jason... I... I could never have coped... the numbers so great, the wounds so severe...' Simon's despairing voice tailed off.

'I am not unfamiliar with the surgeon's heavy load, with the bloody burden and, indeed, with the acute urgency... the senses... the senses being so greatly heightened in the hour of crisis,' this in a whisper, Simon's desolation becoming plain to Tripe, his fears for his friend's well-being confirmed. 'You have my most sincere sympathies. May God preserve them all.'

'Thank you, colleague. I take that very well,' mumbled Simon very quietly.

'If I may be of any assistance... the smallest thing...'

'Thank you. I am persuaded that Marston and I have no further immediate fears for the men; their recuperation is underway... progressing satisfactorily... at least they give no pressing concern these past few days,' Simon sighed, his head inclining as if his shoulders were burdened by all the ills of the world.

'It is the great weight you seem to be carrying... How do you fare yourself?'

'Myself? Why, I can scarcely believe how greatly tired I am... and a cursed vexation inflicts itself upon all my thoughts.'

'I am most concerned to hear it, dear friend,' murmured Tripe.

Simon sighed, 'I have been contemplating on the processes of the mind, on mental recovery after trauma... such an unknown.' Tripe nodding sagely in agreement, Simon continued, 'Whilst the matter of physical recovery is generally greatly more familiar to us, that of the intellect, regrettably, remains so much a mystery.'

'You are in the right of things there, to be sure,' this offered more guardedly, Tripe's feelings, his rising concern for his fellow physician flagging a degree of caution whilst he pondered how best to press his enquiry, to help his friend.

'I have attained not the least conclusion in that matter, I regret to say.' Simon sighed once more, his face gloomy, despondent, his attention seemingly not wholly on the conversation.

'Allow me to feel your pulse.' A minute more, 'It is more rapid than might be considered desirable, colleague; indeed, it is. You must take care not to agitate yourself in the slightest. Will you consider of a tint of Kearsley's *Efficacious Tincture*, a trifle of laundanum perhaps?' Simon looking doubtful, Tripe persisted, 'I confess there was a time, an eternity of distressing events it was, long in the past, when I made my own thankful escape in a dozen of drops,' this said in a voice which did not wholly obscure a hesitation in the stated number, for he had for long spells indulged in far more, and being a physician a degree of guilt lingered still.

'Your suggestion has merit, no doubt... and I cherish you for it. The precious tincture oft seems the most valuable of panacea,' Simon hesitated, 'I have myself, on occasion, considered of an Almoravian draught; however, my mind is turned elsewhere, to another resolution.'

'I desire no explanation,' Tripe murmured in apologetic tone.

The tiniest of smiles returned to Simon's face, 'I am inclining towards practical measures, to a visit to the Isles... to cold mornings, wet days and quietude... to hallowed tranquility... with nothing of the shipboard routine pressing upon me, no sound of the bell, nothing of the customary nautical discomfort. A dream it is I indulge in, no doubt... the present calls on my time are so pressing.'

Tripe had been observing his old friend extremely closely, with a professional eye, a thoughtful pause elapsing before he replied, 'My dear Ferguson, I anticipate that I can be here in Falmouth for some considerable time, and so I will call upon you and your men at your convenience.'

'That is exceedingly generous in you, dear colleague,' Simon looked up, the offer of assistance striking a welcome chord.

'Not at all. The Dear knows that a modicum of cordial exchange, the smallest of assistance... will be greatly beneficial in the crises we oft encounter in our capacity as physicians.'

Simon, after a brief pause and in a low voice, whispered, 'I trust you will allow me to share a small confidence?' A smile in reply, offered encouragingly, and Simon resumed, 'It is my most earnest hope that I may return to my home, to blessed Tobermory in the near future... the very near future. That is to say when the wounded are recovered and my attendance is no longer necessary.'

Tripe, absorbed in studious recollection of his own physiological reactions following the more memorable of his own surgical experiences, nodded again, 'An admirable notion, no doubt.'

'A glass with you, Doctor Ferguson!' cried Edward Pellew, feeling that the private dialogue between the two physicians had endured too long and was to the detriment of the social occasion. The attention of all at the table was captured, voices were lowered, words faltering to a general silence.

'Thank you, Admiral,' replied Simon, raising his glass. 'Whenever I find myself in a gathering, I observe that there is always reason, discussion and argument... but we mariners,' Duncan and Pat took a sharp intake of breath, '... we mariners, I oft believe, too often simply tell stories.'

'Very good, sir,' Edward Pellew's voice boomed out again, 'A glass with you, Captain O'Connor.'

'Samuel, dear brother, the bottle stands by you,' said Israel.

'To the valiant *Surprise*!' declared Edward Pellew.

'Hear, hear,' the response echoed with firm determination around the table, 'THE VALIANT *SURPRISE*!'

'And all her men!' Pellew proclaimed with great vigour.

'AND ALL HER MEN!' Minds, blood and memories pulsated within the Surprises, their glasses emptied as one and set down, the thoughts of each man racing with painful recollections.

Thoughtful moments of silent deliberation for all followed, all chatter paused, until Edward Pellew resumed in the most authoritative of voice, 'Captain O'Connor, you will take her to Plymouth Dock... *to Devonport* as we must now call that place... later this week perhaps?' Admiral Pellew's definitive proclamation precluded any resumption of prior conversations, was expressed in a tone which hinted at stridence and suggested he could not conceive of a refusal.

Pat, his name indistinctly registering as he emerged from staring with unconcealed pleasure and considerable anticipation at a particularly thick slice of divine beef, looked up, his attention caught; indeed, demanded. He swallowed hard, 'Yes, sir, in a day or two. Once I have completed my stores and water, and the carpenter is minded the worst of the leaks are stopped.' His thoughts unsettled by the imminently possible prospect of *Surprise* being condemned, and striving once more to focus his thoughts in best fashion, O'Connor stared at the admiral, his former slavering interest in the divine appeal of the meat fast fading. 'She must come out of the water, and I cannot see that such is possible in Falmouth. She is too large for the yard in Flushing; I am minded their limit is of the order of a hundred tons, no more.'

'Very well,' declared Pellew, giving nothing more away and turning his head towards Duncan. 'A glass of wine with you, Commander Macleod. Give you joy of your promotion.'

'Thank you, sir,' a smiling Duncan, his face shining with grease, hastily set down his knife and reciprocated the admiral's compliment with a raise of and a generous gulp from his glass before returning to his beef with determination.

Utterly beatific minutes passed in a return to blissful, gastronomic pleasures, and divine silence reigned until a murmured query crossed the table, seemingly so innocuous - or was it? Pat wondered. 'Your ship, Captain O'Connor; I see she is a trifle low in the water, her pumps unceasing,' this from Israel Pellew.

Pat looked up again, grave dismay plain on his face for all to see, 'For sure there is plentiful sprung caulking.' O'Connor's reply was short, low, reluctant. He resumed his meal, guardedly taking another extremely large slice of meat from the tray, his eyes unseeing, vacant until switched to his plate, his mind enduring a momentary setback, one which did not pass unnoticed by Simon, engaged in secreting his own napkin - filled with surplus beef slices from his plate - within his pocket: such would be the most welcome morsel for supper, *Surprise's* own provisions not yet replenished, at least not with anything like this particularly delectable treasure.

'The Falmouth schooner *Lavinia* was lost in the great storm,' remarked Edward Pellew, 'and a Bideford sloop too, so we understand.' No reply was forthcoming from anyone, least of all and perhaps significantly from the Surprises.

For the next fifteen near silent minutes there were no further storm- or *Surprise*-related comments; only food compliments were voiced, "capital eating" and suchlike, all replies concurring, the Surprises particularly saying little save for murmured pleasantries in reply to all, everyone present munching contentedly on the divine beef: sublimely tender, succulent, the crisped and still attached fat melting in the mouth with an explosion of flavour, and the wine fast diminishing, until came the next question, another asked innocently enough by Israel Pellew, 'Perhaps, Captain O'Connor, you would be kind enough to tell us a little of your experience of the recent tempest?'

All three of the Surprises looked up, faces frozen, minds recoiling from the mere thought of any recitation, for it was something they had not the least wish to recall let alone recount. An instant and unsettling wave of mental dread, of physical nausea had befallen them all: vivid, frightening, alarming; in fact, terrifying; near panic was returned and pressing hard upon minds seared by the horrific experience. Pellew instantly regretted his question, its reception so obviously and deeply unwelcome. Knives and forks were simultaneously set down by three persons, three faces instantly blank; in three minds all thoughts were suspended, frozen; three tongues were stilled. Duncan Macleod stared down in deep dismay at his plate, acid bile surging up within him, his appetite shrinking, all pleasure in his sublime dinner whipped away as if by a return of the roaring, raging hurricane wind itself. Utter silence descended upon the table, all the hosts recognising that the question had not been well received, acutely aware and embarrassed that such enquiry was fiercely unwanted, had produced social catastrophe.

'I beg your pardon, Captain O'Connor,' offered Israel Pellew, acknowledging the disaster of his own making, every man present staring at Pat.

Hands all around the table reached for wine glasses. An interminably long pause, an excruciating near minute which dragged like the longest of hours, time seemingly frozen within the bleakest of temporal desert, and Pat took a large gulp of his wine. 'Admiral Pellew...' he shivered, that hand clutching his wine glass trembling - his nightmares, vivid and horrific since the cataclysm, had denied him necessary and recuperative sleep - '... your enquiry is deserving of a reply, sir.' The cold words were uttered with civility, yet were distant, and ears all around the table pricked up, all eyes fixed firmly on O'Connor, whose gaze was unblinking, his demeanour so very severe. He was staring at Israel Pellew, not with overt hostility, Pat was too gracious by far for that, but with an infinite reserve and a decent attempt upon politeness; yet his cold eyes betrayed him, illuminating a depth of inimical feeling. Slowly, so very slowly he found his words, uttered with reluctance, considerations of potential personal implication wholly cast aside, his reply quietly spoken, 'Never in all my years at sea have I ... have I *ever* encountered such fury... and found such fear... as that day and night.' Pat took another deep draught of his wine, remained immobile whilst gathering his thoughts, searching for his words, absolute silence reigning, no one interrupting; an air of charged expectancy hung around the table, every face gazing with apprehension, a nervous caution and a polite reserve prevailing.

'Please,' Pellew spoke up, concern in his voice, 'do continue.'

'I have not the least doubt that I gazed upon waves a hundred feet above me; indeed, I venture a hundred and fifty or even greater was more the measure of them.' Pat sighed again, a long, long exhalation of breath, looked to frozen faces around the table, and slowly set down his glass, 'If ever I thought I would experience that tumult... such terror... once more - *Mother of God, Saint Patrick preserve me* - then...' his heartfelt words were now no more than a whisper, '...'tis sure I would never go to sea again... even were His Majesty personally to press upon me to do so.'

The shock of the words, spoken with such evident emotion, rocked every man present, the enduring silence still gripping all at the table and persisting for near a minute save for an astounded Edward Pellew coughing wine from his windpipe. The meal was instantly forgotten, all pleasure in the social occasion swept away, the experienced sea officers stunned, all speechless, every mind whirring frantically in search of some suitable recovery.

A loud cough, 'May I trouble you to pass the salt, colleague?' Simon's words, the weakest of bridge, fell flat, found no reception, passed unheard and unnoticed, all eyes still fixated upon O'Connor.

'By your leave, sir,' Pat, staring vacantly, turned to Edward Pellew, 'I am at a stand, all thrown out. I beg you will allow me to leave the recounting of that day to another time.' Pellew nodded, no words could he find himself.

Monday 29th November 1824   08:00   The Wesleyan Chapel, Falmouth

The dawn found Simon Ferguson entering the Chapel to attend the wounded recuperating there. It was his daily routine, had been since the morning after *Surprise's* arrival. To his immense satisfaction there had been no more deaths amongst his charges; such benevolent outcome had brought to him the greatest of relief, for he had struggled with an unceasing crisis of personal morale for all the months since the end of the second battle to defend Samos from the Ottoman invasion when, in the immediate aftermath, he had become overwhelmed by a momentary breakdown in his resolve, his fortitude withering whilst treating the many casualties, a number dying before his eyes, immense personal anguish arising with his inability to save them. Fortunately for all aboard his acute crisis was brief, and he had returned below after a very few minutes of panic, of mental collapse on the quarterdeck, Pat soothing his angst and despair with calming words, with his own concerns, with gentle praise and great emphasis on the reliance of all aboard on Simon, himself included, and never more acutely than at that moment; and it was Murphy's shout, his plea for Simon's urgent attendance which had restored his determination and carried him below, back to the enduring blood and vile distress of his table.

The ambience within the Chapel was so utterly different to that day of horror upon bloody horror: calm, restful; merely the low murmurings of the patients audible, the ambience one of quietude, peaceful; all of which greatly aided the restoration of mental strength, the benevolent recuperations of untroubled physical rest bringing thankful relief to both the wounded and the surgeons. Simon stared the length of the hall, four dozen beds in four rows the length of it, all the customary benches set aside. In that gloomy, weak winter light which reached the hall from the small windows at the brighter Market end he could see men sitting up - the fitter ones - whilst at the far end, no windows with the hill directly behind the hall and no natural illumination, in the muted glow of lanterns Simon could perceive two men: one he thought familiar, a slight figure and somewhat indistinct in the gloom, standing at the side of the bed of a man who had been particularly badly wounded, who had lost a leg to a large splinter struck from the smashing of the companionway structure. It was his old friend and colleague, Cornelius Tripe, talking with Marston. Simon hastened down the hall.

'Good morning Doctor Ferguson,' said Tripe warmly, turning to greet Simon with an affable smile. 'I was afflicted by a sleepless night and rose early. My accommodation a mere street away, I determined upon a visit to your fellow shipmates, worthy souls all. I have been here an hour with your most admirable colleague, Marston.

'Good morning, Doctor Tripe, Marston,' replied Simon as positively as he could manage, for during the discussions of the prior day he had, after the lengthy exchanges with Tripe - his friend's effort to help him realised - reconnected with his longstanding opinion of him as a fellow spirit, truly a man dedicated to his profession, and that after the briefest of reacquaintance in the Customs House. He was greatly familiar with most of Cornelius Tripe's published works and his comprehensive analyses of those of fellow physicians. He had often re-read his colleague's notes on Stephen Maturin's famous and excellent treatise *Suggestions for the Ameliorations of Sick-Bays* with particular interest, and had always sought thereafter to apply Maturin and

Tripe's philosophies to his own circumstances; but his meeting again with his former colleague, as was ever the case, had crystallised his belief that here was a great medical man, truly an innovator, a creative surgeon and an inquisitive doctor, a physician for a new age in medicine; and that, as far as Simon was concerned, was badly needed within the fleet specifically and in the world of medicine generally. Moreover, Tripe was the most genuine of persons, wholly lacking in those lamentable vices such as arrogance, airs of superiority and ignorant indifference to the views of others, vices regrettably so oft encountered within many fleet medical men; at least that was what Simon had observed on several occasions he had met with such men aboard other ships and at Royal Navy establishments. The two men had reconnected with each other within minutes of their meeting; indeed, had rapidly welcomed the meeting of minds of kindred spirits.

'Doctor Tripe is minded that your surgery, your technique is of the very finest,' pronounced Marston with deep conviction. 'He has attended my cleansing of the men's wounds this morning.'

'Most kind, colleague,' murmured Simon with bountiful pleasure, extremely gratified, for such was praise indeed.

'I have for some months been in contemplation of assisting Doctor Tripe at the Dock upon our return, a position I understand you occupied before your departure for Greece,' said Marston.

'Yes, Doctor Tripe and I became the firmest of friends,' Simon replied, still pleasantly gratified by the compliment. 'He is the most exemplary of men; indeed, he possesses greatly meritorious aspirations for his city; doubtless he will serve Plymouth well in years to come.'

'No doubt,' murmured Marston.

'I have asked of Admiral Saumarez this morning by letter leave to reside for some weeks in Falmouth,' said Tripe. 'He is not greatly pressed with sickness in Plymouth, in Devonport, the fleet reduced so. It would please me, Ferguson, were you minded to allow me to assist you here, to stay until all your comrades are healed, are fit to leave this place, this sanctuary. That is... with your permission, of course.'

Simon, his thoughts swimming, his sense of duty and obligation - which had long seized his every waking moment - relenting just a very little, allowed his mind to trifle with the luxury of relief, blessed relief, which was only now seemingly appearing; the help of the most exceptional and gifted surgeon in the navy, perhaps in the country, was at hand; indeed, it was proffered. 'Why, I would be honoured,' Simon was deeply touched, 'greatly honoured. It would be the most magnificent of privilege to work with you once more, dear colleague.'

'Then you may count on my endeavours until such time as we have effectuated the recovery of all of your patients. May I beg you to tell me about these men, their injuries, such that I may consider further how I may be of help? A very brief account of such generalities which may afflict them all, or several of them, would suffice before we turn our attentions to the particulars of each man.'

'Of course.'

'Is there any fever of the blood?'

'Not in these men. Those who were afflicted by it... that is to say after the battle... those men... unfortunately...' Simon's voice faltered, '... died... in Cephalonia. I regret I was unable to save even a one of them. It grieves me to this day. So much so that I had considered... I remain in some doubt... that is to say... it may... it may be that my talents are not suited to the case...' Simon's voice tailed off, Marston staring agape, for such a thought had never entered his head, his respect for Simon so absolute.

'I must decline to differ,' not the least hesitancy in Tripe's reply, 'My observations are profoundly all of a like; your surgery is of the finest, dear Ferguson... the very finest; there can be no doubt of that, not the least. Indeed, I have rarely seen its measure: a singular precision in amputation, the most careful of sutures and stitching. I believe Guthrie himself would be impressed. May I offer my own, *my personal* congratulations, colleague?'

Simon, the words an uplifting comfort in his diminished state, in his self-doubt, managed the smallest of nods, a silent minute elapsing, precious relief, a degree of restoration of his wavering self-confidence coming to him as he silently thanked God and all in the heavens before continuing in a whisper, 'Thank you. I take that most kindly. For many of our patients there remains considerable pain as broken limbs repair; in others the scars of amputation are healing; these men endure it well, for the most part hold themselves in good cheer, yet sleep eludes them in their difficulties, the consequent fatigue oft leading to dismay and - it is understandable - ill-temper.'

'I venture a little more of laudanum will answer the case. It is a comfort.'

'Several of these poor souls suffer still with lingering wounds... to the stomach, the chest, the abdomen and such places as will leave them with an enduring discomfort; they eat little, oft refuse food. I was contemplating this morning on the prospects for those particular men.'

'A low diet, a thin water gruel... thrice a day... will provide all that is required... or almost all. In Plymouth we are minded that an honest glass of stout in the evening will also be greatly beneficial for the humours.' Tripe turned to Martin at his side, 'Would you be so good as to excuse us for just a minute or two, Martin,' he murmured, 'if you please?'

'Of course. I will look to the breakfast, see how it is coming along.'

'It is scarcely decent in me to suggest, Ferguson, that you are yourself downcast, melancholic... and, will I say, were we in contemplation of your personal disquietude then some remedy might come to mind.' Tripe's consternation radiated from his face, a most earnest stare, 'What ails thee, pray tell?'

A long pause, the quietest of reply from Simon, 'Some may consider it a trifling matter, but it is a long while since I was at home.'

'I beg pardon, there is not the least thing trifling about such a concern. A benevolent restorative it surely will be. I have myself gained necessary recuperation from many an ill affliction of the mind whilst striding over the Dart moor on a fine day.' The surgeons gazed at each other for a few moments, mutual empathy already forged strong. 'I collect that it is your pressing desire to visit your home in Tobermory, is that not so?'

'It is indeed, yet I could not countenance these men without me. I must answer for them to my conscience, and without my care, my presence, it would be a mere contemptible scrap, one not worth a ha'penny.'

Another long minute of reflection, both surgeons weighing the other with a wholly benevolent gaze, reflecting upon their calling and the necessary Falmouth immediacies particularly, until Tripe spoke at last, 'That is most creditable in you; indeed, it is, but you are to consider, dear Ferguson, that - unless I am much astray - there is not a man here whose ailment is beyond my own medicinal capacities. I see no man with the Plymouth Dock Disease, the rot of the flesh... all of them are healing - every one of them. To be sure, you have served them all well; every man is - *with the blessing of our Lady* - recovering, in good heart; and that is most surely thanks to your dedication and your competencies; of that I have not the least doubt. You have saved many of these men with your ministrations, *your personal ministrations*. Go home. I will attend them whilst you are away. It is no great burden, I do assure you. Have no fears; Mr Marston is here as my companion, as my assistant, and he is tolerably familiar with every one of your charges.'

Simon, a powerful surge of emotion arising within him, felt overcome, his fragility of composure so utterly overwhelmed by the kindness of someone who was, whilst not a total stranger, a colleague of the past. 'I am greatly obliged to you...' he could only mumble his words, his heartfelt thanks, '... greatly obliged; thank you... that is immeasurably benevolent in you, thank you.' He choked back the smarting beginnings of tears of gratitude in his eyes and the rising turbulence within his chest, for such would not do; he was a greatly reserved man, and the raging emotions unleashed within him these past months sat ill with him, in fact had brought his natural reserve to a most public collapse at the supper table within the Metaxata household after the Samos battles: Mower's words, the lieutenant's emotive poetry quite overwhelming him. His mind whirring and his obligations pressing hard upon him, he ventured his reluctant conclusion with a shake of his head, 'I could not leave this place, these men.'

Cornelius Tripe despaired, wracked his brain, and then - long familiarity with the sometimes self-serving and creative inclinations of the naval mind prompting a thought - he recalled a particular conversation, one so long ago that it seemed akin to a different life, the recollection vividly coming to mind; he pressed on, 'It is, of course, a regulation; indeed, it is a singularly well-founded statute, a most humane one, that ship's surgeons, returned from any campaign where there has been an engagement, must - *and I do say this most emphatically* - *must* go on leave directly. Why, to do otherwise might be considered in some quarters - *doubtless less-enlightened ones* - to verge upon a gross insubordination.'

'What a benignant regulation,' mumbled Simon, a degree of confusion coming upon him, 'though with so many men wounded I could not in good conscience take advantage of it.'

'Oh, but such is not an option, a choice is not open to you; no, it is certainly not...' Tripe persevered. 'For where would we be without it was observed... no, no, that would never do, Ferguson. Allow me to say, dear colleague, that this particular regulation is invariably respected in the service... *invariably*, so it is,' Tripe's persuasive techniques were reaching hitherto unsuspected heights, 'May Joseph and Mary forgive me,' the unspoken thought coming to his mind before his finale, 'Why, even Beatty was minded to comply after losing Nelson at Trafalgar.'

A long stare, 'With such illustrious precedent it might, perhaps, be considered reprehensible to hold to any exception.' A rising relief began coursing through Simon's every fibre, but then a momentary hesitation, 'Must I not stay?'

A moment's pause and Tripe replied, 'Listen now: will you do me a kindness? Pack your chest, go to your home with contentment, without reservation. You must allow me to insist.'

'Yes... yes, I will,' Simon uttered the words very quietly, a first degree of resolution in the timbre of his voice, 'I am fully persuaded.'

'Then that is settled,' pronounced Tripe, espying Simon's confusion evaporating, a growing conviction evident in his countenance. He seized and shook his hand, 'May the blessings of God and all the saints be with you; give you joy, dear colleague.'

Monday 29th November 1824   09:00   *Surprise, Falmouth*

Aboard *Surprise*, Pat, with a bare score of men with him, had fussed all about his ship since returning to her shortly after the dawn. He stood on his quarterdeck in the cold, dry morning air, a thin mist rising from the still waters within the harbour, the early morning silence conducive to his musings on the work underway, thoughts which were blighted only by the uncertain prospects for his ship. That *Surprise* was *his ship* registered deeply within his mind, though he gave that no conscious thought, but it did subliminally drive his determination to do what little he could to restore her to readiness for the short passage to Plymouth. A dozen men took turn and turn about industriously serving at the pumps, some of them not Surprises though all were Falmouth men, every one a relative of someone who had recently served in his crew. Indeed, the majority had served aboard *Tenedos* when Pat had commanded her and were greatly pleased to be of help, of service to him once more, and an easy atmosphere reigned amongst them all; cheerful words, "good mornin' sir" and companionable nods in passing from all men were extended to Pat as he moved about the ship, Pat reciprocating with a brief greeting or a friendly acknowledgement of an old comrade. His longstanding steward, Murphy, appeared on the quarterdeck to oblige Pat's passion for the very strongest of hot black coffee, passing him a steaming tin mug. His second steward, Freeman, remained ashore, in close attendance of Doctor Ferguson and Michael Marston, assisting the surgeons with the tending of the wounded. Indeed Freeman's stock with every man of the Surprises had never been higher, for he had stuck doggedly to the care of the casualties since assisting in the second Samos battle, the surgeons being swamped, subsumed in so many bloody amputations and life-saving operations. Pat could not bring himself to order him back aboard, and so it was Murphy, the greatest grumbler of all the world, the most pernickety of pedants in the matter of scrupulous care and cleanliness of Pat's clothing, who remained to attend him. Of his few skills and talents, his ability to make the finest coffee was probably at the top of an extremely short list.

'Well, sorr, will 'ee be wantin' a clean, pressed uniform... Admiral Pellew comin' aboard...' Murphy's whining voice dropped to little more than a whisper, '...an' you in them old rags?'

'Pipe down, Murphy; not at present,' Pat replied offhandedly, his mind fixated upon the state of his ship and his recent tour to investigate progress. The carpenter, Stuart Tizard, with three helpers was working at the bow, slung over the side in the bosun's chair and tapping small wedges into the more visible of the gaps occasioned by lost caulking; the bosun, Nicholas Sampays, a Portugese of long Royal Navy service and also a *Tenedos* veteran, similarly strived to clear and replace the last of the ripped shards and torn remnants of the severed rigging which had been cut away when the mizzen was hacked down in the hurricane. *Surprise* had been knocked down when so far over in her turn when falling off the wind that her yard tips had been subsumed in the raging water, her sinking mere moments away. Five panic-stricken minutes of terror, axes wildly flailing, the mizzen crudely hacked down, all rigging manically slashed away and the deadly drag of the mast was released; *Surprise* had managed to complete her turn downwind and, with only mere moments left to her above water, miraculously righted herself. Pat shuddered as he recollected the horrifying desperation of the near catastrophe. For now, he was reconciled to the fact that a replacement for the lost mizzen mast would have to await the frigate's return to Plymouth; doubtless seasoned timber for such could be procured from the mast pond at the Yard if, that is, *Surprise* was not condemned to the breakers. He sighed, his fundamental uncertainties, his gravely unsettling doubts surging to the fore once more in his confusion of thoughts. He looked all about him: Murphy had gone.

Of Pat's officers, Duncan Macleod was below, gathering his dunnage, preparing to leave on *Eleanor* within the hour, slack water just prevailing and the tide nearing the ebb. Abel Jason too was clearing his tiny cabin off the gun-room, and all the officers were puzzling over the mysterious summons of the First Lord. Pat was long aware of Macleod's semi-official role as an intelligence gatherer and Jason's abilities as a linguist, but he could not fathom why, *Surprise's* Greek adventures seemingly at an end - for in her present lamentable state the brief transit to Plymouth was all that she was fit for. In truth he neither wanted nor cared to enquire of either of his officers; not that they themselves knew anything of the reasons for their summons anyway. His Second, Tom Pickering, was also on deck, supervising the most modest of restorations which were underway to the sails. At least some new canvas had been procured in Falmouth, a dozen bolts of it, and the sailmaker had been particularly busy these recent days, for all of *Surprise's* staysails had been torn away, the canvas flying into the darkness of the tempest, whilst several of her square sails had ripped from top to bottom under the great strain of the hurricane wind. Notwithstanding these remedies of stricken canvas, of severed rigging and wedges crudely blocking missing bow caulking, the sum total of all possible repairs was barely sufficient to take *Surprise* safely to Devonport in anything other than a flat calm.

Lieutenants William Reeve and William Codrington were presently both aboard *Eleanor*, readying her to make passage to London: Reeve to command her for the voyage whilst Codrington would return aboard and remain with *Surprise*. Lieutenant Mower remained wholly unfit for duty and remained with the wounded within the Chapel. The master, Jeremiah Prosser, was ashore, his local connections facilitating the arranging of provisions for the wounded and those few men still aboard the barky, for almost all of the crew had been discharged as soon as she arrived at Falmouth, as was the custom. Pat's cox'n, George Barton, was away in the captain's new found jollyboat, purchased on the day after arrival, all of the frigate's boats being torn away from their ties and smashed to smithereens in the hurricane. Barton awaited Admiral Pellew at the Town quay.

It was a strange day, a deserted *Surprise*, so few of the long familiar faces present, both Pat's close friends absent or about to become so and only a skeleton crew aboard. He leaned back on the damaged taffrail and gazed forward, past Sampays and his men to the waist; the gap, the space left by the absent mizzen was so glaring, so empty, and his heart sank just a little. Was she truly now fit only for the breakers? It was a saddening thought. And how was he to bring her to Devonport with a bare score of men, half of them not really of his crew but former shipmates of the *Tenedos* years and, strictly stated, unpaid volunteers? It did not bear thinking about. Perhaps he would speak to Pellew about it. Neither was his wife the happiest lady in town, Sinéad arguing that it was no longer his task to deliver *Surprise* to Plymouth; rather, it was time to return to Ireland, to Claddaghduff in Connemara on the far Galway coast, to the farm, to home, *blessed home* - the real one. He wondered absently where Murphy had gone: probably to the liquor store, likely to idle his time away below.

With rising confusion, his mind in a minor degree of turmoil and a significant feeling of uncertainty besetting him, for such a return to Ireland did not hold great appeal for Pat - he had long recognised that he was no potato farmer - he reigned back as best he could all such depressing thoughts of *Surprise* being scrapped and an end to his seafaring career approaching. In consequence of that particular eventuality he had long before engaged with promoters to commence a small gold mine on his two acres of land in the Gannoughs, in the very smallest of hills, a rocky promontory on the Connemara coast where the promoters assured him that it was the very same granite bedrock as that where, late in the year '95, gold had been found in the Ballinvalley river in County Wicklow. However, no gold had been found at Claddaghduff, at least not yet; but despite the scepticism of his close friend, Simon Ferguson, Pat had not wholly given up all hope of a miraculous discovery of such metallic bounty. As more time had gone by the ever more obvious and real likelihood of failure of that exceedingly speculative venture did bear more heavily with him co-incident with his realisation that it was the sea, only the sea, where he was in his element, where he was truly familiar with and comfortable in the world about him. His mind so very much disturbed by so many and varied fundamental doubts, his thoughts returned to that which he customarily understood so well: his sea-going life and *Surprise*. He did not much care to contemplate a return to duty in Greece, to the rather uncomfortable service outside of the official Royal Navy, for in truth the Greek organisation, or lack of it, would try the patience of a saint; certainly he had found it extremely taxing, only the long spells of *Surprise* voyaging alone bestowing some modicum of relief from the disorganisation, the anarchy that was the Greek navy; indeed, if it could be called Greek or even a navy at all, for it comprised of many and disparate tiny flotillas, armed merchantmen all, of Hydriots, Spezziots and Psariots, many of whom had been feuding between themselves before the war for independence from the Ottoman empire. What therefore did the future hold for him? He had no idea, for that was the truth of things. Where now lay the foundation for his future? He knew not. He sighed, drank down the last of his coffee and determined to go below to his cabin. He stepped to the undamaged companionway, the other still missing, smashed by a Turk ball strike, and he descended to the gun deck, slowly entering the coach, his steps slow, his mind awhirl with a confusion of thoughts and an intolerably heavy burden of despond.

'Well, here be your first breakfast, sorr,' announced Murphy, bursting in behind him. The steward passed Pat by, marched through to the great cabin without ceremony, set down the toasted cheese on Pat's table, fussed about polishing Pat's plate and cutlery, and presented a bright, white napkin.

'Thankee, Murphy,' Pat cheered a little. 'Please to tell me when Admiral Pellew approaches. I will be here in the cabin. Now cut along and rouse out another pot of coffee if you will.'

'Well, 'tis just a'comin' up, sorr, d'reckly,' this accompanied by a determined effort, a near indiscernible smile from Murphy.

Pat sat in his chair, the cabin exceptionally tidy; Murphy had rectified the saltwater flood of the tempest, removed all the sodden books, charts and clothing. His cot lacked its mattress - hanging still over the hammock netting and drying still - but his desk, table and chairs remained, upright once more, wiped down; the familiar surroundings to a small degree diminishing the melancholia which had settled upon him, providing a modicum of a feeling of normality, at least within this, his personal province. He munched speedily through the food, realising he was very hungry, the meal demolished in mere minutes, Pat feeling the better for it.

'Well, now sorr, here be the coffee, an' *if 'ee please*... will 'ee put on these here clean vestments?' Murphy's return and his insistence, so unusually welcome on this occasion, broke the train of Pat's maudlin thoughts.

'Why thankee, Murphy,' Pat's spirits lifted. 'That is tolerably welcome, indeed it is; thankee.' He smiled, a tiny glimmer of good cheer contrasting with the gloom of the day so far. He stripped off his working clothes and began to don with rising pleasure the crisp, clean uniform of the Royal Navy, the prominent epaulettes and insignia more significant in his appreciation than ever they had seemed before, and now restored to his pressed blue jacket: Murphy had not been idle.

Eleanor's boat bobbed and rocked alongside *Surprise*, Lieutenant Reeve staring with a face of anxiety from the schooner's deck, twenty yards off, slack water long ended. Macleod and Jason stood with Pat on his quarterdeck, making their farewells. 'I bid you swift passage, Duncan,' said Pat, striving to present as much cheer as he could summon.

'Och aye, I'll be with ye again in a week or twae,' declared Duncan, shaking Pat's hand. 'Havnae doubt of that.'

'Take care, Mr Jason... Abel,' said Pat, gripping and shaking Jason's hand with an intensity of great goodwill. 'It is my most fervent hope that we will all meet again in Plymouth in the coming weeks.'

'And indeed that is my own particular wish, sir,' Jason's words, emphatically declared and as warm as they were surely meant to be, could not disguise his own reservations, the unwelcome tinge of uncertainty, of doubt.

Without further adieu Duncan and Jason clambered down into the boat, the crewmen immediately hauling hard on their oars, cognisant of Reeve's many reiterations of urgency, greatly mindful of the flowing ebb tide.

'Good day, Mr Reeve!' Pat shouted across the intervening gap, waving, 'and safe passage!'

The schooner rounded the shallows of the Bar and disappeared within a quarter hour behind the Pendennis promontory, the watchers aboard *Surprise* remaining at the rail, unmoving, every man immersed in his own thoughts. After a mere five minutes the reflective torpor was broken as Barton's jollyboat arrived, tying alongside, Admiral Pellew coming aboard. Though no formalities were customary on arrival at the larboard side, where Barton had correctly anticipated Pat's strong preference, 'Larboard side,' he had shouted to his shipmates rowing. Any ceremony in receiving Pellew aboard was inconceivable: Barton knew there was not a man aboard the ship at this moment who was dressed in other than the scruffiest of slops.

A uniformed Pellew ascended the companionway with a literal spring in his step, a broad smile on his face, wholly disregarded convention and saluted the quarterdeck with considerable enthusiasm. Pat, grateful in that small moment of restoration of tradition for Murphy's attention to his own clean and pressed formal uniform, doffed his hat and saluted the admiral. 'Welcome aboard, sir,' the words offered with a civil nod.

Pellew extended his hand, 'And the finest of good mornings it is too, O'Connor. Indeed, it is a damn fine morning whenever I find myself aboard ship these days; there it is... too many infernal days ashore, but enough of that else we may run foul of speaking of higher authorities, and I would not care for that.'

'Top of the morning to you, sir. How I most heartily wish the ship was in better order for your visit.'

'It don't signify in the least, not at all. I do so hate a flash ship,' replied Pellew in a friendly tone and with the kindliest of look.

'I regret, sir, that we have enjoyed neither the time nor the materials to remedy her prodigious damages during these past days...' Pat's voice tailed off.

'Never be so concerned, O'Connor. Do not stand on ceremony,' declared the admiral with great benevolence.

'You are very good, sir.'

'Now, pray be so good as to show me the barky, and perhaps we will enjoy a tint of coffee later... *you do have coffee?*'

'Be so good as to follow me, sir,' Pat was feeling a little more relaxed, Pellew's informality a huge relief. 'Yes, it pleases me to say we have a fine coffee, a Turkish coffee, so it is.'

'Excellent, pray lead on.'

Pat paced slowly about the quarterdeck; that there were none of the customary carronades present was readily apparent. To a fighting man such as Edward Pellew the glaring vacancy loomed large. 'The smashers went overboard, sir, to lighten ship,' said Pat, anticipating the admiral's question, one plainly framed in his face if not on his lips, '... so much water in the hold... seven feet at one time...' The admiral's smile vanished and his face darkened; he nodded his understanding. They turned at the taffrail to gaze forward the length of the ship; the void presented by the absent mizzen mast was stark, glaring. 'The mizzen was cut down to release her, when she was knocked down in the storm,' explained Pat, 'a beam sea... the drag of the mast in the water preventing her from finishing her turn... to fall off the wind, the fury of it pressing her down.' Pat swallowed hard, the recounting of the terrible minutes of disaster in progress constricting his throat, his breathing coming faster, his tone of voice deepening. 'She would not come back... rise up... until the mast was gone, the rigging severed.'

'Good God Almighty!' Pellew gazed at the stump of the mast in something akin to disbelief, his mind struggling to visualise the scene of horror, 'An infernal close run thing, I venture?'

'Indeed it was, sir,' the whispered reply, 'Perilously close.'

Pellew stared hard at the deck planking, walked slowly forward to the rail overlooking the gun deck, all the time gazing down; to his practised eye the indelible dark stains in large patches on the oak planking - holystoning long accepted in the fleet as being utterly useless - could not be missed, could be only one thing: blood, buckets of it, dried in the sun to a permanence. There was no other explanation for such that he could think of. His eyes narrowed, yet he said nothing, the bloody causation of the now near black residues perfectly plain to him. Together they turned and paced aft again, past the compass housing to the wheel, the admiral lifting his gaze from the deck, turning once more, the length of the ship before them. 'The foretop don't look like anything that ever came out of Pompey, O'Connor,' remarked the admiral, 'Cut short, would it be?'

'Yes sir; the original was struck by Turk shot, cut away, cast overboard...' Pat's spirits were diminishing by the minute even as his heart, it seemed to him, beat louder, burning anxieties rising.

'On my life...' Pellew muttered to himself and, more loudly, 'She was damnably knocked about.'

'I regret she was, sir,' Pat waved his hand toward the remaining companionway as if to lead the admiral away from further scrutiny of more ravages, unrepaired and greatly demoralising. 'Please to step this way.' Pat started quickly down the steps of the surviving companionway, as if in so doing it would hasten Pellew's practised eyes away from the sight of so much more yet unseen damage, perhaps towards rather safer havens. 'The other was smashed by a ball strike, off Samos,' declared Pat, anticipating the admiral's obvious enquiry.

Pellew nodded, thinking hard. He reached the bottom of the steps and stared down the length of the gun deck. 'In the storm... the carronades gone... you did not care to cast the great guns overboard?'

'It was not for want of intention, for with never less than one or two feet of water all over the deck, no sails and rolling most severely...' Pat shuddered as he spoke. '... I dare say she was heeled over to some sixty degrees, and it was not possible... we dare not untie them... we could never have held... controlled them... else they too would have gone...' Pat's voice tailed off.

'I am fully persuaded of it,' the words were uttered quietly, the gravity of *Surprise's* situation revealed with crystal clarity, the depth of her distress and that of her men all clear to Pellew, and his tone of voice was low; the terrifying nature and extent of the ship's catastrophic danger had registered with him as they paced the length of the deck to stand under the foc'sle. The admiral gazed in silent astonishment at the bow hull, hundreds of tiny wooden wedges remaining tapped into the gaps in the oak timbers where, bereft of the caulking which had dried and shrunk in Greece's summer and which had then been battered out by the repetitive pounding of monstrous wave after storm wave, the seawater had pressed in, the accumulation of a myriad of tiny jets becoming an unstoppable, unceasing and flooding torrent, much worse on the decks below where it could find no escape.

Pat led on, down the steps to the lower deck. In the immediate area at the bottom of them, a dim light persisting, Pellew noticed more enduring stains proliferating on the planking, many of them large indeed. Shocked and unspeaking, he looked down all about him in dismay, dozens more of the dark blotches were visible, stretching away into the far gloom. The illumination of the solitary lantern not affording him any more than an impression of the whole of the deck, an image, a picture came to mind, his imagination affording him a vision of the surgeons working in this dark place, dozens of wounded men lying here in their agonies, bleeding, crying, dying. The admiral's steps and words were halted entirely. He stood in enduring silence, rigid, unmoving, staring the length of the lower deck.

Eventually, a grim nod from Pellew and they stepped on, down to the orlop, halting above the hold, two feet of water even now still swilling about, for the extra pumps procured from ashore had enabled the water depth to be reduced from the former six feet still present on arrival but no further. 'Good God!' exclaimed Pellew. That so many pumps were still working he had noted on his arrival aboard, great streams of water visibly gushing out in a torrent from the larboard side where he had boarded, the same being visible from the deck on the starboard side; and then the rhythmical, noisy, mechanical workings of the pumps could not fail to reach his ear even now, six of them going non-stop, always a dozen men working them, the laborious toil unceasing, day and night.

Up they stepped, up from the near absolute darkness of the hold to the enduring gloom of the lower deck, both men uncomfortable, aware they were returning to the surgeons' scene of horror; slowly they stepped towards the stern, towards the gunroom, Edward Pellew dawdling, deep in reflection, Pat striving to quicken his step but reluctantly holding back to stay with his distinguished visitor, the admiral taking in everything about him, every detail, every nuance, every visible vestige of record of the events. Pat too began to reflect on the battle; he stared as if seeing for the first time the old bloodstains, never completely cleansed since the battles of Samos, and the fresh ones from injuries reopened by the hurricane's horrors. All had been scrubbed a dozen times since the Falmouth arrival, but with very limited success, and Pat too was now reduced to keeping his silence; indeed, he would have omitted the lower deck from his tour, had that been possible, for the unspeakable horrors he had witnessed in the aftermath of the Samos battle endured painfully in his mind, and simply being here, in the place where Simon had endured the gruesome and ghastly burdens which had precipitated his brief breakdown, was hard, deeply distressing, the horrors so recent. The admiral, Pat's long silence registering with him, reined in the innocuous platitude about to escape his lips, bit down on his tongue, turned and faced his guide, shaken, deeply moved, unsettled, his heart turning within him. He was tolerably accustomed to bloodshed and death aboard ship, but plainly what *Surprise* had suffered was of a different scale. He stared at Pat, spoke after the longest of minute, his voice a mere whisper, 'I have been afloat since I was thirteen... on many ships... in many battles. I have seen unspeakable horrors at sea... terrible things which no man would care to reflect on,' Pellew took a deep breath, '... but it is plain to me, O'Connor... it is perfectly plain to me,' he reiterated, '... that you and your men...' a long pause, 'you and your men... have been to hell.'

Chapter Three

Wednesday 1st December 1824 08:00 Falmouth

The additional volunteers had come aboard a short while before the lightening of the dawn sky, pulled across from the quay in a flotilla of fishermen's boats: two score of men to join the handful of Falmouth men already helping the three dozen of those Surprises who had been re-engaged in service, all others including all wounded being discharged. Quite unbidden, the experienced veterans of prior years, men of *Tenedos*, Pat's prior command, every man a shipmate of Pat's former voyages and for the most part old in years had come in ones and twos from all across the small town; coalescing with a resolute unity of purpose, with a steely determination to seize the opportunity to serve with Captain Patrick O'Connor for what many presumed would be the final time, the last voyage, *Surprise* sure to be paid off once the ravages inflicted upon her became plain to the authorities, specifically the Commander-in-Chief Plymouth, Admiral James Saumarez. Quietly and without fuss they climbed up and on to the gun deck, cordial greetings passed from man to man, to join their neighbours and former Royal Navy comrades. With no instruction necessary they busied themselves about the ship, attending to the familiar and customary preliminaries for departure; for the time had come for *Surprise* to make passage for Plymouth. The weather and conditions were clement: a gusting south-westerly breeze, a benevolent sea-state and - joy of all things - nothing of the customary winter rainfall of those parts, though it was exceptionally cold indeed, near freezing, vapours rising from the still harbour waters.

In the great cabin Pat sat at his table, shivering, his breath steaming. Simon, Pickering and Prosser were with him, all savouring the last of their coffee, their second pot; each man seemingly reluctant to shift from this place of comfortable familiarity, few words exchanged between them, an ambience of gloomy resignation prevailing; even Murphy's customary grumbling was muted, near silent, and everyone present looked to his fellows, all lost in thought. There had been for half an hour a suspension of activity whilst stock was taken, the seemingly bleak prospects considered, the ebb tide in prospect. 'Will we fetch Plymouth Yard before the evening gun, Mr Prosser?' ventured Pat at last.

'Forty-five miles,' offered the master eventually with a deadpan expression, and then, with a confidence which was familiar and so deeply reassuring to all present, 'With the south-west wind so... and the neap tide so greatly favourable, she may make 'tween six and seven knots. We are starting in slack water... until we leave the Roads, and then, so close inshore, we will be favoured with near six hours of making tide with us... and one more of slack in Plymouth Sound. I venture we will reach Devonport at sunset or thereabouts.'

'Very good,' pronounced a subdued Pat, Prosser's declaration gratifying, the moment bearing heavy upon him and calling for his decision, 'Well, let us lose not another moment; we will get underway directly and with all the sail she will bear.' And so it was, the anchors hauled up, catted and fished, her yards braced to capture the freshening wind, *Surprise* shifted away steadily in the brightening light from the inner anchorage; the quays, in contrast to the grand spectacle that had been her arrival, remaining bleakly deserted. The frigate, ungainly sight that she was whilst bereft of her mizzen, rapidly gained way as she headed east towards the low hanging orange sun, weak and diffuse behind the thin mists of the eastern sky, *Surprise* within mere minutes reaching the Carrick Roads and thence bearing south with a little east. Out within a half hour more, out from the waters of the great haven, out into the bay, free of all constraints and setting up for the expected steady and straightforward passage to that famed reservoir of ship repair capabilities and the great resources of Devonport's Yard; or might it be, as Pat still wondered, to the hands of the breakers therein, for he still did not know what would ultimately be ordained for his ship.

His doubts had crept up on him again at first light as Barton had rowed him out from the quay to the ship, rising worry becoming a persistent anxiety, insidious and corrosive. Although he had commanded *Surprise* for only the one voyage, she had become completely familiar to him; indeed, she was an exceedingly swift sailer on all feasible points of the wind, and he had little doubt that with her full set of sails flying she would leave any other ship in her wake; she was delightfully responsive to the helm and, more important perhaps than her sailing characteristics, she was *his ship*, a most precious treasure in these straightened times of fleet diminution. He did not care to think that in her present damaged state she might be condemned as unworthy of repair for further service, relegated to a hulk for storage purposes or for prisoners, maybe even broken up. Such an event would also be disastrous for his loyal band of men, most of whom he had known since earlier days in command of *Tenedos*. No other frigate would ever be based in Falmouth, Devonport near and its yard expanding so, and his men, a reliable and trustworthy crew, would doubtless be unemployed for a long time to come.

It was a gravely unsettling train of thought indeed. Admiral Pellew had ordered her departure during the prior evening, after a day of intense talk, all thoughts of the seafarers being mindful of and looking to the weather on the morrow. The night had been calm, a stillness about the air, a sense of inevitability filtering into wondering minds, unease persevering during a tense and sleepless night, ultimately melting away to a firming conclusion when, in the early hours, the decision was made, the dye cast: *Surprise* was to go once more to sea, and - the despairing thought for many - perhaps it really was for the last time. All about Falmouth town in the darkness before the dawn many a goodbye had been whispered, and many a tear too had trickled down the face of a severely distraught Sinéad, once more reiterating her heartfelt plea for a return to Connemara.

Over the prior evening's supper Pat had talked at length with Admiral Pellew, debating the prospects for departure, several hours passing with Pat struggling with a great deal of profound uncertainty, unsettling anxiety, and he had pressed the admiral as far as he dared decently venture without protocol was utterly abandoned, enquiring about the First Lord's particular interest, and then the admiral's own opinion of the prospects for the ship, his personal wishes for the barky, the dear *Surprise*: for such would always be Pat's perception of her. After the finest beefsteak Wynn's Hotel could serve, after copious quantities of an excellent Burgundy had been consumed, the port wine flowing freely thereafter whilst great stories of the prior *Surprise* and other ships had been recounted, a tide of nostalgia rising across the table, a somewhat moved Edward Pellew had offered his private thoughts; given not reluctantly, but without any mind of preserving the proprieties, the customary practices, reservations and conventions as are between officers of differing rank. The cordial evening to that moment had passed with a rising accord between the two men; indeed, a growing mutual liking was forming, the cautious barrier as is the beginning between two strangers meeting for the first time melting away in the warmth of their reminiscences, until the crux arrived: Pellew's words had been issued with a visible conviction, offered upon the acutely pressing matter which plainly was exceedingly close to his own heart, about a ship which carried the venerable name of *Surprise*, a name which he and many others in the service would always revere. 'In confidence, O'Connor, I will tell you of some tolerably secret matters; the First Lord is singularly minded that a frigate must return at the earliest moment to Greece, to support whichever regime emerges when the civil war is finally ended,' so began Edward Pellew's confession.

In the cold light of morning the recollection of the prior evening burned brightly at the forefront of Pat's thoughts; beforehand he had been firmly minded that he would never return to Greece, but now he was plunged back into a confusion of incompatible aspirations: principally, his wife's hopes for an Irish homecoming conflicted with his concerns for his ship, for *Surprise* and her future, and for his men. He recalled Admiral Pellew's loud, fond recollections of his own sea service, ever more garrulous as the wine had diminished. That had struck a chord within Pat's own heart, one which so rarely resonated in the mundane lives of most men, and during that profound moment, whilst he had strived to understand the measure of it, he could say nothing. He had looked to his hands, had withdrawn them under the table; he had hoped that the admiral had not noticed the trembling which had accosted them or the nervous tic inflicted in that instant in his eye upon Pellew's enquiry: 'Would you return, O'Connor...' The admiral had stared hard at Pat, '... to Greece?' nodding gently as if in encouragement, 'Would you?'

The question posed, Pat's mind had raced, jolted from the slowing, settling influence of drink, violently torn away from the pleasant torpor of enjoyable reminiscences, of memorable old times recounted. 'Why...' he temporised, '... I would have to consider of it, sir.' The scene was still perfectly stark in his recall; he could see it now, his mind drifting, the image of an earnest Edward Pellew so clear: the admiral nodded again and continued, '*Surprise* being reported by Macleod as having endured the Samos battles with a deal of damage incurred... and then the hurricane... and so potentially needing of considerable repair - *the First Lord does not yet know the extent of that* - he is considering of *Diamond*, of the veteran, *Shannon*, and also of the new ships coming off the stocks.' A solemn Pellew paused, almost a tone of disappointment registering in his report. 'However, a man-of-war in ordinary, as those particular frigates are, bereft of all guns, their masts dismantled and all yards removed... laid up with neither stores nor crew, no shot - you follow the general line of my thoughts O'Connor? - cannot be made ready to go to sea in a few weeks... it ain't possible.' He looked closely at Pat, lowered his voice, 'It is my most earnest wish that *Surprise* will be restored, will serve again in that function. That such is feasible is undeniable, but with Boney long gone and a plentiful surfeit of ships...' He frowned and continued after a brief pause, '*Trincomalee* is but one of them that comes to mind, and she is only recently commissioned... and there is also *Unicorn* readying at Pompey.' A deep sigh, 'We cannot know for sure if Melville will decide that your ship *will* be repaired... that such *will* happen. I do, though, most sincerely hope that it does, that such will be his conclusion.'

Pat had stared, fascinated, unblinking, his long years of seafaring wisdom entirely failing him in the moment of Pellew's very personal statement, his mind in a turmoil of indecision, conjuring a myriad of varying visions in the same instant, monopolising his responses; his body seemed frozen to immobility, his muscles wholly incapable of movement even as his thoughts whirred frenetically. Forcing his thinking back to the tangible, to the admiral's revelation, Pat's power of speech returned as a silent Pellew patiently awaited his reply, and the words were eventually formulated and uttered, 'Sir, time being so short, when will his Lordship hear of *Surprise*, her present poor state, the prospects for her repair?' Pat's voice had betrayed a burning concern, one which had settled insidiously upon his mind since his awakening in the early hours of that morning before the dawn, pressing with increasing weight as time had passed, ultimately during the afternoon becoming an unpleasant burden which he could not shake from his thinking, adding to his confusion of the several prospects he faced, all unwelcome; for he could not perceive quite how his future would emerge without his ship, without *Surprise*, without his veterans, his comrades. The profound realisation that collectively they most assuredly represented a haven, one of immeasurable depth and personal significance within his very being, had been dawning upon him all evening as he had listened to and enjoyed Pellew's tales, the admiral's feelings of regret for the passing of his own shipboard service plainly revealed as time slipped by, two bottles of port following the two of Burgundy, the tinge of sadness in his voice increasingly discernible by the time the last bottle was set down dry and as Pellew had ultimately recounted the eventual paying off of his own final ship.

'Oh, Macleod will carry my letter to the First Lord,' Pellew had declared in a rising tone, one not wholly convincing, as if seeking to cast off all the ills of the world.

'But... sir...' a rush of dismay had flooded Pat's thoughts in that jarring instant, '... Macleod has departed already... with *Eleanor*.'

The old face shifted from a picture of internal reflection, 'Yes, he did. It had not escaped my notice, O'Connor,' Pellew brightened, 'and bearing my letter.'

'But... but you had yet to inspect her, sir?' exclaimed Pat, astonished.

'Oh, indeed; but a glass from the quay was all I required. I dare say there is a deal of bow and perhaps other caulking to remedy -

that is perfectly plain to the eye - and a new mizzen with all its rigging to install, but doubtless there will be a plentiful supply of suchlike at the Dock; likewise a new suit of sails.' Pat could only stare agape, speechless as the admiral had continued, 'She is in want of a trifle of paint... but we will pay that no mind; it is no matter... and she may be in need of some little of attention to her copper, no doubt...' Pellew looked directly into Pat's anxious gaze, lowered his voice, 'but I could not - *may Saint Patrick preserve me,* as you yourself might remark - I could not, with the best will in the world, give the First Lord the smallest doubt that she should be preserved; indeed, she must be restored, and without the loss of a moment.'

'That is hellfire good of you, sir!' cried Pat; the significance, the consequence of what Pellew had just said sinking in, he fairly gushed with effusive thanks, 'That is exceedingly generous in you, sir; handsome, so it is; I take that very kindly, more than I can ever say.'

Pat's heart raced, a tide of joy surging through his every fibre as Pellew continued, 'Since he is a landsman, the gentleman may find it something of a difficulty to reach a decision about the ship; indeed, he may come to that particular conclusion which I do not much care to consider of.'

'Sir, I am very much indebted to you... I am so,' Pat found his voice at last, a tide of warmth for Edward Pellew, *wonderful Edward Pellew* engulfing him, happiness unleashed once more and, it seemed, from a very distant place within his being, so cast down had he been; no wonder this man was long a legend within the service. 'Upon my word, that is exceedingly handsome in you, sir,' *and uncommon irregular* the unuttered thought even as the strain in his face relented and softened with a tentative smile.

'We must not concern ourselves with a guinea or two of honest expenditure here and there,' Pellew had grinned without the slightest hesitancy, his face radiating unfeigned pleasure, '... a trifling consideration it is, for sure. Where would we be, O'Connor, without we could read of the reports and voyages of an active *Surprise* in the fleet, eh? Something is surely to be done, for all love.'

'I am much obliged, infinitely obliged, sir,' Pat's words had been whispered, barely audible, coming concurrent with a sudden and illuminating revelation cutting through the fog of his uncertainty, through the confusion which had beset him since shortly after the Falmouth arrival. The raw, burning flush of realisation of how dearly he wished to see his ship restored and to be with his men, *his shipmates* aboard her once again had become a lifting conviction, a purpose of great importance, of strong merit, one much subduing the unwelcome confusion he had endured since the aftermath of devastation inflicted upon him by the hurricane.

Pat's thoughts returned to the present as *Surprise* sailed on across the bay in tranquil fashion, the absent mizzen rendering her helm flighty, her hastily repaired courses and topsails carrying her along with the most modest of heel, her topgallants - in far better order than her courses and topsails - flying aloft, but struggling to bring any contribution. On, ever eastwards through the tranquil waters, her wake barely distinguishable from the merely rippling sea surface, the gentlest of swell; on she swept, past the towering rocky extremities of the Dodman abeam as six bells rang in the forenoon watch, the bright sunlight unobscured by any gesture to cloud, the view in every direction brilliantly clear. On his quarterdeck a contemplative Pat reflected once more on Pellew's comforting words, on his inestimable generosity of spirit, of faith, his attachment to what was evidently for both of them a tradition, one of the highest order, of the very utmost value, Pat's own spirits rising. What a satisfying pleasure it had been - still was - in a kindred spirit found, and such an invaluable friend as Edward Pellew had turned out to be: for after they had seen the end of four bottles they had at long last said goodnight with a firm handshake, a grip signifying the utmost goodwill and mutual benevolence. 'I am in the evening of my career, indeed my life itself, O'Connor,' Pellew's final words, '... a little orphan boy travelled a long, long way... and in these days of the blessed peace I have but little to command save my feelings, and this is my heart speaking...'

The admiral had sighed deeply, as if emptying his lungs, Pat recalled, before his touching conclusion, Pellew struggling to keep his words within bounds, without any exhibition of the so-strongly welling feelings within him, staring, Pat's hand still tightly held.

'I ain't much of a one in the philosophical line - your shipmate Ferguson is your man there for sure - but I will speak frankly.' It was all Pat could do to nod. 'It was a long time ago... I set sail from this fair town in my first ship, the *Nymphe*... a fine frigate she was... but all I could muster for a crew were miners! *Miners* they were, O'Connor... yes, *tinners* and good Cornishmen all!' Pellew's eyes burned brightly with a self-evident passion, and Pat marvelled at it as the admiral uttered his closing words, 'Where would England be, O'Connor, without she had a fleet and men enough to fight for her, eh? Revel in your fine ship... I urge you so... and treasure every moment with her whilst she floats still.'

A particularly stronger wave and Pat, savouring coffee from an old tin mug, started from his recollections as he sensed the greater roll of his ship under his feet, the movement restoring his attention, his train of thought to the present, to an awareness of the comfortable substance of *Surprise's* timbers beneath him. He stared at the solidity of all about him, the familiarity so greatly warming, and he returned to reflect again on the admiral's parting words - even now they moved him, his heart a'flutter - but what did the admiral mean "whilst she floats still"? Was she now to be scrapped? Did Pellew know something which he did not care to tell him? Pat taxed his mind, trying to recollect all the admiral had said, striving to recall his particular words of support. He did remember Pellew's commitment to his ship, and that was a precious consolation. He could not recall any facet of their exchanges being worthy of particular caution, and so with a determination to return to the here and now he tore himself away from his reflections, deciding upon a tour of the decks to reassure himself that all in his seaborne world was well, remained the same, would be so for a long time; at least he hoped with all his heart that was the case. He stepped down the companionway with a vague feeling of contentment, an indistinct but rising inclination that all would be well, for both *Surprise* and his men. Slowly he paced forward along the gun deck, Admiral Pellew still very much in his mind as he nodded or spoke briefly to all those men with staring faces of enquiry, their own uncertainty plain as he passed by, Pat offering kindly words of encouragement, of good cheer; and he was immensely pleased to see that his men were visibly heartened by his gestures of amity. He prayed like never before that his confidence in Edward Pellew was well founded.

Noon and the sighting found *Surprise* halfway through her passage, Fowey far abeam, all weather conditions remaining benign, the following south-westerly carrying the frigate along gently, no concerns necessary for her general deteriorations, but all the pumps were still working constantly. By four bells of the afternoon watch, Rame Head was off the port beam and *Surprise* making her turn into Plymouth Sound, Penlee Point swiftly coming up on the port bow. 'Where is the breakwater, Mr Prosser?' asked an incredulous Pat of the master, *Surprise* making her way into the Sound.

'Washed away, sir, in the tempest,' Prosser's reply was measured, as if such an event was inconceivable, 'Two hundred thousand tons of stone gone. Sure, 'tis there still, but shifted and below the surface; the *Coromandel* was wrecked upon it. Her crew were saved, thanks be to the Lord.'

''pon my word,' mumbled Pat, astounded.

A half-hour later, five bells ringing, 'Hard a starboard,' ordered Prosser, shouted in a tired voice which signified the nearing end of the voyage. The helmsmen hauled on the wheel, *Surprise* beginning a short dogleg turn, the ship aided by the favourable wind alternating between astern and abeam, away from the rippling vestiges of breakwater, a glimpse of it emerging as *Surprise* neared the remnants and faced into Cawsand Bay. Another quarter hour and the master barked, 'Hard a port,' Pat content to simply observe. At six bells, Prosser called out once more, 'Hard a starboard,' Saint Nicholas Island fine on the bow. The wind was falling away in the lee shelter afforded by the peninsula and *Surprise's* speed easing to a bare two knots, the sunset near upon them off the larboard beam.

'Well done, Mr Prosser,' remarked Pat, *Surprise* slowing more as she rounded the turn to bear near directly west, Mutton Cove on the starboard bow, Devonport a mere breath of wind away. The breeze, though reduced to a scant zephyr and no more than the most minor retardant on the port bow, slowed the ship ever so slightly; a small helm adjustment ordered by Prosser brought her head round gently to fall off and so towards the centre of the channel; gaining a little more of pace she crept up the Tamar towards Plymouth Yard, to precious sanctuary, to a place where competent and skilful hands could tend her, where men who cared to do these things would remedy her many wounds. The sound of eight bells fading and at the dying of the light and of all wind, *Surprise* dropped her anchors in the long shadows over the waters of the Hamoaze, every man standing on deck, all silent, all staring about them, looking to their shipmates, the unanswerable query pressing upon them all: could this really be her final voyage? The disturbing thought harangued Pat's own troubled mind.

Thursday 2nd December 1824, 08:00   *The Hamoaze*

Dawn, severely cold, a chill wind rattling the rigging, every man of *Surprise* stood on deck, hungry, staring across the water to the Devonport basins and quays, signs of life emerging in the Yard as the sun, rising beyond the Sound, began to cast its diffuse, weak light over the new day, the Yard in early shade. That it would be an enduring day of uncertainty was sure, a difficult day, Pat thought, rubbing a bristled chin and his tired eyes, for he had slept little. The evening in the great cabin had enjoyed little cheer, supper a miserable affair, Murphy moaning about all and sundry whilst a tired Simon had been no company at all, not present for long and going below to gather the little of personal baggage he possessed in preparation for his planned departure for Scotland, to Mull and Tobermory. Eventually, Pat, sitting by himself, had enjoyed a generous whisky libation, from a bottle long given to him by Duncan and secreted against Murphy's predations, until, at the mournful ringing of six bells, he had retired to his cot to shiver sleeplessly through the cold night, the uncertain prospects for *Surprise* rarely out of his disturbed thoughts.

'Coffee's up, sorr,' Murphy's voice was, for once, very welcome.

Sipping the bitter brew, Pat gazed across the grey expanse of the Hamoaze, watching a cutter pulling away from the indistinct darkness of the Dock quay, several figures within wrapped against the cold and the thin drizzle of the past half hour. Five minutes more and the cutter had pulled all around the ship. 'Doubtless an inspection,' mused Pat, before its occupants were clambering up the side, coming aboard at the gun deck, shaking the water from their oilskins and staring all about them. Pat passed his tin cup to Murphy and stepped down the companionway to greet his visitors.

'Good morning to you, Mr Churchill,' declared Pat, in some little uncertainty, the Master Shipwright shaking his hand, 'and to you, Mr Sidley,' the Master Attendant visibly pleased to greet him.

'Welcome back, Captain O'Connor,' Edward Churchill pronounced with warm cordiality, 'Will I say 'tis a pleasure to see you again... though,' the shipwright's voice dropped, 'the barky is sorely in need of remedy; I am sorry to see her so.'

'For sure she is in want of your most admirable attentions, no doubt, Mr Churchill, I regret to say.' The visitors nodded gravely. 'And it is my most earnest wish, Mr Sidley,' a brief lightening of Pat's mind, a small foray into jest, 'that she will not be in need of yours, that she is not to be condemned into ordinary.' The visitors managed a strained smile, *"or worse"* being the generally unspoken thought.

'I can see a deal of work here, sir,' offered Churchill. 'The absence... *the loss* of the mizzen is plain... and the pumps be working mighty hard... I see the bow state is truly shocking... the caulking, indeed it is... I have never seen worse in all my years,' this said with a decent tone of commiseration, his voice tailing off as if he did not much care to prolong the pain.

A frowning Sidley continued the gloomy litany in the most dolorous of voice, 'There is plainly much of the bulwark timbers to repair, a number of gun ports to replace... and I see at least the pair of shot hole patches in her hull... and very doubtful patches they be.' It was all Pat could do to nod, his spirits swiftly sinking to fresh depths. All his men gathered nearby exhibited the most disconsolate of glum faces, anxiety evident all about them. The Master Attendant concluded his wretched report, 'The companionway gone... stumps, shards and splinters all that is left of it... I venture she will be here some time... indeed, months it will be...' He sighed, 'For sure we are in need of a great deal of time to remedy her deteriorations, Captain... in and out of the water... so much to do, so very much to mend... and I do not care to imagine the likely cost...' The latter point hung in the air like a maritime sword of Damocles, naval dockyard budgets so greatly reduced since the death of the dictator on Saint Helena.

Friday 3rd December 1824, 09:00   Arlington Street, Westminster

In his office at home, Lord Melville stood up as the arrival of Duncan Macleod and Abel Jason was announced by the servant at his door, both visitors swiftly entering to stand before him as he moved round his desk to greet them. The First Lord shook hands with Duncan first, 'Welcome back, Commander Macleod.' The words were spoken with an inflection of warmth, with gracious civility, Melville's smile genuine and lingering, before he turned to Jason. 'Mr Jason, good morning. We have not met... however, I may say that Macleod speaks well of you in his reports.'

'Thank you, sir,' uttered Jason in a voice little more than a whisper, overawed to be in such an illustrious presence. The grandfather clock in the nearby corner chimed to announce nine o'clock, and Jason started, his head swivelling towards it. He stared at it with interest, the collector within him intrigued. 'A most fine time piece,' he murmured, no one taking the least interest.

'Good morning, sir,' declared Duncan, Jason's attention restored, '... and may I thank ye for supporting my promotion... to Commander... 'tis an honour, sir, to be here.'

Melville smiled again, an affable smile, the astonished servant staring at him in silent query, the First Lord not exhibiting his customarily rather dour demeanour; indeed, taciturn might best describe him normally, particularly in the presence of his more junior visitors, ones of considerably lesser standing, mere commanders being wholly within that category. 'And well deserved it is, of that I have not the least doubt; my most sincere congratulations, Macleod. Please, sit down gentlemen; here, take a seat.' Melville paused as the tray of tea and coffee was deposited on the leather writing surface of the expansive walnut desk. 'Italian,' thought Jason absently, marvelling at the exquisite craftsmanship and the quality of the burled olive wood on the sides. The servant departed on Melville's nod. 'May I help you to tea... or coffee perhaps?' Their choices made, the drinks poured, Duncan and Jason sipped in anxious silence, an air of expectancy prevailing, an indefinable sense of something of importance about to be revealed to them, the anticipation bearing down upon them. Melville leafed through his file for several minutes of scrutiny before a throat-clearing cough, and he began, 'I have received no news, no reports of your return home... save for the simple announcement of the arrival of *Surprise* in Falmouth. I trust that the tempest was not excessively vexatious to you... to your ship?' To that exceptionally painful enquiry neither man could offer the least reply, and so they sat, staring, dumbfounded, more than a little apprehensive, cautious nods offered whilst concluding that the capital had, presumably, escaped unscathed. 'Doubtless you are wondering why I have summoned you here to London?' Emphatic nods this time from both visitors, and Melville, sensing their anxiety, smiled encouragingly, the gesture seemingly artificial and wholly unconvincing to either of Macleod or Jason.

'Sir,' Duncan interjected, his memory functioning again, 'I have here a letter from Admiral Pellew, and I believe it may refer to the ship.' The letter was handed over, Melville staring at it for a brief moment, unopened. Duncan continued, 'She was badly damaged in the hurricane... for that it surely was... nae doubt of that.'

'I will come to that later, Macleod,' said Melville, setting the letter down. 'For the moment, allow me to explain my purpose in asking your attendance, if you will.' Duncan and Jason simply nodded again. 'I have it on good authority that the civil war in Greece will not long endure, must draw to an end this winter, if it has not done so already.' Dumb faces before him, the First Lord drained his coffee and paused briefly for thought. He resumed in a somewhat lowered voice, as if the walls might have inquisitive ears, 'Gentlemen, there are great powers with an interest in this war - the Greek struggle against Ottoman rule that is - and it is plain that His Majesty's Government is obliged to act with the utmost prudence... with due attention to any ultimate resolution... and one will surely emerge in due course...'

No reply from his visitors, Melville stared at them. Duncan simply nodded when the First Lord's gaze fell upon him, no words could he find. Melville switched his attention to Jason, noting that his visitor's eyes had wandered again towards his clock: he had, in fact, at last decided that it was a Thomas Tompion piece. Melville raised his voice once more, introducing a firmer tone, one he was much more accustomed to as First Lord, 'Excuse me, but I am blathering... Are you attending, Jason?'

Jason started, nodded; 'I am indeed, sir,' he whispered; he stared hard at Melville; Duncan fidgeted, uncomfortable.

Melville's tone had delivered the message: concentrate! His next words were unexpected, a bolt from the blue, 'I am sending you to Russia.' Duncan shot to a perfectly upright posture in his chair, as did Jason, all eyes wide, two minds racing. 'To Saint Petersburg,' Melville elaborated, 'without the least delay.'

The loud ticking of the clock was the solitary sound in the hush that followed, Melville staring intently at his visitors, awaiting a response. The immediate shock relenting, the seaman in Macleod registered the looming potential difficulty with such a voyage, and he interjected, a degree of concern rising in his voice, 'Sir, winter is nigh upon us... the Baltic will freeze over. I dinnae see there is a deal of time left for us to reach that place.'

'Quite, Macleod...' Melville, a little irritated, nodded, '... and that is why you are departing as soon as your vessel is provisioned... not later than the morning. This is not a matter to wait on our pleasure, Macleod; it is of the utmost urgency, the very utmost. Am I plain?'

The merest hint of a nod from both Macleod and Jason preserving Melville's silent stare, both men nodded more emphatically; 'Aye, sir,' mumbled Duncan at last, trying hard to recall the December Baltic sea state, the extent of ice. Saint Petersburg was at the very north-east extremity of the Gulf of Finland, would likely be the first location to freeze, and even the London weather was cold now. What would the Baltic be like? Perhaps it was frozen already?

'Gentlemen,' Melville resumed, his voice softening to a more gentle tone, as if recognising that such a shock demanded something of reassurance, of comfort to follow, 'Allow me to explain, if you will...' No words could either Macleod or Jason find in response, both men's minds plunged into turmoil, whirling in confusion, not even the slightest nod found; they simply stared, the shock enduring.

Melville rang a tiny bell and the servant returned to remove the tray; he looked round curiously and noted the stunned immobility of the guests. 'Will that be all, sir?' the question expressed much more in its inflection, inferred that a response was required, a prompt towards a necessary aid for the visitors, one oft seen by the servant in this office in similar circumstances.

'Perhaps a roborotive modicum of the malt will render my guests a trifle of comfort,' declared Melville, recognising the hint, nodding in reinforcement. 'Will you kindly bring glasses, Perkins, and did I smell fresh shortbread baking this morning?' He reached into the cabinet behind his desk, a depleted bottle emerging. The servant returned immediately with the glasses and left again. 'I will endeavour to be clear,' the First Lord resumed as he uncorked the whisky. 'There are persons... of... of some standing within Russia who are minded to support their Orthodox Christian brethren in Greece...' Melville poured his own rather generous measure, 'You will join me in a whet?' he looked up.

'Thank you, sir,' whispered Jason, Duncan more emphatic in his reply, his head moving firmly in corroboration, 'I widnae care to say nay to a dram, sir; thankee.' The measures were generous, the aroma divine, the promise beatific. The first sip was all that Duncan hoped for; he smiled. Jason coughed: the malt was strong.

'We understand that the Tsar has concluded, after the June conference in Saint Petersburg, that there is no interest - either from Austria's Metternich or the Prime Minister - in his January proposal to reconstruct Greece as three principalities with the lightest of Ottoman suzerainty,' Melville began, adding almost as an aside, 'and doubtless within the sphere of Russian influence.' Polite nods from the now bemused visitors, Melville continued, 'Canning does not care to see England become a buffer between Russia and the Ottomans, and so has declined the scheme. Hence the Tsar has determined that *unilateral* Russian aid for Greece is now appropriate. His treasury reserves substantially accummulating, he is minded to send financial aid to the formative Greek government... *when*, that is, the civil war has ended.' A bemused Duncan took another large sip of whisky, Jason did not care for more. 'Gold, gentlemen...' Melville's words re-engaged both visitors' attention immediately, 'Gold is mined in Russia. We are reliably informed that the Urals production has risen eightfold, from one quarter of a ton in the year '20 to two tons last year... a remarkable increase indeed. Naturally,' Melville continued, 'the Tsar is mindful that he shares a border with the Ottomans, and therefore his advisors urge the utmost caution, the most careful of approach to any such supportive venture.' Melville replenished his and Duncan's glasses. 'In fact the initiative was reported to have originated from his former Foreign Minister, a Greek in fact - Capodistrias - who presently resides in Switzerland, in Geneva, since leaving the Tsar's service in '22. This man has not, however, been held in the highest esteem by His Majesty's own ministers. He is believed to be still, in essence, a tool of the Tsar, and he - Capodistrias - is presently supporting the side of the renegade Kolokotronis in the civil war. Hence the Tsar's secret proposal of a loan has been some considerable time in consideration, the civil war rendering the scheme moot. However, since the Prime Minister received a letter from the Greeks, despatched to him in late August - that is to say *before* the civil war resumed in October - and which he received early in November... a letter most urgently requesting his help... he has decided to look afresh at the situation, the prospects for their assistance.'

Duncan was somewhat more relaxed since he had rapidly consumed his second whisky, believing it would be beneficial for his anxieties, setting down his glass carefully beside Jason's; in fact he had surreptiously started on Jason's, not wishing to waste it - as he saw things. His curiosity rising, a trifle of courage discovered, he ventured a few words, 'Sir, this is high politics... that is to say, I am just a humble seafarer from the Hebrides, an insignificant commander... and I know nothing of such things...'

'A captain, Macleod.'

'Only a *commander*, sir,' Duncan offered his correction.

'You are now a captain, a post-captain,' Melville insisted, 'promoted... captain it is. I give you joy of your promotion.' The servant, just coming through the door, overheard this and a chuckle escaped him, the reason for his earlier bafflement in Melville's so overt pleasure revealed. The First Lord glaring, he deposited the tray of biscuit triangles and left the room rapidly, without a word, barely able to contain his mirth.

Duncan's gasp, however, was very audible, Jason's whisky glass let slip as Macleod choked on the mouthful of whisky he was about to swallow, and Duncan's exclamation was heard by the departing servant, far along the corridor, 'WHAT! SIR? A captain?' Further words failed him.

'You are indeed... yes... I say it again, you have been promoted, *Captain* Macleod,' reiterated Melville, a smile escaping. 'The order is being prepared by my clerk at the Admiralty, and that will follow presently. I congratulate you, I do.' Melville raised his whisky glass.

'Will I give ye a toast, sir?' ventured Duncan, recovering somewhat and feeling obliged to speak, to offer at least a few words on the so unexpected but welcome news.

'Please do, Macleod,' said Melville with some reserve.

'Ye's a Scot, aye, and doubtless ye will know the words.'

Melville nodded, the tiny degree of acquiescence he felt to be appropriate.

'Here's tae us! Wha's like us? Damn few, and they're a'deid.'

Melville recognised the old Scots toast and managed the smallest of smile, 'Thank you, Macleod... I will say I do concur.' Without pause for reaction, for further unwelcome interruption, the First Lord pressed on without the least hesitation, 'Notwithstanding your promotion being wholly merited... for we do receive reports, Macleod, the very briefest of reports from Captain O'Connor in despatches, all of which describe your conduct as the most exemplary of any officer witnessed by O'Connor... and hence your promotion is undoubtedly warranted, fully deserved; but that is not the particular reason for... for *advancing* your promotion so soon... exceptionally swiftly after rising to Commander...' Melville drained his bottle, refilling the glasses once more, 'No, we could not send a Commander on a mission of such political import. A mere *Commander* - and I say that, Macleod, with not the least disrespect - will not suffice, most certainly will not; but neither could an Admiral fetch up in Saint Petersburg without it was brought to the attention of all in - will I say - *diplomatic* circles. No, a Captain must be sent, with the utmost despatch, and with an ostensible purpose, for no mention of the real one must ever emerge. Am I making myself clear, Macleod... Jason?'

'I think I know the sense of it, sir,' said Duncan, but in truth he did not, he was still reeling from the shock of his utterly unexpected elevation, his glorious promotion, the First Lord's explanation heard but only half understood, his first mental endeavour an effort to accept that his illustrious step - his long cherished dream - had really been bestowed upon him. More than that he had not greatly absorbed.

'Mr Jason, do I understand that you speak the Russian, and, if I am correct in that, to what degree of fluency?'

'I am quite fluent, sir; indeed, I am entirely comfortable with the language, written and spoken.'

'Excellent, as I thought. You will accompany Captain Macleod and translate for him. It may be that not all persons he meets with in those parts will be acquainted... that is to say will be *familiar* with his... his *brogue*, the accent of the Isles. Indeed, Scotsman that I am, I confess the smallest of difficulty myself.'

'I quite understand, sir,' Jason could not suppress his grin; Duncan simply stared, unspeaking.

'With such rich resources at hand, the Tsar is minded to provide half a million of pounds to the Greek government... something akin to that loan raised by the so-called London Greek Committee,' Melville explained. 'Ostensibly it will appear to be a sum similarly raised by subscription... within England; for such also entirely accords with His Majesty's Government's declared policy of non-intervention, no support for either side in the war; particularly so as we are bound by treaty with the Ottomans; and hence the gold will come here first... to London, conceivably to be cast into coinage, thus obliterating all trace of Russian origin, whence a private English vessel will convey it to Greece. Tell me, Macleod,' Melville turned his head again towards Duncan, 'I am no mariner myself - your vessel... *Eleanor* is it? - will she safely convey three and a half tons of gold, for such is the weight equating to the value of half a million of pounds?'

'Wi' nae difficulty, sir. It may be that we will take out some of her ballast, she carries at least that in kentledge.'

'Kentledge?'

'Cast iron ballast, sir... ingots of it, in the bilges.'

'I see. Well, that would seem to be an admirable notion. Now to business once more... the Foreign Secretary has only yesterday written to the Russian Government in reply to the Tsar's letter of earlier this year. A secret codicil has been appended to Canning's letter, pledging His Majesty's Government's support for the carriage and handling of the Tsar's secret loan. You are *not* to convey this communication, *I emphasise not*, Macleod, Jason, to His Majesty's ambassador in Saint Petersburg - I believe Sir Charles Bagot remains there at present pending his expected replacement. The information is for the ears of General Chernyshev alone. The diplomatic community is most certainly *not* to be apprised of this matter, which must remain wholly secret. The delivery of this letter, gentlemen, and the collection of the gold are the true purposes of your mission. However, the *ostensible* purpose will be declared to be no more than a consultative military visit, an exhibition of goodwill from the government and the Royal Navy, to assess the prospects for English assistance, the Russian fleet at Kronstadt known to have been lately so very severely damaged - a severe flood from the Neva on the 19th of November, so the report which I received but a mere three days ago describes.' The First Lord looked up, 'Macleod, you will endeavour to take note of the Russian fleet losses and damages... in as much detail as is possible.' Duncan simply nodded. His briefing finished, Melville concluded, 'Well, gentlemen; my messenger will deliver your orders in detail to your lodgings later today: the Feathers Tavern within the Liberties, is it not?' Firm nods of confirmation, and Melville concluded, 'Very well.' A momentary hesitation, 'Do you have any questions, Macleod?'

'If I may trouble ye with jus' the one, sir?'

'Please do,' the First Lord managed the weakest of smiles.

'What is to happen to *Surprise*, sir?'

Melville's faint impression of pleasure vanished in an instant, the longest ten seconds in the world then passing as if an age; at least that was Duncan's feeling, before the begrudging reply, hesitancy slipping away to be succeeded by the merest hint of irritation in the smooth voice, 'I understand, Macleod, from your own report, that the ship is particularly severely damaged...'

'Aye, sir, that...'

'... and that she suffered greatly in the storm, *the turbulence* encountered before she returned to Falmouth...'

'The tempest, sir.'

'Precisely, *the tempest*... as it was reported to me from every port on the south coast... and that your ship will undoubtedly require significant time and substantial monies... *very considerable monies*, Macleod, to rectify her deteriorations. Is that not the case?'

'I dinnae doot for a minute, sir, that she will need a deal of work...'

'Exactly so. Allow me to tell you, gentlemen,' Melville's voice was raised, 'The Navy Estimates being so very substantially reduced in the present times - a trifle more than five and a half millions this year - the repair of ships... *old* ships, Macleod, is not something that can be comfortably countenanced; no, indeed it is not. Presently you will learn what is to be done and what cannot be done in the matter of your ship.'

'Sir,' Duncan, recovering quickly from the shock of what sounded like the death sentence for *Surprise*, his spirits sinking faster than a lead line, blurted out his last desperate throw, 'Admiral Pellew's report... there it is, sir.' Duncan pointed to the unopened letter atop the desk, 'His report may cast a deal of light, gie ye some guidance on the magnitude of the task... the work... the time it may require.'

'Well... I will say this is uncommon irregular...' Melville frowned, looking sharply at his visitor, piqued and acutely aware that Macleod was treading on the very edge of impertinence; but sensing the despond, the anxiety, something plaintive in Duncan's voice, he held in check his rising indignation and paused for a short moment in reflection. He seized up the letter in rather demonstrative fashion and tore it open, the wax seal ripping into flying fragments which scattered all over the expanse of his desk. A silent two minutes passed, Melville reading intently, the visitors hardly daring to draw breath, before the First Lord spoke in a more moderated tone; perhaps as gently as this man might ever offer, thought Jason, studying Melville closely, watching for the meaning in his face, to measure whether it accorded with his words. 'Admiral Pellew is minded that the damages to HMS *Surprise*, exceedingly ghastly as they may appear to the observer in the first instance...' Melville looked up, significantly, '... are neither substantial nor excessively costly. That is to say, were they to be rectified by experienced shipwrights... and with the necessary and appropriate materials to hand.' There was an audible sigh of relief from Duncan, Jason too at long last allowing himself to exhale, a great release of tension coming to each man. 'Pellew continues,' Melville resumed, 'with the observation that "Devonport is home to the very finest of shipwrights, the most capable of such men to be found anywhere within all the ports, yards and harbours of His Majesty's realm", and he has no doubt whatsoever... "not the least doubt" so he says...' Melville raised his eyebrows, '... that "*Surprise* would be swiftly restored at Dock were she favoured with the attentions of the most excellent craftsmen therein" and...' Melville appeared to deflate, to relax as he concluded the report, '... and, says Pellew, "were they endowed with the most trifling of budgets to do so". Well, Macleod, it seems...' the First Lord gazed more kindly upon Duncan and spoke with as much levity as he could manage, with a voice that was generally reserved for halfwits, whilst Jason had rediscovered his keen interest in the clock, '... it would appear that your concerns are unfounded and that your ship is, in fact, in the very finest of fettle after all! What d'ye say to that, eh?'

The briefest of pause before an astonished and delighted Duncan replied, 'That is a comfort, for sure, and I am entirely in accord with Admiral Pellew's way of thinking, sir.' He could not suppress the tiniest of waver as he feigned conviction so badly, his words emphatically spoken but resonating with the hint of guilty tremor, and wholly unconvincing, which did not escape Melville; indeed, Jason stared at his friend with candid astonishment.

'Very well,' the First Lord conceded an exceptional degree of benevolence, his visitors palpably relieved. 'A frigate will be required to transport the Tsar's gold to Greece... to ensure its safety... but such cannot be a ship of the Royal Navy. That is why *Surprise* has already served in the capacity of a private vessel. However, whether *Surprise* will be that necessary ship must remain an unknown for the present... doubtless Admiral Saumarez will render his own report from Plymouth in due course, when we may then further consider of her future, her prospects,' Melville pronounced his last word on the subject, had evidently tired of the matter. He rose from his chair, stepped around the desk and extended his hand to Duncan, 'I offer my most sincere congratulations once more for your promotion, *Captain* Macleod, and I bid you both safe passage; indeed, a swift passage, the very swiftest... and, gentlemen... please endeavour to make haste... before the ice precludes your return.' Macleod and Jason nodded, staring at Melville, nothing more of meaningful response could they find, the servant ultimately showing them out, Macleod still reeling from the words "Captain Macleod", all thoughts of *Surprise* receding and the shock of his promotion recalled: it was akin to a fire burning fiercely, raging wild within his mind, his thoughts wandering haphazardly and recollections of Melville's words ringing loud - "turbulence" indeed!

Friday 3rd December 1824, 09:00 *The Hamoaze*

In the great cabin, Pat sat with Simon drinking coffee, a meagre first breakfast consumed with few words spoken, Murphy flitting in every few minutes, listening attentively, aware that the mood was prescient, both men seemingly avoiding a conversation which would be unwelcome to both. The coffee consumed, Pat stared at his friend, 'How is Mower these recent days?' his effort to break the impasse.

Simon appeared to welcome the question, 'Oh, his recovery is proceeding admirably. I am pleased to say there are no complications... I believe - *mind, I do not assert it* - I venture he will fully regain the use of his limbs. Doubtless he will press you to put him to service in a month or two. Half-pay holds little prospect for a lieutenant, as you yourself know too well. He lifts with his wounded arm - healed of course - striving for a full recuperation... and he walks with a limp... slowly, tiring after an hour, but I am minded that will pass as he gains strength; his leg muscles have wasted... so long in his bed.'

The sparse, jaded conversation shifted reluctantly towards the uncomfortable subject. 'On which day do you depart?' asked Pat eventually, gazing with infinite concern at his friend.

'I am leaving today, at 10 o'clock, dear... from the Dock gate.'

'Oh, so soon... that is uncommon bad news,' the deep disappointment was plain in Pat's voice, the cold shiver of angst, of tremor audible within it.

'A carriage is arranged which will convey me to Exeter whence a stage coach, so I am assured by Mr Churchill, departs for Bristol at three bells... or would that be seven bells? He mentioned a number of them... late this evening it is. I am intending to visit James Prew in that place; he is a famed surgeon-dentist... of singular talent, so I am informed. I hope I may familiarise myself with his particular techniques. Doubtless such would be of use in the future. There is little, indeed nothing of such ilk in the Isles.'

'And thence to London, no doubt?' Pat's spirits sank.

'Perhaps not directly. I believe I may first take the waters at Bath. Did you know that the town hospital has long boasted a plethora of renowned physicians of all disciplines?'

The merest mute shake of Pat's head; the crushing realisation that his friend was leaving showed so plain in his face. Murphy, near the door, stared intently at the deck, the steward much discomfited, striving in the silence borne of profound disbelief to appear not to be present at all. 'Murphy,' said Pat in a resigned tone of voice, 'Please to fetch Doctor Ferguson's baggage from his cabin.'

Simon resumed, 'I have corresponded with an eminent physician there, Caleb Parry, for some years. In fact, I was invited by his son, Charles, only last year, advising of his father's death... a sad loss. There is too a distinguished chemist residing in Bath, Charles Pepys, a fellow of the Society, and possessing of an analytical laboratory. I am minded that he may offer some interesting observations on Edward Barlow's *Essay on the Medicinal Efficacy and Employment of the Bath Waters*; Barlow is a physician at the hospital there...' Simon's voice tailed off, his tour itinerary plainly holding no interest for Pat.

'When would you expect to fetch home, to Mull? 'tis a plentiful long way, and greatly tiring by coach.'

'For sure it will be a journey of some tedium... arduous and certainly tiring as you say... but no matter, I am minded that I have had my fill of the sea, of Neptune's temper particularly... and doubtless there is much of interest to observe en route.' This was offered without the least gesture to enthusiasm, a waver in Simon's voice, his thoughts interrupted by *"ding-ding"* the ship's bell ringing in definitive announcement.

'Are you fully persuaded of your course... would you care to reconsider?' asked Pat plaintively. 'Perhaps you would care to reflect for a while. It will greatly set back the men - all of us.'

With a so sad demeanour of infinite regret Simon rose from his chair, 'I cannot express to you how much and how deeply I lament my departure, Pat... from friends the likes of which I will never find again... but... I must beg to decline.'

'Oh well, I dare say there's no convincing a decided mind.'

A silent pause, an excruciating minute, and with at least an expression of resolution, Simon continued, 'There surely is a tide in the affairs of men, as the bard remarked... and I have been minded these past weeks that mine is on the ebb... and so I must away...'

Pat sighed, Simon's words quashing his hopes brutally; he stepped, infinitely slowly, around the table to stand before his dearest friend in all the world. 'Perhaps there is something in your notion,' grave regret in his voice, 'I dare say even da Gama tired of discovering America...'

'To which da Gama do you refer?'

'Eh, the explorer, *da Gama* - was there more than one?'

'If you are referring to the generally better known one, the Portugese, Vasco it was - and I venture that is your intention - I believe he sailed east... to the Indies, never seeing America.'

'Oh... then I dare say it was one of the other ones.'

'Doubtless so.'

Pat gazed in dismay at Simon, floundering for something, *anything* he might say to change his friend's mind, all thoughts wholly inadequate to the task until, with an utter collapse in spirit, he conceded, 'For sure the cabin will be a quiet place... when you are gone.'

'For some time I have floundered in the uncertainty of whether to return home or to stay within this nautical parish. It has been the most difficult of decisions and - you will allow me to say - I am far from sure... it may not be the best one.' Simon stared at Pat, so much distress evident on his friend's face, 'However, I remain anxious that you yourself should feel more at ease in your mind... more contented in your own circumstances. I am sure that you have acted upon the purest of principles... and doubtless there are times when several may conflict... life is not a bed of roses...'

'No it ain't.'

'No indeed... but I remain confident that you are equal to any exertion of mind... or body for that matter. No person admired you more than I for your heroic conduct and example in saving this ship and all souls within her from bleak catastrophe in the tempest.'

'Ain't you coming back, Simon?' cried Pat, staring at his friend, aghast, the awful realisation dawning. No words of adequacy; indeed, no words at all could he find in his distress, and he seized Simon in an embracing bear hug, the longest of painful minutes elapsing.

'Farewell, Pat... farewell, brother.'

Chapter Four

Saturday 4th December 1824   07:00   *Billingsgate, London*

The wintry dawn was imminent, its diffuse glow rising in the distant sky over the downstream Thames, the air in the Pool of London cold, a low-hanging blanket of wispy vapours hanging over all the width of the congested river, skeletal masts protruding everywhere from within it in the near and far distance, the distinctively pungent smell of coal smoke hanging heavy in the grey air. The first signs of life were emerging on scores of colliers and fishing boats tied up at the wharves on both sides of the great commercial waterway as *Eleanor*, both her gaff topsails hoisted, inched away from her berth alongside the Custom House on the Legal Quays, favoured with the lightest of westerly winds and in the beginnings of the ebb tide to begin her passage downriver. Within moments she reached midstream, and her crew rapidly hoisted her jib, foresail and mainsail, the schooner's progress swiftly improving such that she reached the Tower within mere minutes, her crew all on deck and shivering as they stared at the impressive edifice as *Eleanor* glided past. With a compulsive and particular interest they stared hard at the infamous Traitor's Gate, Jason pointing it out, the rippling, oily Thames water washing about it, before all gazed further afield to a rising bustle of activity taking place aboard a hundred and more merchant ships of all ilks, and thence curious faces turned up to the grand landmark buildings towering high above the growing clamour and commotion at the waterside. Everything all about them was entirely unfamiliar to the spellbound Cornishmen, fascinated Falmouth minds wholly absorbed in studying a landscape and spectacle the scale and likes of which they had never before seen in their lives as *Eleanor* gracefully swept by a myriad of mercantile trading scenes; for tiny Falmouth and even familiar Plymouth had nothing to compare with the vibrant activity of this grand metropolis. For all that such novelty widened deeply tired eyes, both stupor and torpor pressed heavily upon them; indeed, most of them remained much the worse for wear, and several were also wholly impecunious, having spent many a curious hour wandering the Billingsgate precincts and beyond in the prior afternoon and evening, a number of them having encountered the most doubtful and costly of acquaintances in close proximity to the quays. The news that they were bound for Saint Petersburg across the chill of the North Sea to face the great freeze of the winter Baltic and were not returning home to the relative warmth of Falmouth - as all had expected - had received the most garrulous of mixed receptions: the younger men were curious, for of the essential purpose of the mission they knew nothing; however, they were pleased to be engaged longer in paid service, but for the older men the assured discomfort of the bleak winter voyage held little attraction.

'Mr Reeve, did ye take aboard the extra rum cask?' asked a smiling Duncan, looking all about the schooner in mild inspection, his enduring pleasure since the glorious promotion beatifically obvious.

'Yes, sir, that I did.' Lieutenant William Reeve, his breath steaming, cognisant of his captain's roving gaze, turned and shouted at his indolent men, nothing of note or attention actually being remiss or required for *Eleanor*, but he was striving to banish sloth - as he saw things - and such was his purpose, the crew seemingly clumsy, slow, nothing of their customary attentiveness present so early in this particular morning; but he himself was now directly under the command of a post-captain, Jason having made the greatly pleasing announcement upon his return to the schooner with Macleod, and Reeve did not care to see his crew's bumbling tardiness in Duncan's close gaze. However, Reeve settled and relaxed as the minutes passed, and *Eleanor* surged on, swiftly gaining pace, the relative early dawn absence of shipping activity giving her clear passage into and around the great loop of the Isle of Dogs, the twin towers of the Greenwich Hospital looming prominently into view to starboard.

Macleod and Jason stood, rather politely thought Reeve, on the larboard side of his tiny quarterdeck, Macleod entirely content to leave the ship handling and captaincy to his lieutenant. For the present he preferred to enjoy the Thames vista whilst contemplating his mission and privately celebrating his promotion.

'Baltic bound, *Captain* Macleod,' Jason's jarring pronouncement, reading Duncan's mind, a face of absolute contentment giving all away.

'Aye, that we are,' a delightful surge of pleasure coming afresh with the word, that particular word, one so long awaited, its glorious significance a long cherished desire. 'I confess a grand pleasure sits with me today, Jason. *Captain Macleod*... aye. D'ye know, I would never have thought it just a month ago. For many a year I have wondered whether I would ever make post, ultimately hoist my flag, precious little influence available to me.'

'I have no doubt it is long deserved, sir.' A thoughtful few minutes and Jason spoke again, 'Can we reach Saint Petersburg before the freeze, would you think?'

'I dinnae know for sure, 'tis the wind we need. A strong south-westerly blow - nae too strong, mind, I havnae forgotten the tempest - and eight knots will see us there in... in ten days I venture... 'tis near eighteen hundred miles. The Gulf begins to freeze from late November... from the east, Saint Petersburg first. A cold winter and the freeze comes sooner. There isnae time to lose, nae doubt of that. Melville cannae be sure we will fetch his gold.'

'He places great trust in you, sir; that is plain,' offered Jason with a sage nod of his head.

'Aye, and I dinnae care to disappoint the man, first command and all. Would ye care to take breakfast with me now?'

Monday 6th December 1824   9:00   *Devonport*

Pat received the communication from Admiral Saumarez as he ate his meagre breakfast, no provisions having come across from the quay since *Surprise's* arrival. Steeped in gloom as he was and most unsettled about the prospects for his ship, the unannounced appearance of the admiral's aide presented an immediate surge of apprehension in his mind, the pit of his stomach receiving it within mere moments. Murphy hastened to procure the proffered fresh coffee, supplies of that being ever at the forefront of the steward's concerns - on pain of flogging, the threat frequently made but never actually actioned. The cabin was cold, the ambience uninviting; Murphy's swift return from the galley was most welcome to Pat and the Lieutenant. 'Mr Hemming, please, do take a seat whilst I read these orders,' murmured Pat cautiously, sipping his coffee, a most welcome roborative for a cold morning, and one which both men drank with evident satisfaction. Murphy remained in close attendance at the table, ostensibly to replenish the cups, but his real purpose being to listen attentively to what might be said. 'Are you familiar with these orders, Mr Hemming?'

'I am, sir,' the Lieutenant nodded his affirmation. 'Indeed, they are written in my own hand. The admiral dictated them this very morning... after a telegraph from the Admiralty was received shortly after first light. They are sent with his compliments, sir.'

'Mighty curious,' remarked Pat under his breath. He continued to read swiftly through the customary preamble to reach the detail, the meaning of the orders, setting down his coffee cup with a rattle on his saucer as the substance became plain to him. 'Why, I am to warp *Surprise* across to the quay without delay!' Pat looked up, the excitement in his voice was unconcealed, Murphy's face reflecting Pat's astonishment. 'She is to be be hauled into the New Union Dock directly. What is at hand here, Mr Hemming, pray tell?'

'I do not incline towards speculation, sir. I may say that - as far as Admiral Saumarez has cared to enlighten me - *Surprise* is to benefit from close inspection of her varied damages.' He nodded in emphasis in case there could be any doubt in the matter, 'That is to say... *without delay*.' Pat staring, mouth still agape, he pressed on, 'The Master Shipwright has received orders to that effect this morning, sir.' Hemming stared, his message plainly disturbing Captain O'Connor in his self-evident deep depths of worry - as had been writ in the captain's dour countenance since the Lieutenant had come aboard. It gave him some small concern himself; indeed, the yard speculation for a week had been that *Surprise* would be hulked, possibly even broken up; and those few of her crew who had ventured ashore since arrival had all returned to ship with the bleakest of outlook and with the most miserable demeanour, every man aboard becoming greatly downcast, the dire mantle of depression settling upon them all.

'Murphy!' shouted Pat, oblivious to his steward's attendance, Murphy hovering just behind his captain's sight, but near enough to the table to listen in. 'There you are,' Pat looked up with a cold glare, 'Ask Mr Codrington and Mr Pickering their attendance - their earliest attendance - if you will.'

'D'reckly, sorr,' Murphy moved towards the door with alacrity, his customary complacency wholly abandoned, the keenly awaited bearer of tidings for the ears of every man aboard. What they signified he did not know.

'And Murphy,' shouted Pat sharply, his steward at the door, 'You may care to run!'

'Yes sorr!' the door crashed shut.

Monday 6th December 1824   10:00   Westminster, London

The public saloon of the Feathers tavern, off the Strand and within the Liberty of Westminster, was busy with its customary morning clientele: men of many professions, the majority of them hugely enjoying coffee with noisy abandon and loud discussion; others were partaking of rather stronger libations, for the tavern had become a minor legend within all the Liberties for Mrs O'Donnell's warm hospitality. Her home-cooked Irish food was only the smallest shade behind in its popular appeal, the fame of her particular delicacy, soda bread, having reached the wider environs of much of central London. It was into this rather raucous ambience that a deeply fatigued, hungry and thirsty Simon Ferguson stumbled, clutching his small overnight bag; for such was sufficient to carry all his belongings in the world save for the oldest and most worn items of his meagre clothing which remained aboard *Surprise*. Unshaven as he was, recognition by the hostess was not immediate, and he shuffled wearily towards the fire roaring fiercely on the hearth, the bright flames a magnet for his chilled body, warmth an urgent necessity, for the mail coach had offered him only an outside seat for the sixteen freezing hours from Bristol. He inched towards a chair he espied near the fire, not the least energy to move any faster, stepping with the difficulty afforded by his frozen legs closer to where he might embrace the glorious warmth offered by the burning logs; his frame protesting, he leaned momentarily on the back of the chair and closed his eyes, his thoughts drifting back to his day of taking stock, to his decision. He had cancelled his plans to linger in Bristol and Bath, a severe melancholia settling upon him even as he had departed Plymouth, and he had determined upon the most direct return to Tobermory. The 4 p.m. departure had necessitated the most uncomfortable overnight journey, and the coach, an hour late because of interminable delays over deteriorated winter road surfaces, had delivered him to the Westminster General Post Office in Gerrard Street only at 9 a.m., the subsequent final mile taking him an excruciating hour to reach the familiar oasis of the Feathers, calling upon every last vestige of his failing strength to walk it, Simon being a careful man and not caring to spend precious pennies on a chaise.

'Why, Doctor Ferguson, so it is!' exclaimed Mrs O'Donnell, coming upon Simon whilst busying about the room to greet her many patrons. 'The Dear knows you look so cold. Here, my love, take this,' the glass of gin was thrust into Simon's trembling hand, his bag wrested from his frozen grasp and set down, his cape seized by Mrs O'Donnell as he slumped with her help into the fireside chair, words too difficult in his absolute exhaustion. 'Emma!' shrieked Mrs O'Donnell to the girl collecting the empty coffee cups, beckoning vigorously. 'Coffee, a pot of it... and toasted cheese, a plentiful plate... quickly now, away ye go, go!' The jovial, red-faced hostess turned back to Simon; he had drained the gin and was rubbing cold hands together.

'It is a pleasure to see you again, Mrs O'Donnell,' the words were whispered with obvious effort, Simon shivering uncontrollably about all his body.

'Sandra!' the shout was directed at an inquisitive young lady approaching the hearth. 'Fetch a blanket, directly... quickly now.' Within moments the two girls had returned, the blanket draped over Simon's shoulders, the hot coffee poured, the toasted cheese promised within a very few minutes.

'Bless you, weans,' the quiet words were offered with a thin smile, the coffee a glory amidst Simon's chilled misery.

'Here it is, sir,' Emma proferred the plate of steaming food, Sandra seizing the coffee cup, the girls kneeling each side of the armchair.

'Well, and 'tis a pleasure to see ye, sir. Indeed, it is,' said Mrs O'Donnell, Simon chewing with determination on his first morsel since a hasty dinner in Bristol before boarding the coach. 'Will you be with us for long, sir? Mr Macleod's room is kept free. I'm sure he will not mind if ye take it.'

'Thank you, Mrs O'Donnell, but it is just the day I am in London. I had intended a week in Bath before going home, to the Isles... to blessed Tobermory... to my abode, but yesterday my intentions changed, my thoughts all ahoo. I became minded to leave directly; I have reserved a seat - an inside seat, thankfully - on the *Express* to Carlisle, leaving tonight at eight o'clock, and thence I will take the *Independent* to Glasgow. With the blessing, I will fetch home on Sunday.'

'Then may it please you to take dinner here, sir. There is a fine ten days hung side of beef and six brace o' partridges in the larder.'

'That will give me the utmost satisfaction, my dear; may the blessings of all the saints be upon your fine house. May I beg another pot of coffee?'

Mrs O'Donnell smiled with all her being, leaned down to seize Simon in her arms, kissed him on both his cheeks, the last slice of the toasted cheese sliding precariously towards the edge of the plate before Simon hastily rescued it, and she waved the girls away with an imperious growl, 'More coffee, d'reckly... and whisky; bring a jar; get along now!'

Monday 6th December 1824   10:00   *Devonport*

The Master Shipwright had pre-empted efforts to warp *Surprise* to the quay by sending four boats and two score of men to tow her the quarter mile to the dock, the tide making. On her prow Pat talked with Codrington and Hemming, the bosun in close attendance. 'High tide is at six bells, sir,' said Hemming, adding by way of belated apology, 'Doubtless you remarked that yesterday.' Pat scowling, he resumed, 'I venture, once she is hauled into the dock, the gate will be closed directly, all the pumps set going, and she will be propped and chocked before the evening gun.'

Pat had his doubts about the validity of the lieutenant's belief in the efficacy of the dock, its pumps most particularly, and he was cautious towards Hemming's enthusiasm, but all he said was 'Thank you, Mr Hemming,' even as his stare remained fixed on the lieutenant, his mind remaining in a state of worried pertubation.

'It would give the greatest of pleasure, sir, to escort you to the office of Admiral Saumarez.'

Pat's racing thoughts afforded only the briefest of acknowledgement, 'Most kind...' At this moment there was a loud cough from behind the officers, Murphy making plain something was amiss, saying nothing. Pat frowned at him with unqualified suspicion, the realisation then registering. 'Mr Hemming, I have to attend my log for the briefest of moments, would you care to excuse me?'

'Of course, sir; there is plenty of time to spare. I venture she will be near the quay in twenty minutes and within the dock in a half-hour, little more.'

In the cabin, Murphy handed Pat his clean, pressed uniform, item by item, as Pat hastily changed out of his unkempt slops, a grateful smile offered by Pat when he emerged in all his finery, a gratified Murphy exhibiting a rare, near completely toothless grin of triumph.

Monday 6th December 1824   noon   *North Sea*

The noon sighting was taken in glorious bright weather, the heavy rainfall of the past twenty-four hours mercifully left behind, the wind biting sharp, a freezing north-westerly bringing a little of sleet, but favourable and steady on the port quarter, the sea state choppy with whitecaps breaking everywhere; *Eleanor* was progressing well, her progress reckoned to be at the anticipated eight knots. The bosun piped "Up Spirits" and the first half of the grog ration was handed out and gratefully received, for it was severely cold, breath freezing in the air, every man shivering, even the faces of the old hands - men long inured to the winter North Atlantic - pinched, their eyes hollowed, precious little sleep gained. 'Lads,' cried Duncan to the small gathering, eight men only serving with Lieutenant Reeve, 'I am minded we will increase the grog ration...' general mutterings of consensus were heard. 'There will be an extra half-pint issued, beginning at dawn tomorrow...' Hearty words of thanks ensued, as might be expected, Duncan waving his hands in the air within moments to restore quietude, 'Cut half and half.' More cheering - this would be strong stuff, the customary blend being diluted four parts water to one of rum.

'Is that not a trifle strong, sir?' whispered Jason, a degree of anxiety in his voice.

'Aye, so it is, but there isnae any cause for concern, there is precious little else to do on this voyage... no prospects for any action.' Duncan laughed, 'and 'tis a mighty cold night to endure.' He looked up to the gathering of happy faces to deliver his *pièce de résistance*, 'Your attention, lads... there will be another issue after the sunset... to set ye up for the night.'

Glorious uproar followed, 'Three cheers for Captain Macleod... Huzzay... Huzzay... Huzzay!'

Monday 6th December 1824   12:00   Devonport

The Plymouth Admiral's office in Admiralty House atop Mount Wise overlooked the Hamoaze, where Admiral Saumarez was comfortably ensconced in his work, a quantity of papers strewn before him as his aide opened the door to show Pat in. The admiral rose, stepped round the desk to greet his visitor with a civil hand outstretched, a genial smile on his face, 'Captain O'Connor, I bid you welcome... please, take a seat. I hope I see you well.'

'Thank you, sir, most kind,' declared Pat cautiously

'Mr Hemming, please ask my steward to attend. Thank you.'

'I am, sir, confounded,' Pat spoke up, his exasperation and misgivings combining with his personal quandary to get the better of him. 'My ship ordered in such uncommon haste into the dock...

and we have been cooling our heels... indeed we have been *freezing* 'em... these four days... no orders... no word at all... *confounded.*'

'Indeed, so am I,' pronounced Saumarez with sympathetic emphasis. 'I gazed upon your ship from this very window,' the admiral waved his arm, 'as she entered the Sound. Plainly she was in need of repair, and every moment since I have considered of her with a profound uncertainty, no word about her coming from their Lordships, the vessel plainly not fit for sea. Yet... yet the reports I hear from the Yard, from the Superintendent's office - wholly speculative of course... and without any standing - suggest she is worthy of repair...' the admiral paused as if in consideration of what he might say, resuming with a sigh, 'but precious little are the funds available for such tasks these days. The blessings of the peace are undeniable... save for, I am minded to think, our own endeavours in this particular place.' The steward entered bearing a tea pot, a coffee pot, cups, glasses and a decanter which Pat particularly noticed, and which was filled with something stronger, a burnt-orange tint to the liquor. 'What will you take, O'Connor?' the admiral waved dismissal to his steward, a nod signifying his thanks.

'I will never refuse coffee, sir.'

'And perhaps a whet of this fine malt? I believe we may have something which is deserving of a modest toast,' teased Saumarez with the most genuine of smiles.

'Certainly, sir,' Pat replied, controlling his curiosity with difficulty; it would not do to interject when an admiral was speaking, his ship's very future hanging in the balance.

'The telegraph at first light brought orders from the Admiralty... from the First Lord himself,' announced Saumarez, his tone declaring the event unusual if not unprecedented. The two men stared at each other, weighing the undoubted significance of the words to come, the admiral's words ultimately softly spoken, uttered almost with disbelief, 'Your ship, O'Connor, is to be restored...' Pat's gasp was audible even to the lieutenant standing at the door, a tidal flood of relief washing through his very being, engulfing him in that instant, '... and without the loss of a moment.'

'Most excellent news, sir,' Pat, recovering from the momentous shock, uttered the few words in barely more than a whisper.

'Most irregular... and profoundly perplexing it was too,' declared the admiral, 'That is... until I read the secret protocol attaching to the order.'

'The secret protocol, sir?'

'Indeed, O'Connor, the secret protocol. Naturally some news of your ship's exploits in Greek waters has reached Devonport and Plymouth these past months... much of it speculation, I grant you... but enough to conclude that your ship has seen action... my first sight of her as she approached the Sound confirming that beyond doubt at all. Yet, their Lordships did not care to afford us here in the southwest any official report of her mission... of her role these past two years.' The admiral sipped his coffee, Pat remaining silent, 'and so we have heard snippets... mere snippets, O'Connor, and precious little more... from packet captains, from merchant vessels returning from the Mediterranean, from the Ionians particularly.' The admiral looked to his attentive aide, 'Mr Hemming, will you excuse us?'

'Of course, sir,' the lieutenant, who had been listening most attentively, exited the room.

'I understand that your ship is to return to the Ionians and thence to resume her former role in that place, which is... as I now understand, O'Connor... which is to assist the formative Greek government... and in an entirely *unofficial* capacity - that is made plain to me in their Lordships' telegraph.' The admiral poured the whisky, exceedingly generous measures, and decided upon a diversion, a necessary one as he saw things, Pat's face a picture of uncertainty, 'Will you join me, O'Connor, in a toast to your ship... and to her crew, for I gather that she has suffered an intolerable number of casualties - I heard that from Dr Tripe, his report from Falmouth. It seems that you have participated in a number of actions - this gleaned from several of your men who Dr Tripe is treating - and indeed you have gained the most meritorious of victories. Is that not so?'

'I confess, sir, that *Surprise* and my men have been struck hard... very hard indeed, when... when assisting the Greeks. Too many of them have been... been left behind, sir... we suffered many deaths, too many... it pains me greatly to say.'

'I am dismayed to hear it, I am so.'

'Thank you, sir.'

'And now, let us raise our glasses, Captain O'Connor... this is surely a moment which calls for a salute to your comrades, valiant men all... of that I have not the least doubt. You will allow me to propose the toast...' The admiral stood up as if to demonstrate his profound respect, Pat following.

'Sir,' Pat nodded, picking up his tumbler.

'TO THE VALIANT *SURPRISE!*' the admiral's voice boomed out throughout all the room.

'The valiant *Surprise!*' Pat echoed the emphatic words, in truth finding the moment bearing heavy upon him.

'And to all those brave souls who sailed in her!'

'To all those brave souls...' Pat was finding the rising sentiment hard, powerfully overtaking him, his stomach and his emotions both churning, the feeling of profound relief that his ship was to be repaired fighting with the grave dismay he felt as he recollected in that fleeting instant a flurry of memories of those men who had been lost, in his raging emotions finding any further words at all too difficult. He drank down his whisky in one, stooping to set down the tumbler exceedingly slowly, turning away from the admiral to obscure his confusion, a rising distress coming upon him, his sleeve serving to quickly wipe his moist eyes.

The admiral, perhaps recognising Pat's discomfort, urged another coffee upon him; the offer passing unnoticed, he allowed another minute to pass in reflection until he spoke again, 'Allow me to freshen your glass.' Saumarez poured more whisky. 'O'Connor, I am tasked by His Lordship to ask of you a most important question... of the utmost importance, as is made plain.'

'Sir?'

'Melville desires me to press you on this... precious little time available to arrange any alternative... and none that he cares to contemplate...' a pregnant pause, Saumarez staring intently at Pat, 'O'Connor, would you care to return to Greece?'

Monday 6th December 1824   18:00   *Westminster, London*

Simon, plentifully filled with beef and warmed with copious quantities of whisky, picked up his bag and stepped towards the door, readied for departure. Macleod's nieces, Emma and Sandra, in close attendance pressed their farewells upon him, for he was the most welcome and well-regarded of guests, though more customarily at the inn with his close friend, Duncan, and rarely by himself. Not a tall man, the girls had little difficulty stretching to bestow kisses on his cheeks as each hugged him in turn, both of them perfectly aware of how close his friendship was to their uncle and benefactor, for it was Macleod who had brought them to London after the death of their father, their mother long predeceasing him, and no means of support available to them in the Isles.

'Will ye pass my thanks to Mrs O'Donnell, weans?' murmured Simon, the hostess oddly absent.

'No they will not!' boomed out the loud voice approaching from the kitchen door. 'I am a'comin' with 'ee, to the coach,' declared Mrs O'Donnell in a voice that reverberated throughout the room and down much of the street.

Simon smiled, still greatly heartened by the warmth of his several welcomes at the Feathers after the cold and exceedingly dispirited mood of his journey from Bristol. 'That is most kind of you, Mrs O'Donnell,' he declared, 'but allow me to say it is wholly unnecessary, I do assure you.'

'An' I'll be a'takin' that, sorr,' boomed Mrs O'Donnell in a tone which would brook no contradiction whatsoever, seizing Simon's bag from his hand. A final wave to the girls, and they started down the Strand, Mrs O'Donnell enquiring of Simon's preparedness for the long journey to far distant Scotland, a sure wilderness she had oft heard mentioned by her guests and visitors, one which she could only vaguely imagine as something similar to her Irish origins, but much more remote, a place she had never visited and likely never would. A few hundred yards at the slowest of pace, Simon plainly sunk in introspection, and they turned right into Garrick Street. Simon offering only the briefest of replies to her sustained queries of concern, Mrs O'Donnell sensed his underlying unhappiness and determined to press him for an explanation. She stopped, set down his bag, 'Sorr, ye will forgive an honest lass from the County Clare, I'm sure, when I ask... what ills trouble ye so?'

Simon started, shaken at last from his private concerns. He stopped too, stared at his companion, 'Why, Mrs O'Donnell, 'tis nothing but the wanderings of a mind which is homeward bound... with all the time in the world to dwell on the prospects for precious peace of mind, of home... all onerous obligations, nautical and medical, left behind.'

'No it ain't,' spluttered Mrs O'Donnell, the timbre of indignation in her voice. 'I may be a simple Irish lass from the Burren, I grant ye that, but 'tis plain there's a deal o' worries on yer mind... sorr.'

'Will I share a confidence with you, my dear?' said Simon, shivering in the cold wind, a minute of reflection passing, his tone resigned.

'If ye care to, sorr.'

He sighed, 'I have... I have lost a deal of patients on my table this past twelvemonth... men I had known for many a year; indeed, several I was pleased to think of as friends... it grieves me so...' Mrs O'Donnell seized his arm, Simon so evidently in consternation. He resumed in a whisper, 'I know... that is to say... I doubt the finest surgeon in all the world would have saved any of them... poor souls... their wounds so greatly severe... that they were... but no, I am minded that... I am minded that clarity is lacking, Mrs O'Donnell, clarity... my very purpose is become in doubt these past weeks. Will I persevere within the mariner's watery realm? Will I ever return to the sea... to face violent, bloody death once more... or should I remain in Mull, a landsman for the future... serving my peaceable and ruly neighbours? I am all thrown out. What is to be done? It is a damnable confusion.'

A long and thoughtful stare from Mrs O'Donnell before she spoke, 'Sorr, all those years ago, I fetched up in London, a penniless orphan straight off the boat from Cork, an' my uncle a tyrant I was pleased to leave behind.' This was offered in the soft voice she rarely had occasion to use, with infinite kindness and with all the natural warmth of Ireland within it, 'My own fears were much the same. What to do? I was come to the big city... to find my way; just a cousin here to give me a bed... precious little to do fer a young girl in the County Clare... save I was to marry some ruffian an' grow potatoes for evermore.' She squeezed Simon's hand, 'Time, sorr, plenty o' time... heals all the ills o' the world... well, fer the most part much of 'em, so it does.' She pressed on valiantly, Simon's face a picture of doubt, 'I dare say a spell in yer home... with old acquaintances there, fer sure... will bring that precious peace o' mind, so it will.'

'I am sure there is something in what you say, Mrs O'Donnell... from the philosophical perspective,' mumbled Simon, 'and I am most grateful for your thoughts, profoundly grateful. I thank you most sincerely.'

'There will always be a welcome fer ye at the Feathers, sorr.'

'That is and will remain a comfort, my dear, as I find my course... whilst I am adrift upon this... this sea of uncertainty.'

'Come, Doctor Ferguson, let us get along now.' Mrs O'Donnell seized up Simon's bag from the pavement. Twenty minutes more of companiable walking brought them to the Post Office, a score of coaches and their horses, their breath steaming in the cold evening air, standing ready for the concurrent 8 p.m. departure to their many destinations.

'I will bid you goodbye, my dear,' said Simon, 'and my thanks once more for your kindness. May our paths cross before too long.' A fierce hug from Mrs O'Donnell and Simon, his spirits restored a very little, stepped back and looked with visible anxiety towards his coach.

'Here, sorr, take this,' Mrs O'Donnell pressed her own bag into Simon's hand, '... 'tis a brace o' roasted partridges an' my last jar o' Killaloe whiskey... the treasure o' the blessed County Clare, so it is... here, I beg you will take it... fer the journey.'

Monday 13th December 1824   13:00   *Gulf of Finland*

The eventual clearing of the fog which had persisted all morning and into the early afternoon presented a view of distant Kotlin

Island, *Eleanor* inching along at no more than three knots in a weak wind, a powdery dusting of snow on her deck, thin and broken surface ice abounding all around her; indeed, all through the long night every man had been kept awake by increasingly noisy brushes with it, praying that nothing of greater solidity would strike the schooner, for all knew only too well that a calamity in the freezing Baltic water could not be survived by all, *Eleanor's* small boat of a size for only four men. For several days the grog ration had been exceedingly well received, the deep bone-chilling cold of the Baltic winter entirely unfamiliar to everyone, and all had endured the past three nights with constant shivering, in extreme discomfort, sleep proper quite impossible, a precious few hours of uncomfortable dozing all that any man had achieved before rising in the darkness to stumble up to share a watch. Ice had long formed on all the schooner's bulwarks, rigging and deck, and whilst it remained thin and insufficient to affect her stability, her decks were slippery, making movement hazardous; and the first deep breath of the air inflicted an assault on the lungs, every breath condensing into a steaming cloud as teeth chattered, every finger numbed and freezing despite their woollen gloves, all faces blue and pinched with cold.

Macleod gazed through his glass, the Kronstadt naval base becoming discernible, cloaked in white, the masts of many ships protruding above the persisting low-lying fog. 'I doubt we will safely make Saint Petersburg,' he offered to Jason, standing alongside him on deck. 'This ice is thickenin' by the mile... 'tis near seventeen miles beyond the island.'

'Then what of our purpose?' exclaimed Jason, dismayed.

'Fer sure, nothin' will be served by being frozen in for the winter,' Duncan replied in a voice heavy with resignation. 'We will tie up at Kronstadt and make our enquiries o' the ice... and any open passage to Saint Petersburg through it.' Another two hours, the island close, the fog all cleared at long last, and *Eleanor* shifted her course towards the snow-covered quay, the most pitiful sight of dozens of badly damaged ships becoming plain before them. Frigates, larger ships - seventy-fours - and some of the behemoths of the Russian navy, 110 and 120 gun ships, all presented their pictures of abject desolation. On every one of them topmasts and yards were struck down, no trace of canvas on any ship; several hulls were perilously pitched over to an alarming angle, only the smallest movement away from capsize, buoys abounding all about the sorry sight. Boats of many sizes, scores of them, were hastening to and fro, men everywhere hauling on lines to rectify this and that, precious little success did they appear to have achieved; and all over the anchorage floated swathes of debris: timbers, planks, shattered fragments of unknown origin and various sizes, broken yards, gun port doors, the remnants of great cabin windows, blocks - hundreds of them - and general detritus of all forms including bloated, drowned rats in their thousands, above which the gulls - hundreds of them - soared with excited curiosity, rising and swooping, their eyes gazing down to select their next morsel to eat.

'Jason, will ye take a look through the glass... those ships. I cannae read the Russian. Tell me, if ye can, their names, and I will write it down.'

'Of course, sir,' Jason stared, as did every man aboard, many of the ships canted far over, presumably their ballast shifted, others low in the water, some exhibiting smashed and vacant gun ports, the armament missing, presumably crashed out through the missing doors to sink. The received reports of catastrophe were true: this fleet could not depart for many a month, if ever. 'I see *North Star*... there, that one,' Jason pointed.

'A seventy-four,' declared Duncan, scratching away, the ink kept liquid against his chest, clutched precariously within his coat, '*North Star* did ye say?'

'*North Star*, yes... and there is *Hamburg*... *Katzbach*... and *Jupiter*.' Macleod scribbled hastily as Jason resumed. 'I see *Finland*... and *Prince Gustav*.' *Eleanor* moved on in circuitous approach, passing by the distressed fleet. '*Three Hierarchs, Three Saints*... *Borei*.'

'A wee slower, if ye will, the damned ink is freezing. Timmins, there is a charcoal stick on the table in the cabin... swiftly now.' A boat had put off from the quay and was approaching.

'*Sviatoslav*... another seventy-four, *Arsis, Brave* there, the larger ship,' declared Jason.

'I venture she is at least a 110.'

'*Leipzig*, another 110... and *Hard*... she is doubtless a 110 too... and... *don't touch me.*'

'I wilnae,' exclaimed Duncan, taken aback.

'No, sir; it is the ship's name... *Don't Touch Me.*'

'I see,' declared Duncan doubtfully, for who had ever heard of a ship's name such as that.

A hail from the Russian boat, near alongside, interrupted the observations, shouted instructions to tie up at the quay translated by Jason, and the schooner shifted her course again. Fifteen more minutes and she was coming alongside, Russian sailors throwing lines fore and aft, a Russian officer immediately coming aboard with a greatly officious demeanour. 'We are summoned by Admiral Senyavin,' pronounced Jason.

'Oh dear,' sighed Duncan, 'That is damnable bad luck. Let us pray we will nae be interned for the next year.'

'Interned?' asked Jason anxiously.

'Aye, the admiral spent a year in Portsmouth with his five ships in the year '09... the Tsar having declared war on Britain. A rum affair it was. I will tell ye about that later. First, let us get ashore, your man there is getting anxious. I dinnae care to become unwelcome.'

Monday 13th December 1824   15:00   Tobermory, Mull

On the quayside, Simon paced up and down in solitary thought, pausing to stare from time to time across the choppy waters of the Sound towards the distant grey outline of the hills of Ardnamurchan, the low sun and diffuse light reluctant to cede the day to the gloom of the approaching dusk. He shivered, the air so very cold, a brief recollection of the warmth of the Greek summer a pleasing memory. With more than a little apprehension he awaited the arrival of his sister-in-law, Flora MacDougall, with her two daughters coming from Islay, brought by fishermen. Simon's very recent arrival home, only the prior day after an interminable, freezing journey from London on coaches that were slow, delayed and even halted in the wild winter weather, had given him not the least time for recuperation. His first task of the morning had been to cast wide the shutters and the windows of his tiny house, to vent the unpalatable stench of damp and the sooty odours of his unsuccessful fire of the prior evening: more smoke than flame as his logs had hesitated to burn; and so he had sat in the near darkness close by the small vestige of doubtful warmth at his hearth, a solitary lamp flickering its dim yellow light his sole companion as he reflected on the absence of his wife, his beloved Agnes, the lady of this particular house, her graceful image still so very clear in his mind. She had died in the year '13, wasted away with the consumption, his inability to help her and her eventual loss a still fiercely burning fire of distress within him all these years on. His first evening at home for a very long time had not been a happy one. That his housekeeper had neglected the house for many a month was obvious, a cold ambience of dust and a sense of abandonment was evident throughout. It had not been the homecoming he had hoped for, and no opportunity had he found to meet any of the old friends of his former life before the Edinburgh medical college and the navy had taken him away from the village. His thoughts returning to the present, he halted his pacing; he looked up and stared across the choppy water, a leaden grey sky holding only the promise of a downpour and adding to his gloom; he pulled tighter his coat against the chill of the gusting wind, the first spits of rain in the air, and he pondered what food he might offer his guests, the little in his larder hastily procured during the late morning, the postmaster pressing upon him the letter from Flora announcing her arrival this day; since when he had eaten nothing, and the first pangs of hunger were stirring within him.

 The small fishing boat came into view, fairly swept into the tiny harbour from the outlying Sound, closed swiftly on the quay, the tide not quite yet at slackwater, approaching to tie alongside. Simon's eyes gazed, then stared in sharp focus at the huddle forward of the helm which was the passengers, his anticipation heightening as the sense of uncertainty brought a waver, a tremulation within his mind: this was the sister of his wife; she would be with him within mere moments. He had never met the woman; what would she be like? What might she say when they spoke of his dear Agnes, her sister? Closer now, the crewman, a youngster, leaping from the bow across the tiny gap to the quay, heaving on the line, pulling over the hawser, tying it to a rusty, encrusted bollard, the boat swinging closer, the stern now touching and the older skipper throwing the second line.

From the deck emerged two young girls; they leapt on to the quay, and then came their mother, swathed in a tightly gathered, buttoned cloak with the traditional mutch of white linen wrapped over and around her head, the folds obscuring any sight of her face: doubtless a protection from the cold and the chill wind. The boat's skipper, Simon noted, hurried to take her hand as she stepped gracefully over to the quay without any difficulty. She beckoned her daughters and turned back to the man, a few words and a tight embrace between them before the lines were checked, the crew leaping back aboard to clew up the sails, the boat swiftly prepared for a night at the quay, the small baggage heaved ashore.

Simon, twenty yards away, waved his arm and stepped towards the arrivals; the girls, their age about twelve he reckoned, were plainly excited to be at this new place. His sister-in-law threw off her headcovering and, gathering her daughters within her arms, shepherded them along with her. Simon halted, stood perfectly immobile, stock still, his heart racing so violently that he feared a heart attack was overtaking him even as he experienced a shortness of breath. He stared, wide-eyed, at the approaching woman: it was the greatest shock of his life.

Monday 13th December 1824   16:00   New Union Dock, Devonport

Barely fifteen minutes before the sunset and the labourers were preparing to leave *Surprise*. The removal of the old and putrescent gravel ballast had been going on for much of the week and carpenters had descended upon the ship in force, likely every single one the yard employed, their numbers so great. Her oakum caulking was being prised out from all over her hull where there was the least doubt of its integrity, nothing of it remaining in her bow. A weary Pat sat at his table within the great cabin reflecting on a tumultuous week. He had been about to begin to read a letter from his distant cousin, Canning, the Foreign Secretary, which he put down on the desk as, unbidden, Murphy brought in the extremely welcome coffee pot, Pat nodding absently to his steward, reluctant to break his train of thought, the letter and also Admiral Saumarez's question monopolising his thoughts. He looked up, Murphy lingering near his table, 'Yes, Murphy?'

'Beg leave to say, sorr; there is a deal o' mutterin' with the men...'

'Muttering?' Pat looked up at his steward's shrewish face, immobile, giving nothing away.

'Yes, sorr.'

'What do you mean, Murphy?'

'Well... the men is a'wantin' to know if they should go home, sorr, to Falmouth... the yard men handlin' the barky's repair.'

'I see,' Pat finished his coffee. 'Please to tell them I shall be with them in a minute or two... on the quarterdeck if you will.' Despite the instruction Murphy remained, hesitant, plainly agitated. 'Go on,' prompted Pat in the tone he employed to coax confession from his steward, usually upon the discovery of an absence in the stores.

'Well, sorr,' Murphy swallowed hard, spoke again with obvious reticence, with a degree of uncertainty, nervousness even, 'The men, sorr... they'se a'wonderin' if their captain is a'stayin'... wi' the barky that is... Doctor Ferguson an' Mr Macleod both gone.'

'Cut along, Murphy; I will be there presently.'

'D'reckly, sorr,' Murphy crept out of the cabin.

Pat, his mind wavering between several matters, grave indecision to the fore, resumed reading his cousin's letter,

Gloucester Lodge,
London.
December 8th 1824

My dear O'Connor,

Would that we might find the occasion to speak of these matters personally, and until such time presents itself when we may do so my written congratulations and grateful thanks must suffice for the sterling service you have rendered His Majesty's government these past eighteen months.

Mention must also be made of your most valiant officers and men. It is with my most sincere condolences that I remark upon those of your men who have, sadly, been lost; I have not the least doubt that they are heroes, all of them.

I state this in the most frank of terms: it is a matter of immeasurable significance to His Majesty's government that your invaluable work of these recent times, and also that of your men and ship, must be perpetuated. In that matter, it is my understanding that your ship will be repaired and replenished for a return to that invaluable duty, the political situation in that region to which I am referring being generally significantly deteriorated and "our friends" acutely requiring of urgent assistance.

It is therefore my most earnest hope that you, dear cousin, will resume and return to that onerous and exacting task when your ship is restored. As was plainly the case previously, no other officer - in my own estimation and also in the opinion of the First Lord - is more suited to those requirements, to that particular service.

I have the honour to be
your obedient servant,

George Canning

Pat sighed, a black cloud of apprehension, of enduring obligation filling his mind; he put the letter in his desk drawer, pulled on his uniform jacket and picked up his hat; he stepped out through the coach and up the companionway steps, the vigorous murmurings amongst his men dying away to silence as he appeared. Slowly he put on his hat, paced steadily aft to stand at the stump of the mizzen mast and looked about him to inspect his men. There were over seventy present, three dozen of them his regulars - enlisted men - and about forty volunteers. Devonport boasting several taverns close by the Yard, he wondered whether the blank faces he saw were consequent to drink: *Surprise* being within the dock ready access was afforded to many and various local pleasures. Certainly none of the men could be described as being drunk, for the drunken state of a sailor on leave so affected was unmistakeable; no, there were a few who seemed unsteady - the ship unmoving within the dock and the tie of its supporting props - but undeniably Pat detected a whiff of drink in the cold air as he paced further through the gathering to stand at the stern rail. The hands were sober enough, in full possession of their senses, enough at least to know their purpose, to exhibit their unease and unhappiness with their lot; Pat could see that.

'All hands aft,' Pat shouted, no dire imperative in his tone, rather a call to assemble about him. It was a formality, everyone already as far aft as the deck would permit. The men shuffled a step closer. 'I am not here to make a speech,' he declared. 'We know one another well enough after all these years, and so I will speak frankly.'

He stared about him at many of the familiar faces, all glum, their dejection plain to see in their demeanour. The takeover of the packet service from Falmouth's private contractors by the Admiralty had promoted great concern within the Cornish port, employment in fishing the only alternative, but one which for a long time had not been greatly remunerative, fish catches much declining. The loss of *Surprise* would be particularly painful for the small town. Pat took a few minutes to allow his eyes to wander across as many men in the gathering before him that he could see directly. His shipmates of the recent past in Greek waters were perfectly familiar to him, and so he looked with particular interest to the volunteers. They were generally veterans of prior voyages with Pat in years gone by, *Tenedos* men, older hands who had relinquished their shipboard places to their younger brothers, to their sons and nephews. His gaze passed from man to man, recognition prompting the smallest nod of his head here and there. Few were unfamiliar to him, though he could not see all at the back of the crowd, so tightly were they standing together. Silence, expectancy and despond seemed to be common to every man, all of them dejected, morose, waiting; the despondency was plainly general. The sun had departed, the muted light of dusk all that was left to them; the Yard's men were all gone; even the wind appeared to have graced the moment by falling away to insignificance, though the severe chill of the day remained. He saw nothing but uncertainty and a measure of unwillingness on the dour, blank faces before him. 'Lads,' he began, calling upon his natural benevolence - for any display of command authority did not seem appropriate on this occasion - and upon the small reserve of diplomacy he possessed, but it fell dismally short, not a man stirred. He began again with a small jest to try to spark some uplift of spirits, 'What is at hand here? I pray this is no mutiny... eh? Else you will all be obliged to be hanged!' This rather fell flat, not the least show of mirth evident, his words having no effect whatsoever. He resumed in a rather more stern voice, 'Gather round.' The men shuffled forward again, the shifting about presenting a most familiar face at the front of the press: Jelbert, a volunteer, a topman in years gone by on *Tenedos*, a man who had subsequently introduced his son to join *Surprise*; he had been the captain of the aftmost larboard gun in the *Tenedos* great cabin when Pat had assumed command, later promoted to master gunner, so gifted was he with the aiming of the great guns and the training of their crews, retiring to cede his duties to Boswell as master gunner. Pat gulped, his mind raced frantically, an unpleasant surge of something near panic welling up within him; he had not encountered Jelbert in the voyage from Falmouth nor in the days since whilst the ship had lain in Devonport. Jelbert's son had been killed in the first battle to defend Samos. The unblinking gaze of both men lingered on each other, no words spoken, the moment a truly dreadful one for Pat; for Jelbert had pressed him before *Surprise* had left Falmouth to look after his son, the youngster following in his father's footsteps as a gunner, and Pat was acutely mindful that in the most important thing in all the world for the man standing before him he had failed, failed utterly. It was a thought he had sought to put out of his mind for many months, never with complete success. That particular death and that of so many others was the foundation of his own uncertainty as to whether he himself would persevere, would continue to captain the ship, Saumarez's question still unanswered even in Pat's own mind, Pellew's valued advice of the evening before the transit to Devonport not quite bringing him to the conclusion he so much sought to find, and his cousin's letter - despite being the most considerate plea for his return to Greece with *Surprise* - still leaving his decision cloaked within a painful swathe of uncertainty, with no notion of what he would choose to do. His mind raced, but no words would come.

Monday 13th December 1824   16:00   Kronstadt, Gulf of Finland

Macleod and Jason waited, with some small degree of tension, outside Admiral Senyavin's office, the Russian marine standing at the door unmoving, his eyes staring directly ahead, his rifle presented with bayonet affixed. 'You mentioned internment, sir?' whispered Jason. 'I cannot say I care for these climes.'

'Aye, 'tis the strangest of tale. It was the summer of the year '07 and Senyavin had defeated the Ottoman fleet off the island of Tenedos, forcing a treaty between the twae powers. On his way back home, to the Baltic, the Tsar made peace with Boney and then declared war on Britain - would ye believe it? And Senyavin, his ships then halfway home... in Portugal, in the mouth of the Tagus, was blockaded by Admiral Cotton... this after Senyavin had shaken the hand of Admiral Collingwood on the Rock.'

'Well, I never...' exclaimed Jason. 'Quite extraordinary.'

'Senyavin was ordered by the French to bombard the Portuguese and the Spanish, allies of ours, and to come out to fight with Cotton. This was in the summer of '08.'

'Fascinating! What did he do, pray tell?'

'Senyavin refused all French orders, declared Russia was not at war with Spain or Portugal, and accepted Cotton's invitation to be interned in Pompey until the end of the war.'

'I venture he was a principled man.'

'He left for the Baltic in the autum of '09,' Duncan concluded the rather strange tale of great powers. 'So ye see, I widnae be sure the admiral wilnae keep us here for a year or twae - if he is so disposed.'

'But surely our mission, acting in the Tsar's personal interests, will override any... any inimical intentions of Senyavin?'

'We can but hope so... if, that is, the admiral is aware of the Tsar's direction in this matter. That isnae sure.'

At that moment the authoritative aide summoned Macleod and Jason into the room, Senyavin rising from his desk with a rather dour expression, stepping forward to greet them. 'I bid you welcome to Kronstadt.' The aide translated before Jason could do so for Macleod. 'Please, sit down,' this spoken rather sharply. The aide, on Senyavin's nod, brought coffee and vodka, a large jar of it, pouring the coffee for the three seated officers.

A first cup of coffee diplomatically enjoyed, Jason spoke up, offering in Russian, 'Sir, my name is Jason, and I am aide to Captain Macleod, here beside me. We are here at the bequest... *the personal bequest* of His Imperial Majesty... that is to say Tsar Alexander.'

If Senyavin was impressed he failed to show it, merely blinking and turning to speak to his aide; the admiral's reply was echoed by that officer, 'Captain Macleod, Admiral Senyavin is, of course, knowledgeable about your purpose, your mission. Indeed General Chernyshev himself - anticipating the ice - came to Kronstadt a week ago to brief him, bringing out from Saint Petersburg a considerable cargo... cargo in sealed crates... not to be subject to any inspection... military or Customs.'

'Sir, are you... are you familiar with the contents?' ventured Jason to Senyavin, rather cautiously.

'Mr Jason... the Tsar has a thousand serfs tending his gardens at the Palaces...' The admiral paused momentarily, Jason and Macleod wondering what the significance was. 'Do you think I care to join them?' The admiral laughed out loud. His aide smiled. 'Of course I do not know the contents of the crates... did I not make that plain?' Senyavin reverted to a frosty look of irritation, 'Chernyshev departed for Saint Petersburg immediately the guard was in attendance, fearing for the channel - it was beginning to freeze over.'

'You are aware, Captain Macleod,' added Senyavin's aide, rather pompously and no longer smiling, 'that the thaw may not come until the spring?' He refilled the coffee cups.

Macleod nodded; Jason breathed an audible sigh, whether of relief or anxiety could not be perceived, replying immediately in Russian, 'Then, if it pleases you, sir,' looking to Senyavin, 'we will begin loading that cargo this very day, without delay... without the loss of a moment; the ice is a most considerable concern.'

Senyavin, relaxing, nodded his understanding, his consent, and spoke briefly, 'Gentlemen, I have a file of marines standing ready to assist you.'

'Thank you, we are most infinitely obliged to you, Admiral,' declared Jason.

'Admiral,' ventured Duncan cautiously, 'Your ships... we passed them as we approached the quay... May I enquire what happened to them, so greatly damaged they are?'

A grimace from Senyavin, the subject obviously acutely distressing to him, his aide's scowl suggesting such a question was impudent indeed. The admiral appeared to reflect, perhaps deciding the question to be an honest one, the natural curiosity of a fellow mariner. 'It was a great flood of the Neva... on the 19th... Saint Petersburg was submerged under water to the eaves of houses, more than 500 souls drowned in the city...'

'Mother of God,' Jason exclaimed.

'... a sudden thaw... and an ice dam on the river broke, so it is said, the water behind it flooding the city, the levels there rising so very swiftly... twelve feet within three hours, and the river torrent sweeping through the city and carrying all before it... many people swept away with no chance to flee... nowhere to go, the rising water depth simply overtaking them.' A long draw from his coffee and the admiral continued his dreadful litany, 'The city lost more than three hundred houses destroyed... over three *thousand* were damaged. It is calculated that the cost of the various damages to the city will be in excess of twenty millions of roubles.'

'That is truly lamentable, Admiral, catastrophic indeed... but your ships...?' Duncan prompted gently, the aide translating.

'My ships...' the admiral sighed, a long exhalation perhaps signifying a reluctance to allow his mind to contemplate that particular subject. He finished his coffee before resuming. 'The city's disaster followed the most extreme of winds from the west during the prior day... the 18th it was... and all through the night. The anchorage was assaulted by them... a long fetch sea all the way from the southern Baltic... no doubt of that. Plainly my captains could not leave the anchorage... the westerly winds so strong and the Gulf - it had been exceptionally cold in the days beforehand - was frozen for much of its surface east to Saint Petersburg.' Senyavin sighed again, nodded to his aide who poured from the decanter into the glasses on the desk. 'And then the wind dropped on the 19th, which we prayed would be our salvation, but the wave heights became greater still... I could perceive the sea heaving and swelling in the most unaccountable manner, and this despite the lesser wind. The waves appeared to be standing still, no longer shifting but rising ever higher... yet no wind to drive them on... a perplexing mystery indeed... and increasingly we were becoming engulfed. You may judge of the height of these waves when I inform you it was so shocking that I could scarce believe it. I stood some time and observed the ships tumbling and tossing about as if in a violent storm; the quays - indeed, all the island - then wholly awash, all the wooden buildings simply crushed and swept away, the fortress itself damaged, and our ships shifting violently at anchorage. Some had broken their cables... and they were carried to smash, ship against ship... and all this later in the morning without any wind of significance, which seemed the more astonishing. At the same time, a great number of boats and small vessels, all anchored, were swallowed up, as if in a whirlpool, and nevermore appeared, nothing to see save for the masts of larger ships... projecting from the waters next day.' The admiral gulped, the recounting of the story was evidently distressing him. 'Worse was to come in that vile day... *next* came the tidal wave from the east, from the river, in the afternoon, conflicting with the huge waves from the Gulf. All day the air had warmed... and the thaw of the Neva unleashed floating mountains of ice borne along atop it... our ships' anchor cables were ripped away in the flood, and several of them - frigates for the most part - were crushed on the quay... others were whirled around with incredible swiftness; several were turned keel upwards; there was nothing we could do to save them,' the admiral's despairing voice tailed off. He nodded to his aide, indicating the vodka.

'And your intentions for repair?' prompted Duncan cautiously, keenly aware that the admiral's answers would be of great interest, of fascination to Melville upon his return home.

'Only twelve vessels have survived out of ninety-seven lying in the harbour. The remainder have been condemned or... as I expect... will be so when the extent of their damage is truly plain to the fleet surveyors.'

'Eighty-five lost!' Duncan could not refrain his exclamation.

'Indeed, large and small.' Senyavin, his shocking story concluded, relaxed a little and smiled for the first time, raising his exceedingly well-filled glass of vodka, Macleod and Jason duty bound to follow. 'But now, a toast... to an old acquaintance. To Admiral Cotton!'

'Admiral Cotton!' the echo was followed by Senyavin downing his glass in one and Macleod's sterling attempt to follow - pausing at half - but Jason, striving but failing after the merest sip, coughed out his unfamiliarity with such strong spirit.

'The Royal Navy!' Senyavin shouted, his glass already swiftly refilled by his aide.

'The Royal Navy!' came Duncan's equally enthusiastic cry, his doubts about the admiral's feelings for his former imprisoners wholly cast aside. Jason's toast was expressed in more moderate voice, followed by his faintly disguised but unconvincing attempt to sip the vodka.

'And now to work - eh?' beamed Senyavin.

Monday 13th December 1824   16:15   Tobermory, Mull

Flora MacDougall's fishermen companions had made their greetings with a silent and still shocked Simon before moving off along the quay towards the alehouse, perhaps detecting his enduring state of distress and wondering why that might be, but politely not caring to ask. The elder was Flora's brother-in-law, the younger his son. Flora's subsequent entry to an exceedingly subdued Simon's house was not propitious in the least: they shivered immediately on stepping across the threshold into a cold and gloomy room, for the fire had burned out, the hearth and range were cold, and the dusk was upon them. The solitary oil lamp still burned, casting its weak yellow glow, the dim light sufficient only to preclude falling over the sparse furniture: two wooden chairs, the smallest of table and a tiny sideboard with a mirror above.

'Here... Mrs MacDougall... allow me to help you to this chair... May I take your cloak? Perhaps not... with the cold so I am sure you are inclined to keep it on...'

'Doctor Ferguson, is this the only lamp you have?'

'Why yes, my dear, save for the one upstairs.'

'Then do you have candles in the house?'

'There may be some in the sideboard. I will look... yes, a half-dozen, to some small degree burned - for the most part that is.'

'Then, if it pleases you, let us light them.'

'Of course... directly. I will do so now.'

'Annag,' Flora looked to her daughter, 'a half-dozen of the driest, smallest logs, if you will - look out the back. Rhona, will you help your sister and search for some paper. Thank you both.'

'May I offer you a glass of whisky?' asked Simon nervously.

'No, thank you. Where is the kettle? Would you have tea in the house?'

'That is doubtful, I confess, but there is a trifle of coffee in the jar. Would you care for coffee?'

'I would not, thank you.' Flora stared all about the uninviting room, her gaze eventually fixing on Simon. 'Doctor Ferguson, you were expecting us today, were you not?'

'Yes of course, my dear Mrs MacDougall, most certainly I was expecting you... indeed, looking forward with considerable pleasure to your coming, I was so, but... but the precise day of your arrival was not known to me until today. I fetched up here myself only last night... from London... and my post, that is to say your letter, was made available to me only this morning.'

'I see,' Flora scrutinised Simon carefully. He was pale, thin, and it was clear he was in need of many a good meal. 'Might I enquire... do you have any provisions in the house?'

'Why yes, of course...' Simon paused, appeared to rethink, 'Actually... precious little, I regret to say.'

Flora reached for her own bag, 'Then we shall eat the loaf and the fish I have brought from Islay. Will that suit?'

'Admirably so, I have a particular taste for... for fish... and indeed for bread, most certainly I do.'

'Then allow me to light this fire, and presently, while the fish is cooking, we will see to our accommodations,' declared Flora, Simon's head nodding, his eyes closing, no suitable words in his grasp to explain the deficiencies of the other bedroom; indeed, the house generally, but a growing appreciation of Mrs MacDougall rising within him, even as his mind was slowly accommodating the thunderbolt inflicted upon it in seeing the twin of his wife; now a little older, a little more rounded, but the resemblance, her presence and character particularly, was near indistinguishable from her deceased sister, and it was the shock of that which had overpowered him utterly.

Monday 13th December 1824   16:30   the quarterdeck of HMS Surprise

'Mr Jelbert,' a whisper, Pat struggling to find his words, his chest feeling tightly constricted. He stepped closer to his old shipmate, the two men staring intensely at each other, until Pat spoke at last, 'It pains me... it pains me greatly... that is to say... I am deeply sorry that your lad... your *son*... was lost...' Jelbert's murmured reply was inaudible, even to Pat, now standing only a foot in front of him. 'He... he was the bravest of souls... an admirable man, so he was... a capital fellow and an uncommon skilled gunner.' Jelbert's pain and dismay was plain to all standing about them, general silence abounding and the conversation heard by a dozen of men, the few men still speaking at the back pressed to silence by their fellows, every man aware that some significance was attached to their captain's dialogue, and every man strived to hear the quiet exchanges. 'How are you? How do you fare?' Pat's gentle words conveyed his deep concern; his face radiated his anxiety, such a profoundly difficult moment for both men.

'Tolerably well, sir,' Jelbert's mumbled reply could not be perceived as anything but a fiction, so great the visible pain in his face that all watching, including Pat, were intensely moved, two of his shipmates, kindly men, close by his sides pressing on his arms, their personal gesture of support the tiniest crumb of comfort.

Pat, his own spirits sinking as fast as the best bower ever disappeared, spoke very softly, his face radiating his own heartfelt distress, plain to all, even as he strived with his words for warmth and benevolence, 'Will 'ee care to come to the cabin when we are done? Perhaps we may speak further of your son, of your own intentions?'

'I will, sir; obliged... most kind... thankee; but my intentions are plain... *sir*... if ye will?' Jelbert spoke with resolute conviction, his voice firming.

'Please do... your intentions...' Pat found himself whispering once more.

'If ye please, sir... I wish to join the crew o' the barky.'

Pat's mind recoiled in small shock, Jelbert no longer a young man, a thoughtful pause passing before he spoke again, 'Ye wish to join the barky's crew? Did I hear ye plain?'

'Oh, I am no longer fit for the tops, sir, but I can fight a gun, haul on the braces... as well as any man here... I can so.'

'That's right,' echoed the shouts of a dozen men, the old hands of *Tenedos* particularly loud.

'That is most commendable, Mr Jelbert... admirable, but...' Pat hesitated, his concern for an older hand staying his words.

'Falmouth town needs this ship, sir...'

'That is the case, yes... but 'tis a long time since you served with us... on *Tenedos* - aftmost larboard gun in the cabin...' Pat sighed, '*Billy Warr* it was, if my memory does not fail me... and then master gunner for the last twelvemonth. It surely was a long time back.'

'My son can no longer serve... sir,' Jelbert resumed pointedly, 'but I will... that is to say... if ye will have me.' A silent Pat staring, Jelbert, unwavering, pressed his case with plaintive words, 'Will ye consider of it, sir? I beg ye will.'

In that moment, every man on deck listening intently, the spell of silence was broken, not a man present unmoved by Jelbert's most earnestly spoken request, his determination so plain: clapping broke out from all the men and shouts of 'Huzzay!' from a number of them. Pat was himself greatly moved, infinitely humbled, 'Well, Mr Boswell plainly is injured and doubtless will be...' He hesitated no longer; he seized Jelbert's hand, gripped it tightly, a tumultuous surge of feeling, of relief engulfing him in that profound moment of revelation, his catharsis found in the most unlikely of quarters, his mind powerfully made up, 'I will be most heartily pleased to have ye aboard, Mr Jelbert.... It will be an honour to serve with ye again, for sure it will.' More and louder shouts of 'Huzzay! Huzzay!' rose from the assembly, louder clapping, scores of feet drumming hard upon the deck, unfettered jubilation abounding from every man, Pat's flood of conviction, his relief plain in a widening smile.

'God love 'ee, thank 'ee, sir,' shouted Jelbert, shaking Pat's hand harder with a crushing determination before turning and looking all about him to the faces of his Falmouth friends, his shipmates; his two closest companions lifted him off his feet and into the air as the cheering continued, wild, raucous, 'Huzzay! Huzzay! Huzzay!'

A minute longer, the tide of feeling within him subsiding a very little, and Pat raised his arms in the air, the hubbub dying away. 'Lads... Lads!' he shouted. 'I ain't a man minded to blather on...' Quietude descended on the gathering. 'The Lord knows we have seen our share of infernal trouble these months gone...' nods all round from all, 'and 'tis a damnable setback of the first order to lose so many of our shipmates... good men, all.' A general chorus of "Aye" from the gathering. 'And for many a day I have asked myself... what is to be done... and... and what is to happen to the barky?' The return of silence was followed by a long, long interval with not a word uttered by anyone as Pat stared round at his men. In little more than a whisper he resumed, 'I have been cast down by these ills... I have... so low in spirits... and I know... *I know* that you have been too... 'tis plain to see.' Murmurings of agreement, another pause, a supportive nod to several of his men, and Pat continued, still very quietly, 'But the time comes... when enough is enough... when blasted confusion don't answer... and 'tis plain... the hour is upon us when we must pump, the barky so low in the water...' Many confused faces stared, Pat's marine metaphor less than clear to them. Recognising the confusion in his men, Pat spoke up, 'Yes, 'tis time to pump... as hard as we can. Lads, the time has come to cast off the damnable devils of the mind... to look for'ard... and no longer aft.' His thoughts firming, Pat raised his voice further, 'and I am minded the compass is telling me plain... 'tis time to look to tomorrow, to the bright new day...' Further murmurings of consensus stirring generally, Pat pressed on, 'If Marston were here, he would say it plain... better than any words of mine, so he would...' He looked up momentarily as if for further inspiration, 'I collect the words of Doctor Ferguson... in Greece... It is time to contemplate precious hope once more... and to cast away our afflictions of bleak despair.' A subdued chorus of "Hear, hear" resulted, and Pat, brightening a little, continued, 'You know... you have doubtless *heard* that our dear *Surprise* is to be restored... I have no doubt Murphy has mentioned that...' A hesitant burst of laughter all round, 'Aye, he is the font... the fount... the source... of all knowledge on this ship... that's sure...' Another spell of laughing, louder, hearty, '... but I will tell you this myself... and Murphy ain't heard it yet...' a rising cacaphony of laughter from the men, 'Lads... I tell you this today... I am a'stayin' at the helm... with the barky!'

An uproar of shouting, and then came the loud bellow from Clumsy Dalby, 'Three cheers for the Captain!' Every man responded, as loud as ever they could shout, 'Huzzay! Huzzay! Huzzay!' and dozens of hands were pressed upon Pat to be shaken for interminable minutes until his own ached painfully.

Monday 13th December 1824   19:00   Tobermory, Mull

The simple repast was consumed with the relish of hunger, the girls then sent upstairs to share the double bed, fully clothed and wrapped in blankets to hold the chill of the night at bay. Simon and Flora remained close by the fire, the logs since near an hour burning brightly, the light and warmth of the flames dispelling the previous gloom. 'Mrs MacDougall, I thank you again for my supper. I will endeavour in the morning to replenish my stores, to offer you the repast that you deserve...' Flora smiled, and Simon continued, 'As may be obvious, my house... my home... is a modest one, a trifle spartan, the plainest of accommodations...' a wider smile from Flora, 'but I see that does not greatly dismay you.'

'Doctor Ferguson, I have not the least doubt that your home will appear... that is to say *will present itself* on the morrow as a comfortable abode; an hour or two with cloth, soap and water... I am sorry, I beg your forgiveness, I meant no disrespect.'

'None taken, my dear. Have no cares of that. You will recall that when at sea I live in the tiniest of wooden box, six feet by three,' Simon laughed, his first for a very long time, 'and no window, no warmth, and the cot - for that is all I have within - is perpetually in motion. The house is a palace in comparison... though I grant you there is plainly a want of attention.' Simon paused in thought before adding in a kindly tone, 'Will it suit you to stay here? I am, as my letter made plain and as the house itself exhibits, in need of a housekeeper... yet the remuneration is precious little... small indeed.'

Simon's words appeared to go unnoticed, Flora staring at the flames, eventually turning to face her host, 'Doctor Ferguson, that is no matter, not the least of concern, I do assure you. On Islay, my daughters and I were dependant upon charity, my brother-in-law willing to support us, but it was a great burden for a fisherman, one with his own wife and four bairns. No, two more and myself - welcome as we were - could not endure; hence I did not care to be longer there. Your offer was most welcome, generous it was; have not the least doubt of that.'

'I am pleased to hear it,' Simon murmured, with a decent attempt to control his emotions, for in truth he was exceedingly relieved to hear it, more so than he could ever have imagined.

'I say that... because...' Flora hesitated, '... because when I saw you at the quay, when I stepped from the boat... I... I... that is say your countenance was greatly severe... and that is a concern.'

'Mrs MacDougall...'

'Flora, Doctor, if you will. We are kin... please.'

'Mrs... *Flora*, you do so closely resemble your sister... my beloved Agnes... my precious wife... my late wife. It was a shock, I confess, a most considerable one. There before me... before my gaze... a vision - no, a living reality - I was contemplating on my late wife, and it seemed as if it was dear, dear Agnes standing there before my eyes... I could say nothing, could not speak, could not think of anything else... save her.'

'I am so sorry, sir.'

'There is not the least thing to apologise for, I assure you... nothing at all. Will I say that the shock is gone now, but its successor... I beg you, do not fret; allow me to explain... there is now a turmoil, a conflict within, and I know not what will be the outcome.'

'Would you prefer that we left on the morrow?' asked Flora, great dismay in her voice. 'Mr MacDougall is leaving at first light.'

'No, no, no, my dear; the quandary is entirely a puzzle, an endeavour to come to terms with something of significance... of brilliance... with the... your likeness... the striking resemblance to Agnes. These past ten years, I realise... I see... I have... I have been married to a memory, to a ghost... and now she is here again; I see her... in your face; I hear her in your voice, and surely no widower could ever find any greater gift?' Flora plainly remaining in great consternation, Simon, perceiving that she was weeping, his own heart beating frantically, pulled back from the brink of relaying thoughts which could not possibly come to good, ones which he realised he would regret immediately, and he resumed with all he could find in the most difficult of moments, 'But let us say no more of that, else it may lead us - as a mariner with whom I am familiar with might say - into uncharted waters.' He took her small, trembling hands into his own, 'Here you must stay. I beg you will cast aside any other notions.'

Chapter Five

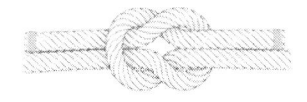

Sunday 19th December 1824   15:30   Øresund Strait

The tedious day and its hard-working hours, beating against the prevailing and strong south-westerly, were near gone, a diffuse sunset mere minutes away as *Eleanor* approached the maritime choke which was the Øresund Strait, the wind reduced in the past half-hour to the most gentle of breeze, the mere chill of a relentlessly grey day rapidly falling towards the unwelcome, freezing cold extremes of recent nights. Duncan's eyes stared all about *Eleanor*: astern, the light quality was fast fading; ahead, the low sun, though weak and indistinct, made any sighting and all detail difficult. His mind was absorbed with the acute worry of passing through the narrows without let or hindrance from Øresund Custom House vessels serving the Helsingør port. Doubtless the Danish officials would expect the customary toll to be paid, but he had neither money nor papers, having left London in great haste, and he did not care in the least to expose *Eleanor's* immensely valuable cargo to even the most cursory of inspection let alone risk bureaucratic delays or a disaster such as the gold being impounded were it to be discovered. Such a catastrophe could not be contemplated; the magnitude and monetary value of the contents of the Tsar's crates was immense, let alone the political significance, and Duncan had not the slightest idea of what he might offer by way of explanation to any Customs officer discovering the gold. For this potential event Melville had given him no instructions; indeed, so inadequate had the preparations for departure from London been in their haste that *Eleanor's* men had relied on Admiral Shenyavin for food provisions for the return home, and during all the short winter days and cold, sleepless nights since leaving London for Saint Petersburg Duncan had taxed his mind to find a solution. The Customs cutters were particularly swift vessels, necessarily so, and no doubt easily capable of closing on *Eleanor,* for although she was a relatively speedy vessel for a schooner, with the bluff bows and hull of her Garmouth heritage - not intended for speed so much as carriage - she could never outpace any cutter; hence to flee could not possibly succeed. Every man of *Eleanor* stood on deck, sensing that their cargo was irregular, though why they knew not, and all were observant of their captain's evident and rising agitation, but more than that they did not know or understand; consequently unease and apprehension was general amongst them, every man concluding there was some inherent need to preserve the secrecy of the cargo from Customs and pondering their prospects of doing so.

Twenty more minutes, *Eleanor* moving slowly, near drifting, the day coming to its tiring close, an unsettling silence decending, like the cold, all about them. Grey, boundless grey stretched away to infinity, ultimately to an indiscernible confluence where sky met sea, the cloud blanket so low, the light so poor. 'I venture now is the time for the lanterns, Mr Reeve,' exclaimed Duncan. The lieutenant simply nodded, unmoving, as if still digesting the words, some evident semblance of uncomprehension about him. The message had carried in the near completely still air, dense, heavy, every man jolted to an alert sense of immediacy.

'Surely lanterns cannot conceivably be in our interest, Mr Macleod?' ventured Jason, confused. 'Is not darkness the better prospect for us, to slip through unseen? There is precious little light, and this low cloud can only serve our purpose... surely so?'

'Unless and until we're sighted... aye... and then the game is up. Lanterns!' Duncan shouted to the man near the wheel. 'Trannack! Go below, at the double; fetch the lanterns we've readied... make haste!' Trannack dived down the steps.

'Lanterns, Mr Macleod?' asked Jason again, astonished. 'Pray explain.'

'Aye, lanterns; four of 'em to hoist up. I venture that will make her visible from the Helsingør quay.'

'But... but surely...' Jason stopped, mystified, the quay several miles away and not at all distinct in the near ethereal light of dusk. 'But will the Customs cutter not call us into the harbour, our...' his voice dropped to a whisper, '... our precious cargo revealed, our purpose undone?'

'Mr Reeve,' shouted Duncan, looking away, 'The yellow flag... it is readied below?'

'Aye, it is, sir.'

'Fetch it up. Let it be hoisted without the loss of a moment.'

'The yellow flag?' Jason was now utterly bewildered. 'Does that not signify disease?'

'I venture there isnae a Dane who has forgotten the great plague... Danish ships bringing it ashore...'

'The plague?' cried Jason, instantly alarmed.

'Aye, eight hundred died here in Helsingør, a thousand and more in Malmo... and would ye believe fifteen thousand in Copenhagen... a quarter of the population dead there.'

'Oh my dear God!' exclaimed Jason, fright now raging within.

'Duncan relented, 'Never fear, 'twas a century ago... but they wilnae have forgotten that. We must take our chances, Jason... I havnae been able to conceive of any better plan. D'ye speak the Danish at all?'

'Precious little,' murmured Jason, angry, the shock subsiding only slowly. A minute of simmering reflection before his grudging continuation, still feeling annoyed and vexatious about Duncan's teasing, 'It has similarities with Low German, with which I have some familiarity, and of course that is also the language of mercantile trade here in the Baltic... doubtless every Customs inspector will understand it.'

The lanterns were lit, four of them, one affixed at the top of each mast, the third hanging off the bowsprit, the fourth at the end of the boom, and the yellow flag was hoisted atop the main, though it did not fly so much as flicker, the wind so weak. 'Barton, change course,' shouted Duncan, 'Towards the town... hard over before she falls in irons. Hear me! Every man below, swiftly now... the Turkey red... on your faces, on your hands. Dyer, stay at the helm.'

'Turkey red?' spluttered Jason, incredulous, another challenge for his imagination, and similarly ill-received.

'Aye, 'tis a dye... madder. I asked Admiral Senyavin for a flask of the stuff, 'tis the red of his officers' waistcoats... and for that matter our own army's jackets.'

Jason sighed, mystified, offering no further question. Twenty minutes of rising anxiety, Duncan, Reeve, Jason and Dyer remaining on deck, lit by the lanterns' radiant glow, as it seemed in the dwindling final vestiges of dusk's feeble light, and out of the gloaming verging on darkness emerged the cutter they feared, her long bowsprit so prominent, her fast fore and aft rig leaving no doubt of her purpose, quickly closing off the larboard beam even in the lightest of winds. Her helm hard over for a swinging change of course, she closed skilfully to put herself on a parallel to *Eleanor*, just ten yards away, the cutter's own lanterns held up by curious men on her deck; and then came the hail, 'What ship?'

'Up, lads!' shouted Duncan, and from below five men of *Eleanor's* crew scrambled rapidly on deck, the combined brilliance of all the lanterns of both vessels starkly illuminating the glaring, bright red hands and faces of the men, a frightening shock to the Danes who visibly recoiled, shrieking loud exclamations; and then up came the last two of the Eleanors, struggling to haul a large sack between them, tied up close with hammock netting, struggling with it to the side. 'Overboard!' screamed Duncan. The two men heaved with all their might, the sack so obviously of great weight, ultimately splashing violently into the water between the slowing, near stationary *Eleanor* and the close Customs cutter, a visible spray soaring upwards; shocked, fixated Danish faces stared in unmitigated horror, Jason's bewildered thoughts similarly hurled into a paroxysm of complete confusion.

Monday 20th December 1824   16:00   HMS Surprise, Devonport

The short winter day, the afternoon in particular, had seemingly raced by and appeared to be hastening towards its dismal end, the sun sinking ever faster as each hour passed, for such was Pat's perception. A weak, cold glow still hung over Millbrook, bright reflections glittering all across the puddled mud flats of low water on the far side of the anchorage and sparkling on the rippling waters of the Hamoaze itself, the sun seemingly gifting its last vestiges of energy, most benevolently, on behalf of those who laboured still at the dock. The low tide, to the fanciful mind, appeared to be concurrent with the energies of the toiling men, all of whom had visibly tired as the strenuous day had passed. For two weeks the seventy or so crew of *Surprise* had worked cruelly hard, aided by three score of the yard hands, to shovel and carry out in sacks and buckets the fouled gravel ballast, stinking and putrescent: twelve years of human waste deposits had progressively accumulated - occasioned by the heads oft being dangerously inaccessible in severe storms and seas - and no amount of flushing and subsequent pumping out had wholly alleviated the vile stench; nor indeed could it, the gravel ballast inaccessible and unshifting for much of its sprawling extent. Every man, albeit well accustomed to the unwelcome task, wore a gag over his nose and mouth as he shovelled, deep in the stinking confines of the hold, a human chain passing up and out the detritus-polluted gravel.

'How goes it, Mr Churchill?' asked Pat, turning from his gaze over the waters of the anchorage to greet the arrival, and feeling in rather better spirits than he had felt in all the recent months. The horrible year was nearing its end. It had been, without the least doubt, the worst he could ever recall, and the fundamental anchor of his life was becoming ever more obvious to him as each day had passed since his decision to continue, to persevere with the ship and her irregular venture. The necessity to be within his familiar maritime world, so valuable to him, notwithstanding the greatly irregular pay and all dangers set aside, had become as clear as the dawning of the new day; as was ever stronger the affinity he felt for his men, his regulars, his old comrades; for he had also determined that he could not bear to contemplate *Surprise* and his men departing without him when she returned to her clandestine Greek mission. Naturally, his wife had not been best pleased, remaining in Falmouth whilst considering a return home to Galway, and a rift had arisen between them, one which he had not the least idea of how to heal. Oddly, his children had seemed to better understand his decision: a mystery which he had concluded was quite beyond the self-evidently meagre limits of his own comprehension.

'We are near finished taking out her shingle, Captain O'Connor,' the Master Shipwright replied in cheerful voice, 'One hundred and twenty tons of it... near all is gone. Tomorrow should see the last of it.'

Pat shivered, recollecting the violent shifting of the ballast in the worst of the hurricane, many tons of the gravel shingle sliding dangerously from side to side as the ship had risen and fallen on the monumental waves, the maelstrom blasting her far over on the crests only to recover in the troughs, the acute and justifiable fear of capsize lingering in his memory. He nodded and sought to expunge that particular thought from his mind, focussing instead on the iron ingots which would replace it: kentledge, pig iron or simply pigs as they were customarily termed within the Yard.

'She still has ninety of iron to be left within... all is firmly fixed,' Churchill continued, 'but doubtless you collect, sir... there is much more of that yet to be installed. The first of it is promised for the end of the week. The pigs will offer better stability than the shingle, sir... a stiffer sail... and the new will also be fixed in place.'

'Mmmm,' murmured Pat, 'I most certainly hope so. Very good, Mr Churchill... and her hull?'

'Coming along, sir,' replied the Master Shipwright, nodding sagely. 'Coming along. The caulking above the waterline is all prised out where there is the smallest doubt of its firm fixing, and that copper hull sheathing which was missing has all been replaced...'

'That is handsome news, Mr Churchill, prime, so it is... Tell, how many more pigs of kentledge will there be?' Pat indulged his mild curiosity, his thoughts wandering back to the ballast stowage.

'Another one hundred and ten tons is promised, sir... hence there is a necessity for seven hundred and seventy more pigs.'

'And what size would they be?'

'Each pig is customarily a trifle more than five and a half inches square and a yard in length, sir.'

'Tolerably large, indeed... and how heavy would one of these sizeable monsters be, pray tell?' remarked Pat offhandedly, losing track of the numbers.

'They are three hundred and twenty pounds in weight... seven pigs per ton.'

'God help us!' exclaimed Pat. 'Three hundred and twenty pounds! May Saint Patrick preserve the men who shift 'em, eh?' He did not care to think of lifting one, even with plentiful assistance; he recoiled from the very thought, so heavy! It was a rare task indeed when Clumsy Dalby came to mind: the man himself had stayed aboard the barky, Pat recalled, although he had not been one of those few men who had been officially re-engaged, and Pat could not but commend him for remaining despite his many misgivings for Dalby's other traits and limited capabilities. He had certainly demonstrated his value as a comrade when he had rescued Simon Ferguson and Abel Jason from Turk pursuit when the Ottomans had invaded the island of Kasos, and he had also saved Pat's life in the hurricane when the raging sea sweeping the quarterdeck was about to carry him, utterly exhausted, over the side. Doubtless he would, at the very least, be fed by his particular friend, the men's cook.

'These pigs won't fly,' declared Pickering, who could not resist laughing.

'A task for Dalby, Mr Pickering,' Pat laughed too.

'Yes indeed, sir,' Pickering smiled, his captain's spirits were visibly improving by the day.

'And the precise storage of these ballast pigs is exactly calculated, I collect you said?' asked Pat. Churchill was in the most genial of mood; indeed, Pat recalled he had never heard a single grumble from any of the Devonport men, despite the unpalatable task they were engaged in, and he remembered too that every man of the Yard had cheered *Surprise's* original departure after her first refit, a most unofficial blue pennant flying aloft before he had noticed it as the anchors were hauled up.

'Most certainly it is, sir,' Churchill replied, 'The substantial majority of the pigs, nine tenths or thereabouts, will be fixed in place... either side of the keelson... and before the main for the most part, leaving one hundred and forty of them free...' His audience's attention plainly wavering, both of them simply staring, Churchill swiftly pressed on with his explanation, '... which will allow the bosun to make such shifts as he believes may be for the better stabilisation of the ship when you are at sea.'

'I'm sure,' murmured Pat, all interest lost in the matter of the ballast. 'Most excellent news. And what of the water tanks?' Iron water tanks were planned to replace the wooden butts.

'The new water tanks are standing ready, near the mast pond.'

'However,' Lieutenant Pickering interjected, noticing his captain's attention waning, 'that will be after the final pigs are stowed. That is to say the water tanks will be installed above all that pig ballast which is to be fixed in place.'

'Yes, yes, Mr Pickering,' Pat had heard enough of such things. 'I am sure the Master Shipwright and the bosun together will accommodate the changes... all in Bristol fashion... no doubt everything will be ship-shape... eh, Mr Churchill?'

'Another week, Captain O'Connor, and I venture she will be ready to go back into the water, and then we will instal her new mizzen. It remains curing in the pond at present until the last moment, when the work in the hold is completed and the men are out of the way of the carpenters,' Churchill concluded his report, Pat and Pickering nodding vigorously, a profound satisfaction enveloping them both.

Life in the great cabin during the past two weeks had been a somewhat lonely experience, Pat's two closest friends, Simon and Duncan, both absent, and he had not the least idea whether either man would return to rejoin him when the barky departed again for Greece. When that would be he did not know either. His own letter of reply to his cousin, Canning, had been posted, acceding to the very personal request that Pat remain in command of the ship, but as yet he had received no further instruction, and hence his time was wholly spent at the yard, aboard his ship in the dock, the basin pumped dry and four score of shipwrights engaged in the necessary repairs, the yard plainly pulling out all the stops, every conceivable one and more, every man working with an energy, a purpose, one so rarely exhibited in all those yards which Pat had had occasion to visit over many years. Certainly he had heard no mention of any bonus remuneration being offered to the yard's men, and therefore it seemed plain to him that their industry was surely something of significance. He had not the least doubt about that. His own men fraternised with those of the Yard, and it was therefore a safe bet that near all in Devonport had heard of *Surprise's* exploits, battles and casualties. Perhaps the Yard men felt they were doing their bit, making their contribution, assisting the Surprises as best they could.

Wednesday 22nd December 1824   noon   Tobermory, Mull

For Simon, the single week within his home had been a revelation: hard toil for the first four days, cleaning, cleaning some more and then painting: walls, ceilings, doors, windows; every day ending in severe fatigue, yet Mrs MacDougall had never wavered, never stinted in her own endeavours before subsequently cooking the evening meal after each tiring day; though it had not escaped Simon's notice that her two daughters' zeal had tapered away by noon every day with precious little contribution coming from either of them by the end of the weekend. He minded not the least, for his own zeal was also much diminished; not that he could admit or show such, his new housekeeper a stern inspiration, a demanding one, which, in truth, he was more determined to live up to than anything else he could recollect in his life. The somewhat frightening reality was dawning upon him: he had fallen in love with his wife, again; and here she was before him after eleven years in her grave. The truth of that had shocked him to the core; he was dumbfounded, had not the least idea of what to do, to think; and so he floundered, observing all formalities, profferring excessive politeness, his attentiveness close to Flora's every word, his compliments for her culinary presentations flowing, until, the glorious vista of the evening meal on the table - the same roasted chicken, buttered stovies and neeps of his childhood flashing to mind in silent, nostalgic recollection - Flora had shattered the great strain of his fragile composure at a stroke.

'Annag, Rhona... you will go upstairs.' Flora's abrupt words brought looks of confusion from her daughters, the steaming food just placed on the table. The girls hesitating, Flora resumed, 'Girls, if you please, will you allow Doctor Ferguson and I ten minutes, no longer... and then you may return?' Mystified nods; the girls accustomed to their mother's regime, they left the room in silence. 'Doctor Ferguson, it is a matter that greatly troubles me...' Simon simply stared, could say nothing: what could conceivably justify the room being vacated immediately after the food, piping hot, was served? He could not think of anything warranting such an extreme measure, and so he waited, a degree of trepidation arising within him; Flora was nervous, that was plain. He nodded in small encouragement. 'Doctor Ferguson... I am minded... that is to say, it seems... I will be returning to Islay.'

'Excuse me, my dear?' Simon recoiled in shock, could say no more.

'I am minded... it is not the easiest thing to say... will you forgive me?'

'Go on... please,' Simon found his tongue with difficulty, alarm ringing loud in his mind, waves of panic washing uncomfortably through his stomach.

'I am minded that I am not welcome here...'

'Pardon!' Simon was deeply shocked. 'Excuse me... if you will, but why, my dear, would you hold such an ill-founded notion?'

'You say so little; it is as if I am merely tolerated, not really welcome here, an irritation to be endured for the sake of my dear... my late sister... is that not the case, Doctor Ferguson?' Stunned silence followed for only a second before Flora burst into heartfelt, shaking fits of sobbing, streams of tears flowing in profusion; they were not solely Flora's.

Thursday 23rd December, 16:00   *New Union Dock, Devonport*

Sunset fast approaching and the shadows were lengthening over the placid waters of the Hamoaze, their long fingers reaching to embrace the masts of *Surprise* within her dock and to touch upon the whole of the Plymouth Yard quays generally. The ambience seemed wholly appropriate to every man, for a deep fatigue, nigh on absolute exhaustion, was upon them all. Long present as the week had wound towards its weary end, the men of *Surprise* and the Yard together, seamen, shipwrights, carpenters and labourers, were self-evidently flagging, their enduring hard work of the prior few weeks winding down, the Devonport men for several hours in pleasant anticipation of the morrow, Christmas Eve, the Yard working only until the noon bell and then the first of two days of rest and recuperation, and that was a rare occurrence. The Surprises, it had been arranged, would depart at the dawn for Falmouth, Admiral Saumarez having arranged the unprecedented privilege of a cutter to carry them, the roads deemed too slow; thence to return on the Monday after New Year's Day to the unceasing, hard schedule of restoration aboard the frigate; at least, Pat hoped, the men would return. Unexpectedly, Lieutenant Mower had arrived from Falmouth two days before, ostensibly citing the need to see the barky, to experience her refitting, to be once again aboard his maritime home; and his presence had cheered on the Surprises, even the Dock veterans seeming to be mightily impressed with his dedication and enthusiasm, to the extent that he could never shift far on his crutches without the offer of assistance from the nearest man, whatever his inquisitive location. Yet Mower's primary purpose had been to bring letters from Falmouth, most particularly one for Pat from his wife: it was a declaration of her intention to return to distant Claddaghduff, and very soon.

Pat, Pickering and Mower were in the cabin awaiting supper; a meagre ration it would be, they had no doubt. It was a muted table. 'How are you, Mr Mower,' asked Pat, deep concern in his voice, the lieutenant plainly extremely tired, fatigued, his few movements giving him pain.

'Bearing up, sir, bearing up,' Mower tried to be cheerful; it was not convincing. He sighed, 'In truth, I manage for most of the day, sir, the evenings giving me some difficulty; but I am always in hope that the next will be a trifle easier, that I will be better recovered.'

Pat merely nodded, wondering what to say to offer cheer, and Pickering interjected, 'Were we moons, some days we would be in the full, in others a mere slip of our real selves, but the full always returns.'

'Thank you, Mr Pickering; I could not say better myself,' said Pat affably. 'Allow me to pour you both another glass.'

The Yard's men having departed, the Surprises were contemplating their own modest but imminent supper, an hour away. The second half of the grog ration being dispensed on the gun deck, the men clustered near the hot galley for a trifle of warmth in the cold, exceptionally chilling evening, deep fatigue relenting a little of its choking grip as the warming grog slipped down, *relaxing the fibres* as they all joked; the sharp edges of utter physical exhaustion relenting to reach an accommodation with mere tiredness, and every man bathing in a sense of satisfaction that their efforts were indeed bringing about that restoration which every man longed to see, and for a much cherished ship. The muted banter of weary men continuing, from the side of the dock came the sound of a wagon, the squeal of wheels on stone cobbles, several horses snorting, the noises plainly approaching, closer, and to a stop. Curiosity brought the men up the companionway steps to stare over the hammock netting from the waist and the quarterdeck - the captain's privileged preserve long forgotten, or at least ignored. The wagon driver, without the least delay, doubtless mindful that it was not long before the onset of darkness, tethered the horses to an iron mooring ring in the quay, and together with his mate each slung a substantial bundle wrapped in a canvas sheet over their shoulders, marched across to and stepped noisily up the rattling wooden ramp to enter *Surprise* on the gun deck, hastening through the open gun port to arrive near the galley. Acute interest - not to say a degree of excitement - arose within the Surprises; the most wonderful of aromas were emanating from the mens' heavy loads, their carrying sheets wet and stained; fat and cooking juices - for obviously that it was - dripped in profusion over the men's backs and clothing generally.

'Roast mutton, lads!' shouted the wagon driver, easing the bulk of his heavy burden gently down to the deck close by the galley. The cook, who had been for some time in daunting contemplation of his aged and rather poor quality salted pork - steeping had revealed copious fat, bone and gristle - was pleasantly stunned. Joyous shouts rose from three dozen of men who had hurried back from above to see what it was coming aboard, their growing suspicions gratefully realised. Within two minutes all the remaining Surprises had arrived, Dalby assisting his friend the cook to lift the roasted mutton carcasses on to the stove to preserve their warmth. The wagon driver and his mate hastened back ashore, to return with two sacks of fresh loaves. 'May it please you to hear,' he shouted over the vigorous hubbub of loud excitement, 'May it please you to hear... Admiral Saumarez has sent his gift.' This was received exceedingly well, the loud hubbub reaching new heights.

At that moment, Pat appeared, brought out of his cabin by the raucous exclamations of pleasure of his men, Codrington and Pickering in train, Murphy a single pace behind them, to gaze upon the unexpected development. The sheet wraps being removed, the smell of roast mutton had filled the still air, had wafted aft towards the cabin. Pat stared, the mens' bright faces of anticipation radiant in the flickering yellow glow of the lanterns. He paused for the merest second, his eyes fixing upon the roast mutton; he nodded to the cook before turning to Murphy with a face of great pleasure, 'Murphy, Dalby there, go below d'reckly. Another issue of grog, if you will.' The cheering being immediate and general, Murphy needed not the slightest elaboration, swiftly disappearing. 'Lads,' said Pat with joy in his face, gratitude filling his thoughts for this so very welcome turn of events, the boisterous noise dying away, his men awaiting his words; 'Happy Christmas...' the only ones he could speak, his thoughts a'fire with his recent momentous decision. His evening thus far had been spent in searching reflection, his wife distant in every respect. His friends, Duncan and Simon, were both absent; and now a feast, a modest one but no less welcome for that, was before him; it was cheering and uplifting, his officers and men no longer resigned to a most dour evening, as it had seemed to be, and for that small mercy he was profoundly grateful. He pondered his plans for the morrow as the mutton was passed out, sipping Murphy's proffered tumbler of grog - not greatly diluted he noticed - as he stood amongst his happy men, a rising contentment firming within him.

Friday 24th December   07:30   *Devonport*

The air intensely cold, the Surprises boarded the Yard's new cutter, *HMS Bramble,* in the weak pre-dawn twilight for their return to Falmouth, the wind blowing its customary south-westerly. 'About ten knots, gusting twenty,' thought Pat, 'It will surely be an invigorating passage,' his cautionary remark to Mower. The first half-hour, before the sunrise and within the shelter afforded by the Cremyll side of the estuary, was perfectly placid until, Saint Nicholas's Island left astern and her course changed, *Bramble* was flung about in the violence of the chop and heeling, Pat guessed, at least three and often four strakes in the water. Her lieutenant, mindful of his own intent to make best speed, kept as close to the wind as the cutter would bear, but despite its exceptionally favourable windward rig he was swiftly forced to a more southerly course until, the visible remnants of the breakwater close ahead, a series of vigorous tacks brought the cutter around it to bear south once more, all the time nudging a little to the west, every man's eyes on the sail edges. Within a further and most uncomfortable, half-hour - none of the Surprises minding in the least; after all, they thought, this wind was no hurricane - Penlee Point was passed, prominent off the starboard quarter, and Rame Head was coming up off the starboard beam, Pat admiring the lieutenant's determination even if he did not much care for the aggression and discomfort of his chosen course, the wind and its creation, long fetch waves, so fine on the bow.

'A trifle more than forty miles, sir,' offered Prosser, the master plainly enjoying himself, 'I venture it will be late when we fetch home... long after the sunset with this wind agin us.'

'I'm sure you're in the right of it, Mr Prosser,' Pat nodded.

'Good morning, sir,' Mower limped up to the deck, Old Jelbert hovering at his side in case he fell.

Pat smiled, 'Mr Mower, how are you feeling? It is tolerably rough to be up here... with your... your *incapacities*, will I say.'

'I will pay it no mind, sir,' declared Mower.

'Good man, but please... have a care and do not dwell up here if... if it becomes a difficulty,' offered Pat with infinite affection for his shipmate in his gaze.

Friday 24th December 1824   noon   *Tobermory, Mull*

It had been a momentous few days: the tearful and mutual collapse of sorts over the dinner table two days previously had left both

Simon and Flora in emotional confusion; Simon's painfully heartfelt reassurances and his passionately declared wish that she should stay had been accepted by Flora without the least doubt, no hesitations attaching to Simon's confession. He had admitted his own feelings, his heart and mind aflame, a heart-rending turbulence raging, the likes of which he had not felt since his wife's death; since when for eleven years all such thoughts had been closely constrained, suppressed, left for some distant, future time when he believed he might better cope with the emotional perils of them, but in the presence of his wife's twin his resolution had crumbled, every defence had melted and burning emotions had been unleashed in an outflowing flood which he had been shocked to realise in that cathartic moment that he could no longer contain. All of this had become apparent to Flora, few actual words of explanation from Simon required; her own uncertainty and insecurity, her own anguish - her husband lost only in the prior winter - had been set aside to gently respond with infinite sympathy to Simon's so obvious plight. The girls had merely peeked round the door, the dinner by then cold, before fleeing back upstairs where they had remained hungry for several more hours until the summons back to the table had been shouted by Flora, the salvaged meal eaten in near silence save for the most innocuous of pleasantries, substantial depletions inflicted by Flora on a bottle of wine, one of whisky near wholly consumed by Simon.

    A new start had been made, a mutual accommodation reached whilst both Simon and Flora reflected on matters, both anxious to place not the lightest of burden on the other, both attentive yet with the tiniest of reserve, not cold but cautious. Slowly, a stabilisation was taking place; perhaps - Simon dared to wonder - even a foundation, but for that he had insufficient courage to allow hope to root, for any aspiration or dream to become established, and so he contented himself with conversations on and discourse about the wildlife of the Isles and the pressing need of the populace for physicians; perhaps in doing so his train of thought was indicating his leanings, Flora seemingly a perfectly contented listener, each of them beginning to understand and to know the other.

Friday 24th December 1824   20:00   *Green Bank quay, Falmouth*

HMS Bramble tied alongside the pier. The cutter's lieutenant had received an education from Prosser since passing the Black Rock and entering the Falmouth Roads, and both men were on the most amicable of terms, the former now possessing a knowledge of the Falmouth currents and depths at all stages of the tide and the preferred passage in every conceivable wind direction; after that, his return to the Hamoaze, he was sure, would seem like simplicity itself. The Surprises stepped ashore with friendly goodbyes to the Brambles, Pat thanking the lieutenant and his crew personally, Prosser revealing one or two final marvels of maritime minutiae to be considered by the lieutenant for *Brambles'* return to Devonport on the morrow.

In stark contrast with the evening of *Surprise's* return to Falmouth, the quay was dark and deserted. No words found, none seemingly necessary, every man picked up his small baggage and began the southbound trudge through the darkness into the town, a still weak Lieutenant Mower near carried along by a rotation of a half-dozen men as the minutes slipped by, a slow and most muted procession. Not that a welcome had been expected by any of them; indeed, it was not known whether any news of their intended passage in the cutter had actually reached Falmouth beforehand, for such was most unlikely, Admiral Saumarez's declaration made known to the Surprises themselves only during the prior day in an unexpected noon appearance by the admiral, his inspection greatly pleasing him, becoming the occasion for his decision - the gift of his cutter for passage to Falmouth - the works of *Surprise's* restoration moving along so well.

A hundred yards of walking in near silence and then, from amidst the baleful procession of seventy men, a lone voice - Beer's was recognised immediately by all - struck up a song,

'*Christmas Eve, and home we go,*
Our shipmates fine, now we know;
The barky's fixed, all a-tanto,
Falmouth's men all set to go;'

The chorus echoed out from his friend, Knightley,

> *'Way oh, way oh,*
> *Her yards braced up,*
> *and what a blow;'*

Beer singing again, the second verse found a few more contributors,

> *'Salt pork vittles, full stocks below,*
> *Shot 'n' powder, ready to stow;*
> *Surprises all, every man we know,*
> *Off to the ship, we're set to row;'*

Beer and Knightley's arms now waving vigorously in encouragement, rising numbers joined the chorus,

> *'Way oh, way oh,*
> *Her sails all filled,*
> *and what a blow;'*

By the top of Dunstanville Terrace a tide of good cheer had settled upon every man, and as they descended the High Street all the Surprises, enlisted men and volunteers together - Mower carried aloft in jubilant spirit - were singing at the top of their voices,

> *'The wind set fair, and off we go,*
> *Prizes sure, when we will crow;*
> *Black Rock ahead, off the bow,*
> *Back to sea, the tide a'flow;*
> *Way oh, way oh,*
> *Gale wind astern,*
> *and what a blow.'*

On they strode in rising, boisterous celebration, the Chapel being the intended destination, those few Falmouth citizens on the street waving as they passed by; others, staring from doors and windows, clapped and shouted greetings, many townsfolk recognising relatives amongst the crew, loud hails following their passage until they halted in good cheer in the Moor where a hundred and more relatives and friends, all gathered in their wake, stood in noisy discussion and loud exchanges. The news of the homecoming had spread swiftly about the small town and more people were coming out by the minute, another hundred rapidly appearing to greet the arrivals, an increasing gathering accumulating about the returned Surprises. Out of the Chapel stepped Marston, in a state of some small umbrage, to investigate the uproarious noise which had disturbed many of his patients, several of whom had been sleeping. Swift recognition of the Surprises washed away his indignation in an instant, and he stepped rapidly towards his captain, Pat standing speaking with an exuberant but obviously flagging Mower, the lieutenant still supported by two men.

'Mr Marston, there you are,' roared Pat, 'Mr Mower may be in need of your attentions,' this in obvious jest, the noise of the growing crowd necessitating shouting.

'Welcome back, sir... 'tis a pleasure to see you; indeed, it is,' cried Marston, offering his hand, seized and firmly shaken by Pat and then Mower. 'How are you, Mr Mower?'

'You would scarcely credit how pleased I am to be home in dear Falmouth town for Christmas, sir.'

'Good man,' Pat patted his lieutenant gently on his lesser wounded shoulder, his affection plain. The returned Surprises gathered all about him, Pat looked to Marston and nodded towards the Chapel, 'Will we see the men now?'

'Come in, please; it will cheer them greatly,' Marston led on. Pausing momentarily at the door they saw that some small semblance of a return to normality had begun with the restoration of some of the pews before the altar at the far end of the hall, half the wounded Surprises having recovered sufficiently to shift to their homes. The diffuse light of lanterns illuminated those who remained, a score of men, most within their beds, some sitting, several talking with attendant family members or friends, others who had been seeking sleep and recuperation now stirred to wakefulness, every patient turning to see the entrants coming into the hall. Pat stepped forward, leading Codrington, Pickering and Mower, followed by the two dozen of the enlisted Surprises just returned. The arrivals dispersed throughout the rows of beds to greet particular friends, Marston explaining their improving health to Pat as they paced from one man to the next, 'How are you coming along, Collins? The arm is healing well, I see,' and 'You will doubtless favour that leg, Penrose, for some time yet, eh?' All of the convalescents were gratified by their captain's visit. 'I see you are bearing up well, Trevelyan.' Cordial greetings were exchanged, acknowledgements offered in good humour, 'Thankee, sir,' the pleased reply from the men, the officers listening attentively.

A most uplifting hour passed in many spirited conversations, Pat relieved and gratified to see his men in good heart, amicable exchanges enjoyed until the rising fatigue of the wounded became evident in the low voices and fading attention of all the patients, when *Surprise's* returnees made their farewells and departed for their own homes and families. The officers walked swiftly along Market Street towards Wynn's Hotel, Pat pondering whether the welcome he might find there from a somewhat estranged Sinéad might be as warm as that given by his wounded men; he dearly hoped so, but he could not shake the foreboding that when she learned of his decision to return to Greece that would surely be the end of all pleasure in Christmas.

Saturday 25th December 1824   noon   aboard Eleanor, the Dover Strait

'Mr Macleod,' declared Jason, rubbing frozen hands, his breath condensing in a tiny cloud before his eyes, 'The white cliffs over there... I venture there is a tolerably similar resemblance to those particularly famous ones... at Dover; is that not so?'

'Aye... they're the cliffs, the very same,' Duncan, his deep fatigue evident in his voice, his reply gruff, took a large swig from his tin mug.

'But... we are no longer returning to London... with the... the cargo?'

'Nae London... as I have been reading just now... well, after the dawn... Melville's orders,' Duncan shook away the dregs of his cold coffee before shaking his head, as if such might similarly throw off his tiredness; he turned away from gazing forward into an unrelieved grey merger of sea and sky - save for the indistinct cliffs on the starboard beam - to face Jason, a smile on his face just discernible within the unkempt and heavy fresh growth of facial hair, everywhere peppered with tiny moisture droplets. 'Sealed they were, aye,' Duncan resumed, 'sealed 'til we're approaching Kent. We're to return directly to Devonport, nae London. Time... pressing it is, so he says; and so much the better... Kathleen and the bairn are in Falmouth, a little ways on... and I didnae much care for London. Merry Christmas, Jason. At noon I think we may allow ourselves a wee dram with the weevil and biscuit, eh?'

Jason grimaced at the thought, the servings of the galley better described as scrapings these last two days, 'When will we reach Plymouth, Mr Macleod?'

'Eighty-five leagues... the wind nae helpful... aye, and strengthening all morning... If it does nae come too much further west of south, we might fetch the Wight on Monday and tide it down to Plymouth sometime on Tuesday... three days... four perhaps,' muttered Duncan with something akin to a sigh.

Saturday 25th December 1824   14:30   Wynn's Hotel, Falmouth

The Christmas dinner for Pat, for his and Duncan's families, and his officers was ordained strictly for 3 p.m. and not a minute beyond that specific time, Pat having no truck with the increasingly fashionable drift to later dinners; and so the dining room was filled from 2pm, all present sipping ale or wine, a crackling log fire in the hearth; holly, ivy and mistletoe aplenty fixed to the dado and picture rails, and draped about the furniture, the ambience of relaxation and genial contentment greatly contrasting with the recent weeks of frenetic activity at Devonport, and for that Pat was deeply grateful. The place smelt of Christmas, of all things that were homely: divine aromas of roasting meat - and thankfully nothing of olive oil - were wafting into the room from the kitchen, and Pat immersed himself for a few minutes within fond thoughts of days in his Irish home as a child. He wondered whether he might call for a plate of boxty; he smiled at the thought... and served with apple sauce. He was mightily relieved and pleased to be sitting at his wife's side at the table - his doubts during the crossing from Devonport of whether that would be so thankfully dispelled. Kathleen sat at his other arm, the three youngsters close by; Codrington, Mower and Pickering were seated opposite, and

Marston, called from his attendance of those two dozen men still at the Chapel, completed the table. Behind Pat hovered Murphy, Freeman remaining with his wounded shipmates, *his* charges as he had come to see them, Doctor Tripe having gone home to Devonport two days beforehand, no longer any pressing urgency for a physician for the care of the recovering wounded, all in good heart.

The waiters appeared at the appointed time with silver serving dishes, the gentle hubbub of conversation dwindling away, all eyes looking to Pat after they had sat down. He tapped his spoon on his glass, 'Ladies... gentlemen... if you will, may it please you to welcome our most valued of friends, Michael Marston, to say grace.' A polite accord rippled around the table, expectant silence descending.

'Thank you, sir... ladies, gentlemen,' Marston rose to his feet. 'Before I do so, you will allow me to speak of another matter... I have been long enough aboard our gallant vessel... the barky,' a small laugh from the officers - Marston generally never used the mariner's slang - 'to become acquainted with the several toasts particular to each day... and today the Sunday toast is most timely.' The officers, silent, all nodded. The ladies looking quizzical, Marston resumed, 'Please remain seated for the toast, as is the custom; I give you... ABSENT FRIENDS!' The words, so appropriate - as was recognised by all - were echoed by everyone, by the five Surprises with loud emphasis, all their thoughts flashing painfully back to momentary recollections of the several dozen of their shipmates killed in Greece, images of Simon and Duncan then coming to Pat's mind; 'Hear, hear,' the officers added in heartfelt endorsement. Marston resumed, 'Our wounded so long accommodated in the chapel of our Wesleyan brothers, it seems entirely appropriate that our prayer this day is one that is customary to them...' Polite murmurs of accord from everyone present, and Marston concluded, 'Be present at our table, Lord. Be here and everywhere adored. These mercies bless and grant that we may feast in fellowship with thee. Amen.'

'Amen,' the acknowledgement resonated around the room, Marston sitting down to Pat's words of thanks. Pat waved to the waiting servants who sprang into rekindled activity. The food was deposited, the wine poured, the joyous exchanges of banter commenced and the serving dish lids were removed to universal gasps of delight as the feast was revealed - Murphy's exclamation being particularly loud, his eyes induced to shift from a sideboard heavily burdened with wines, a cask of ale and plum puddings - ones which he felt sure would be heavily laced with alcohol of one kind or another - to the festive banquet of laden silver trays and tureens offering a chestnut soup, a whole chine of beef, two geese, four ducks, a dozen of cod in an oyster sauce, and a side of mutton; the meat and fish complemented with carrots, artichokes, cabbage and a large bowl of old-fashioned frumenty. The eyes of the four officers burned in pleasurable astonishment, for a feast such as the likes of this none of them had ever seen before.

Sunday 26th December 1824   noon   *Tobermory, Mull*

'There... over there, beyond the buoy... the small bird; it is a black guillemot,' said Simon, pointing, as he walked along the quay with Flora, the day pleasantly clement, very cold but dry. Christmas Day had been a joy, blissfully relaxing and unlike any such day of tranquillity of recent years; not that there had been many of those whilst in Greece, he recalled. There had been an ambience of mutual accord, of cordial pleasures in simple conversation between him and Flora such that he could not recall unless he allowed his mind to wander back in time to his wife, but he did not - could not - care to do that.

'But it is grey... grey, not black.'

'Yes, my dear, but that is its winter plumage we see. In the summer it is black. Look, over there now... the seal... and she is most certainly a grey.' Fifty yards at the gentlest of pace and Simon halted, 'Flora, please forgive my enquiry... you seemed greatly contented yesterday... I venture my observation is not greatly amiss... yet leaving Islay must have presented some difficulties after all those years in that place?'

'For sure it did, Doctor Ferguson...'

'Please... if we are to enjoy such... such modest cordialities as these walks together, I beg you will refer to me as *Simon*... if you will. There is a reticence, an unwelcome one, with an excess of formality... do you not think so?'

'*Simon*... of course... yes, I miss Islay very much; I do, and my daughters have left their friends there; they were born on the island... but it is a poor place, as must be many of the isles. There is a living to be found from fishing... not a fat one,' Flora laughed, for the first time, Simon noticed, 'and many have employment in the whisky distilleries, but for a widow, one beyond marriage age as I am, it is a bleak prospect... and I did not care to be an imposition upon my brother-in-law and his family, precious poor that they are.'

'I see.'

'So, Doctor... I was grateful indeed for your offer of a position as your housekeeper, I was... and I remain so. You forget, perhaps, I grew up here myself, with my sister. The village is greatly larger than in those days, it surely is, but it is not unfamiliar to me, and the girls possess that great resilience of youth... I believe that we can be happy here.'

'I am tolerably pleased to hear it,' murmured Simon, his throat constricting, a particular thought emerging in his mind. 'I would not incline to the view, my dear, that you are beyond marriage age, no, certainly not.'

'Why, thank you... *Simon*,' Flora blushed; not that Simon could see that, his eyes become moist, focussed into the distance but seeing nothing, his thoughts all a'jumble.

Monday 27th December 1824   18:30 *Wynn's Hotel, Falmouth*

'Sir, these gentlemen are just arrived from... from Peninsula Metal Alloys, the fabricators...' announced Pickering. 'Allow me to introduce Mr Benjamin Peddler,' this to Pat, handshakes all round, '... together with his colleague Mr Edwin Perkis. Mr Peddler is known to Doctor Ferguson, sir... they are acquaintances from youth and school in Scotland.'

'Good evening, Mr Perkis, Mr Peddler,' said Pat, offering his hand. 'Mr Peddler, it particularly pleases me to meet you. A friend of Doctor Ferguson is a friend of mine; how are you?'

'Most kind, Captain O'Connor, I am very well, thank you.'

'If it pleases you, may I ask... how did you make Doctor Ferguson's acquaintance?'

'We grew up as mere striplings in the same Mull village, Tobermory, sir, together on every day, weekdays and weekends, inseparable as children, we were... and as youths as we grew older. We started our first school in the same class, brothers in friendship, yes... until the day came when Doctor Ferguson left for medical school, and our paths most rarely crossed after that... perhaps on occasions such as Christmas times when he returned to visit his parents in our village, but our careers were diverging. I have seen precious little of him these past twenty years; a tragedy it is.'

Pat nodded sagely and turned to the older of the two men, Perkis; he was a short man, of about fifty years of age, near completely bald-headed, and carrying his middle age as fat around the waist, 'Mr Perkis, a pleasure to make your acquaintance. You are, sir, I presume, an alchemist ...' blank stares all round, and Pat, his error dawning, swiftly continued, 'that is to say a *metallurgist*, no doubt... what with the interest in iron, eh?'

'Not all all, Captain O'Connor, my principal avocation is stockbroker; my interest in Peninsula Metal Alloys arising since following my friend, Mr Peddler's investment in the firm. I also have a modest shareholding in it... but I advise, sir; I advise on stocks. The market is particularly bouyant at present, as may have come to your own notice.'

'Indeed it has, Mr Perkis; most certainly,' replied Pat. 'It had not escaped my interest that the index is risen most spectacularly since September; I received the Times, a very late copy, from Zante when I was in the Ionians. As an Irishman it pleases me greatly that the editor, John Barnes, is most sympathetic to matters relating to Ireland and its affairs. But I digress, I collect the Times reported the index as it then was at 140, and now... why now it approaches twice that!'

'Indeed it does, sir. You are well informed; you are an investor?'

'No, no; I have an interest... I do, certainly, but I have only the most modest of investments in stock...'

'It is assuredly the most exciting time I can recall to be an investor,' Perkis interrupted.

'... and a gold mine,' Pat finished what he was about to say.

'A gold mine!' exclaimed Perkis, visibly rocked on his heels.

'Sir, these gentlemen...' Pickering interrupted, the train of discussion neither holding any interest for him nor seemingly relevant to the purpose of the meeting, and his supper was nearing, '... these gentlemen are intending upon a return to Plymouth this evening. They are here to discuss the particular requirement for the kentledge, the ingots being prepared this week for delivery to Devonport next week, commencing on Monday... and the... *the additional ballast* which is to be delivered to these gentlemen for... for appropriate preparation. I'm sorry, sir, but this is something of which I know nothing at all, if you will forgive me.'

'Of course, Tom,' Pat's thoughts returned to the refitting of *Surprise* and the awaited pig iron, but neither he nor Pickering knew anything of Duncan Macleod's mission, and so the reference to the additional ballast was a mystery to him too. Pickering disappeared to call for refreshments.

Perkis spoke first, 'Captain O'Connor, as you may collect, *Surprise* is to receive seven hundred and seventy ingots of cast iron from our own foundry. We are here to determine if there is any - will I say - *particular* requirements you may perceive necessary before it is delivered to the yard for embarkation.'

'That is most courteous of you, gentlemen,' offered Pat, mystified, for no one had ever asked his opinion on the matter of ballast ever before. 'I cannot think of any such... such requirement,' he said, scratching his head, thinking hard; was there something he had not thought of?

'The customary size, Captain... a yard in length, a trifle less than six inches square in profile... does that suit?' Perkis persisted, much to Pat's perplexity, racking his brain now for anything he might have missed.

'Well, they are a trifle heavy, for sure,' Pat replied guardedly, his conversation with Mr Churchill coming to mind, 'three hundred and twenty pounds. Indeed, Doctor Ferguson oft laments that so many of the men have hernias.'

'Then perhaps it would be most beneficial for your men, your crew, were the ingots to be cut down... halved in length... and, of course, halved in weight... they will certainly be more manageable... what do you say?'

'Why, that would seem to be a capital notion,' offered Pat, wondering why such a useful, indeed excellent idea had never presented itself to him ever before, or to anyone else for that matter.

Peddler spoke again; he was a younger man than Perkis, taller, bearded and bespectacled, and similarly running to a little fat, 'Captain O'Connor, you are aware that there will be additional ballast to follow that of next week from our foundry... to be installed within your vessel when the *iron* is fixed within?'

Pat could not fail to notice the emphasis on the word iron, but to what Peddler was referring he had not the slightest idea, though he did not care to admit such, to reveal that he, the captain, was not in possession of all the facts relating to his ship's refit, and so he temporised whilst continuing to think hard: what were these men about? 'Mr Peddler, the distribution of all ballast within my ship is most carefully calculated by the Master Shipwright, Mr Churchill. I have no reason to doubt his... his intentions in the matter of the... the location of the ballast, additional or otherwise. Is there some particular... some *attribute* attaching to the additional ballast, pray tell?'

'No, no, not at all!' Perkis interjected, realising that Pat was unaware of the purpose of the additional ballast he had referred to.

'Mr Perkis, pray explain... I have heard nothing of additional ballast these four weeks... why then is such required, eh?'

'Captain O'Connor...' Perkis smiled - entirely unconvincingly thought Pat. Pickering, who had returned, was also staring as Perkis continued, 'Captain O'Connor, the workings of the maritime mind, the shipbuilder, are not something with which I am familiar; no, far from it. Indeed, I am a mere wholesaler of metals... of all kinds... cast iron being one of them... one wholly suited to ballast.'

Perkis perpetuated his smile, 'A gold mine, you say?' and in that instant Pat formed something of a reservation about the man.

Friday 31st December 1824   16:30   *Falmouth*

Eleanor arrived at the Green Bank quay just as the sun set beyond the hill behind the town, the dwindling last light of the dusk near gone, the schooner swiftly disembarking most of her men before Reeve and two others anchored her midway between the quay and the Flushing side, no concerns for water depth necessary there, the three men swiftly hastening back to the quay in her boat. All together, the Eleanors stepped along the familiar road towards the town, their heads filled with visions of their families, Christmas sadly missed. It was the end of a voyage of unremitting strain: Devonport's quayside had been reached only the prior day, the cargo unloaded by Yard hands in the presence of Admiral Saumarez and a file of marines, the bemused and tired men of *Eleanor* looking on, thoughts of Falmouth pressing hard in their own minds. Later, the night severely cold, purgatory had been avoided by Admiral Saumarez's gift of a small cask of rum and half a roasted pig sent aboard, the consolation most welcome after the prior three days subsisting on soft biscuit and five-water grog; and then came the freezing new day and an uncomfortable passage to Falmouth against the building south-westerly, rain persisting all the way, the Black Rock never before such a welcoming sight.

Friday 31st December 1824 22:30 Wesleyan Chapel, The Moor, Falmouth

The beds of the wounded having been cleared aside in the morning, the townsfolk of Falmouth were congregated within the Chapel for a special Watchnight Service, every man of the Surprises present save for Simon, as Pat so painfully recalled. All the wounded were clean dressed, fresh bandages applied where called for, and they were sitting in the front pews. The hall had been filling for an hour, and was lit by the glow of a score of lanterns; it was filled to capacity, bursting with the crush of standing persons all the way to the back, the doors left open to the Moor, another two hundred people or even more standing outside in the darkness save for candles held by dozens of relatives of the Surprises, the latecomers. The service proper still a half-hour off, Pat walked about at the front of the hall - great difficulty found in the press of people - to speak with his men, venturing gentle enquiries of their wounds and their progress to recovery, kindly words of encouragement offered to every man individually, his every word most gratefully acknowledged.

It was to be an informal service; the minister had welcomed Pat's suggestion that Marston might say a few words; indeed, even Mower was intending to recite his latest work from the pulpit, the event exhibiting a latitude which pleased many that customarily attended the stricter format services of other denominations.

Tired and overheated in the crush, unable to gain a seat within the Chapel, Pat determined to retreat to the colder air outside, to speak with his men there. On the fringes of the gathering he noticed the arrival of several of the Eleanors, but he had no opportunity to speak with any of them, the press of Falmouth people gathered on the Moor ever more intense. He was there when the service began and he was still there, fatigued and flagging somewhat, as midnight approached when the call went up to announce the end of the service - except for Mower's words, held back until the end at his own request, the lieutenant not caring to intrude upon those religious conventions with which he was generally unfamiliar. There was a buzz of interest amongst the Surprises outside the Chapel, and all pushed forward to enter the hall, a squeeze developing as the sides of the room alongside the pews were packed ever tighter until eventually every man of *Surprise* was inside, within the mass, not the smallest of space remaining to move, to turn even. The air within the hall was heavy, excessively warm, the light poor, the oil of several lanterns burned out, the residual acrid smoke lingering; and as the crowd quieted, all looked forward to the front, to the altar, up the steps of which Mower struggled, plainly still fragile, in some little difficulty even with Old Jelbert taking his arm and assisting him at the steps until Mower eventually leaned against the lectern, manifestly fatigued, but his determination to speak shining through all his incapacities in his voice which was resolute. 'Good evening, people of

Falmouth...' a wave of murmured reply washed through the hall. 'It pleases me to stand before you on this so special evening, at this moment of great tradition... I am, myself, a son of Falmouth... This is my town, the place that beget me, this port for the great Atlantic... and 'tis surely my beloved *home...* and home too for all my shipmates... my *brothers*. From here we sailed... together, all those months ago, but sadly... it pains me greatly to say... many of my comrades are not here this evening...' He gulped water from his glass. 'With those men I toiled and fought; I saw the sweat in their faces... Falmouth men they were... every man a hero... the flesh of my flesh... and I miss them, every one...' Mower paused, in obvious difficulty, a minute passing, the hall spellbound, utter silence prevailing. He raised his head once more and resumed, 'It is the final night of a year which for myself and many of my shipmates has been the most memorable of our lives... We have returned from far away Greece, fount of civilisation... which is now plunged into the most barbaric of wars... *God help those people...*' A general murmur of 'amen' echoed all about the hall, 'but not all of us have returned. Many of my... of *our* shipmates will never return... from that far place...' quiet words were spoken in echo by many of the Surprises packing the hall, '... but for all of us who are here tonight... all of us who have returned from that bloody strife... we must look afresh to our future, to a new year... a year without that hatred which did, I confess, for a short spell consume us all...' loud endorsements from many in the crowd, '... and so I will conclude tonight with kindlier words for the new year. After all, this *is* a time to celebrate the *future*, to celebrate *hope*... and it was hope...' his voice fell to a near whisper, 'so precious to me when struck down...' Mower looked all about the hall again; he raised his voice once more, '... it was hope, precious hope... which preserved my own spirits when wounded in Greece... and for a long time since in my sick bed.' Mower paused, momentarily overcome, taking another sip from his glass. 'I will read my own poem, written here in this Chapel these past weeks whilst I have lain sick, recovering...' General shouts of loud encouragement were rising now from the Surprises, loud shouts - the lieutenant was very popular. 'If you please...' Mower, self-evidently struggling, raised his arm. A few seconds, the general noise of hundreds subsiding to expectant quietude, and Mower shifted to a more comfortable stance for his wounds. His voice wavering just a little, he began to speak,

'It is New Year's joyous eve,
Our thoughts are filled with affection;
A small stitch in time's brief weave,
When we will pause for reflection;

It is New Year's genial eve,
All our hopes are rising anew;
But for friends lost we grieve,
Those most precious of few;

It is New Year's festive eve,
The time of all times;
But we must take our leave,
After that clock chimes;

It is New Year's hopeful eve,
So let us send joy and prayers,
Give thanks for all we receive,
Love for all those we have cares;

It is New Year's thoughtful eve,
Before the next year arrives;
But before we do leave,
Think! It is the time of our lives.

Chapter Six

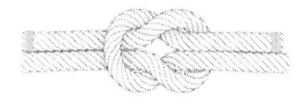

Tuesday 4th January 1825 07:30   *HMS Surprise, Devonport*

'There has been precious little occasion to speak with you since your visit to Saint Petersburg,' declared Pat to Duncan as they sat in the great cabin, cold and shivering in the gloomy half-light before the dawn proper. They were sipping coffee whilst patiently awaiting the small pleasure promised in Murphy's burgoo. 'I grant you the days have been a trifle busy but your few words before the Chapel service hardly served as an account, eh? It could not be described as more than the most economical of log entries... and that with the wind astern,' Pat laughed, trying hard to shuck off the rising sense of burden, of obligation creeping over him, clouding his thinking. 'Why did you go to Saint Petersburg, Duncan, pray tell?'

'I venture if there is nae prospect of that stove being lit, I swear I will remove to the Port Superintendent's office,' Duncan's growling retort was filled with discontent. He was shivering even though well-wrapped, the cold so extreme. 'I havnae doot it was warmer in the Baltic, in Kronstadt.' He rubbed his hands together, 'We didnae reach Saint Petersburg, the ice already present to the east of Kotlin Island... aye, and precious little time did we dwell there... just the one night... and we were away at the dawn. I will say, Admiral Senyavin was a most gracious fellow; without his provisions we would have starved on the passage home.'

'Well, here be the burgoo, sorrs,' Murphy entered. Pat was distracted from his query by the welcome anticipation of at least some warmth - even if it was only in the porridge - and the matter of Duncan's Russian trip was let slip, Pat making a grovelling request to Murphy to attend the stove as the steward was leaving the cabin. A bare minute more had elapsed, both men oppressed by vigorous, recurring bouts of shivering, and the door was knocked again, the Master Shipwright entering on Pat's shout.

'Good morning, Mr Churchill,' declared Pat, striving for a welcoming voice.

'Good morning, Captain O'Connor, Mr Macleod,' replied a cheerful Churchill. 'Sir, may it please you to know that it is intended to flood the dock later this morning, before the ballast is all loaded... so that we may see how she sits in the water as it is affixed in place... most carefully and tidy-like.'

'Very good, Mr Churchill. Is the kentledge here yet... in the yard? I understood it had not arrived last week,' Pat recalled his meeting with Perkis and Peddler in Falmouth.

'The first of it was delivered yesterday, sir, and some of the ballast installed... I dare say near sixty pigs, and that near the keelson, forward of the main mast. A half-dozen of wagons arrived with it; ye will see the dung of their horses all over my yard, an unceasing deposit of it all day there was. I have set two men to work to clear it.' A minor cloud of annoyance passed across the Master Shipwright's face, 'I do so like to keep a clean and tidy yard.'

'Quite so, Mr Churchill; you are of my way of thinking; a tidy yard and a tidy ship, doubtless they make good bedfellows, eh?'

This latter comment of Pat's odd humour confusing Churchill - struggling but failing to see a particular association - he offered no reply. Murphy entered at that moment with the kindling and the coal, 'Well, will ye be a'wantin' more coffee, sorrs?' He was ignored by all, and scowled, letting slip the kindling with a crash to the deck near the stove.

'If only looks could kill,' the unspoken thought in Pat's mind as he glared at Murphy before turning back to his visitor as Churchill resumed, 'There will be more wagons, this morning and this afternoon, Captain O'Connor, a deal more... I dare say.'

'My lads are ready to help with the stowage, Mr Churchill. When you are ready.'

'Thank you, Captain. I will be on the dock side all day, save for dinner, if you require anything of me.' Churchill made to depart. A thought apparently occurring to him at the door, he hesitated, turned back, 'Those wagons, sir, of yesterday... they removed

Eleanor's cargo... from Admiral Saumarez's office it was, on his order, sir, a dozen of marines going with the wagons.'

'Most strange,' thought Pat, but he merely nodded, deciding to ask Duncan about that later, his thoughts on the subject interrupted by Murphy's efforts to light the stove not being greatly successful: the cabin was filling with stinking, acrid smoke, both Pat and Duncan coughing. They seized their bowls of burgoo and stepped out to the gun deck to eat in cleaner air. Both men shivered again, it was most certainly freezing cold. They stared upon a string of men, coming up the ramp and through the open gun port, two at a time, each pair carrying one of the heavy cast iron ingots of ballast, the kentledge. Every ingot was being manhandled with obvious and considerable difficulty across the gun deck to and down the aft companionway steps to the lower deck. From the for'ard steps a slow stream of men came up from below, freed from their heavy burdens, to dodge through the gun port between the pairs labouring across the ramp with more pig iron. The burgoo gone cold, Pat and Duncan ate it anyway, setting the bowls down on the deck before stepping up to the quarterdeck for a better view of what was going on all about the ship and the dock. Three wagons were halted on the dock side, the unloading taking place at the first one, the others waiting in line, their drivers standing around a roaring brazier, rubbing their hands. old caulking being the burning fuel judging by the black smoke, the drivers giving it no mind, all sipping from silver flasks. Likely gin, thought Pat, the idea of a warming tint of whiskey crossing his mind, but he dismissed that for later, making a mental note to check that Murphy had not plundered his modest stocks again - at least not excessively.

The final hour of the working day had arrived, the ship's bell clanging out a discordant six bells of the afternoon watch, and the bosun appeared in the cabin to report. 'Come in, Mr Sampays, and close the door if you will,' called a hungry Pat from behind his table, nothing eaten since his second breakfast, and the cabin after the whole day with the stove lit still only a degree or two warmer than the freezing air outside, his breath steaming. 'How goes the loading?'

'I venture we have installed sixty pigs, sir,' said Sampays hesitantly.

'Sixty! *Only sixty?*' cried Pat, 'Is that all? It seems precious few.'

'I dare say, sir; but 'tis a devil of a job to clear the last vestiges of shingle... to ready the place for the pig afore it is affixed down flat and firm... nails and batten, sir... nails and battens, firmly affixed. It would not do were it to shift... no, no. I would not care to countenance that, sir... in the hurricane it was all ahoo.'

'I'm sure you are in the right of things, Mr Sampays,' Pat replied, a frisson of fear passing through him as he recollected the terrifying instability of the ship during the hurricane, the ballast lurching from side to side, *Surprise's* yard tips in the water, the ship a mere few minutes from sinking, before the terrifying five minutes of axes wielded with frantic desperation, their blades biting manically and repeatedly into the mizzen mast before it was eventually snapped and ripped away with all its rigging; swept away into the watery maelstrom by the hurricane winds, the ship only then beginning to right herself.

'Each one is taking near ten minutes to set in place,' the bosun continued, 'the weight... so greatly heavy... is not helpful, no, it ain't.'

'Well, do your best, Mr Sampays,' Pat declared in an encouraging tone, mentally calculating how long the entire task might take; more than two weeks being his conclusion. The bosun departed, Pat returned to his paperwork at his table and Murphy entered with another bundle of firewood.

'Well, an' what would ye care to eat for dinner, sorr... an' will Captain Macleod be dinin' in the cabin?'

'*Commander* Macleod, Murphy... *Commander*... has departed the ship... only this morning, returned to Falmouth, to take leave... his wife taking great exception to his absence at Christmas,' declared Pat. 'As does Sinéad, me being here,' he thought, but he did not look up from his accounts, a damnably tedious report to be finished for the Yard victualler, and he was in something of a quandary, his number of men - with the volunteers - considerably exceeding the fiction of his official numbers, his enlisted men. He was missing his purser, missing Jason's presence, for he had remained in Falmouth to assist Marston.

'Captain Macleod... Captain it is, sorr,' Murphy's irritating voice was triumphant.

'What are you cackling about, Murphy? Captain indeed!' Pat looked up, his irritation overtaken with a swiftly rising sense of curiosity. 'What drivel is this now? *Captain?* Pray explain yourself, you maundering idiot!'

Monday 7th March 1825   20:00   *Tobermory, Mull*

It had been two months of unprecedented mental turbulence for Simon since the momentous shock of the instant on the quay when he had first glimpsed Flora, and although he was accustomed to the most exhaustive analysis possible when any patient consulted him, on all the occasions in her company he had floundered, the experience and effect upon him utterly outside of his customary analytical and investigative approach. Naturally he strived for accord in every aspect of daily life in his small house, on some days receiving local people who, having heard of his return to the village, sought his professional opinion on their ailments. On other days, in clement weather, he took himself for long walks along the shore or into the hinterland of the island, equipped with sandwiches, a flask and a glass, to observe Mull's oft spectacular bird life. During his walks he pondered with difficulty on his burning predicament: whether to explore a more intimate dialogue with Flora or to let sleeping dogs lie, to leave seemingly satisfied dogs well alone lest they up and run away. He had no answer. Certainly the relationship with Flora was friendly, warming as the weeks had passed by, and yet it seemed to Simon that it had reached something of a plateau, a levelling off in something akin to mere cordiality; and he so much aspired, indeed yearned to reach a higher plane, to grasp a closer relationship, but he had not the least idea of what to do. There were positive indications: the comfortable adoption of Christian names, a growing familiarity with preferred routines - his own particularly - and pleasantries between them in every matter of the household; but that was no longer Simon's vision, for the absolute resemblance of Flora in every respect to his late wife, Agnes, had stunned him. Whether Flora truly recognised that he did not know and could not possibly ask. His predicament seemed without solution, and he strived, not always successfully, to conceal it from Flora by busying himself in renewing old acquaintanceships, encouraging the villagers to consult him and generally keeping as busy as he possibly could. Yet in the dark winter evenings, sitting at the fireside with Flora, the girls retired to bed, the turmoil of his dilemma pressed hard upon him.

'May I ask, what matter it is that preoccupies you?' murmured Flora gently, Simon sipping a whisky and deep in thought.

The words presented him with a golden opportunity, unasked, and a gift it was for sure, but Simon hesitated to grasp it. A silent minute more of introspection, a fire of anxiety and indecision raging throughout his thoughts, but he shrank from the brink, fear of rejection holding him back, and instead he steered for rather more placid waters with his careful reply, 'Oh, I do apologise, my dear, for the rudeness of my solitary reflections; I do. I have received a letter from Falmouth yesterday... from Michael Marston, chaplain on *HMS Surprise*; indeed, he is more than that... he is a beloved colleague of mine and assistant surgeon on the vessel. He describes the progress of our patients... such is exceedingly encouraging, barely a handful remain in his care, all others discharged to their families or, it pleases me greatly to say, they are fit once again.' A silent Flora nodding cautiously, Simon continued, 'His letter refers to a particular patient, our dear friend Mr Mower; most severely wounded he was, and for many a week after he received his dreadful injuries I feared for his life, but he is mending; indeed, he spoke in the Chapel on New Year's eve, his words finding a most appreciative audience... so Marston reports. He was carried from the pulpit by several shipmates, greatly fatigued, but gloriously happy... as am I, it pleases me to say.'

'And I am happy for you... for your friend too.' A momentary pause, 'Is it your intention to return... to your ship... to rejoin your comrades?' Flora's softly spoken question, it appeared to Simon, carried with it the most tiny tremor of unease within her voice; even so, he could not find the courage to seize upon another possible opening for the exploration he so much wished to embark upon. Flora continued, her voice firming, 'You have a following in the village... a deal of folk with never a doctor... save they must go to Oban, which most cannot afford.'

Simon's nerve failed him; he hesitated, and the moment of decision was lost, gone; a safe return to earth chosen, with both feet firmly planted, no courage to risk the soaring heights of closer personal communication. He sipped his whisky and pondered, ten minutes elapsing before he determined on the smallest of foray into unknown waters, 'Flora, my lo... my dear, I have been this past week in contemplation of a return... to Falmouth... a temporary one that is, and of singularly short duration. Marston mentioned that the men of *Surprise* are to embark once again upon another voyage, and I am minded... that is to say, it is a concern of mine... to see that... that all is in the finest of fettle aboard her... with her men, before she departs.' Simon stared closely, believing that he glimpsed the minutest flicker of uncertainty passing across Flora's face, though he was not wholly sure of that. 'I would wish too to see my friends once again, before they do depart... our last voyage was of eighteen months duration.' He did not care to mention that twenty-two men did not return.

'When... when would you choose to depart?'

Flora's words most certainly carried the tint of concern, and there was anxiety there after all, Simon observed, but the precise nature of that would merit much more thought. Perhaps more dialogue whilst discussing his plans might well bring the, thus far, absent clarity he so much sought. 'I am minded to consider further,' he temporised, 'The weather is not presently greatly clement for such a journey.' He had not forgotten near freezing to death, huddled next to the guard, on the outside of the Bristol to London overnight coach in December.

'Perhaps it would best serve to await the spring?' the words conveyed a modicum of solicitude for which Simon was most grateful. He simply nodded, his face graced with a trace of a smile.

Monday 21st March 1825 10:00   HMS *Surprise, Devonport*

The wagons arrived as usual, bringing the last of the kentledge, the drivers assuming their customary indolence once upon the quay, taking station at the burning brazier to talk amongst themselves. From the quarterdeck, *Surprise* now floating within the dock, Pat gazed down upon them enviously, the deep cold of January persisting to make life aboard perpetually uncomfortable. 'Mr Churchill, there you are,' he shouted, the Master Shipwright stepping up the ramp and coming up the companionway.

'Good morning, sir,' the affable reply, Churchill usually in good spirits. 'The fresh canvas is coming aboard this week, sir, after the new mizzen is fitted. My shipwrights will begin to instal that this very morning. They are fetching it from the mast pond. Give you joy of your ship, sir!'

'Thank you, that is handsome news; indeed, it is,' Pat smiled, rubbed his hands together fiercely, 'and what of the replacement carronades, Mr Churchill?'

'The armourer has set aside replacements, sir, so he has. They are ready to come aboard once the new mizzen is in place, the rigging completed.'

'Admirable,' declared Pat, turning his gaze, his attention caught by two civilians stepping up the ramp: Perkis and Peddler it was.

'Captain O'Connor!' shouted Perkis from the gun deck, looking up to Pat and Churchill, leaning over the rail near the companionway. 'Good morning, sir!' Pat nodded, waved his arm to beckon them up.

'I must away, sir,' declared Churchill, and with a nod of farewell he turned and stepped down the companionway.

'Good morning, Mr Peddler, Mr Perkis,' cried Pat, wondering what was the purpose of the unannounced visit. 'Will you care to step into the cabin... take coffee with me perhaps?'

'Thank you kindly, Captain,' said Perkis.

'To what do I owe this honour, gentlemen? Murphy, Murphy there... a pot of coffee... if you please.'

'It is the last of the ballast to come aboard today, Captain O'Connor, and we are here to ensure all is stowed correctly, the delivery concluded, to secure the receipt to be provided by the Yard authorities and... and to determine that you are satisfied with our endeavours in this matter. I trust that you are?'

'Why, yes... indeed, I am, gentlemen.'

'Excellent,' said Perkis. 'Then, if you will excuse me, Captain, I will speak briefly with my men... ensure all the remainder of our ingots are brought aboard, and then perhaps we may enjoy a modest whet together?' Pat nodded, he suggested Perkis speak with the bosun.

'I have received a letter, Mr Peddler,' said Pat, 'from your childhood friend... from Doctor Ferguson... yesterday it was. He is minded to visit us in a few weeks time, before we go to sea.'

'It will give me great pleasure, sir, to see him again after all these years.'

Deep in the hold, Perkis accompanied his two men struggling to bring the first one of the final delivery of the kentledge, the bosun staring in fascinated query, for it was plain that they were in considerable difficulty with the weight of it. A puzzled Sampays could not fathom it, his own men had manhandled all the prior ingots aboard without such evident strain as the two men exhibited. 'Here, let me help you with that,' he offered.

'That will not be necessary,' declared Perkis emphatically. 'These last ingots, Mr Sampays, they are all to be stored together in this particular location, I understand?'

'Yes indeed, sir. Mr Churchill said to leave room for them... just here, in the bow... for the last two dozen or so we are expecting... right here, sir, under the for'ard platform,' the bosun pointed, an evident and vacant space awaited the ballast abreast the keelson.

'Excellent, Mr Sampays... my own men will bring them all aboard if you will,' said Perkis, nodding to the pair still struggling valiantly to come forward, eventually lowering the first ingot with extreme difficulty, the strain evident on their faces, and both plainly sweating despite the extreme cold, their heavy breathing producing swathes of condensation. The bosun nodded and gladly left them to their unenviable task.

Back in the cabin, Pat talked with Peddler, a half-hour slowly slipping by in pleasantries until Perkis re-emerged from the hold. 'Ah, there you are,' said Pat, 'Please, take a seat. Allow me to pour you some coffee. How are things coming along?'

'Thank you, Captain O'Connor. It pleases me to report that the last two dozen of the ballast ingots are now aboard the ship, on the deck out there, and awaiting the attentions of my men to stow them in the hold. The first three are affixed in their position below... as determined by Mr Sampays.'

'Then all of our pigs have come home to roost?' Pat laughed; Murphy, attending, laughed louder; Peddler and Perkis stared.

Ten more minutes, the coffee finished, the visitors preparing to leave, and then Perkis halted, appeared to remember something, 'Captain O'Connor, I was reflecting on our first meeting... in Falmouth a few weeks ago, just before Christmas it was.' Pat simply nodded and Perkis continued, 'The stock market index continues to rise magnificently... 390 it was yesterday, up from 140 in September.' Pat nodding again Perkis pressed on, 'You said, sir, that you are an investor... would you care to consider... in the present most favourable of times in the cycle... consider of expanding your portfolio? My fees as broker are exceedingly modest... and for yourself I am sure a significant reduction is in my contemplation.'

'That is most kind, Mr Perkis, most generous of you. However, I have very little available to me in cash deposits at the present time. The Admiralty is... you may not know, exceedingly slow in paying its officers and men, and the quarterly remittance is oft delayed... *much* delayed, I regret to say.'

'I collect you said that you are the owner of a gold mine, Captain, in Ireland.'

'I am, yes, in the County Galway, in Connemara; though its development is more akin to the exploratory stage and its production can hardly be said to be prolific,' Pat laughed again, 'but I must not bore you with fanciful tales of that.'

'Nevertheless,' Perkis continued, 'These are surely exceptional times... I have not the least doubt that collateral such as a gold mine represents would be considered most favourably by many a bank owner in my acquaintance... should you be minded, that is, to borrow to invest.'

'I should have to consider of it, Mr Perkis,' said Pat, carefully refraining from any indication of interest.

'Here is my card, sir, and now we must away. I bid you good day.'

'Good day, Mr Perkis, Mr Peddler.'

Saturday 2nd April 1825   14:00   HMS Surprise, Devonport

Pat sat with Duncan in the great cabin. Macleod had returned only very late the prior evening, near midnight, from four weeks leave in Falmouth, time spent with his family prior to the impending voyage. The Yard workmen had all departed the ship an hour previously. They had worked hard, their attendance on Saturdays not customary in the winter, but the Superintendent, on Admiral Saumarez's urging at the behest of the First Lord, had promised a generous bonus.

'I venture another week and the barky will be ready for sea,' said Pat, a significant note of uncertainty in his voice, an indecision, something of doubt lingering. 'It has been a greatly taxing time, these recent months... arduous indeed.'

'Aye... and I will be pleased to see the back of this dock and the barky afloat out there,' Duncan strived for resolution in his reply, Pat's tiny waver detected. 'Ye know I am staying with ye... as your First?'

'I'm sure that before we know it you will be Captain,' Pat laughed, 'that is to say... of this ship, eh? You have never explained, Duncan, the purpose of your visit to Russia... and the promotion to Captain, so swift... 'tis unheard of... why, I venture Galileo's meteors never shifted so fast... *Galileo's meteors!* Hah hah! What a wit I am today!'

Pat's wit had not registered with Duncan. 'I am sworn to secrecy by Melville, Pat, as is Jason. We cannae speak of it - save to yourself; why, if we did, I havnae doubt I would be cashiered, struck from the list, and Jason likely locked up... myself too, aye.'

'Go on...' Pat prompted. A knock at the door and Pat, still wondering what the mystery was about, shouted, 'Come in.'

'Well, may it please ye, sorrs... here be a visitor,' Murphy could not keep the widest of grin from his countenance - an unusual event, and one Pat customarily regarded with deep suspicion.

'I am come to visit,' Simon declared, letting fall his tiny bag, his great pleasure evident on his face as he entered the cabin, Pat and Duncan leaping to their feet to greet him. Handshakes utterly inadequate, Simon was hugged by his dear friends, first Pat then Duncan, Murphy hovering close by in obvious pleasure to see the joyful reunion, finally exiting the cabin in anticipation of the shout for suitable refreshment. Within minutes, another tap on the door, and Mower arrived to join the celebration, stooping, hobbling a little and aided by a stick, considerable mutual joy found in his greeting of Simon, who had saved his life, so many wounds had he suffered in the Samos battle.

'Mr Mower,' said Simon, seizing his hand, 'it gives me immeasurable pleasure indeed to see you, your wounds so greatly healed,' great satisfaction in his observation, 'and I give you joy of your recovery.'

'Thanks to you, Doctor Ferguson... thanks to you. I will never doubt that... I have kept all my limbs because of your efforts, your care... I will for ever be in your debt... that is as sure as the sun will rise on the morrow...'

'Come now, the surgeon's skills are oft exaggerated,' replied Simon. 'You were struck down with all the fitness of youth, the recovery sure...'

'With the blessing,' added Pat cheerfully.

Pat's cook, on hearing of the return of both Duncan and Simon, had redoubled his efforts at the galley and with great Scottish emphasis for the imminent dinner, Murphy eventually bringing into the cabin a large silver platter piled high with barley-meal flatbreads baked in mutton fat and rolled, stuffed with the finest cuts of fresh roasted mutton meat.

'Bannocks!' exclaimed Duncan, 'A feast for the eyes. I confess to a grand hunger, nothing this morning, aye, nae even a wee tait to eat since Falmouth. Forgive me, I will begin.'

'That is a most welcome sight,' murmured Simon, 'I am without breakfast, too, leaving Exeter town in great haste.' He seized upon one of the bannocks without ceremony, eating it within a minute, the fat dribbling down his chin until he wiped it away on his coat sleeve.

Pat gazed with infinite pleasure at his friends, contenting himself with pouring the wine, the two arrivals swigging it down in mere moments to wash away the first bannock, both seizing a second without delay, the pile swiftly diminishing. Murphy re-entered within five minutes with the second platter, looking about keenly to assess the mood of the gathering: beatific it plainly was. 'Compliments o' Wilkins, sorrs,' proclaimed the steward setting the second course down upon the table.

'Collops!' Simon took a long sniff of the meat, 'Beef collops! Upon my word, Wilkins is doing us well... and roast potatoes. Here, Murphy,' Simon grubbed around in the depths of his coat pocket, a grimy silver threepence and two halfpennies retrieved and appearing in his palm, 'This is for Wilkins; I trust you will ensure he receives it?' The latter words were spoken with an unblinking stare at the steward, Murphy nodding, no comment offered. 'You may keep the halfpennies,' Simon shouted to Murphy as the steward reached the door, 'Indeed, two dozen of them make a shilling!' all at the table laughing out loud.

Duncan started on his first of the collops without delay, 'Mmmm, grand... fried onions... plentiful salt and pepper...'

'Sweet herbs too... rosemary - such a divine addition to any meat - and, I venture, sage - would it be?' added Simon, inhaling the rising fragrances of the collop, seized in his hand despite its enduring heat. He took a most determined bite.

The persisting severely cold temperatures of winter had relented a little and the small stove had somehow managed to create a tolerable warmth in the great cabin, the ambience at the table one of absolute cordiality, the old friends reunited, eating with enthusiasm, the wine slipping down at a prodigious rate, three bottles swiftly finished and the port wine served, when Wilkins concluded his sterling efforts with a sublime fruit pudding, the top crust of baked shredded bread and suet uniformly crisp, fragments of burnt edge adding to the delightful taste, the lower level bursting with the flavour of rum-preserved apples, blackcurrants and gooseberries, and served with thick cream of the west country preference, clotted, cloying and sticking to the crust as it melted.

'Will I read you a poem I wrote when in my sick bed?' ventured Mower, licking the cream from his lips and pulling a small notebook from his pocket.

'If you please,' said Pat pleasantly, 'It is surely a capital moment for a verse,' his contentment knowing no bounds, for he was no fan of poetry generally.

'I *am* a Cornishman, Falmouth born and bred, as you may recall.' Mower began to read,

'Sweeter than the odours borne on southern gales,
Comes the clotted nectar of my native vales –
Crimped and golden crusted, rich beyond compare,
Food on which a goddess evermore would fare.

Burns may praise his haggis, Horace sing of wine,
Hunt his Hybla-honey, which he deem'd divine,
But in the Elysium's of the poet's dream
Where is the delicious without Cornish cream?'

The poem was followed by loud applause and cheerful congratulations from all, Simon raising his glass with a wide smile of deep satisfaction, 'A glass with you, my friend!'

'A most admirable creation, Mr Mower,' said Pat graciously.

At the end of the meal, none of the men felt able to rise from the table; Murphy, similarly and surreptitiously satiated, struggled to serve the coffee before he, with a degree of clumsy difficulty, replenished the stove's wood fuel. Time, utterly forgotten, passed by unnoticed, slipped away pleasantly in jovial conversation, Simon in particular embracing the cordial ambience of longstanding friendship. The daylight was fast fading, diminishing to the softer luminescence of the dusk when Pat ventured a suggestion, 'Will we scrape for an hour? The instruments are still here in the coach... and a whistle too, Duncan.'

'A most admirable idea, brother,' declared Simon, for in truth he had not felt as relaxed in all his days at home in Tobermory.

'Aye, a wee spell with the whistle will serve,' said Duncan with enthusiasm, stirring a little from the torpor of gross indulgence.

'My instrument is below in my cabin,' pronounced Mower, a proficient player of the Spanish guitar.

Pat stepped into the coach, encountering a tipsy Murphy on the other side of the door where he had been listening attentively. Pat picked up his cello, Simon's viola and the pennywhistle. He despatched Murphy below for the guitar. A violin remained in Pat's glance, belonging to Michael Marston, still in Falmouth with the wounded. Murphy returned, a few minutes passing with the squealing adjustment of the strings, the damp having taken its toll and much of every instrument considerably out of tune.

Pat shouted, 'And so to an old familiar, if you will!' and began to play the hesitant opening bass notes of the first movement of that so very memorable Bocherini quintet in C major *Night music of Madrid*, the high chords of *l'Ave Maria* slow and hesitant, no sheets needed, the music so very familiar to all of the musicians and much beloved by them; everyone followed Pat, joined in, until the cabin resonated with a loud, ragged procession of sound, not all keeping precisely the same tempo - Simon grimaced at several notes - until, too quickly, the lull was passed, the second movement and its mournful beginnings ceded to the faster reiteration of the beginning of the next, flying by in an outpouring of exuberance and enthusiasm until *Los Manolos* brought another rise in the tempo, Simon backing Pat's vigorous and rising lead until the dying conclusion was reached in eventual harmony, all the players seemingly striving to conclude concurrently and finishing with great smiles all round.

'Well, what did you think of that then, eh?' asked Pat, his pleasure shining on his face.

'Capital, capital. I doubt if Luigi himself could have done better,' joked Simon, before laughing more than he could remember doing for a very long time, 'An invigorating delight indeed, though your bow did knock over the wine bottle, and a particularly palatable port it was. Would there be another bottle?'

'And now to something more melodic, if you will,' cried Pat, enthused and not taking the least notice of either the spreading puddle or Simon's enquiry, 'We will make our attempt upon a favourite of mine... *Boccherini's Guitar Quintet number nine*, the *second* movement, the *andantino*. It is a trifle slow... yes it is, but it will afford Mr Mower the lead, and we will support him. Here are the sheets.'

The musicians began with a degree of trepidation, haltingly, Mower appearing to be in some little discomfort as he played but rising valiantly to the melodic repetitions of interval between Pat's 'cello, Duncan venturing brief improvisations with his whistle which were never in Boccherini's contemplation. Simon's viola maintained a continuity which set the pace, a slow one as was originally written and the best that Mower could manage, his hands still exhibiting the lingering vestiges of his injuries to his upper arms, absolute precision of control beyond him and bringing a note missed here and there as his arm strength began to fade by the third minute. Ultimately all reached the glorious end, Mower patently tiring, great pleasure found by everyone even with the many minor discrepancies, all the musicians far out of practice.

A small pause for refreshment, Murphy entering with two bottles of sherry, a particular favourite of Simon's. He lit the lanterns, the afternoon progressing and the light beginning to fade. He stoked and replenished the coals in the stove before making his exit, his intentions set firm on a sherry or two for himself and perhaps something a trifle stronger to follow before he set to with making the supper of toasted cheese, which he knew Pat would shout for sometime during the last dog watch. He heard the squeal of the first bow striking the strings as he stepped down towards the hold, the music resuming, resonating and echoing all around the near empty ship, almost all the hands ashore, joyous notes following him for a half hour as he shifted from liquor store to pantry to galley.

In the great cabin, the glorious playing concluded and the instruments were set down; the music, though sometimes discordant, had been greatly uplifting for tired spirits, and each man offered vigorous applause and the most cordial of congratulations to his fellows for their musical contribution, a greater pleasure found in the amity and unity of their gathering, the joyful reunion.

Thursday 7th April 1825   09:00   HMS Surprise, Devonport

Surprise had been out of the confines of her dock since the prior Friday and was once more anchored in the tidal stream of the Hamoaze, slackwater upon them, the true strength of the ebb a half-hour away. The day was benevolent, the dawn mists relenting to bright sunshine, the wind a warmer south-westerly. It would make egress a little difficult until the breakwater was far astern, but neither Pat nor the master gave that any mind. All along the quay thronged hundreds of the Yard's workers, all watching the fruits of their long labours preparing for her departure. It was seldom these days that the men of the Yard saw off a ship to active service, particularly one which they had themselves restored, and every man knew of her destination and of her prior duties in far distant, eastern Mediterranean waters despite the supposedly confidential nature of her mission. Every man knew too of the fearful casualties she had suffered, for the Yard grapevine worked exceedingly well and the Surprises had become firm friends with many of the shipyard workers, benevolent good wishes for the future being bestowed by scores, indeed hundreds of the Devonport men. A pinnace pulled out, swiftly crossing the hundred yards or so to tie alongside *Surprise*, its occupants coming aboard and up to the sacred quarterdeck. Admiral Saumarez it was, with the Master Shipwright and the Master Attendant.

'Admiral, welcome aboard, sir,' said Pat, great pleasure in his voice, 'Mr Churchill, Mr Sidley.' He shook hands with all three, every man present delighting in the moment, a job well done, a success; a plainly deserving frigate - one with a name belonging to her illustrious forebears before her own reputation, history attaching to her - was restored to service and ready to go to sea;

and for the visitors that was cause indeed for great satisfaction in the present times of economies, of thrift verging on penny-pinching; for that is how they saw things, the Admiralty budget so substantially reduced.

'Captain O'Connor,' declared Saumarez in loud voice, many of the Surprises having appeared as if by magic about the waist, some venturing cautiously upon the port side of the quarterdeck, as if to belatedly polish the restored carronades a trifle more or attend the new mizzen's rigging, 'We are here to wish you a safe passage to Falmouth, to bestow the best wishes of every man at the Yard... I swear all of them are idling over there now, every one of them watching!' The admiral laughed, all on deck laughing with him. There was something of a commotion from the admiral's pinnace, a shout, and a cask of rum was hauled up with a crate following. Saumarez turned about to face the gathering of men staring at him. 'Here be a farewell gift, lads... from my men at the Yard to the men of *Surprise*... a cask of rum for the run home to Falmouth!'

Clumsy Dalby it was who called out, 'Three cheers for the admiral!' Every man of *Surprise* followed with loud shouts of 'Huzzay! Huzzay! Huzzay!'

'And here is a crate of the finest wines from my cellar, for yourself and your officers,' Saumarez added. Pat thanked him profusely, and the admiral, mindful of the tide - now visibly on the ebb - wished them all safe passage and shook hands with Pat and his officers for the last time, swiftly climbing down into his pinnace, his men pulling strongly for the quay.

'Stand by, Mr Macleod, Mr Codrington!' shouted Pat.

'All hands!' bawled Duncan, 'prepare to make sail!'

'Lay aloft!' shouted Prosser, sending men scrambling out on the yards. 'Rig capstan bars, bring to the messenger... man the bars!'

Surprise was anchored port side towards the quay, the current tugging harder at her solitary stern anchor since the tide had begun its full flow, the best bower hauled up since fifteen minutes, the south-westerly wind a little forward of her starboard beam.

'Breast the capstan,' shouted Prosser.

'Up anchor!' ordered Pat.

'Up anchor for home!' echoed the master with great enthusiasm.

'Heave and a-weigh!' cried Duncan.

The cable began to be wound in, the men singing, *'Walk her round and round she goes, way oh, way oh.'* It was not the regulation standard of *"two-six, two-six"* but no one gave it any mind.

'Up and down!'

'Thick and dry for weighing!' shouted Prosser.

The topmen meanwhile had cast off the gaskets, were clutching the canvas under their arms and waiting. The tierers were hauling in the last of the cable, and the stern anchor was hauled up out of the water. 'Standby aloft, let fall,' bawled Prosser. The bosun whistled *peep-peep, peep-peep*.

'Let fall! Sheet home, sheet home, hoist away!' the master shouted. The topmen dropped the sails, swiftly unfurling in their fall, flapping wild within mere moments; and then the men hauled on the braces and *Surprise's* yards were tied off, her sails beginning to fill, no contribution from them just yet. Slowly at first, the tide doing the work, *Surprise* gained way, within minutes her filled and tautened sails were driving her faster, the strong ebb tide pushing her with ever greater momentum downstream, down the Hamoaze, onwards, on towards the sea, a general feeling of rising satisfaction common to all aboard.

'Keep her close-hauled, Barton,' Duncan, conscious of her lee drift, reminded the helmsman and his helpers at the wheel.

The men heaved the remainder of the stern anchor cable in; the anchor was quickly catted and fished, and within a minute all around her bow and at her stern there streamed white water.

'Mr Pickering,' shouted Pat, 'The salute, if you please!'

'Larboard gunners!' bawled the lieutenant, 'FIRE ONE!' From *Venom*, the forward gun, a bright orange-red flame flashed out, the crack and roar of the blast noise immediate, a black smoke cloud following. 'If I wasn't a gunner I wouldn't be here,' Pickering slowly recited the words of the old custom to gauge the five seconds interval between firing, 'FIRE THREE! *Dutch Sam* roared, and on the firing rippled down the port side, *Tempest, Hurricane,*

Delilah, and so to the aftmost guns, the two in the great cabin, *Daniel Mendoza* and *Billy Warr*, until *Venom* thundered once more to complete the fifteen guns appropriate to Saumarez's rank as Vice-Admiral, and then silence, for a few seconds only, when from the distant quay, from the dense crowds of men thronging all along three hundred yards of waterside, came the groundswell of commotion, a thousand arms waving in farewell, and from a thousand throats came the unreserved roar of tumultuous cheering.

Thursday 14th April 1825 12:00   *HMS Surprise, Falmouth*

'I am awaiting two infernal metal merchants, sir,' a somewhat disgruntled and downcast Pat replied to Edward Pellew's query about the intended departure time, both standing on the quarterdeck. 'They are joining the ship for the voyage. They are damnably late.'

'Mighty odd, O'Connor... metal merchants taking passage... for what purpose?'

'They are bound for Cephalonia... with a coin press, sir. More than that I know not.'

'A rum affair,' mumbled Pellew, and a minute later, 'You have completed all your provisions? She is watered? Powdered?'

'Yes sir, powdered from the hoy in Devonport, provisioned and watered here these past three days.'

'Very good. Will we take a modest whet whilst you await your passengers?' enquired Pellew, sensitive to Pat's air of dismay.

'Of course, sir; let us step into the cabin.'

'Your officers and men are all aboard, I see. Your surgeon too?'

'Yes sir, Mr Marston is aboard the barky as surgeon for this particular voyage. Doctor Ferguson is returning to Scotland on the morrow. I believe he is presently attending the last three of my wounded men in the Chapel.'

'Why is Doctor Ferguson not sailing with you, O'Connor, pray tell?' The admiral's line was a particularly unwelcome one for Pat, much set back by Simon's absence, and he did not care to dwell on that let alone construct any reply.

They stepped down the companionway and passed through the coach and into the great cabin, brightly illuminated by light pouring through the repaired glass at the stern. At the captain's desk, writing in obvious haste, sat Simon, Murphy fretting all about him. 'Murphy, if you please,' murmured Pat, greatly surprised, '... the admiral and I will take a glass of... of... Admiral, what would you care for?'

'I will take a dry sherry.' Murphy nodded and hastened out. 'Doctor Ferguson,' cried Pellew, surprised himself, 'It is a pleasure to see you again; indeed, it is, very much so.'

Simon looked up from his writing, 'Thank you, Admiral... and a pleasure to see you too, sir.' He resumed frantic scribbling, his head put down immediately.

Pat stared with utter incomprehension: Simon had been originally intending to take the morning coach with Sinéad, Kathleen and the three youngsters, yet an hour later he had decided to stay for a day or two in Falmouth to ensure the wounded were properly attended in Marston's imminent absence aboard *Surprise*. Indeed, Pat and Simon had already made their painful farewells, in significant mutual distress, after breakfast at the Marine Hotel on the Town quay, yet here he was. 'Over there, sir, let us take a seat in the glorious sunlight.' Pat led the way to the upholstered bench curving below the glass panes, Murphy hastening in with a silver tray, the sherry bottle and three glasses, setting all down on the desk and pouring, the two glasses delivered on the tray to Pat and Pellew, the last left in incongruous isolation at Simon's elbow.

'Doctor Ferguson,' cried Pellew, 'Will you join us in a farewell toast?'

'Of course, sir... my apologies... a minute and I will be with you - once I have finished the sentence. I have but little time to complete my letter, this ship departing any moment...'

'Most strange,' thought Pat, the mystery deepening.

The admiral appeared to lose interest in Simon and his distant, rather rude demeanour, taking a sip of the sherry and turning back to Pat, 'Your wife and children, O'Connor... I did not see them on the quay?'

'Left but an hour ago, sir, as would we were it not for those wretched merchants who are delayed. My family took the coach to Exeter; they are going on to London and thence, after a few days, returning to Ireland, as is Mr Macleod's family... accompanying mine.'

'Admiral, my profuse apologies, sir,' said Simon, moving to join them, a sense of purpose, of decision radiating from his face and resonating within his voice. 'I have finished my letter, and it would give me great pleasure to take a glass... a very little glass with you. How are you, sir?'

'Very well, Ferguson, and yourself?'

'I have been in some confusion... I confess... lamentable confusion, a particularly troubling notion in my head for all the weeks of this year, but that is now settled. I have reached a decision only this morning, and that, sir, is something of a blessed relief.'

'And what would that be, pray, may I ask?' Pellew curious, as was Pat, agape and staring at his friend in bewildered incomprehension.

'I am minded to join Captain O'Connor on this voyage.'

Pat could find no words; he gasped, he blinked, he set down his glass which tipped off the bench and fell to the floor. A rush of relief filled his mind, a surge of joy raced through his heart; the two floods melding together to overwhelm him and leaving him without the least capacity to assemble a cogent sentence. Admiral Pellew, observing Pat's shock, his incapacity, stood up, shook Simon's hand; his own words, emphatically spoken, were not lacking in the slightest conviction, 'I never formed the opinion, Ferguson, that you would do otherwise.'

'It is most kind of you to say so, Admiral Pellew, but I confess I have wavered. It seemed at times that I was not equal to returning to the violence... to the bloodshed, so distressed had I become the last time... but I could not... I could not countenance my shipmates... *my friends* in peril without the prospect of my attendance... downstairs.'

Pat stood up, seized and shook Simon's hand, 'Thank you... Simon... thank you...'

Time itself become seemingly suspended, several minutes passed by, Pat and Pellew scrutinising Simon's face, his stance, wondering about his change of heart; such a welcome change of heart to Pat's way of thinking, before Simon replied to the unanswered question hanging still in the air, silence enduring, 'Where is the man, the coward that shrinks from fighting for such as his brothers? I was afraid... Pat... I was so greatly affrighted that more men would die under my knife... that September day... Samos... so many men killed... a slaughterhouse it was... the blood... so very much blood...'

'It was a damnably tough day, I venture,' offered Pellew with feeling.

'Even worse, sir, even worse,' murmured Pat, 'We were cruelly knocked about.'

Murphy returned in that dramatic moment to announce the sighting on the quay of a wagon arriving, Lieutenant Pickering following him into the cabin. 'Mr Pickering,' Pat collected himself, 'You would oblige me extremely if you would go in my launch to the quay and fetch both the gentlemen accompanying the wagon. There is also a... a device... a press of some form to come aboard. Take Barton and three men to assist.'

Pickering, sensing the somewhat unusual ambience within the cabin, his attention caught by Simon's presence - a puzzle to him too - merely murmured, 'Aye aye, sir.' He nodded to Simon, to Pellew, and departed.

'Murphy! Murphy there,' shouted Pat, 'We will take a tint of something a trifle stronger, if you will. I collect there must be a jar of Brusna pot still, from Kilbeggan, in my dunnage.' Murphy's eyes lit up and he disappeared, returning within five minutes, the whiskey uncorked, the level in the jar to Pat's eye conceivably down an inch, but he gave that no mind, nodding, and Murphy poured three exceedingly generous measures.

Pellew raised his glass, 'Give you joy, O'Connor, of Ferguson's company... and... *Ferguson*... give *you* joy of your decision. I have not the least doubt it is the one you will never regret.'

'Thank you, sir,' mumbled Simon, the previously tense atmosphere relaxing for all the men.

'We seafarers, we mariners are of a kind, O'Connor, Ferguson,' declared Pellew, 'A breed of whom the very wind has swept to all the far seas and oceans. Would that I could be with you.'

'Is that, sir, not within the bounds of your prerogative?' said Pat with boundless warmth in his reply.

Pellew laughed, 'It would give me great pleasure, O'Connor, great pleasure indeed, but I am minded my seafaring is all done.'

Fifteen more companionable minutes passed in cordial exchanges, in talk of the ship's restoration, the weather, the possible timetable to Cephalonia, the prospects for a call at the Rock, at Malta, nothing remotely intrusive arising; and the first glass was consumed, when Murphy, in eager attendance and plainly greatly pleased himself, poured another without delay, no prompting necessary, the second glass of similarly heroic substance, Murphy hastening from the cabin with the residue, as he saw it, the final inch in the jar.

'Would you care to accompany us, sir?' said Pat to Pellew, noting that his reiterated suggestion had produced a palpable sense of discomfit with the retired admiral. He decided on a moderated offer, 'Perhaps as far as the Rock... or even to Malta? I have not the least doubt you could return on the mail packet at your leisure.'

'Most kind, O'Connor... most kind, indeed. Never a day passes without I yearn to return to the sea. I will be sixty-eight in a few months, and I have been at sea since I was thirteen, a rash youngster with all the spirit of the world... yes... put ashore by my captain, I was, after three years... for quarrelling with him - can ye believe it, eh? - but now... now I am too old and too fat... why, climbing aboard is as much exertion as ever I can manage these days.'

'Nonsense, sir... why I venture ye would climb to the tops after a month at sea,' offered Pat, his affection for this man knowing no limit.

Pellew laughed, 'That is most generous, O'Connor, and were I ever to return to sea, to join a ship, it would give me infinite pleasure were you to be her captain, so it would. Thank you. I cherish you for your kind words. No, it is no longer for me, I regret to say. I must content myself with recollections... with memories, and they surely grow more precious with age.'

That the coin press was heavy, inconvenient to handle and damnably difficult to haul aboard was evident by virtue of it being an hour before Pickering reported again at the cabin door, 'All ready for departure, sir.'

'About time too,' was Pat's immediate thought in his growing annoyance with the long delay, only a little moderated by the influence and warming glow of the whiskey, but principally because he was hugely buoyed up by his sublime pleasure in Simon's last minute commitment to the voyage, 'Please to ask Mr Macleod to prepare to get us underway, directly.'

'Admiral, will you take this letter for me, if you please?' asked Simon.

'Of course,' murmured Admiral Pellew. 'I bid you both farewell, a safe passage and all the success you deserve in your admirable venture.'

'Will you give me your hand, sir?' said Pat. 'My best thanks for all you have done for us... for the barky,' he declared, shaking Pellew's hand, a tinge of regret in his voice that the great man was about to depart his presence: the veteran of so many campaigns, the victor of more frigate actions than any of his contemporaries, the destroyer of a French seventy-four - *Droits de l'homme* - on a stormy lee shore - Pellew in *Indefatigable* clawing off, the most decorated frigate captain in the Royal Navy, the holder of the Knight Grand Cross of the Order of the Bath; his hero was departing. Pat gazed at Pellew with something akin to worship; the admiral himself seemed reluctant to leave. 'We are, all of us, infinitely obliged to you, sir, for your benevolence,' said Pat, respect resonating from his every word. Pellew, no words within his powers at that moment, nodded, drained his glass; he shook hands again with the firmest of grip with both Pat and Simon, and he left to go ashore in his brother's Customs cutter, more than a little affected by the conversation and the whiskey, intense feelings of nostalgia raging fiercely within his mind, and burdened by an all-consuming sadness that the fire of his own youth was, to his infinite regret, burned out.

The admiral gone, Pat turned to Simon, 'I am mightily relieved that you have changed your mind, old friend... that you have come back. It is like having the true Saint, Patrick himself... sailing with us, so it is.'

'Oh, what stuff and nonsense, Patrick O'Connor,' said Simon, though he was not entirely displeased to hear the grateful endorsement. 'Pray do not speak of such childish notions. Now, will I have an hour before we leave to bring aboard a further stock of laudanum and other medical stores?'

The tide on the flow and slackwater long gone in the wait for the late arrival of the two metallurgists, Pat was more than a little anxious to depart, his concerns thus far stayed by his amity for Pellew and his delight and satisfaction with Simon's return. The wind at least was favourable, had remained conveniently westerly, was most helpful for their departure, particularly the narrow exit from the Roads; more, once out into the Channel *Surprise* could set up to sail close-hauled along the coast. Now was the pressing time to go, now, immediately, to gain sea room before the fast approaching dark of the night, now, when they might sweep all the way down past the whole of Cornwall at the most splendid rate; and with so much water in the King's Road they would not have to be too particular about her course to clear the Bar, reach the Roads and pass by the Black Rock.

'The tide is at the full,' said Pat. 'Slackwater is gone this past half hour. We have precious little time with the ebb in our favour so.'

'Ah, the tide, the eternal tide. I see I am bound once more by its demands and that of the winds.'

Pat fixed him with the inquisitive stare that Simon had long been accustomed to, 'You was aware we was always sailing on this ebb, this tide?'

'This particular tide? To speak plain, Pat, I had not given much thought to the tide...' and then, he said quietly in a somewhat irritated voice, 'I recollect such, yes, now you refer to it, I do.'

Pat, gazing at Simon in the most amicable of manner, with the utmost benevolence in his voice, added, 'The wind too is not presently unfavourable, but may change against us later. There is nothing sure about the wind, as doubtless you understand.' Pat did have his doubts about his last statement.

'That is to the good, certainly it is, but may I say that if the wind did not exactly serve, there is always another day. Are we pressed by such temporal extremes, such nautical immediacies once more... so soon?'

'There is presently a great advantage, Simon, the wind so and the ebb with us.'

'Indeed,' said Simon, a little despondently, his voice falling away, 'and those are doubtless significant considerations.' For all his maritime life he had felt somewhat burdened; indeed, he was oppressed at times by those preponderant twin metereological factors on frequent occasions when he had wished to linger, to study some botanical discovery of great interest, but always he had been pressed by Pat with a sense of acute urgency; and a reluctance had developed within him, one that never actually made the slightest impression upon Pat's decision, however expressed, and it was always followed by a sense of resignation, of bowing to inevitability, not the least prospect of any other course, and that irritated him profoundly. 'But Pat, for all love, I don't doubt time and tide are marching on - it always has been so for as long as I can remember - but are such matters so greatly relevant to our intentions? Surely there will be another tide later... on the morrow perhaps?'

Pat stared at Simon as if weighing how anyone of the least maritime experience could conceivably be so profoundly ignorant about the desirability, indeed the necessity of exploiting a favourable combination of wind and tide. 'Sure, but it is the present tide that I intend to take.'

Chapter Seven

Thursday 14th April 1825   18:00   *Off the Lizard*

Pat, leaning on the rail, gazed towards Bass Point, a mile distant on the starboard beam. All of the Lizard, its entire rugged coast was in the shadow of the sunset finale, the bright orange orb half gone, a phosphorescent yellow radiance of bright sky all around it, reflections flickering off the water and illuminating the wave crests, low and akin to ripples on an infinite pond. *Surprise*, with the gentlest of heel, was sailing on a bowline in the most clement of conditions, all her canvas hoisted and no call for any reef. A settled air of contentment, of satisfaction abounded throughout the ship, the few men present on the deck standing in the silence of absolute happiness, merely the squeak of the new hemp of the rigging the solitary noise Pat could hear above the muted slap of waves on the hull. He was relaxed, nothing disturbing a spell of tranquillity the likes of which he had not felt for many a month. A solitary gull swooped inquisitively past the side, near within touching distance, and Pat turned his head to follow it; he looked aft, gazed along the white stream of the wake, particularly prominent in the diminished light of approaching dusk, to see *Eleanor's* distant sails just visible far, far astern.

Dalby rang four bells, the loud *"ding-ding ding-ding"* of the end of the first dog watch intrusive but also gratifying, signifying as it did another confirmation of comfortable routine, of returned normality; for it was surely such, to be at sea again, the ship restored, all his men with him, and Simon particularly. There had been no absentees at all, not a one, every man of the prior voyage presenting themselves at the quay for embarkation, save for those wounded men still recuperating; but, Pat reminded himself, all such were beyond danger, their recovery assured, though for many it meant the loss of a limb or at least part of one. Pat reflected on this, the many casualties; indeed, it was the issue which had so greatly oppressed his mind and morale in all the months since leaving Greece in the prior year: that and the number of shipmates left behind, never to return; to the extent that he had doubted whether he would ever again resume command of the barky. It had taken many and varied influences to sway his mind to his eventual conclusion, much painful procrastination preceding it, and only slowly had he come to terms with the fact that he had actually and finally made up his mind; since then he had been striving to come to terms with the substance of his decision, the inherent obligations of it; yet the reassuring conviction had ultimately firmed within him that he had, in fact, made the right call, and for that he was grateful; indeed, he was profoundly relieved. He reflected that his closest friend had suffered a similar quandary, and Simon's decision to return had been reached even later than Pat's own.

'Well, sorr, will 'ee care for supper?' Murphy's familiarly puling, high voice jolted Pat back to the present. 'Will 'ee eat a little somethin'?'

He realised that he was hungry, his dinner a scant affair, a modest beef sandwich eaten in haste with Admiral Pellew whilst awaiting the late arrivals, Peddler and Perkis; his feelings before departing Falmouth largely of anxiety, his family being left behind being most discomfiting, leaving him not the smallest of appetite; even now, despite his hunger, he had no inclination for food.

'In a while, Murphy, if ye please... a half-hour or so. I am reflecting on... on...' He paused, gazed up to the heavens. 'What indeed am I reflecting on?' Pat asked himself. His attention returned to his steward, Murphy waiting patiently, 'It would please me to take an ale, here on the quarterdeck. Would you mind fetching one? My griego too.' A realisation of the chill coming over him, he shivered, the sun all gone, a pale orange glow remaining in the western heavens behind thin rags of wispy cloud.

'D'reckly, sorr.' Yet Murphy did not shift; he stared at his captain momentarily, deciding to linger, to investigate, Pat not usually slow to his table, 'Would that be pale ale or stout, sorr?'

'Eh?' Pat turned to his steward, the question registering, but Murphy was rarely if ever hesitant when directed towards the liquor store. 'Oh, a stout would answer the case, yes... a stout, if you will Murphy.'

'Anythin' else, sorr,' Murphy's persistence was plain; Pat stared, his mind turning, but no direction found. 'Soup? Cheese an' pickles? A slice o' marchpane? That is to say... a... a morsel?'

'No, nothing else,' Pat stepped towards Murphy, smiled, patted him on the shoulder, 'Thankee.'

The steward returned within minutes, Pat turning from his contemplations, from staring absently into the fading, pale yellow afterglow of the sunset, 'Well, here it is, sorr, stout... an' I have brought 'ee your dinner... Wilkins cooked it an' I have warmed it up on the galley... an' here is your coat; now, put it on, sorr, d'reckly; 'tis gettin' cold, so it is.'

'Why, thankee, Murphy,' Pat took a deep draught from the stout, the taste exquisite and wholly satisfying, a further and welcome reminder of the present. 'Life goes on,' he thought, 'even after the worst that comes along.'

'Now, sorr, the coat... put it on before 'ee catch your death,' cried Murphy emphatically, stepping closer, his arms spreading the coat wide. 'There, sorr, ain't that better?'

'Splendid,' said Pat with another smile, buttoning the coat. 'What's this, Murphy, pray tell?' asked Pat, looking doubtfully into the still warm pot.

'Wilkins cooked it special, sorr, the barky a'leavin' Falmouth; 'tis a French dish... *Cock of hen* he said it was...'

'*Cock oh van*, Murphy,' said Pat, 'Foreigners always pronounce better than they spell.'

'...but the sauce has dried up.'

Pat stared at the blackened, shrivelled lump within the pot, 'More like cock up. You may try it with the cat.'

He was still there three hours later, the only illumination afforded by a brilliant panorama of stars within the black expanse, no moon intruding, and Pat gazing up through his glass with acute fascination. Murphy stepped up to the quarterdeck with a particular concern, all his recurring visits to the great cabin with Pat's customary coffee finding it empty, 'Will 'ee care for coffee, sorr... a tint o' whiskey... eh? An' here is a fresh pasty, *right fresh*, hot from the galley.'

Pat, in a rare moment of empathy with his steward - though in truth Murphy was much more to him than a servant despite the differences in rank, in education and particularly in temperament - replied in friendly voice, 'Thankee for your attentions, Murphy... the pasty will serve for an admirable supper...' An enigmatic pause before Pat resumed, 'I was thinking... 'tis the long road we have trodden since the old days... since leaving Galway, eh? A world of miles we have travelled, you and me together.'

Murphy stared suspiciously at Pat, for confidences were a rare thing and usually pressaged a request of one kind or another, often for stores of the alcoholic variety that were no longer to be found anywhere aboard the barky, 'Sorr?'

'I have been contemplating on our shipmate... on Jelbert... *the elder one,*' Pat continued, 'You doubtless collect he was master gunner with us on *Tenedos*...' Murphy simply nodded, wondering where this revelation was leading, and Pat resumed, 'He ain't a young man... but I was obliged to take him on again; no, that ain't right... I obliged myself... that is to say, that day in Devonport... I wished him back... aboard the barky... with *us* again, and I could no more refuse him... his request than I could ever sail the barky square against the wind.'

'Well, sorr,' Murphy, recognising that Pat was in some difficulty, in some confusion, strived to make his own small contribution, 'There ain't no doubt, sorr, he was a splendid gunner... first rate he was... an' doubtless still is,' he murmured, 'an' a capital man with the hands, nothin' too much trouble for him... an' he has taken a shine to Mr Mower... helps him with everythin' he does.'

'Yes... yes, I'm sure... but I was contemplating on his spirit, his most admirable spirit... his son being killed...'

Murphy's own filial aspirations were unclear, even to himself; he had oft suspected that he might have sons of his own and in several of those ports of his more frequent acquaintance, but of sympathy in this plainly poignant and introspective moment for Pat he was certainly not lacking, 'A tragedy, sorr... for sure it was,' he mumbled.

'... his son struck down... in this very ship... in the cabin it was... *in my cabin*... serving his gun.'

Murphy, no fool but realising he was, without the least doubt, a deep fathom out of his depth, fumbled about within his pocket, pulling out a small silver flask which he presented to Pat, 'Take a whet, sorr... here... take it; it will do 'ee a world o' good, the air so cold.'

A long pause, Pat staring intently at his Galway compatriot, 'Thankee, Murphy.' He took a swig, coughed - the whisky strong, burning. He wiped his mouth, patted Murphy on the shoulder in companionable fashion and returned the flask. 'Indeed, there's something in what you say...' he whispered, the burning sensation still enduring in his throat, 'Come, it's time to go below; I am minded I'll have that coffee before I take to my cot.'

'D'reckly, sorr... comin' up.'

Friday 15th April 1825   09:00   off the Brittany coast

Pat was back on his quarterdeck at the dawn, his spirits much recovered, and revelling in the new day. The morning was cold, the wind a moderate breeze gusting to fresh but not a great deal stronger, whitecaps abounding: Biscay was behaving herself, nothing more than a moderate swell. Flying all the sail she possessed *Surprise* sailed on majestically across the great bay, a little more south in her course for Finisterre. Topgallants atop, studdingsails boomed out aloft and alow, and her yards braced for the wind on her beam, on she raced - magnificently to Pat's eye - for mile after steady mile, no call for tacking, not the least deviation for long boards, her lee gun ports occasionally dipping into the white water when the wind gusted. From her bow her wake creamed and sparkled in the bright sunlight, sweeping all along her sides to leave the most turbulent of silver wake; and the copper of her hull - all cleaned to a pristine state at Devonport - gleamed on her weather side, heeled over as she was.

Pat stood contentedly near his helm, Barton, Prosser and Sampays all attending. Every man on deck had demurred from wearing oilskins despite the damp and the chill, preferring proud optimism and comfort of movement before sensibility, though the spray flew up in infrequent showers as *Surprise* dipped after each wave, the deck soaked, the lower yards and sails shedding flurries of water everywhere. Despite this moderate wetness, not so much as an intrusion as an inconvenience, Pat delighted in taking his second breakfast on deck: another of Wilkin's pasties, warmed and consumed with pleasure as all stared east, the much feared rocks of Ushant visible but safely passed at a considerable distance, painful recollections of the hurricane coming back to haunt them for fleeting moments, when on each occasion such unwelcome memories were set aside with a determined resolution, all minds held rigidly focussed on the present, not a man with any inclination to entertain any recollection of the horror and terror of November.

Simon, stepping up on deck to take the air before his own late breakfast, was greeted royally by all the men he encountered, customary reservation thrown away and many pressing their hand upon him to be shaken, his old patients particularly gratified to speak warm words with him, effusive statements of welcome showered upon him by dozens of the hands, for not a man had been easy in the prospect of returning to sea and likely battle without him being aboard; hence delight was found by them all in his return, reassurance gained and personal confidence fortified in his presence.

'Good morning, Simon,' shouted Pat enthusiastically with a beckoning wave as his friend stepped up to the quarterdeck. 'How are you? How do you feel, first night back at sea, the barky shifting along so splendidly? Here,' Pat sniffed, 'do you taste that smell of the salt air, eh?'

Simon blinked; he was long accustomed to Pat's literary melds, 'Tolerably pleased, Pat, tolerably pleased; my olfactory and gustatory faculties are in fine fettle, the finest; though I dare say I will never be as accustomed as you are to the forceful billows, the haphazard nature of the vessel's motions, Neptune's vigorous irregularities and so forth, but I confess it is not entirely disagreeable.'

'Good man,' declared Pat, slapping Simon on the back. 'We have cleared Ushant, and the weather is fair handsome... look, look all about us.' Simon venturing a tiny inclination and turn of his head, Pat continued, 'Look aloft now... *up*,' the general direction emphatically reiterated in case such a mariner's term might not be readily grasped by his friend. 'Have you ever seen such a prodigious fine spread of canvas? Ain't it a wondrous sight to behold, eh?'

'Quite splendid,' ventured a contented Simon, his appreciation not stretching quite as far as enthusiasm.

'I venture we are making nine, maybe ten knots... ain't that the barky at her best, eh?'

'It is indeed a memorable velocity, I make no doubt,' murmured Simon, pleased to see the delight on his friend's face, a glowing and radiant pleasure upon it for the first time in many, many months.

'Why, at this rate I venture we will fetch Finisterre in three or four days, and you can't say fairer than that.'

At that moment the guests appeared, stumbling in obvious discomfort out of the companionway, unsteady, a little grey in the face. They struggled aft towards the helm and across to the sacred starboard side to stand near to Pat, each with one hand clutching the new mizzen mast, the helmsmen turning about, muttering, and giving them blatantly disapproving glances. 'Good morning, Captain O'Connor,' grunted Perkis.

'Mr Perkis, Mr Peddler,' said Pat pleasantly, his welcome moderated a very little by the breach of protocol (not that his guests would know that, he admitted) and so not quite reaching the flowing warmth previously extended to Simon, 'Good morning to you both.'

'Good morning, Captain,' mumbled Peddler, swallowing. He turned immediately to greet the bosom pal of his youth, 'Ferguson, dear friend, what a pleasure to see you again. I hope I see you well? I must apologise for keeping my cabin last night, I was in some little discomfort... the motions of the ship, the severe rolling.'

Pat stared, bemused; he could not recollect any rolling nor indeed any motions, violent or otherwise; the sea had been as calm as ever it was likely to be.

'Peddler, my dear old friend... *Benjamin*,' Simon seized and shook his hand warmly, 'Pay that no mind; I will offer you a suitable draught, a remedy of certain effect... when you are ready. It is such a great pleasure to see you again after all these years... and who would have thought it would be on the deck of a ship, my home more often than not? Is it ten years... perhaps fifteen?'

'Too long, too long by far,' declared Peddler.

'Captain,' Perkis interjected, 'I have been myself somewhat discomfited, uncomfortable overnight, but I am now recovered; and there is a need to discuss the voyage... the timetable, our anticipated day of arrival in distant Greece. I wonder whether we might dine together... in your cabin? The most modest of dinner will serve very well... I have no gastronomic aspirations. Will we say today?'

The helmsmen, a mere two yards away and all striving discreetly to follow the exchanges, turned their heads and stared in unqualified disbelief, utter abhorrence plain in their faces: a passenger daring to invite himself to the Captain's table, to dinner! It was unheard of, and plainly it was also the height of rudeness verging on a shocking disrespect.

'Mr Perkis,' said Pat, smiling and maintaining his pleasant demeanour, for in truth nothing could conceivably spoil his day, at least nothing short of the barky foundering, and that - treacherous Ushant far astern - certainly never entered his thoughts, 'It would give me great pleasure to dine with you and your colleague, certainly it will, but may I suggest, sir... may I suggest that we leave it for a few days... when Mr Peddler has found his sea legs - he is plainly a trifle indisposed at present, and there is plentiful time in which to discuss the voyage.'

'Of course, Captain, most certainly,' uttered Perkis, perhaps becoming aware of the glares of reprobation from the helm. 'I shall await your pleasure, sir, and look forward to your company.' Another fifteen minutes of a rather strained silence on the quarterdeck, Peddler obviously to all still in enduring discomfort, and the two visitors returned below.

'Pat, I will go below myself and attend my friend,' said Simon, 'Peddler's sickness reminds me, and you will recollect my concern before our departure...' a pause before adding 'leaving in our customary haste. I remarked that I must augment my stock of medicines, laudanum most particularly... before... before we are in contemplation of any event which might necessitate calling upon them.'

'Oh, pay that no mind. It is in my thinking to touch at Argostoli, to water and provision there. You can be sure you will find all you need in that place. There is plainly a need, a necessity to speak with Napier... to find out the general situation... the present state of the war. We have no notion of what we might find, but I venture Napier will give us a clue.' Pat settled back to enjoy his morning, nodded to the small group near the helm as if to signify his satisfaction.

All day *Surprise* sailed on under an infinite deep blue sky, unblemished by cloud, hour after hour passing pleasantly whilst she ran on with a seemingly rejuvenated spirit all of her own, only the merest tightening of the halliards and braces occasioned as the new hemp of the rigging stretched in first use. Pat revelled in everything that was wonderful in his world, though his personal tranquillity was not quite perfect as his ears caught the grumbling of the helmsmen; Barton it was, lamenting to the bosun, dissatisfied: something not exactly right and proper as *Surprise* answered her rudder; she was a trifle heavy, a little more reluctant than usual to respond to the helm; perhaps being down a whet at the bow was the cause, and a suitable adjustment to her trim might well answer the case. Pat gave it no mind, preferring to study all other aspects of his ship, the spread of pale new canvas a delight to behold after the greatly deteriorated, shabby and much repaired sails in service for the last six of the months in Greece, no access afforded there to anything new, the sailmaker always exceedingly unhappy and constantly busy.

Pat was still on his quarterdeck at sunset, the wind holding to a firm westerly, *Surprise* shifting to a south-south-westerly track, as close to the wind as she could sail, slowing from her former racing progress. The sense of a memorable day winding down was coming upon her men, Pat particularly; the brightness of the light was diminishing, the meagre temperature falling away to a cold chill, displacing the mild sense of euphoria held by many all day. Pat, shivering, handed over to Duncan and went below to the cabin, grateful for the imminent prospect of hot food which he had postponed all day.

Sunday 17th April 1825   20:00   off La Coruña

Pat and Mower were seated at the table in the cabin when Simon knocked and entered after supper, a bottle of port wine - much depleted - stood alongside its empty brother. They were playing Mower's new game, a chess variant with a board much larger than usual and with a correspondingly greater number of pieces; indeed, whilst each player still had only one king to defend and one queen with which to attack, their expanded command boasted double of all the other pieces, the board presenting a most splendid panorama, fourteen by fourteen squares, most perplexing at first sight. The lieutenant had persisted in persuading the officers when off duty to try his invention, and although chess had previously not appeared aboard with any great frequency over the years, Mower's innovation was seen as an engaging novelty and a challenge which all had risen to with plentiful enthusiasm but little success: the lieutenant, possessing of more practice during so many hours in his sick bed whilst recovering from his wounds, invariably triumphed.

Simon, only recently become familiar with the game, stood behind Pat and stared at his pieces, his strategy plain - a bold advance on his left flank with two bishops, two castles and his queen threatening the black king - exposed since the loss of a half-dozen of pawns and no movement of pieces on the black king's own left flank; yet the threat was enabled because of the outlying position of Mower's own more powerful right flank pieces, their wider ranging distribution together with the far greater range of movement afforded to them by the larger board making any interpretation of intentions beyond the most immediate of moves far, far more difficult. Simon stared, fascinated: in all situations involving ships in battle, as he well knew, Pat might be expected to win, for his mind was perfectly capable of the assessment of a multitude of varying influences and concurrent threats, but such was also the product of practice as well as intelligence, and in this particular chess form Pat almost wholly lacked the former.

Simon, upon Pat's nod and perfunctory wave, drew up a chair and sat down to watch. He helped himself to a glass of the port, sat back and studied the faces of the adversaries, the board losing his interest. Pat was plainly concentrating hard, no movement of his head, his eyes fixated again upon his planned gambit; Mower's face was relaxed, a smile offered in reply to Simon's scrutiny, and that pleased Simon immensely, for in all the months since leaving Greece the lieutenant had exhibited little in his face except the persisting pain of his wounds. He had endured bravely, never speaking of his agonies, never lamenting his difficulties, his constant fatigue and the swift descent to tiredness every day; and he had insisted on joining the new voyage, maintaining that he was almost recovered, though to Simon's practised eye such was plainly inconveivable. Pat had favoured him with the lightest of duties, with short watches to which all the other officers and non-commissioned officers had rallied behind him, standing in as he had always eventually tired, as all knew he would; yet his spirits had remained undiminished, his commitment was unflagging and his enthusiasm could not be challenged. He was always under the eye of Jelbert who took particular care to speak with him whenever Mower was on duty, appearing as if innocently to discreetly check on his strength, his ability to sustain his watch; and it seemed to all observers that Jelbert had adopted an almost fatherly interest in the young lieutenant. Clumsy Dalby, too, seemed oft in attendance whenever even the lightest of physical burden was imposed on Mower, every man aboard understanding that he remained weak and it would be months yet before his strength returned, his muscles having wasted in inactivity.

'Check!' the emphatic announcement from Pat as he stamped his queen hard on the board, the bottles shivering. He refilled his glass, looked up to Mower with sublime satisfaction in his face. Triumph was brief, shockingly so: no hesitation from Mower, a long move by one of his four bishops blocked the attack, the bishop's destination defended by a knight.

'Damn!' Pat pressed on, unwavering, sacrificing a castle to take the bishop, then taking the revenging knight with one of his own; however, that was his undoing, his shifted knight betraying his defence; and the black queen swept in with a long board to take Pat's white queen. 'Checkmate!' pronounced Mower with great satisfaction.

Pat stared in muted disbelief for several seconds, eventually draining his glass. 'It may be that my intellectuals are not very bright this evening,' he declared after a long sigh; 'Congratulations, Mr Mower.' He looked up towards the door and shouted, 'Murphy!' The steward entered immediately. 'We will have our evening coffee, if you will... and bring the whiskey too.' Murphy nodded and left. 'Mr Mower,' said Pat, 'it is plain to me that your own intellectuals are not impaired by your wounds, and I commend you, I do, for your determination to serve...'

'Thank you, sir,' Mower replied, his voice nervous, a little of apprehension within it.

'Yet it is also clear to me that it will be some months before you will recover your fitness, your energies - ain't that so, Doctor Ferguson?'

'That would be my prognosis, yes,' said Simon quietly, also wondering where this was leading and mindful that he had voiced his similar concerns to Pat at breakfast.

'I am decided that you will exchange with Codrington and take command of *Eleanor*...'

'But sir...' Mower interjected.

'You will shift to *Eleanor* when we leave Argostoli... and you will remain with her for all the time when we may conceivably engage with Ottoman ships.' Mower looking crestfallen, Pat continued, 'Mr Mower, I do not care to contemplate losing you in any engagement on account of your weakness - that is plain to see - and neither would any man on the barky thank me if such happened... no, I will certainly not countenance that.'

'Sir,' Mower was crestfallen.

'It may be that the time will come when we need you back aboard the barky... but that time is not now. You can best serve me... and your shipmates by taking command of *Eleanor*. I need you there. I need Mr Codrington here. Am I plain?'

'Perfectly, sir,' Mower's face was a picture of dejection.

'Ah, Murphy, there you are.' Pat's stern demeanour relented. 'Gentlemen, will you take a whiskey with me, with our coffee?'

Wednesday 20th April 12:00   *south of Lisbon*

Surprise fairly raced south, sailing large with the customary northwest wind of that coast on her quarter, making a constant eight knots. The crew had joyfully embraced their return to the shipboard routine, to blessed normality as they saw things, and *Surprise* had run off five hundred miles from La Coruña in just two days. Mindful of the pronounced landward drift of the Portugal current, Pat had kept her far off the coast, particularly during the nights, ultimately a distant Cape St Vincent coming in sight off the port bow at noon as Pat took his sighting. 'Strike the bell, Mr Pickering.'

'Strike the bell, Dalby,' the order was relayed, Dalby ringing the eight bells. From that moment Pat stuck doggedly to his quarterdeck, attending despite his officers also being on watch, a general curiosity rising until, an hour later, Pickering voiced the question on the lips of all on deck. Simon, standing in attendance, looked on.

'Sir, I have succeeded Mr Macleod an hour ago... and I am aware that you have attended near all of his watch and much of Mr Mower's before that; I am sure that you do not doubt us, our competencies - at least to stand a watch - but is there something of particular significance which I must look out for?' A silent Simon stared, his curiosity piqued.

'Oh, I am sorry, Mr Pickering,' offered Pat, 'I am reflecting on something of a puzzle... a maritime mystery... mindful of something of significance which Admiral Pellew mentioned to me whilst we were dining... it was before we departed Falmouth for Devonport.' Pickering merely nodding, Pat began his explanation, '*Indefatigable* in the year '95, Pellew in command, struck an uncharted rock which was reported in his log as being off *Cape Finisterre*. It occasioned significant damage to *Indefatigable*, to her keel and side. With five feet of water in the hold, Pellew inspected the damage himself by going overboard and swimming down to inspect it. The damage - though he did not believe it threatened the loss of the ship - was such that she was making twelve feet of water an hour - *twelve feet!* That was much akin to what *Surprise* was making in the worst of the hurricane. The men were put to the pumps and she made Lisbon in three days for repairs, two months more passing until she could return to Plymouth. I have much reflected on this, on and off, ever since he mentioned it.'

'Pray continue,' prompted Simon, intrigued, Pickering staring.

'I ask myself: why did Pellew go all the way to distant Lisbon and not put into *La Coruña*? Spain was on our side at that time - doubtless you collect it was not until '09 that General Moore was chased out from that place - and it is the closest port of significance. Why did he turn *south* and why then pass by Vigo? Doubtless the wind may have been significant... and the coastal current is always southerly in those parts, though weak, but why then go on another eighty miles beyond Vigo to reach Porto?' Pat's voice was raised loud by now, 'And then why continue even further, on to Lisbon, another one hundred and seventy miles south of Porto?' No reply from his audience, all bemused, Pat resumed, a little more quietly, becoming aware that all the men at the helm and as far forward as the waist were staring at him with keen interest. 'Lisbon is a very long way if you are shipping twelve feet of water an hour, would you not think? No, it does not make a deal of sense. Sure, Lisbon would be the nearest port for a ship in distress if approaching from the *south*, but certainly not from as far north as *Cape Finisterre*.' Pickering spellbound, Simon a little less sure about his geography, near wholly ignorant about all the ports of the Peninsula and saying nothing, Pat continued, 'We were enjoying our second bottle... in Falmouth... when Pellew reported to me that he had recently received reports from the Admiralty in response to his personal enquiries about this rock which *Indefatigable* had struck... and its absence from all charts. The Admiralty hydrographer, John Purdy, was in the course of publishing the new Atlantic chart and the notes thereto; he was in possession of a report of the brig *Briton* - Captain Stokes. Stokes had reported striking a rock twelve to fifteen leagues SSW of *Cape St. Vincent* in December of '21, all aboard taking to her boat, the brig lost; the crew, fortunately, were picked up. Purdy was also aware that some time before that the transport brig *Daedalus* had struck in the same location, was damaged and she had put into Lisbon for repairs... *into Lisbon;* do you follow?' Pat stared at his silent, staring audience in some exasperation, as if staring at imbeciles.

'Perhaps not exactly,' Simon mumbled, Pickering remaining silent, thinking hard.

'Well, don't you see?' exclaimed Pat, 'Could it be that *Indefatigable* did not strike off *Cape Finisterre* but struck off *Cape St Vincent*? Of course Pellew did not tell me that... his log recording the north cape... not the south. I have wondered since whether Pellew was minded or indeed trying to tell me something more... but could not quite bring himself to say it plain.'

'But why would that be, sir, and is that really possible?' said Pickering at last with considerable hesitation. 'Was not *Indefatigable* escorted to Lisbon... by Admiral Waldegrave if my memory serves me? I have read much of Pellew, of course; every junior officer has.'

'When *Surprise* was taking so much water I collect I had not the least care for my own log... and could it be... was it a mistake in writing up his log some time later, a simple mistake; and who cares to admit such... so many years later, eh?'

'Surely it must be doubtful that the log could be in error for three days?' said Simon. 'You are yourself most particular about scribing your own... though with an economy of words, I do concede.'

'Truth is the most valuable thing we possess,' said Pickering, the ship's wit, in a murmur, adding, 'and doubtless therefore there are times when we should be economical with it.' Blank stares from Pat and Simon.

'There is one other thing I remarked,' said Pat, continuing, 'Pellew's orders were to patrol for French ships *in the Bay*; that is to say from Bordeaux to Finisterre; so perhaps he did not care to report that he had, in fact, ventured as far south as Cape St Vincent? Why he would go that far south I have no idea. Was he following a ship or in search of something else? It is all surmising, of course, but I looked at Purdy's notes myself, and there is something to that effect... from a Captain Livingston: he reports that he was informed by *"a very respectable Royal Navy officer who was present at that time, and whose name he did not care to mention"* that *Indefatigable* struck off *St Vincent* and not, as recorded, off *Finisterre*.' Blank faces all round and Pat concluded, 'Well, 'tis a rum affair, no doubt. Perhaps if the man did not care to mention his source by name then there was something fishy about it. I collect... was it not Lisbon where Pellew pressed his fiddler - Emidy - *pressed indeed*, hah hah.'

Not the least reply forthcoming, Pat blinked, adding, 'I like a good story, well told; that is why sometimes I am obliged to tell it myself.' Blank stares of incredulity all round, and Pat, visibly deflated, moved on, 'So, gentlemen, we are here and looking for the mysterious rock; 'tis named the *Daedalus Rock* after the brig sunk by it. Purdy said there had been a rock recorded on French charts before their revision of '86, when it was omitted. No recorded sightings of it since had led all cartographers, theirs and ours, to the view that it did not exist. Pass the word, Mr Pickering, to the men at the tops. I do not care to see *Surprise* suffer the same fate as *Daedalus* or *Briton*.'

Thursday 21st April 1825   10:30   off the eastern Algarve

No sightings made of the mysterious rock, Faro left astern and the fresh meat having all been eaten by distant Cape St Vincent, *Surprise* hove-to amidst the Portuguese fishing fleet to buy their catch of tunny fish, Sampays negotiating the purchase of a half-dozen grand specimens.

'Duncan, our guests are dining at my table today,' said Pat as they shared second breakfast, *Surprise* rocking gently on the mildest of swell. 'Will you kindly explain their purpose... and that of your visit to Russia? The orders I received in Falmouth from Melville were simply to take them aboard and to convey them to Greece... where our old friend, Mavrocordato, will accept their cargo, the infernal great press... and damnably heavy it is too. Why, Sampays ain't stopped puling about it since we left home; he reckons the barky is down near half a fathom at the bow, and the master don't like it neither, him and Barton lamenting she is a trifle slow to answer the helm.'

'I can tell ye now, Pat... now we're at sea. I would have explained all in Falmouth, though I didnae know the whole tale myself, Melville leaving sealed orders for me also. D'ye collect the last of the kentledge comin' aboard... much later than the rest - with Perkis, the man himself?'

'Yes, now that you mention it. It occured to me at the time that something was a trifle strange, the late final delivery... a rum affair.'

'Well, those last twae dozen of pigs were... was *Eleanor's* ballast, taken aboard in Kronstadt, her iron taken out and the new crates stowed below to replace it.'

'What? Her ballast taken out? Out? It was exchanged? Changed for what purpose, tell?'

'Aye, swapped out; it was so.' Duncan paused as if wondering how to explain the strangest of tales. 'Will we take a dram, before I continue?' he hedged, still thinking fast. Pat would not be swayed, urged him to explain. 'The new ballast, the ingots... 'tis nae iron.'

'WHAT! Not iron? Has the world turned upside down and nobody told me?' Well, what the devil is it?'

'I grant ye it looks like iron, but that is - so I am told - a plating of iron.'

'Plating?' Pat's mind grasped for but failed to find any sense in the strange tale. 'And what is it that is plated, tell?'

'Gold...' Duncan was whispering now, mindful of the likelihood of Murphy listening behind the door. '*Gold*. Three and a half tons of gold.'

Pat, after gasping a very full intake into his lungs, his eyes as wide as ever they would be, exclaimed in a loud voice, 'Mother of God! May all the saints preserve us!' An instant recollection of Perkis's suggestion of cutting all the new kentledge ingots in half came rushing to his mind: to reduce weight, to assist the crew's handling of them, so he had said. Pat did not know the relative weight of gold to iron, but he knew enough to know, from the very rare occasions when he possessed a modest pocket of golden guineas, that gold was heavy, heavy indeed; it was far, far heavier than iron: the true purpose of Perkis's apparent benevolence was revealed. 'Three and a half tons?' he whispered, as if such news was akin to Saint Patrick himself coming aboard.

'Aye, in twenty-four ingots.'

'Duncan, tell me...' Pat recovering a litle from the shock, 'What is the value of the... the... *this cargo*?' Pat's own mind was swiftly adjusting to the possibility, the strong possibility; indeed, the likelihood of Murphy's ear at the door.

'Half a million of pounds.'

'Oh my God!' then silence, Pat's mind trying but failing to come to terms with a sum of such colossal magnitude. A new frigate, off the stocks and all fitted out for sea, might cost somewhere in the region of fifty thousand pounds, even in these days of grossly excessive inflation, and that was as much as he could imagine.

'The Tsar has provided it,' Duncan continued, Pat simply staring, 'and we are to take it to Mavrocordato... *to Mavrocordato alone*, and he is to receipt it, nae other person. Seemingly he has nae taken sides in the civil war.'

The knock on the door preceded Murphy's entrance, a straight face and no clue given as to whether he had been listening to the tale of money beyond the dreams of all aboard the ship, a sum beyond all imagination, though Murphy could imagine quite a lot. 'Beggin' your pardon, sorrs, Wilkins says dinner will be at two bells. Will I set the table? Will ye care for a bottle or two?'

'Yes... yes, Murphy... please do set the table...' Pat, stirring, nodded to his steward. 'We will take a bottke of sherry to begin, if ye will. Thankee. Oh, and bring whisky for Mr Macleod... for *Captain* Macleod.' Murphy left.

'*Mister* Macleod will suffice, Pat, when I am here as your First. I dinnae care to hear *Captain* Macleod, if ye please.'

'What? Oh... I see... a capital notion, Duncan, yes... indeed; *Mister* Macleod it is. You will join my dinner table, Duncan? Simon is attending.'

'Aye, for sure I will, Pat... 'tis a long time since I enjoyed fresh tunny.'

'Well, best get underway. Will we go on deck? I must take the sighting.' The huge specimens of tunny fish had been hauled aboard when they reached the quarterdeck: one to be shared between the captain's table and the gun-room, with five for the men. *Surprise* moved away amidst friendly waves and farewell shouts from the fishermen.

'A fine purchase, Mr Sampays; well done. Please to send one directly to my cook; it will serve admirably for my dinner today. I doubt my guests will care for salt pork.'

'Of course, sir,' Sampays face displayed an unconcealed concern, something on his mind, necessitating words. 'Sir, if I may... it is in my thinking to shift about some of the shot for the guns in the hold...'

'And she won't hold so close to the wind neither,' added the master who had been listening with interest, keen to get his bit in.

'... she is down at the bow, and the helm ain't serving properly... ain't exactly right... so, sir, I intend to do what I can below, that is... with your permission,' the bosun concluded.

'Please do, Mr Sampays... do as you think fit.' Doubtless it would serve as a temporary measure pending more time to stow all below again, perhaps to shift further aft one or more of the new and grossly heavy iron water tanks; Pat was fully behind the bosun, for *Surprise* had, in his own observation, a tendency to answer her helm more slowly, to fall off the wind a little when on a bowline - more so than he recalled before - and that was something of a minor disappointment to him after the comprehensive refit at Devonport.

'Very good, sir, and thankee,' declared the bosun, resolute approval resonating plain in his voice.

Dalby rang eight bells and Pat took the noon sighting. Another half-hour passing in no time at all, Pat stepped down to the coach, thinking of reminding Simon of the imminent dinner, of checking on his friend's attire, which he imagined Simon could not conceivably have considered. Pat was astonished to find he was wrong, Simon had indeed dressed for dinner. His chin was daubed with a half-dozen of tiny paper fragments to dry the blood from his shaving cuts and he stood in a new shirt and breeches; admittedly they did appear to be several sizes too large for him: the shirt baggy, sleeves rolled up, the breeches hauled up high by his braces. 'Simon, I confess I am taken aback. I have been greatly shocked once this morning and now is the second occasion. Here I am, expecting to see you looking like an escapee from the Fleet or the Marshalsea, as is your custom,' Pat laughed out loud, 'and yet I find you are garbed in your finest! Indeed, I did not conceive that you possessed anything other than vestments more in the line of rags, eh? You being an untidy cove! Have you mended your ways at long last, tell?' Pat laughed again and slapped his thigh; he always enjoyed his own jokes, however feeble.

'Nothing so merits reforming as the habits of others,' Simon replied, testily.

'Pray explain your regenesis - perhaps I should better say your *clean slate*,' Pat laughed out loud, 'if you will.'

'Have a care, if you please, Pat. These new clothes are gifts... from a dear and most generous individual of my acquaintance. The outfitters in Oban did not possess my exact size. It pleases me to wear them for the first social occasion in near fifteen years with my old friend Peddler.'

'A generous individual did you say... and in Oban? Who would that be, tell?' Pat could not contain his curiosity.

'It was my intention to mention it beforehand, but the occasion did not arise. I have granted the accommodation of my house in Tobermory to my sister-in-law... that is to say Agnes's sister, Flora. She has two daughters, quite the loveliest of bairns, and they are without a home - *were* without a home until they shifted there.'

'Why that is the most benevolent thing, brother; I commend you with all my heart and soul, I do indeed.' Pat slapped Simon enthusiastically on his back.' Simon silent, Pat detected something more, something reserved, unspoken; 'And?' he prompted.

'I had thought such was impossible, could never be... but I find I am... that is to say... I am in contemplation of...'

'In contemplation of what? Come now... out with it if you will.'

Simon looked up from study of his hands, his face one of consternation shifting towards the merest hint of a smile, an eventual whisper forthcoming, 'I am in contemplation of... of marriage.'

'My dear friend... my dearest friend...' Pat seized Simon's hand, pumped it with excruciating force, 'I am delighted... uncommon delighted... my congratulations... may Saint Patrick and all the saints bestow blessings forever upon your house. God bless you! Murphy! Murphy there! We will split a bottle of champagne, eh?'

'No!' Simon exclaimed. 'Not now. Pat, I share this confidence with you, but it is not in my intention that it should become generally known. It is a trifle soon, and - as is generally acknowledged - there can be many a slip twixt cup and lip.'

'Of course... certainly; I will not say a word about it, not one,' Pat whispered, waving his incoming steward away, 'Murphy, 'tis nothing.' A minute's pause and Pat resumed, 'Simon, I have long dreamed of this day... your finding of another... another love. I have never spoken of my hopes... mindful of the depth of your black feelings... that is to say in the matter of the loss of your beloved Agnes, but I always did cherish the dream, the blessed dream that you would... would emerge from that long despair... to find another love, I did so.'

'Thank you, Pat,' whispered Simon, his eyes moistening.

'We must be careful to find in our experiences the wisdom that is in there, and stop there...'

'I have not the least doubt of it,' Simon replied after a momentary hesitation, significant doubt in his face, Pat rarely coming it the philosopher; at least rarely successfully, save to his own way of thinking.

'... lest we be like the cat that sits down on a hot stove-lid.'

'Mmmm,' murmured Simon, striving to express accord, his understanding of where Pat was going wholly foundering.

'She will never sit down on a hot stove-lid again...'

'Doubtless not. Felines, despite their popular perception as curious animals, are certainly cautious creatures.'

'... and that is well, but neither will she ever sit down on a cold stove-lid anymore.'

'No... I suppose not,' Simon pondered, a long pause, 'I think I see... the merit of the analogy; yes... and appropriate it is, I concede. Thank you, brother.'

'Allow me to walk with you into the cabin; Murphy will be fetching our guests any moment. My congratulations again, dear friend... Would you care to remove those scraps of paper from your chin?'

Pat, standing at the cabin door, Simon at his side, welcomed his guests for dinner: Duncan, Pickering, Perkis and Peddler; everyone settling at the table when Murphy busied about pouring the sherry. It was a reserved start, little said other than pleasantries, Perkis perhaps trying to avoid any gaffes, his comments on the quarterdeck and best practice when upon it explained to him subsequently by Simon.

Duncan raised his glass, 'With your blessing, sir, I will omit the traditional toast - I dinnae think 'tis one for today - in favour of one from the Isles?' Pat nodded, he did not care for any mention of it either, "A bloody war" being the traditional Thursday toast. 'A wee few words from the man, Robbie Burns, first, if I may?' Nods all round. 'Wherever I wander, wherever I rove, 'tis the hills and the isles forever I love. Aye, and so it is.' Polite clapping. 'So, to the toast: may ye never want a friend or a dram to give him.'

'Thank you, Mr Macleod, an admirable toast indeed,' declared Pat with feeling. Eventually, the soup consumed and the merest hint of relaxation coming upon the table, Freeman and Murphy returned with the tunny: half of the fish, cut from head to tail and laid out on a long silver tray, the bone removed, the skin crisped; the whole resting in melted butter, diced garlic and herbs floating within the pool; the whole fish surrounded by scores of boiled potatoes. The rising aroma was divine, loud murmurings of appreciation general, every mouth watering in glorious anticipation. 'Doctor Ferguson, would you care to carve; your proficiency is greater than mine, and doubtless we would not care to see that fish swimming again... across the table... fleeing from my knife and casting the butter upon us all!' Pat laughed out loud, more than a little gratified to hear a gentle murmur of humourous accord from everyone else, for it had been hard going thus far, not a great deal of conversation aired; indeed, he had wondered for how long the occasion might endure, the guests looking particularly glum and, unusually, no humorous quips from

Pickering, not a one. The rather restrained ambience did not dampen appetites however, Peddler's particularly; for with his health perfectly restored, as Pat noticed, he ate a great deal of the tunny, returning for second helpings, his hand and attentions wavering towards thirds, as Pat further observed, time grinding on in dreary fashion until the dinner was eventually all consumed. Simon plainly had other thoughts on his mind, as Pat knew, and Duncan, unusually, had not been much help since the toast. At least, Pat thought, if sacrifices were made and the pudding, for which he himself was properly set up for a considerable portion, could be passed over then his own day might be saved by the ultimately forthcoming port, though whether he could endure the tedium for that much longer he had his doubts.

Murphy appeared, and much to Pat's relief his question was spoken in restrained fashion; perhaps he had observed the muted ambience, seen that Pat's interest, his attention at the table was sinking. 'By your leave, sir, will 'ee care for the figgie-dowdy?'

Pat relented, his learned stomach in anticipation overruling his hesitant mind; he whispered his instruction in Murphy's ear as his steward waited to collect the empty plates - to bring only the smallest of portions of the pudding; it would be too much of a tragedy, it having been prepared, not to indulge in at least a smattering, but then to shift as quickly as decency allowed and without a moment lost to serve the desperately anticipated port.

'Captain O'Connor,' Perkis at last offered his belated contribution as Freeman set down the bottles, 'I am with child to hear all about your gold mine. Will you indulge me, sir?'

Pat brightened just a very little, poured the port in haste, 'Oh, 'tis not a fully producing mine... no, not yet at least... 'tis early days, I make no doubt. The excavation is not long underway.'

'But there is a positive prognosis, surely so?'

'Why of course. The promoters... experienced people from Dublin... explained that it was merely a matter of time before their new technique produced bountiful quantities of gold from the anticipated heavily-laden ore.'

'Their new technique? A wholly proven method, I trust; one that assuredly will produce a worthwhile... a *valuable* result?'

'Yes, of course... well, proven at least to their satisfaction. They explained it was a most carefully researched process, a secret one, never used in other parts, in other mines; so they said. I confess I did not fully retain the principles of it. You metallurgists, I am sure, will be familiar with the method; it involves copulation.'

A shocked silence all about the table, save for Duncan who laughed loud and hearty for an embarrassing ten seconds, ultimately spluttering to a halt as the discomfiture reached even him, Peddler eventually speaking, 'You doubtless refer to cupellation, Captain.'

'I dare say... yes, that too.' Pat brazened it out, 'Boundless quantities of gold will doubtless emerge when the furnace is set up in proper fashion.'

'Then it would appear that your mine would present the perfect collateral, sir,' Perkis resumed. 'Did you give any thought to the idea of other investments... in the market... since we spoke at Christmas time?'

'Not a great deal, I confess. I have been greatly pre-occupied with the restoration of the ship and the recovery of those of the men who were wounded.'

Neither the ship's state nor the wounded seemingly interesting Perkis, he continued, 'An unprecedented opportunity is open to us, Captain: the banks are presently lending copiously to individuals of standing... with an evident respectability - such as yourself.'

'I have not the least doubt that you have a far, far better understanding of finances, of money-matters than I; that is plain. However, a man in my position, in my particular circumstances has much else to consider before any notions of investment can be entertained; I'm sure you understand.'

'Why, a captain in the Royal Navy must surely be the perfect client of any bank, eh?'

'I am not wholly with you, sir,' said Pat, recollecting his small bowl of figgie-dowdy, his thoughts wondering towards whether any of it might have survived within the galley for later, and his interest in investment fast waning.

'Why, sir, you are at sea for much of the time, no doubt. Precious little communication and no opportunity of dithering in the matter of *will I take the money out or leave it in? Will I switch from Consols, Navy Fives or even Poyais stock?* Yes, I venture you could borrow a great deal on the back of your mine for new and further investment. I would be perfectly delighted to advise you.'

'I am obliged to you, Mr Perkis, and I am sure your advice is sound, but in the matter of investment my mind is not entirely made up; I see the market has peaked, is off a long way from the 390 it was in January.'

'That is the natural cyclical up and down of the short term; profit-taking it is, a natural greed overcoming the better sense to leave the investment in place. I have not the least doubt it will be rising to reach not less than, say, 500 come the month of May.'

'A man oft has a desire to have more of a good thing than he needs,' observed Pickering, his first words for some time. Pat nodded in welcome acknowledgement, grateful for small mercies.

'Mr Perkis, there is another matter which must be considered; so I have heard of late,' Pat resumed. 'Within those few people in the mercantile community with whom I speak of stores, supplies, foodstuffs for the ship and suchlike, I have heard a deal of troubling talk about the prospect of banks being exposed to hasty withdrawals, particularly after upsets such as this recent fall in the market; and the prospects for them failing is worrying; I confess it troubles me. Not that I have a deal of money anywhere on deposit at the present time.'

'It is absolute balderdash, I do assure you. The fundamentals have never been stronger...'

'I'm sure there is something in what you say, and were all to believe the same, to think alike, then where would be for all love? After all it is the differences of opinion that makes for a horse race, eh?'

Pat's drift into equine directions presenting some difficulty for Perkis to follow up, he simply scratched his head; 'Quite so, Captain O'Connor,' he said eventually. 'Perhaps we will speak more of this another day.'

'Certainly, sir; and I would be most grateful was you to develop your investment proposals at greater length,' Pat was tiring of the matter, 'and in your own time at your convenience.' He paused momentarily, 'and in your own cabin,' he thought, but did not add. 'What I would particularly value at present is coffee, a cup of it, that is... I do not speak of the crop, of investment in the Brazils, no... I would give a day's pay for a cup. Murphy! Ah, there you are; a pot of coffee if you will.'

The dinner finally faltered to its welcome end, at least as far as Pat was concerned, and, when his guests had all eventually departed, he sat by himself reflecting on the table conversation until, tiring of it, he considered briefly whether he might make an attempt upon Bocherini's 3rd movement of his *Cello Concerto in B flat*, the cheerful *Rondo*, but he discarded the idea in favour of an hour in his cot. He lay back, drifted off to that frustrating intermediate state between the restfulness of sleep and tired wakefulness, his thoughts flickering between focus and diffusion, flitting between his men, his ship and his own aspirations for them all; his mind puzzling over Perkis and Peddler, their true purpose, whether they were trustworthy or possessed more nefarious intentions. No conclusions coming to deliver him to either of grateful sleep or alert clarity, he summoned Murphy to bring him a pot of coffee. He lit a cigar and sat smoking on the stern gallery, taking an occasional sip from his cup, alternately savouring the aromas and the tastes of his cigar and his coffee. The clamorously loud ringing of the bell finally disturbed him, and he stepped up to the quarterdeck. He could feel the enduring warmth in the late afternoon, the evening approaching, a softening in the light pressaging the close of the day; he gazed all about him, studied the men at the helm, his eyes wandering to Pickering conversing with Mower near the wheel, Prosser standing by; he gazed up, momentarily admired the new canvas once more, smelled the still-pungent aroma of the new hemp of the rigging; he nodded to those of his men who looked towards him, a sense of all being well with his ship settling upon him, a contentment with his men coming to him, his confusion of thoughts subsiding; yet the small feeling of minor anxiety, of uncertainty would not wholly leave him. 'Infernal scoundrel,' he eventually muttered to himself.

Surprise sailed on, close-hauled and making long boards against the presence of an increasingly warm *Levanter*, Pat's eyes adjusting as the light faded, the customary noises of the ship becoming more prominent to the senses as dusk slipped away to darkness; he gazed up into the eastern sky, more and more stars becoming prominent, bright within the black infinity before the bow, and an awareness of his utter insignificance settled momentarily upon him, a vacancy entering his mind, before his thoughts shifted once again to images of his wife, his children. No, he was not insignificant, and that conclusion was more precious to him at that moment than any he could ever recollect.

Chapter Eight

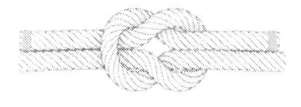

Sunday 1st May 1825   6:00   *Approaching Sicily*

The clang of four bells ringing stridently brought a drowsy Pat up to his quarterdeck. A consistent warmth in all the hours of the days and nights since distant Cadiz, far in *Surprise's* wake, had blessed him with little sleep; he yawned, stretched out his arms and stepped forward to lean on the waist rail. He stared at the sea state, distant cloud to larboard just becoming visible in the pre-dawn twilight, the familiar stars fading in the increasing light as the lingering last vestiges of night ceded to the dawn. At the beginning of the rising of the sun, a few minutes later, he gazed all about him, an indistinct and distant outline of the bulk of Etna emerging off the port bow. A half-hour later and Murphy brought him a welcome flask of coffee, Pat demurring from the offer of his first breakfast. Eight bells and the end of the watch, Pat remained on deck, deep in thought and no interruption to his solitary deliberations save for the odd "good morning, sir" from the members of the incoming watch to whom he offered a vaguely affable smile and a nod; until 'Good morning, Pat,' the familar voice intruded into his musings as a bleary-eyed Simon stepped from the companionway.

'Good morning, Simon,' the reply was offered by rote, for Pat's mind remained pre-occupied with an undefined yet lingering sense of concern, the cause of which he could not pin-point; it nawed away in the background of his conscious thinking, intruded into his concentration, his focus on any task; and because of it he had remained ill at ease since the unsatisfactory dinner with Perkis and Peddler, his recollections of that dolorous occasion rekindling the sense of disquiet he could not shake. 'Oh that the wind might seize and take my concerns as the *Levanter* lifts those gulls... there off the port beam... the *port* beam,' he pointed.

'*Ichthyaetus*, yes, I see them now; Audouins, I venture; the wing tips are the clue. You have been listening too long to Mower, Pat. I dare say poetry does not presently number amongst your considerable talents,' Simon laughed. No response save for a frown from Pat, he continued, 'Your unsatisfactory cerebrations... *your concerns*... to what do you refer, brother?'

'I understand that you were... *are* since childhood great friends with Peddler,' said Pat hesitantly, 'but what do you know of Perkis?'

'I do not personally know the man, but Peddler speaks well of him, tells me he is a man of substance, a thinker - in the commercial sense - of some considerable ability... has spec... *invested* in the market with success; indeed, he has cleared thousands this past twelvemonth.'

'And you are sure... *entirely sure* that your confidence in Peddler himself is well placed?' Pat frowned.

'Why, Pat, we grew up together as bairns; we ran barefoot across the cobbles of Tobermory's streets as children, we shared as if brothers any indulgence which befell us; and, since the age of nine, we played chess after church on Sundays and every evening through the dark of long winters.'

Pat nodded, his expression one of reluctance, a weighty consideration pressing heavy upon him, or so it seemed to Simon. 'Perkis... he has pressed me to invest in the market... with *him*... says he has made profits far, far beyond handsome... uncommon vast profits.'

'Benjamin Peddler has vouched for him, for his integrity... at least to me; but, I regret to say, I have little or nothing to invest myself - not that I am so disposed, I hasten to say. The small funds at my disposal, the *very small funds* remain in the Plymouth Dock Bank where I may call on them at a moment's notice in the possible eventuality of an unanticipated need at home... in Tobermory. I am mindful that I have incurred an obligation there... one, I must add, which I mind not the least.'

'Yes... yes, I wholly understand, I do,' said Pat, 'but as to Perkis and his investment proposal, I am minded to keep to those matters that I am familiar with; that is to say solely *ships*; I will not say *potatoes*,' Pat laughed out loud.

'And gold mining.'

'Oh come, Simon... is a man not entitled to a modest flutter, the smallest of investment... when it rests within his hands... his grasp, his *very close* grasp?'

'I dare say, but in the matter of investment, speculation and the like I am a mere babe in arms; I possess of not the slightest of knowledge; and in the matter of money generally I am a veritable ignoramus. Pat, forgive my pontificating any opinion on matters of which I have not the least credibility... but is not your money less likely to be diminished *and perhaps entirely lost* if invested in the market rather than in digging a prodigious vast hole, one of a size sufficient to cast within your entire wealth? Is that not the case?'

'No, that ain't the case. The venture... *the mine* is not yet afloat... *underway*... so I am told, but Thomas Weaver himself has visited, has expressed an interest in taking a share.'

'Who is Weaver?'

'He is the great man from the Croghan Mountain... from Wicklow, the manager of the mines there; he possesses a fortune made from the lead of the mines.'

'That's as may be, but Pat... I collect lead never has been turned into gold... though many have sought the alchemist's process.'

Pat stared, unsure if Simon was jesting at his expense, 'There may be a deal of stone to be shifted, so I am told, before we have prospects of finding the gold vein.'

'Then perhaps Perkis may also help you find the Philosopher's stone?' declared Simon brightly, smiling.

'Eh? Are you making fun of me?' Pat stared suspiciously. 'Perkis... what am I to make of the fellow? His proposal sits ill on my mind, so it does.'

'That is the very same conclusion I reached myself,' offered Simon agreeably, 'though previously I would not presume to articulate such, nor indeed precisely why that engenders my own disinclination. However, in the matter of monies I will say that I am minded that there are two times when a man should not speculate...' Pat simply staring, Simon continued. 'The first is when he cannot afford it...' this said with a huge grin on Simon's face.

'Infernal clever, Simon...' Duncan appeared at that moment to replace Pickering on watch. He caught Pat's eye, nodded to Pat and Simon before stepping over to the helm to replace his colleague. Pat's attention returned to his friend, 'And the second?'

'When he can,' Simon laughed out loud.

Pat sighed, 'I confess I have reservations, Simon... reservations. In fact I have decided I will not countenance his damnably clever pecuniary schemes... no, I will not. There is something... *something* about the fellow... yet the high and the mighty of the City have placed their confidence in him *and your friend*... have placed a deal of confidence in him, uncommon plenty of it.'

'To what particular confidence do you refer, dear?'

'Why -' Pat stopped abruptly, recalling his own confidences, his orders, the secrecy of the true cargo, and he decided to say nothing of the gold. 'Why, the Treasury has asked them to press the new Greek coin. That is the reason we are conveying that monstrous great weight in the hold, the press... a coin press it is. Greek sovereigns, ha ha.' At the mention of the word "sovereign" the men on the deck edged closer, as unobtrusively as such could be achieved, Simon glancing towards the nearest. 'Perkis showed me one, the model for the... the production,' Pat continued, 'At least he said it was. It carries the image of the phoenix, a bird of these parts... if my memory serves me - Simon?'

'It is certainly a bird of Greek origin, brother... a particularly long-lived one, though decidely rare.'

'No doubt; I have never seen one.'

Duncan approached, the gunner in his train, 'Good morning sir, Doctor Ferguson. Mr Jelbert has a matter for your consideration, if ye care to hear it.'

'Good morning. What is it, Mr Jelbert?'

'Sir, I have been a'thinkin'... of the guns... on what will aid us when we might face a deal of Turk ships,' said the gunner hesitantly.

'Please... go on.'

'Well... the men have told me of the Greek fireships an' the fear the Turks have of them.'

'Yes...'

'Fire... 'tis every mariner's nightmare. I have been thinkin' hard on the matter of fire... the fear of it, and how fire might serve us,' declared Jelbert, warming to his subject. 'There is an ancient weapon... one of fire...'

'Yes, yes; indeed there was; why, you are thinking of Greek Fire!' exclaimed Pat, and more quietly, 'Would that we possessed the secret, eh?'

'The secret?' Simon interjected.

'A liquid fire it was, heated by a furnace and projected by a bellows mounted at the bow. The secret was the recipe, the ingredients... that is not known, never was... save for those few in Constantinople who created it. I regret to say the secret is long lost...' a reflective pause, 'but perhaps that is for the better; after all, it was the Turks who possessed that particular menace.'

'I conceive it would have been the most fearsome threat,' said Simon with an immediate surge of despond, the surgeon within him imagining the dire burns and wounds such a horror would inflict.

'Why, with such a weapon I doubt there is a ship would stand against us... *Greek Fire*... 'tis but a dream, Mr Jelbert; a grand one, I give you that.'

'Sir, that ain't exactly my idea.'

'Go on; what is your notion, tell?'

'I am minded that one of the ingredients of Greek Fire... one which *is* known, was sulphur... from the island over there,' Jelbert nodded to port, '... from Sicily. Were we able to mix sulphur with tar and best red powder, then something of similar ilk might be fashioned.' He paused, Pat deep in thought, 'We have the powder... an' plentiful tar.'

'That's as may be, but we have no bellows, no furnace, no projector,' Pat mused, thinking aloud, his interest stirred.

'The guns, sir... it is; I venture such a mixture would give a spectacle of fiery flame, great clouds of smoke and a... a fair thunderous noise. It would create a fear which must be to our advantage.'

'To be sure, it might so,' declared Pat, hesitating, 'and flame is good, noise is frightening, but it is the ball that does the work.'

'Exactly so, sir! The ball it is... the shot. I am minded 'tis something that can be made... with the mixture within, which begins to burn only as it strikes... to set sails and rigging afire.'

'An explosive and flaming shot! Why, I don't doubt you may have something there, Mr Jelbert; t'would be the ball from hell! Sulphur you say? From Sicily?'

Thursday 5th May 1825   12:00   Approaching Cephalonia

'Michael,' murmured Simon abstractedly as they reviewed the medical stores and cleaned the surgical instruments, 'Have you considered long on immortality?'

'Ours, no. We are precious, certainly, but transient is a word which better suits our particular case. Of the immortality of the soul, I do believe in that, yes... many millions do, always have.'

'They have also believed the world was flat.'

A long pause before Marston resumed, 'Is there something troubling you, dear colleague?'

'I have been reflecting on my past wife, my beloved, *my dear Agnes*. She is oft in my thoughts.'

Marston remained mute, lost for words; he stared momentarily at Simon's face, wondering about this revelation, this unexpected side of his friend. No conclusion reached, nothing more offered he resumed with determination to polish away the discolouration on the blade of the surgical saw he clutched, thinking hard.

A minute and Simon spoke again, 'I hope you will do me a kindness.'

'Why of course,' a frustrated Marston looked up, set down the trephine he was defeated by, more than a little annoyed by his inability to wholly cleanse away the tiny specks of rust: the damp of the hold did not serve the instruments well.

'It is something of a delicate subject, and I trust you will keep my confidence.'

'Most certainly,' Marston stared again at his friend, his face switching in an instant from that of surgeon's dismay for the poor quality steel of the bone saw to one of the receptive concern of the chaplain for his parishioner, his supplicant. 'There is no call for concern; one may say anything, anything at all to a man of the cloth... even the most extreme of statements, and such will go no further... save to our maker.'

'It is... it is a trifle early for... for consideration of... of the necessary motions, I make no doubt,' Simon's face clouded, his look of anxiety deepening.

'Never in life,' Marston smiled, merely the ghost of a smile, but sufficient in his experience with many within his nautical parish to coax the inevitable and reluctant confession. 'My dear friend, here we are today, and what are we about? Why, we are preparing our instruments for the bloody day which we fear... *we know* will come. An hour in preparation is worth a day unprepared; I am convinced of it. I prepare myself every Sunday with prayers for that eventual day which must come to us all. Tell me... surely your preparation will be for a lesser event? That is to say, one less daunting?'

'Yes, certainly it is that,' Simon smiled, a small lifting of his apprehensions, 'It is in fact a joyous event I wish to prepare for.'

'Marston beamed, much relieved, 'Then please allow me to hear of it, if you will.'

'It is not wholly sure... not yet certain, but I am minded to tread this particular path... if...if... That is to say... there is another party...'

'Yes?' in the most encouraging tone, and Marston smiled again.

'I am minded to take the vows... to marry again.' This was whispered, Simon's voice a meld of pleasure and apprehension.

'I am delighted to hear it, I am,' exclaimed Marston with obvious relief, adding after the briefest of reflection, 'Is this an imminent engagement?'

'No... no... I do hope, Michael, you will not suppose that this is a... a direction I have embarked upon lightly. I am a widower, as you know; indeed, I have never entertained the notion that anyone, any lady could replace my former... my most beloved Agnes, no... I could never have conceived such was possible.'

'My dear, dear Simon, we must not contemplate replacement; no, no. Such is wholly inappropriate, invalid... no, we must most certainly never conceive that substitution is the concept we embrace in such circumstances as these; rather it is *renaissance*, a *rekindling* of that essential being, that precious spirit which resides within all of us.'

'It was the tragedy of my life... losing Agnes... none greater. Even now I am mortally cast down to think of it.'

'I grant you it may seem that the fire of life on occasion burns low, low indeed... but I assure you, I do assure you that the precious flame never, never entirely goes out. Treasure your memory of her, certainly... but embrace - I am sure you will - your new love with all your heart.'

'I am grateful... most grateful for your most kind words,' said Simon, a little overcome and finding a deal of comfort in his friend's advice.

'For where would mankind be without wives?' Marston sought to cheer his friend, to lift his spirits, 'Why, we would be scarce, scarce indeed; and that is the truth of it - eh?' His gentle laugh produced another strained smile from Simon.

'She has two bairns, and I... I have no aspirations for more; it is not in my intention to add further to my household.'

'I will concede that children may appear to be, at certain times, a burden, but they are truly so very much more a blessing.' Simon looking unconvinced, Marston resumed, 'And who, may I ask, is the fortunate lady?'

'Why, her name is Mrs Flora MacDougall, a widow herself; she is the sister of my dear Agnes.'

'Oh dear,' exclaimed Marston in a sinking voice of the deepest dismay, as if his entire being was recoiling from the most unwelcome, the most repellant of discoveries.

'I beg your pardon,' huge concern and anxiety in Simon's voice. 'Michael? What is it?'

'My dear friend... my dear, dear friend... whilst I - *and our Lord* - would most certainly welcome your union with your new beloved... with Mrs MacDougall... it inflicts the gravest of pain upon me to say that I ... I cannot perform the ceremony. I am set back... much set back. I am deeply sorry.'

'Michael... why so? Do you object so much to the marriage of a widow and widower?'

'No, no... not at all... oh if that were simply the case... no...no.'

'I beg you will speak plainly,' fear in Simon's trembling voice.

'With an infinity of regret... I must tell you that the law prohibits a man marrying the sister of his deceased wife. There it is, and I confess that I struggle myself to avoid profanities when speaking of such an ill-considered notion.'

'Then the law is a damnable ass, and I do not share your reluctance for profanities,' exclaimed Simon in a fleeting explosion of anger before the burning outrage which wholly consumed him; ultimately a cold realisation rushing in, brutally quashing the rising hopes that he had nurtured for months, smashing upon his fragile spirit with unmitigated shock and violence.

Since the onset of darkness a half hour before, Pat was seated on the padded comfort of the stern gallery, his 'cello wailing with gusto, the bow flying as he strived for the sound he so much sought, each of several repetitions audible as Simon approached the cabin: a sequence of short fragments resonating, each varying higher or lower, faster then slower, all making plain the musician's frustration, his inability to settle upon the exact solution, his recall failing him, too little practice being greatly insufficient. 'Why there you are, Simon,' Pat set down his instrument with some small relief. 'I am for evermore in thrall to a fiddler I once heard in a roadside inn in the County Galway... many years ago when I was a young man... walking to Galway town. I collect his name was Mathew Keane... so it was, and he played the most sublime fiddle that ever reached my ears in all of Ireland. It haunts me now, and I cannot exactly find his sound. I try... from time to time, I do... when there is precious little else to do - not that such is often, mind... but it always eludes me, so distinctive it was...'

'Perhaps then you would better be served making your attempt upon the fiddle?' offered a glum Simon, 'To my ear the 'cello will never sound like its brother.'

'Yes, yes... there is something in what you say, no doubt,' murmured Pat, 'but the essential flow... the movement, the timing of it... the bow on the string, the lingering delay for a fleeting instant, then the touch, the pressure... and then the flash of the leaving note... gone! That it is I am seeking, the pleasure in that note, and it is damnably difficult to find.'

'It will come to you, no doubt... perhaps in your dreams, an unsettled night; that is when recall serves for potent effect... and practice, it is often said, makes perfect,' Simon offered this without the least conviction, for in Pat's case he did have his doubts.

'Will you take up your viola and we will play for an hour before supper? What do you think of another try for Bocherini, that 3rd movement - the *Rondo* - again? What do you say?'

'Perhaps later, my mind is turned elsewhere.'

'Well I find I am damnably hungry already myself,' Pat could not conceal his disappointment. 'Murphy! Murphy there!' he shouted. The shrewish face appeared at the door in an instant, a quizzical stare serving, no words uttered. 'Bear a hand there; toasted cheese for me and the doctor, and... a bottle of the claret, d'ye hear?'

Well, comin' up d'reckly, sorr, so it is,' the door crashed shut as the steward disappeared.

'I am heartily sorry to say, Simon... you look tolerably unhappy, you do. Will you at least sit with me and take a whet?' Pat put his 'cello into its case.

A silent two minutes passed, nothing more than sighs from Simon, his face a picture of depair, and Pat was looking to his friend with concern, with rising apprehension when Murphy returned bearing the wine. He poured two glasses without ceremony and set the bottle down on Pat's table, bringing the filled glasses. 'Well, here it be, sorrs.' He stared at Pat, no reply forthcoming; his eyes switched to Simon, his distress obvious, his head hanging. A silent nod from Pat and Murphy departed, the door closing much more quietly. They supped the wine for several minutes, Pat staring at his friend with dismay.

'I had hoped so much to be married again, Pat; it had seemed that the love of my life was returned, come back to me. For a time I thought myself the luckiest man of the world, I did.'

'What has happened, pray tell?' this in a hesitant low voice.

'Marston tells me... a cursed thing... he tells me a man may not marry his wife's sister.'

'What balderdash!'

'No, I wish it were not true; it is the law,' exclaimed Simon, 'and I am mightily set back. All my hopes for a future with Flora are gone... gone in the bleakest of instants...' His voice fell to a murmur, 'A dream had come to me... and now it is swept away... vanished.'

Pat O'Connor was never a speaker of the least proficiency; such as he did offer when explaining his reasoning was more often than not something of a muddle of several disparate and only vaguely connected elements, his listeners customarily struggling to understand his oft invented analogies, sometimes ones with only the most limited of foundations; but of understanding and sympathy he was never short; he hastened to refill the wine glasses, returned to place a hand on the shoulder of his friend. 'I am heartily sorry to hear that,' he whispered with infinite sadness.

Saturday 7th May 1825   09:00   Twenty miles north-west of Sphacteria

Pat and all his officers had taken to the deck since the dawn. In the three hours since, the men at the tops had reported many sightings of distant sail to the south, and Pat had decided to approach the island with the utmost caution. 'Mr Macleod, heave to and signal *Eleanor*. I am minded the time has come to speak with Codrington and Reeve. Summon all my officers to the cabin when they have come aboard.'

'Aye aye, sir.'

'Captain,' declared an anxious Perkis, present on the deck with Peddler and plainly aware that some form of crisis was at hand, 'may we... Peddler and I, attend you when you speak with your officers?'

'Mr Perkis, I regret these are military matters,' Pat was brief, his thoughts preoccupied, the smallest distraction unwelcome, 'We will speak later.'

'But sir... our cargo, if you will... its safety...' Perkis was ignored; Pat brushed by him and descended the companionway.

The ambience in the great cabin was expectant, nervous even; the several dozen of sail sighted abreast Pat's intended route south and thence into the great Bay of Navarino to the east of Sphacteria had sparked a tide of apprehension in many minds, a tint of fear encroaching. All of Pat's officers sat in silence around his table, looking to him for the inevitable decision they all anticipated. 'Gentlemen,' he began, 'it is plain that there is a deal of activity before us, a multitude of vessels reported by the topmen. Seemingly, so I was told in Argostoli, the Egyptians have since February landed an army at Modon, scarcely seven miles south of Neocastro; that is the port within the Bay of Navarino. That the Ottomans have not yet seized that town in all the weeks since February is near beyond belief. They have been bombarding it for some time with a battery of nine mortars from the heights to the north-east of the town. However, we will remain distant of the land,' Pat looked all about him before resuming, '... and far to the west of those ships... until we see the nature of them. Our orders are plain, gentlemen: we are here to find Prince Mavrocordato. The reports I have obtained in Argostoli lack a deal of clarity, but it is believed that he is somewhere in the regions bounding the bay and is there to bolster the defences of it, Neocastro particularly. The Egyptian general, Ibrahim, is besieging that town since several weeks. Hence, to find the prince it would seem we have no choice but to enter the bay and make our enquiries within Neocastro.' Pat unrolled a chart on the table. 'Here is Smyth's chart. The bay is a great horseshoe in shape, its mouth a half-mile wide to the south. It is bounded by Sphacteria... to the west,' Pat pressed his finger on the chart, '... a very small island, almost three miles north to south and a half mile at most - east to west, much less in most places. North of it is the Sikia Channel, a passage of negligible depth and sufficient only for no more than a boat; it separates the island from the mainland fortress of Old Navarin - still held by the Greeks. Neocastro, the port within the bay, is here, just inside the entrance... to the east on the mainland. That is where we are going.' Glum faces all about the table and Pat moved on without pause, 'Mr

Mower, you are to take command of *Eleanor*, Mr Reeve in attendance...' Mower's grunt was inaudible. '... and you will await my further orders whilst holding to the west of the Sikia channel. Have a great care, Mr Mower; I venture the Turk... or the Egyptian as he may be, if wishing to attack Old Navarin on the north side of that channel, must approach from the south; yet, since he is a mussulman, I dare say he may come up from anywhere. Mr Codrington, you will come aboard *Surprise* as Third.'

'Yes sir,' declared Codrington.

'*Eleanor* on the sea side of the Sikia channel will best aid us were we to become blockaded within the bay by the Egyptians,' Pat explained. 'Our leaving... the bay... with their fleet arrived will mean a sure engagement... and...' Pat's voice fell to a whisper, '... and our escape must be far from certain. In such circumstances I will send Mavrocordato - were we to find him, that is - through the channel in my boat to *Eleanor*... to you, Mr Mower.'

'Understood, sir,' Mower nodded slowly, the magnitude of the looming peril before them had become clear to every man.

'One last word,' murmured Pat, 'If we do not come out of the bay... in the event of the Egyptians having set upon us... you are to sail to Calamata on the Morea. It is still in Greek hands, so I was told in Argostoli. You will take a certain cargo we have been carrying for the Greek government. Prince Mavrocordato will be its recipient. Take care that you obtain a receipt for it from the man himself. Mr Perkis is familiar with the cargo. I will send it, in the ship's boats, out from the bay through the Sikia Channel. Am I plain?'

'Yes sir,' whispered an extremely downcast Mower.

Pat completed a hasty and solitary dinner as six bells of the afternoon watch rang out. He stepped up to his quarterdeck, the brightest of clear skies persisting as *Surprise* approached the southern extremity of Sphacteria, closing on the entrance to the bay. The ships observed earlier had presumably shifted far further south-west, blown by a weak northerly wind away from the island, their identities remaining unknown. As far as the topmen had been able to see, the two masts of every one of those vessels which they could still see all suggested that they were Greek brigs; any

Ottoman fleet - Turk or Egyptian - almost certainly would possess three-masted frigates, and none such had been sighted. The wind had fallen away to a gentle breeze, leaving barely a ripple on the water, without a single cloud in an unbroken blue expanse as the frigate, Greek flag flying, slipped close-hauled past the southerly point of Pylos Island, Neocastro bearing north-east, directly ahead. From far beyond Neocastro the dull boom of siege guns firing every five minutes or so was very audible, an obtrusive and seemingly so incongruous a backcloth to the perfect scene of tranquillity before them which was the great bay. Twenty minutes more and *Surprise* hove-to north-west of the port, letting go her anchor in twelve fathoms alongside two Greek brigs, another four brigs were visible, anchored a cable off the east coast of Sphacteria a mile away to the north-west. 'Please to ready my cutter, Mr Sampays,' cried Pat. 'Mr Macleod, double the topmen; each mast to possess a glass.'

'Very good, sir,' Duncan nodded.

'I am going ashore... for the shortest of time. Mr Jason, would you care to accompany me? I will need your services.' Within five minutes, Pat's men were pulling furiously for the quay in the launch, Pat noting a sense of anxious trepidation settling on all his men within it; perhaps his men had sensed his own.

'Mr Macleod,' cried Perkis, marching across the quarterdeck from the companionway, 'Where is Captain O'Connor? Where has he gone? To what purpose has he left this ship? I insist you tell me!'

Duncan, somewhat taken aback, stared at Perkis with a rising inclination towards dislike. He had never engaged with the man during the voyage to any great degree, had not really found that he cared to, and in the present moment he had no intentions of beginning. 'Mr Perkis, the captain seeks the man to receive...' he lowered his voice, '... to receive our... *consignment*. I dinnae care to say more about that, if ye please.'

'Aahh, I understand... and that person is here... in the town?'

'That is our understanding, but we cannae be sure.'

'I see, but those ships we saw... the reports of the Ottomans approaching... In here we are bottled up like the proverbial rats in the trap, surely so?'

'Mr Perkis... *sir*, there isnae a deal of wind as ye know, and neither we nor any other vessel can shift without it.' At this, Perkis scowled, nodded and stamped off to go below, his seething anger plain.

An hour gone, when Pat's launch returned, to be greeted by the expectant, curious faces of all his officers on the quarterdeck. 'Mavrocordato arrived and departed here on the 4th, so they said ashore, and he was yesterday at Old Navarin, at the fortress there. Seemingly it was attacked by the Egyptians without success yesterday, hence those sails we saw; and this morning some fifty-two Egyptian vessels were sighted at the mouth of the bay.' Pat scowled, 'Where the devil they are now is not known.' He took a draught of coffee from his mug, 'After Ibrahim had attacked Old Navarin, his forces also besieging that place from north of the fortress, Prince Mavrocordato is reported as having left that place to go ashore on Sphacteria... he will be there this very morning,' he declared. 'Those far brigs we see over there, four of 'em,' Pat pointed towards Sphacteria, 'have also shifted from here to carry a number of men to man the guns which have been landed to bolster the defences of the island.' He gazed all about him for several minutes in assessment, the merest light breeze from the north still prevailing. 'Haul her anchor, Mr Macleod, we are crossing the bay to the island, even though we may require sweeps.'

'Aye aye, sir.'

Close-hauled, *Surprise* was barely moving, shifting so very slowly. A half-mile on and she came about, every eye anxiously staring at the sails, for she had little way in the feeble breeze and no one could be sure whether she would come round or fall off the wind. Sail edges fluttering, the bow slowly turned and the ship slowed, near stopped; the rudder as hard over as ever it would go, she faltered, the spirits of all on deck sinking, and then, as if with the last feeble breath of the wind, the tiniest of gusts, she came round at last, slowly, so very slowly, until her bow pointed towards the distant Greek brigs near the Panagia Landing. Her flaccid sails beginning to be pressed aback, the wheel was swiftly turned to straighten her rudder, and *Surprise*, infinitely slowly, gained way: half a knot, a knot, a collective sigh of relief released by all. Inch by inch she closed upon the four brigs, half a cable or less from the island shore, passing by within twenty yards of them, friendly waves and shouted greetings offered by all on their decks as the frigate moved along at a snail's pace, her identity and her previous endeavours in the Greek cause well known to everyone aboard them. Pat ordered another turn, *Surprise* coming about once more and pointing towards the tiny islet of Kuloneski in the midst of the bay, which she approached at a crawl until it was just off her starboard bow, when she turned again, continued for another half mile and anchored. The slow series of short boards had taken her near two hours to make a bare two miles of northing. Now ensconced near the north-west corner of the bay, Pat felt the smallest degree of relief; for, were any Ottoman ships to seek to enter the bay and approach her, the northerly wind and two miles of sea room in which to manouevre would provide the tiniest shred of comfort.

'Mr Macleod, you will go ashore directly and find Mavrocordato. Take Mr Jason as interpreter and six men in the launch. Those four brigs lie in that place where you must go ashore, at the Panagia Landing; there is nowhere nearer, if anywhere else at all. Listen out for the signal gun and hasten back if you hear it... *with or without* the prince.'

'Aye aye, sir.'

'Mr Codrington, take the small cutter with six men and go through the Sikia Channel; endeavour to verify that *Eleanor* is there and awaiting us. Take lanterns, there is but two hours until the sunset.'

At that moment, Perkis and Peddler stepped out of the companionway, Simon, Marston and Jason in their wake. Stridently Perkis brushed by Pickering's ineffectual efforts to halt the procession, and they gathered in front of Pat, who glared with undisguised irritation plain on his face. 'Captain O'Connor, I must press you to explain your intentions. Here in this place... this *cage* for our vessel and our cargo... it is plainly unsafe; why, with reports of the Egyptian fleet abroad, they might arrive at any moment, and what then would become of us?' Peddler nodded vehemently in anxious corroboration; even Simon allowed the tiniest gesture to a nod, Marston and Jason looking on with faces of abject concern.

'Mr Perkis... gentlemen,' Pat adopted a mollifying tone, 'I beg you will allow me to carry out my duty as I see it. My orders are to find Prince Mavrocordato. He was not at Neocastro, but is reliably reported as being on this island before us. I have sent Mr Macleod ashore to find him. There is nothing more to be done save to wait their return. It is apparent, perfectly plain that there is no wind, and for want of wind we are unable to leave this place, but so mired will also be the Turk... the Egyptian. Hence, rest assured, there is no present danger, I do assure you.' The words were uttered with far more conviction than Pat felt. His audience all looking wholly unconvinced, Pat resumed before any interruption might be made, 'Mr Perkis, Mr Peddler, once we have embarked the prince, we will be away as fast as can be, to wherever he wishes to go... with our cargo - that is to say, *the press*. Now, gentlemen, if you please; I must beg you to leave the quarterdeck. I have matters to attend to - of some urgency.' The group moved away, a deal of muttering amongst them, but for the moment the anxiety was quieted, superficially at least, for Pat himself possessed grave uncertainties: Perkis was right, the bay was a trap, and *Surprise* was well and truly snared; fifty-two Egyptian vessels in the vicinity was not a matter to be taken lightly, but Pat could see no other course of action.

An hour passed by with no return of either boat party. From the quarterdeck Pat could see the Greek brigs anchored off the Panagia Landing; he could make out with his telescope his launch tied up there, empty. Murphy brought sandwiches and coffee for Pat and Pickering, both never shifting from the rail, Pat's eye glued to his glass, watching, looking over the whole of the bay, figures glimpsed on the distant Greek brigs, no activity there. The sun descending below the high cliff of Sphacteria, *Surprise* was plunged into shadow. A half hour remaining until sunset, the cutter returned from the Sikia Channel and Codrington hastened aboard. 'She is there, sir, *Eleanor* is there, a trifle north of west of the channel entrance, in fourteen fathoms; directly west the channel be shallow.'

'Thank you, Mr Codrington,' murmured Pat, 'That is welcome news. Go below and get a bite to eat; we may yet be busy this night.'

The long shadows lengthening further and no sight of Duncan's party, dusk descended, a myriad of insects buzzing all about the lanterns above and below deck, the air still warm, humid; the off-duty men went below with the deepest reluctance and only on Pat's order to gain what rest was possible before, as he anticipated, the busy day of the morrow. Indeed, he rather dreaded what might develop in the new day. For sure, the Egyptians were not going away. After a failed attack on Old Navarin the prior day and Neocastro under siege there could be no doubt that their fleet would return. He prayed it would not be in the morning. He wondered what on earth had happened to Duncan and his men: the island was tiny, not three miles from north to south and a slender finger of a quarter mile in width for the most part; it could not take long to find Mavrocordato. At last, as Barton rang four bells of the first watch, the launch was sighted, a tiny lantern glow illuminating it as it pushed off from the island's shore, approaching *Surprise* with tediously slow speed, or so it seemed to the scores of watchers on the deck, all gripped with curiosity, with keen anticipation and a rising sense of foreboding, one which had become general, every man conversing in little more than a whisper, as if to speak louder might carry to alert some unseen enemy, near but out of sight.

'Duncan, there you are,' exclaimed Pat with audible relief in his voice. 'Come below, to the cabin. Murphy, Murphy there!' The steward was behind him, no shout necessary. 'A sandwich for Mr Macleod and - tell cook - food for his men.' They hastened below, every man still on deck pressing about the other returnees, questions coming thick and fast. 'Did you find him... the prince?' Pat could not contain his anxiety and curiosity any longer, the question asked as they passed through the coach.

Duncan nodding, they sat at Pat's table. 'Aye, the man is there. We found him after a half-hour, nae longer. He is in the middle of the island. There's a battery there, four guns facing west out to sea and over a rocky shore. Nae cliffs, and doubtless a dangerous bottom of rocks for any vessel with any draft, but 'tis the place for a landing, for sure.' Duncan seized and bit into the sandwich as soon as Murphy hastened in to place the tray of food on the table, continuing to speak even as he chewed, his hunger necessitating such - as he saw things. 'There is another battery, the three guns brought by the brig *Aris*, brass 18-pounders, on the southern point of the island... to defend the entrance to the bay... and ninety seamen from the six brigs to fire all the guns. But there isnae enough of Greeks on the island, Pat, to defend it - excuse me,' he coughed, a particularly tough piece of gristly beef defeating his teeth, '... from a determined landing; nae, the place cannae be held with what men are there now. I tried to persuade him to leave with me, directly, but the man would have nae of that; he is a staying put with the defenders, so he said.'

'Damn!' shouted Pat, thumping his hand on the table. 'Then plainly our... our *cargo...*' Murphy returned at that instant, bearing a tray with glasses and the whisky he anticipated Duncan would call for, '... cannot be offloaded here, it would be a gift for the Egyptians.' Murphy's ears pricked up. 'Neither do I care to leave it in Neocastro, the town likely to fall in due course. What the devil is to be done, Duncan, eh?'

'I will go ashore on the morrow and will try again. Perhaps the man will by then have realised the island will surely be lost; maybe he will come off with me, or at least come off in one of the Greek brigs. Four of their captains were ashore all day. They've gone to advise on the defence of the island,' Duncan laughed loud in despondent fashion, 'aye, the defence... seven guns against a fleet, eight hundred of men against an army. Precious wee chance they possess. Tsamados, the captain of *Aris*, he agreed with me, Pat, as did the other mon... Votsis, aye Votsis, the captain of *Athina*. There is another Greek there... Sakhtouri; he is Governor of Neocastro, and the man in command on the island is General Anagnostara.' Duncan took a long draft of his whisky. 'There is also a philhellene, Count Santa Rosa, come from Old Navarin where the defenders of that fortress would take nae notice of his experience and advice as a professional soldier... he is a revolutionary from Italy, and so he had resolved to assist the defenders of Sphacteria. He widnae leave either... said he would fight to the death, much tired of being despised by his fellow philhellenes. I fear 'tis a tragedy in the making... such a waste, Pat, a hopeless position for sure.'

Pat's own spirits sank; what was to be done? It seemed the island was a hopeless case, an indefensible position. Yes, all parties had calculated that it was the key to the capture of Neocastro: take it and the bay entrance was closed to shipping, when the port would be cut off from reprovision and evacuation, surrender inevitable. Plainly Ibrahim, the Egyptian commander had realised such, hence the previous attack on Old Navarin, the narrow and shallow crossing of the Sikia Channel from there facilitating the island's food resupply and the movement of water in the opposite direction to sustain the garrison of Old Navarin from the well on Sphacteria. The two were mutually reliant on each other. Take one and the other must fall, whence the port would follow, and Ibrahim would possess the best anchorage in the whole of the Morea, the best in western Greece. *Surprise* and six Greek brigs could no more prevent this disaster in the making than he could... What he could do he never decided, Simon entering in that moment after a peremptory knock on the cabin door.

'Good evening, Pat. Welcome back, Duncan. May I join you?'

'Simon, please do,' Pat waved a beckoning hand, pleased to see his friend, his entry a welcome relief from an insoluble problem, for that is how it seemed. 'How are you? I regret I have been a trifle pre-occupied today, no occasion found to speak with you.'

'Pay that no mind. I have endured Perkis and Peddler for as long as I can, and I seek refuge here. Even now they are engaged with Marston and Jason in the gunroom. I venture my colleagues' patience much exceeds mine. What of our particular circumstances, tell?'

'We are charged by Melville to deliver our... *our cargo* to Mavrocordato and to obtain his note which vouchsafes that it is delivered. Yet the man - the prince - refuses to leave this damnable small island, an island which is plainly indefensible... save, perhaps, in the mind of an idiot. So, should we leave and retain our cargo, and what is to be done with it? Or will we stay and most surely be destroyed by the imminent Egyptian fleet?' A tiny waver in Pat's voice, 'It is a cursed dilemma. What do you say, eh?' His words spoken in a tone of resignation.

'It is as obvious, Pat,' Simon sighed, 'as that the sun will rise on the morrow, as you yourself might say. No words of mine are necessary. To stay and await sure destruction serves no purpose, not the slightest; and I, for one, am tired of seeing our men on my table, blood flowing as if akin to from a tap, their severed limbs in bloody buckets... and precious men - *friends* - cast overboard. I beg you will not decide on anything which might result in more of that ilk. We must depart, and without the least delay; leave NOW, if that is possible. I beg you will haul up her anchor and set sail, all of them, large and small... hoisted up on every mast she possesses.'

Pat silent, reflecting on the passion in Simon's plea, Duncan spoke up, 'Aye, I am with ye there, old friend, I am. Let us away, Pat. I will make my final attempt on the morrow with Mavrocordato, and we will leave this place. I have a bad feeling, aye, this is a cursed place... a graveyard for ships and men,' he added with conviction.

'Very well,' said Pat, his voice firming with his friends' corroboration of his own opinion, 'I am minded you are both in the right of things; I see no other choice for us. Simon, there is precious little wind to take us away this night, and so we will, in the morning, spend no more than one hour longer speaking with Mavrocordato before we depart.' His decision made, Pat brightened a very little, 'Will you take a whiskey with us?'

Simon nodded, Duncan poured, the three friends all greatly uncomfortable yet seeking to find mutual reinforcement from each other, the conversation desultory, hesitant until Simon rose to the challenge, 'I collect, many years ago when I was a medical student in Edinburgh, my tutor urged me to read the classics; one such comes to mind. It was written by Thucydides, who was author of the *History of the Peloponnesian War*. In fact, he was a combatant, an Athenian general. If my memory serves me, he described the successful invasion of Sphacteria by the Athenians, defeating the Spartans; indeed, the memorable aspect... to Thucydides and the Athenians, was that it was the first occasion on which Spartans had ever surrendered.' Not the smallest interest exhibited by Pat or Duncan, Simon laboured on in dolorous tone, 'Will the Greeks do any better, Pat?'

'No, I fear they cannot,' murmured Pat, dislodged from tired introspection. 'They have precious few men, a mere handful of guns... and both east and west coasts of the island to defend were Ibrahim to enter the bay. If the weather were inclement, the Egyptians may find it too rough to land on the west coast, for there is no beach... a low rocky shore affords a landing if the breakers allow barges to reach it. Were the Greeks to possess just three frigates, I venture *Surprise* - with them - could keep the invaders out of the bay. But it is May, not winter, and Ibrahim may reasonably expect benevolent weather, and the Greeks do not possess a single frigate, merely their brigs.'

'But Pat, the Greeks - with only brigs - have prevailed before... at Samos last year.'

'Yes, that's true, but that was at sea, with a great latitude in which to manouevre, but here, in the bay, with no room for such, it will be a shooting match; and the Egyptians have far more and greater guns than anything the Greeks possess. No, given fair weather the island is doomed. It cannot be otherwise, and I do not care to think of *Surprise* - and us - being here when they come. It pains me to think of running away and abandoning those men... but we have no choice.' A few minutes elapsed and Pat spoke again,' Duncan, on the morrow when you go to the island, listen out for our signal gun. If you hear it, hasten back at all speed. I confess I am fearful of the Egyptians returning. The weather... the wind of yesterday was not greatly helpful for holding station off the island; hence, we must presume they have drifted away... perhaps to return to Modon?' Duncan nodded, no reply offered; it was a most bleak prospect indeed.

Sunday 8th May 1825   06:30   in the Bay of Navarino

First light and not a breath of wind, nor even a single cloud in an unbroken blue sky save for a low sea mist on the far distant horizon which could be glimpsed only through the entrance to the bay. The men pulled steadily, in silence, across the flat calm of the water.

'Come aboard!' shouted the Greek sailor as Duncan neared the *Aris* in *Surprise's* launch. 'Prince Mavrocordato awaits you!'

'Did ye know what the man said, Jason?' asked Duncan, the Greek words unintelligible to him.

'It was an invitation to step aboard. The prince invites us,' offered Jason with relief in his voice as he reported his translation, their prospects seemingly brightening.

'Dalby, seize the line, we're going aboard,' shouted Duncan. They clambered up the side and were welcomed by Captain Tsamados himself. Duncan had already formed the opinion during the prior evening that Tsamados, a Hydriot, was a brave and modest patriot, well-meaning and striving with such precious few means that were available to help the defenders of the island. Consequently he was pleased to shake his hand and to follow him into the cabin.

Mavrocordato did not rise from the table where he was attended by a black servant and eating in the company of his secretary, Monsieur Grasset. Also at the table were Sakhtouri and Captain Nikolaos Votsis of the brig *Athina*. 'Good morning, Captain Macleod,' the prince offered, 'Please, join us. We are breakfasting before we go ashore.'

'Good morning your Highness; I regret I dinnae have the time to join ye. Captain O'Connor is minded that he will take *Surprise* out of the bay within the hour... he wilnae stay longer. As ye know from when we spoke yesterday, she carries an important cargo - *the coin press* - it is of significance for all of Greece... and surely that must rank as greatly more important than ye staying here on this rock, the Egyptians sure to return at any moment?'

'You are quite in the right of things, Captain Macleod. I have been considering that very point since we parted last night. Indeed, I must leave, I am obliged to do so... and with you, aboard *Surprise*. However, I beg you will allow me to make a final visit to my compatriots, the defenders of this island. I have obligations as a leader of men... you do see that? And sometimes such duties may not be exercised from the safety of places far distant from the theatre of war. There are brave men here... on this island, Captain Macleod; indeed, I have not the slightest doubt that they are braver men than I. It will not do for them to see me hastening from this island, the place where every man knows it is entirely possible that he will meet his death... today or tomorrow... Who knows when? But that time is coming - and soon. The frightening inevitability is recognised by all the defenders of this place. I will, *I must* make my goodbyes, Captain Macleod, speak my parting words with the defenders, and I trust that Captain O'Connor will bear with me for an hour or two, no longer.'

'Very well, sir. I thank ye for your plain speaking, and I will send your communication to *Surprise* with the men of the barge. I - Mr Jason too - will remain with ye and embark later in your company.' Jason translated Duncan's reply into Greek, nods and smiles from Mavrocordato and Tsamados signifying it was well received. Duncan and Jason returned to the deck. 'Dalby...' Duncan bawled down to the waiting barge, '... Mason, come aboard. Fisher, ye will take the launch back to *Surprise*; his Highness will be embarking with us in an hour or twae, nae more. Tell the Captain and then return with the barge to collect us. Am I clear?'

'Aye aye, sir, 'tis plain!' shouted Fisher. Dalby and Mason climbed aboard the brig. The launch was untied from the line and the remaining four men pulled away as swiftly as they could.

The breakfast finished, Mavrocordato, his servant, Grasset, Tsamados, Sakhtouri and Votsis climbed into the brig's boat, Duncan, Jason and the two Surprises squeezing in with them, the short pull to the Landing accomplished in mere minutes. An uphill walk of a few hundred yards brought them to the low point of the ridge forming the backbone of the island: to the left or south a low scrub-covered hill stretched away, to the right the ridge climbed gradually to the pinnacle of the island, five hundred feet or thereabouts, so Duncan recalled from Smyth's chart. All along the east coast of the island were cliffs, and any landing from the sea from the bay side would be exceedingly difficult unless made at the same place they had stepped ashore. Duncan knew there was one other potential landing site within the bay, a quarter mile or so further to the south: rocky and less favourable. On they went, approaching the west coast after another short walk along a beaten path through the dense scrub thickets to where a gathering of a few hundred men clustered around a gun battery. Two of the brig captains were chattering with the gunners. Tsamados introduced Duncan to the Spetziots, Captain Georgios Orlandos of *Achilleus* and Captain Theofilos Moulas of *Poseidon*. He mentioned that their compatriot Spetziot, Captain Santos, remained aboard his brig *Lykourgos*, as did the Hydriot, Captain Boudouris, on *Aleksandros*; the two brigs remaining anchored near Neocastro on the far side of the bay.

The battery, of four guns, overlooked a length of the coast of about a half mile where there were no cliffs, but neither was there any beach. The sea washed up on a low rocky shore, shallow - Duncan judged - breakers extending to thirty yards out. Yes, boats could land men here, but they would surely suffer some damage to their hulls in anything but the most clement weather. That was the weather today, he observed, the sea at its calmest, no wind to speak of. If Ibrahim was ever coming, if he could get his ships here, today was the perfect day for an invasion.

'Captain Macleod,' Mavrocordato hailed from within the ensemble with a wave of his arm. Duncan stepped through the crowd, looking right and left at faces lined with weary anticipation, with a degree of doubt and apprehension in many eyes. 'Here are our guns. We have plentiful powder and shot.' Duncan cast about him: the guns seemed to be well attended, shot stacked about them in piles, the smallest supply of powder standing ready but more in casks set back behind stones. Certainly the guns commanded a splendid field of fire out over the shallow water, and they were served by men brought ashore from the six Greek brigs, four of them anchored off Panagia Landing, but four guns was hardly enough to deter even one ship - and Ibrahim commanded dozens. Duncan nodded cautiously. 'And now, we will go on to the southern point of the island, to our second battery,' declared the prince in loud voice. Jason studied him carefully: his face, his demeanour - it seemed to Jason - all suggested that Mavrocordato was putting on a brave show. That the man was highly intelligent there was no doubt, that the Egyptian intent to capture the island was realised by Mavrocordato was sure, for to think otherwise was simply incredible. 'He is putting a brave face on matters,' thought

Jason, an enquiring glance towards Duncan, a mutual nod exchanged suggested he thought similarly. On they trudged, uphill, the morning beginning to warm as they walked along a well trodden and beaten narrow path through the dense scrub vegetation prevailing over almost all of the island, only a very few trees evident and most of those in the vicinity of the central or western battery, near the water well. They emerged, hands and faces bloodied by thorns, at the second battery, another three guns which faced towards the entrance of the great anchorage which was the bay, guarding its approach; at least to the extent that the tiny battery could do so. Duncan pondered the inadequacy of just three guns. Gathered all about them were another four dozen of seamen, also brought across from the brigs within the bay. They were talking quietly amongst themselves, a poor breakfast being eaten, until a commotion arose, beginning with a few men who previously had been seated and who were rising to their feet in some excitement, a noisy sense of alarm spreading immediately to all, the whole gathering staring out to sea, to the south and to the west. Duncan, alerted by the voices, getting ever louder, shrill shouts of exclamation becoming general, followed their gaze with a rising foreboding. He stared with wide eyes, the clarity of the morning displaying everything in crystal clear detail: in the distance and approaching from both south and west were dozens and dozens of ships' masts protruding above the sea mist; it could only be Ibrahim's invasion, the numbers so great, the Greeks not possessing of anything like this fleet. The shock was brutal, instant, a great wave of fear flushing through mind and body in the most violent of surge, every man present similarly and visibly affected. Duncan gasped, 'Will ye look to that?'

'Oh my God!' exclaimed Jason.

Chapter Nine

Sunday 8th May 1825   08:00   *in the Bay of Navarino*

'Where is Macleod?' cursed a frustrated Pat, his anxiety rising, staring through his telescope, his pacing across the quarterdeck halted momentarily. He had, with growing concern, anticipated Duncan's return within the hour, but looking into the approaching launch he could see only four men, Duncan visibly not one of them. Simon, waiting patiently next to him, could only grimace, Pat long beyond anything resembling sociable conversation. Coming alongside, the men clambered aboard to face their captain's glaring presence, his unhappiness and vexation radiant on a hostile face.

'Where is Mr Macleod, Fisher? Where the devil is he?' barked Pat abruptly.

'Mr Macleod is attendin' Mr... er... beg pardon... *His Highness*... attendin' the Prince, sir,' offered Fisher cautiously, Pat's unsettling demeanour and ill-temper rarely so evident aboard the barky.

'What in God's name is he doing staying with Mavrocordato?' cried Pat in a loud voice that raised eyebrows as far forward as the waist, Fisher and his companions looking most unhappy.

'Well, sir... the Prince has agreed to come back to the barky... with Mr Macleod... but only after he has said farewell to the men on the island... the defenders.'

The words struck a mollifying chord with Pat, and he calmed somewhat, 'Very well, go below and get your breakfast. You will pull again for the island in a half-hour, no later - is that plain?' Vigorous nods from all four men who disappeared in haste.

'Pat,' Simon spoke up in gentle tone, 'I am sure your references to the biblical luminaries were not greatly helpful.'

This was ignored; Pat turned away to pace up and down from the stern rail to the waist, deep in thought. Simon could only look on in dismay. Murphy's enquiry as to whether Pat wished for his breakfast was peremptorily dismissed with a wave away, his uneasiness increasing by the minute. Pausing, he gazed again through his glass at the Greek brigs, several dozen hands visible on each of their decks. He looked to the Panagia Landing, no one there. He strived to make out figures higher on the island, but the scrub vegetation covering all made it quite impossible to pick anything out. Finally he acceded to another suggestion by Murphy that his "toasted cheese was better ate up hot", and he reluctantly went below, fuming, the meal eaten unnoticed, no taste registering whilst his thoughts raced over the vexing situation.

It was plain that the weather was most propitiate for an enemy landing - if, that is, their ships could arrive in the present near complete calm. The fact of their attack on Old Navarin two days before suggested that they had a determined objective to attain, and he had not the least doubt that it was the island of Sphacteria, for that was the key to the capture of the town and fortress of Neocastro and the valuable bay itself. Once the harbour was in Egyptian hands it would provide the secure anchorage in all seasons that they and their Turk confederates lacked; indeed, its capture could greatly influence the course of the war. That Ibrahim had recognised such was obvious, his forces had besieged Neocastro by land for some time without success, its heavy guns denying his fleet safe access to the bay.

He sat by himself with his coffee, wondering what, if anything, he could do, until *"Ding-ding"* two bells rang out and the hasty arrival of Pickering - no knock or waiting - threw Pat into a heightened frenzy of agitation, 'Sir, come quick,' Pickering was greatly flustered, 'Masts - beyond the bay - *dozens of 'em!'*

The rush up the steps of the companionway had never been accomplished faster, Pat clutching his glass. On the quarterdeck, an excited murmuring evident amongst dozens of men, Pat gazed towards the bay entrance, near three miles distant, the morning mist still present but clearing. A dozen ships or more were indistinctly visible beyond the mouth, perhaps two miles distant to the south of it: brigs, schooners, even a few frigates. Pat was alarmed to see the latter, for it meant only one thing: the enemy was upon them, the Greeks possessing nothing more than brigs. It could not be other than the Egyptians.

In that dreadful moment of realisation - *Surprise* was trapped in the bay - came the distant sound of a great barrage opening, many guns firing - heavy ones such as could only be aboard ships - the thunder coming from beyond the island, from its western side, that which was exposed to the sea. The tension of all aboard *Surprise* soared, Pat's nervousness shooting to new heights. He hastened to sweep the bay with his glass: from the Sikia Channel in the northwest, a quarter-mile off, to the south entrance, three miles distant. As far as he could see, the Egyptians showed no interest in entering the bay and braving the Neocastro fort's guns; for that battery, Pat had noticed previously, boasted sixteen heavy pieces, eight of which were 36-pounders, and such would do frightful damage to any intruding frigate or corvette. Nor could any vessel swiftly pass by that danger in the near absence of wind.

With a deep sigh of despair, Pat lowered the telescope, 'Mr Codrington, fire the signal gun. Mr Pickering, ask Mr Sampays to attend - without the loss of a moment.' The bosun was duly summoned and hastened from the forepeak where, with a score of others, a hundred more men now all along the rails, he had been watching the far fleet. 'Mr Sampays, that final delivery of ballast in Devonport... the one which came much later than the rest... *the last twenty-four pigs*; do you recall?'

'Aye, sir,' Sampays replied rather circumspectly, 'It was stowed below the steps... in the hold.' He turned his head, Perkis and Peddler, both with an exceedingly anxious demeanour, had appeared on the deck.

'You are to fetch it up to the gun deck, directly; is that clear?'

'What is happening, Captain?' cried Perkis in strident tone, rushing over and plainly alarmed by the sound of the guns.

'Mr Perkis, I regret to tell you, but we are bottled up in the bay by the Egyptians; their fleet has arrived. Here, if you will, take a look.' Pat passed the glass and pointed.

Peddler fidgeted whilst Perkis focussed the telescope. Perkis, the focus at last sharp, gazed upon his worst nightmare, rising fear verging on horror filling his face; 'Jesus Christ!' he shrieked. Pat and many others present frowned. 'Our valuable... the go... *our cargo*, Captain... what is to be done?'

'I have asked the bosun, Mr Sampays here, to fetch that up from the hold. We will send it out to *Eleanor* through the Sikia Channel in our boats.'

'Peddler,' cried Perkis, 'Go with the bosun! Do you remember where the... *the cargo* was stowed?'

'Of course,' said Peddler, in a tone suggesting injury, for how could he conceivably forget such treasure and where it was.

'Get away now, make haste!' declared Perkis, Sampays halfway to the companionway.

'Mr Pickering,' ordered Pat, 'lower the second cutter and find men for all three of the boats, six lads for each.' *Surprise* possessed only a launch and two cutters, no more had she been given at Devonport. 'Send another eight men to the hold to bring up Perkis's *particular* pigs - lose not a moment.'

'Aye, aye, sir,' said Pickering, plainly perplexed; for who, at such a time, would be in the least concerned with shifting ballast. 'Particular pigs, sir?'

'Yes, *most particular ones*, Mr Pickering. Mr Peddler will show you if Mr Sampays cannot remember which ones they are. Crack on, lose not a moment.'

'Yes sir,' Pickering nodded, bewildered by the peculiar order and strange task, but he hastened after Sampays and Peddler, a passing shout offered to Barton to launch the larger cutter.

There was no one more bewildered by now than Sampays, and plainly to all present he was extremely flustered, hesitant to speak or shift; for what on earth was he doing removing iron ballast, particularly when the enemy fleet imminently threatened; it was utterly beyond his comprehension. Peddler had assumed seniority in the task, ordering the eight men sent below to shift precisely the ingots he recalled seeing stowed in Devonport. In the cramped, confined space below the stairs within the darkness of the hold, it was plain that none of the men appreciated the seemingly absurd task in the least: curses and profanities were uttered without any constraint, no mind given for who might hear. The men struggled and sweated to lift out their heavy burdens, a half-hour elapsing until twenty-four exceedingly mystifying pigs lay on the gun deck, a hundred men and more staring at the perplexing sight. Pat ordered *Old Nick* rolled back from its port, and the ingots were lowered, four into each of the three boats, all of which settled deep in the water as the last of the six rowers settled on the thwarts. 'As I feared, it will take two trips to take them all,' declared Pat with another deep sigh of despond. 'Mr Codrington, into the larger cutter if you please; Mr Perkis, will you care to embark in the launch? Mr Peddler, you may attend the second consignment.'

'Sir,' interjected Pickering, 'what of Mr Macleod? There is no boat to fetch him off the island.'

'I am aware of that. If pressed he will have to embark aboard one of the Greek brigs,' replied Pat gloomily.

'But sir,' Pickering could no longer contain his pressing curiosity, 'why are we shifting ballast, sending it to *Eleanor*... and now of all times?' The lieutenant had uttered the blindingly obvious question, one burning within the mind of every man aboard, at least within that of every man unaware of the true nature of the ingots. A score of men standing close by stared, very eager to hear the answer.

'Mr Pickering, if you please, for the moment we will pay that no mind,' declared Pat in a stern voice that ended all words on that particular subject.

A wave from Pat and the three boats, all loaded and manned, moved away, the men pulling hard for the Sikia Channel, a quarter mile to the north-west, all the men of *Surprise* watching from every yard of the rails, their own confusion melded with grave apprehension: the morning mist was long evaporated and the distant warships were all in plain sight beyond the entrance to the bay.

On the island, Mavrocordato's immediate entourage with Duncan and the Surprises gazed down at the chilling sight of the great armada. The Egyptian fleet had split into three parties: the first, bound for the mouth of the bay from the far south, was a squadron which was plainly charged with bottling up any attempt at Greek exit from within. It boasted a frigate, a corvette and four brigs. Further distant, to the west, were two dozen more ships including another nine frigates, five corvettes and ten brigs; that squadron seemingly standing off at some distance out to sea, perhaps four miles, waiting for and presumably a safeguard against the possible return of Admiral Miaoulis. Two miles off the west coast of the island, directly before the Greek gun battery but out of range of it, were ten more brigs and a dozen transports; they were obviously the intending invaders.

From the high ground behind the battery near the south peak, Duncan heard *Surprise's* signal gun boom out, the sound exacerbating the nerves of every man, rising fear and trepidation common to all. From the high southern point of the island the land felll away to the north for near two miles, down to a narrow central waist, before it rose steeply towards the north summit, another mile further on. He stared in the direction of the Panagia Landing at the low point on the east side, but he could not see it nor anything of the Greek brigs from his present position. Duncan therefore had no idea whether any boat had arrived to collect him and his men. He turned to Mavrocordato, urgency in his voice, 'Yer Highness, we must away d'reckly, with nae a moment lost.'

'Mr Macleod, I share your concern, I do; yet I believe there is no imminent danger, and my men are preparing their guns for firing. We will see if they will give the invaders a bloody nose. I shall linger for a short while and see what happens here. I would not care to be called coward.'

'But sir,' an exasperated Duncan tried again, 'Captain O'Connor will be wanting to take the barky out of the bay, and he cannae wait for us... the Egyptians already here at the mouth.'

'Exactly, Mr Macleod; the enemy is here, arrived, is upon us; it makes little difference if we leave - *if your ship leaves* - now or in an hour, none that I can see. As you say, they are already approaching to blockade the bay entrance. Will your ship clear the bay before they are upon us?' Duncan could not bring himself to admit that such was most unlikely, the wind so weak, and so he simply stared, racking his brain for something to offer which would bring Mavrocordato to his senses.

His Highness's decision to dwell did not accord with others either, Duncan noticed: Captain Orlandos of *Achilleus* and Captain Moulas of *Poseidon* had set off near immediately to return to their brigs, a frisson of discord audible within the seamen standing ready to serve the guns on the heights.

Struggling to subdue increasing apprehension, Mavrocordato's party hastened at a swift pace and in great anxiety down the hill and back to the first battery at the low point on the west coast. In the instant they arrived there the nearest Egyptians opened fire from three-quarters of a mile offshore, "BOOM, BOOM, BOOM" a rapid succession of shots erupting from scores of guns, the ball projectiles flying in every direction within a hundred yards of the Greeks, much falling short and splashing into the water; a very few shots, richochets, flying up to fall short of the battery. 'Fire!' screamed General Anagnostara, the anxious Greek gunners desperate to let fly with what little response they had. It was a futile response: four shot against more than a score of vessels.

'Cease fire!' roared Captain Tsamados angrily. 'We will await their barges. We must save our shot and powder.' The enemy firing did not relent, the Egyptian brigs firing at long range; fortunately with no great effect or loss for the Greeks, the distance too far. There was little to no wind, Duncan noticed, and he presumed that their captains did not care to come closer for fear of running aground were a stronger and adverse off-the-sea *Maestro* to strike up as the day warmed, which was the usual event, and certainly at present there was a very real risk that any ship so close would surely fall in irons, near powerless - save for the help of her boats - to avoid a calamitous drift ashore and striking on the rocky outfalls which were plainly visible for a great distance north and south.

'Yer Highness,' said Duncan eventually, 'May I suggest that we retire a wee way up the slope... a few yards or so, nae more. We are a target here, near the guns, and can better see what is happening over more of the island from back there.'

'Very well, Captain Macleod. I accede to your concern, and well meant it is, I am sure. My servant here,' Mavrocordato nodded towards the black man, 'can go back and forth with any messages and news. Lead on, if you please.'

"*Ding-ding, ding-ding, ding-ding*" the strident tones of the bell reminded all on *Surprise* that an anxious hour had passed by since the boats had departed, the distant firing from the far side of the island continuing incessantly and no sign of the awaited boats. Pat, fretting about those men, about Macleod marooned and the invasion seemingly started called his only remaining officer to a minor conference conducted in whispers on the quarterdeck. 'Mr Pickering, unfortunately we can give no mind at present to Mr Macleod and his men - we have no boats. However, if they must escape the island in haste... there are the Greek brigs at the Landing... though I doubt they will linger if the Egyptians look like overrunning the island.' Pat sighed, 'We have no wind of any worth, a mere breath, no more; hence, shifting is beyond us... and when the boats return they have another passage to make with the remaining pigs...'

Within moments the sound of firing from the distant guns had ceased. An eerie minute of silence followed, Pat noticing a flurry of wind in the rigging, and then came the distinctive sound of signal guns. Pat's face become a picture of apprehension, his words a strained whisper, 'I venture that is the signal for the landings to begin.'

On the lower slope of the ridge, two hundred yards behind the Greek battery, Jason glanced at Duncan and then to his watch; it was eleven o'clock and the Egyptian brigs had ceased fire, an air of expectancy settling upon the waiting Greek defenders. Five minutes passed, two signal guns were fired, and from all the transport ships came the repetitive *"boom boom"* of bass drums as their boats were being lowered to the water, fifty of them carefully counted by Macleod with his practised eye as a part-time intelligence officer; he estimated thirty men packed into each one. The monotonous drumming continued, a persistent and foreboding backcloth. The filled boats began to pull for the shore from the transport brigs which had closed to only a half-mile offshore. Mavrocordato despatched his servant to speak with Tsamados.

'Here they are, sir!' exclaimed Pickering on the quarterdeck, his face flushed with relief, the three boats just coming out of the Sikia Channel mouth; the men, apparent even at distance, were visibly still pulling hard. Fifteen more minutes, the Surprises all along the waist shouting loud encouragement, and the boats were alongside, the exhausted rowers hastily brought aboard, gasping for breath and pouring with sweat. They were swiftly plied with plentiful water, the grog ration advanced and being particularly well received. Fresh men boarded the boats, the remaining twelve pigs were loaded as rapidly as possible, not a moment lost, a nervous and uncomfortable Peddler climbing aboard the larger cutter on Pat's nod.

'Away ye go, lads,' shouted Pat, waving vigorously, his pained face urging speed. The three boats were heavily loaded, sat deep in the water, their gunwales with precious little freeboard. With no wind of significance and their sails no use, their men would have to work hard. 'Doubtless they will be invigorated by the guns,' thought Pat absently, eye returned to his glass, staring to the south, to the bay entrance.

'Wait, wait... hold fire,' screamed Tsamados to his gunners. On came the boats, six hundred yards, five hundred, four hundred, 'FIRE!' bellowed Tsamados. The four Greek guns all roared at once, the shot flying the short distance into the midst of the barges near instantly, the low trajectory giving a momentary glimpse of the ball before it struck or, more often, splashed alongside a boat before richochetting into the distance. A direct hit would undoubtedly ensure total destruction, the power of the shot undiminished over such a short range. Sure enough a ball from the third fusillade flashed through one of the leading boats, carving without hindrance through the men aboard, hurling broken and dismembered victims aside - flung backwards or high into the air - disintegrated bodies splashing down into the water or splattering neighbouring boats - to the dismay of their desperate occupants; some shots striking obliquely and smashing other boat hulls to fragments, large groups of men cast into the water, floundering, drowning; even those few who could swim were dragged down by the weight of their ammunition and pack.

'FIRE!' Tsamados continued to scream, his orders going wholly unnoticed in the frenzy of gunners swabbing their barrels, shoving home the powder charge, the wad, the ball, ramming all home before leaping aside before the flash in the touchpan and the roar and flame of the discharge, the guns leaping back violently on their trucks. At all four guns the seamen sweated blood to ready and fire as rapidly as any shipboard gunners would ever do. Duncan marvelled at their energy, their determination. He looked at men the likes of which he had seen aboard *Surprise* many times when she had fought; he studied grizelled, determined faces, those of minds wholly possessed by their strenuous task and driven by the fear that settled upon all men in such circumstances, a cold fear which was controlled, managed by practice and experience. They did not come close to the abilities of *Surprise's* experienced gunners - four shots in five minutes not considered to be anything exceptional - but the Greeks, who were really merchant seafarers for the most part, maintained a most creditable rate of fire. He looked out towards the barges to assess the effects of the barrage: some crews were wavering, a few turning back; the heat of the cannon fire, so close, so bloodily destructive, was surely terrifying and demoralising.

Three hundred yards and perhaps four boats had sunk, the Greek guns discharging frenetically, without let up; more boats were wavering, turning away, some shifting north or south along the shoreline; others were pulling as hard as could be back towards the transports. Behind the boats a brig had closed up, towards the shore, at least as close as its captain dared, rocks evident all about the vessel and unobscured by wave, the water hardly influenced at all by precious little wind. From the brig's deck the officers bellowed and the wavering boats turned back once more, pulling again for the shore, likely for the lesser of the two dangers, summary punishment for cowards most likely to be meted out immediately after the action. Several Greek shots struck the brig low in her hull, showers of wood splinters and fragments - remarked by the gunners - flying high in the air. The waiting Greek soldiers now fired from three hundred muskets, a discouraging torrent of lead flung towards the small boats. Yet still they came on, the nearest a hundred yards off, the Egyptians visibly pulling hard, straining every sinew and muscle. The Greeks depressed their cannon as low as could be, still firing frantically: another two boats disintegrated. The musketeers continued loading and firing, loading and firing with dogged determination and without the slightest let up. Duncan, a fascinated and fearful observer, counted: some thirty boats were close to beaching before the Greek guns; another ten had diverted north or south and must also be very close to land. Twelve hundred frightened and furious Egyptians were close to coming ashore. He looked all about him in assessment of the prospects for a successful defence: three hundred and fifty Greeks or more, he estimated, stood ready with muskets, pistols and the short, curved blade yatagan - the Greek equivalent of the cutlass. Many Greek musketeers had already begun firing at those few men already scrambling ashore on the rocks, others still directed their muskets at the easier targets that were the boats, knocking down many men aboard them, their slumped bodies cast out so as not to hinder the rowers. 'At such short range the Egyptian casualties must be dreadful, their wounds very severe,' remarked Duncan to a very frightened Jason, who did not reply.

From the leading boat, Egyptians spilled out, their officer leaping ahead of them onto the slippery rocks, waving his sword arm and bellowing encouragement to his men, more and more leaping ashore every minute, all taking mere moments to find their footing on the rocks, no beach on the western side. The Greek gunners had long switched to grapeshot, swathes of metal fragments hurled out to strike down a dozen or more men caught in the blast each time. But four guns could no more hold back the surviving thousand Egyptians than Canute could hold back the onrushing tide. For the most part the Egyptian infantry still had dry powder in their muskets, and they began to fire back from the rocks where they huddled down to stay below the hurricane of Greek grapeshot; others bounded to the left and to the right, Greek musketeers cognisant of the threat of being outflanked, firing upon them. The gunners, man after man, were realising that their job was near done: it would be the Greek infantry who must win the battle when the Egyptians determined to close on the guns or - as they could see was already happening - go around them. Indeed, that was the undoing of the Greeks: those boats that had pulled frantically to the north or south to escape the Greek guns had since landed their soldiers, and those men were coming on in greater numbers, coming ever closer from landings two hundred yards or even more afar, pushing through the dense and prickly scrub vegetation to approach on both sides of the Greek battery.

'How long could several hundred Greeks stand against a thousand Egyptians?' wondered Duncan, sticking closely to Mavrocordato's side; 'Not long,' he quickly concluded. 'Your Highness, I beg ye will hasten away. The battle is near done; your men have fought well... but cannae stand for much longer. Look all about ye, the Egyptians are coming on twae sides... 'tis sure death to dally here.'

Mavrocordato needed no convincing, his face was white, he trembled, his breathing was unhealthily fast and his face poured with sweat. He seemed to welcome Duncan's suggestion - was grateful for it - nodding immediately, turning his fearful eyes away from the sight of onrushing death, beckoning his secretary, Grasset, to follow.

Duncan looked all about him once more: some of the Egyptians had brought drums ashore, and to their loud, pounding beat and with resounding cries of "ALLAH, ALLAH" they were closing ever faster upon the Greek defenders. Dozens, scores of invaders crouched to fire, ducked down whilst reloading, skipped forward to shelter behind the next rock, ever closer, a hundred yards off, seventy-five, their green standards waving. The game was up, Duncan realised. 'RUN!' he screamed, hauling hard on Mavrocordato's tunic, 'RUN!' The prince did just that - without the least hesitation - panic showing plain on his face. Together with his immediate entourage he sprinted towards the low point of the spine ridge behind them, Duncan guiding him with fierce tugs at his arm, pulling him on as he faltered, frantic exertion straining his unaccustomed legs, panting, his breath coming ever faster.

Duncan glanced back for a second; the Greeks as a fighting body were crumbling; Egyptians with fixed bayonets were striking gunners down at the battery, stabbing fallen men, no quarter given. No Greek possessed a bayonet, many of them being seafarers from the six Greek brigs and, unaccustomed as they were to such fierce hand to hand fighting, seaman and soldiers alike were fleeing in ever greater numbers, hastening for the heights of the ridge, running north, oblivious to the tearing thorns, musket fire exploding behind them, men falling, stumbling, desperation and panic become general. Duncan violently grabbed Mavrocordato's arm, the prince had tripped again; he hauled him up, looked around briefly: the Egyptians were fifty yards behind, no more, muskets cracking, balls whistling above and all around them. 'Come on, sir,' he shouted, dragging a struggling Mavrocordato along, 'RUN!'; Grasset, his secretary, was ten yards ahead with Jason, neither man looking back. Another forty yards and Duncan halted to give the prince a very brief moment to catch his breath; he stared again at the mêlée around the guns, thought he saw Tsamados and Santa Rosa struck down amidst a fighting flurry of Greeks all around them, muskets swung down to smash upon those who had fallen, swords flailing into the flesh of wounded men. He tore his eyes away from the distressing scene, horrified, and pressed on; with Dalby's help dragging Mavrocordato along, his legs and lungs protesting, the ridge nearly attained, every muscle in his body shrieking "enough!" He could feel his heart was pounding fit to burst; sweat, pints of sweat flowed from every pore of his body, his clothes were utterly soaked. On they all struggled, fighting back panic, lungs protesting with searing pain, overloaded, chests panting frantically. On, on, running, fear endemic, legs thrashed by terrified minds. His muscles straining so hard, Duncan thought they must tear away from his jarring, jolting bones; he looked ahead: twenty agonising yards more to the ridge. Run! RUN! His legs no longer seemed to want to comply with his wishes. The top and a few seconds respite from the slope gained, a hopeful glance afforded towards the Greek brigs and safety. He gazed anxiously down upon the bay. He simply could not move for a few moments even were the pursuers to fall upon them: crushing physical depletion gripped him and his lungs burned red. Even so it did not stop him fretting, aware that the Egyptians were no more than one or two minutes behind.

Pat stared through his glass to the south. The two brigs at Neocastro were leaving, frantic activity visible on their yards and decks. His spirits sank. Another ten minutes passed, his eyes glued to the glass: *Athina*, a brig at the Panagia Landing, had also cut her cables and was edging away from the island. The first two brigs were soon underway, their sails filled but gaining little from the still weak wind. Pat felt it had become a little stronger, a light breeze, force two perhaps. It might give them a knot or two.

On the island ridge, Duncan, struggling to breathe, his burning lungs coughing spittle, stared all around him; he could see hundreds of Greeks running north towards the heights, bounding from rock to rock to avoid being cut off by the widening spread of Egyptians, many of them hastening up towards the rocky path which ran along the spine ridge; he stared down into the bay, gazed in shock at the sight of two brigs a distant mile off the shore on the other side of the bay, their sails aloft: both Boudouris on *Aleksandros* and Santos on *Lycourgos*, the two brigs at Neocastro, had hauled their anchors and were fleeing. The brig *Athina*, formerly anchored off the Landing, evidently had decided to follow them shortly after; she was visible, had shifted not far, perhaps a quarter mile, and was a little distance off from her three sisters still remaining there. Momentarily his thoughts crystallised to a particularly unwelcome conclusion for a mariner: *Athina's* departure seemed a little strange when her captain, Votsis - he felt sure - was still somewhere behind his own group of fugitives.

He looked closely and with a rising sense of fear at the last three remaining brigs, men on the decks of two of them in the act of cutting their own cables, axes in the hands of men frantically swinging. Evidently Captains Orlandos of *Achilleus* and Moulas of *Poseidon*, both of whom had both set off earlier to return to their own brigs, were now leaving. Only *Aris* might remain when they reached the Landing. Grasping for the residual strength rekindled by the tiny recovery in his lungs and legs, he urged his companions on, no further time could be afforded for recuperation. All together they rushed down the slope on the well trodden path towards the Landing. If *Aris* departed without them, death was close and certain - of that he had not the least doubt: the Egyptians were demonstrably in no mood to take prisoners after their own mauling; he had seen dozens of Greeks cut down who plainly were trying to surrender. His lungs still on fire, his legs trembling uncontrollably, the brief pause no real respite at all, he shouted again, 'RUN!' With a wave of his arm Duncan urged his party on, every man self-evidently exhausted, energy all expended, muscles aching painfully, red raw lungs gasping, struggling for air that would not come. He pulled Mavrocordato forward, but the prince was finished, had nothing left to carry him on and he collapsed to the ground. 'Dalby! Mason!' he screamed at the two Surprises, both a yard or two behind, cutlasses drawn as if to fend off any closing attacker; 'Here, bear a hand, your mon is done.' A nod from Clumsy Dalby to Mason and both men passed their weapons to Duncan and hauled up the prince between them; Mavrocordato was too shattered to even speak, his face grey and breath coming in short, fast spasms. On they struggled, a hundred yards more remaining to reach the shore. They could see a boat, four men within and two standing on the rocks, waiting. 'Brave men,' thought Duncan, near finished himself. 'Bang' a musket cracked behind them, a Greek brought down, no one with the strength to turn back, to assist. 'On, quickly now, faster!' shrieked Duncan, as if such was possible. Even Dalby was tiring, hauling the prince along and still fifty yards to go to reach the boat. A party of Greeks had clustered around their fallen compatriot, were fighting the Egyptians with their curved swords, the agonising, terrifying screams of dying men and the shouts of their attackers reaching the ears of the runners - loud, closer. To the shore at last, no hesitation, splashing without pause into the water, the Greek boat crew heaving Mavrocordato aboard, a near lifeless dead weight, absolute exhaustion for Grasset and Jason too, both getting in only with the greatest of difficulty, then Dalby and Mason, the black servant the last man into the boat. And then, a shout, a final desperate leap amidst great splashing through the water and a robed priest clutched frantically for the gunwale, the hands heaving him across the sternboard so as to avoid capsizing the heavily laden boat. No room left on the thwarts, the priest clung on for his life as the seamen pulled away, rowing hard for the last remaining brig, *Aris*, the occasional musket crack from behind them, the ball heard whizzing past, the boat at the extreme range of accuracy of the Egyptians firing from high up the slope. Three minutes of desperately necessary recuperation, the merest of respite for lungs burning red hot, for muscles spasming in the acute pain of cramp taking hold, and then they were at the side of *Aris*, men reaching down to haul them from the boat, the terror still with them, the panic subsiding only a very little.

The boat was swiftly emptied of its refugees, and its crew pushed off once more, Duncan marvelling at their bravery, shots coming in small fusillades from the heights; more and more of Egyptians were appearing at the ridge. The last party of Greeks, the final rearguard as it had seemed for them, were running down the slope, men turning to swing yatagans at close pursuers, several falling, wounded Greeks and Egyptians hacked down in a microcosm of the devastating bloodbath that the battle for the island had become, the pursuers plainly taking no prisoners.

The boat had reached the shore once again, the last survivors of the Greeks were scrambling across the rock and through the water in panic, the Egyptians near upon them. The boat swiftly filled and then - disaster. Duncan and the rescued Surprises looked back in horror; the boat was overfilled and had capsized, every man thrown into the water. From the Greek brig muskets cracked and a few Egyptians fell; others waded into the sea to club down the drowning Greeks, a few swimming valiantly even as more shots splashed into the water all about them. The Greek crew on the brig were frantic; a dozen kept up their own fire upon the enemy, four stood ready in great anxiety with axes to cut the cables, but somehow held themselves back from the act, a few swimmers still being plucked out, near drowned. A dozen men clung on aloft - ready to let fall the canvas, another score heaved on the braces to position the yards so as to catch the strengthening breeze; Macleod had already noted it was picking up.

Aboard *Surprise,* her boats had returned and the men were scrambling up the side in haste, every man mindful of the cessation of firing from the heavy guns, aware too that the sound of muskets cracking on the island was much more desultory, and all presumed the battle was over, finished; the pursuit, capture and perhaps killing of the final surviving fugitives was the bloody business they could still hear.

Surprise swung at single anchor, the other hauled up, catted and fished for an hour since, Pat desperately keen to depart. For fifteen minutes he had wavered with his intent to haul up the best bower, keeping his nerve and holding his order back with great restraint, the pressing urge to flee weighing heavily upon his own mind, his concern for Duncan, Jason and the men ashore burning as a fiery presence within his frenetic thoughts.

'Mr Pickering, let us weigh anchor! Swiftly now! All hands to make sail!' Pat shouted the long delayed commands, reiterated by Pickering, Sampays and a dozen other men passing it along, all of them anxious to be gone.

Pat gazed through his telescope: at least two or three score or even more of Greeks were trying to escape the island by swimming across the Sikia Channel. It was particularly shallow at the near, eastern end adjoining the bay and, Pat thought, likely presented no great difficulty for even a poor swimmer. He returned to a view of the more distant Panagia Landing: only one brig, *Aris*, remained near; the last two of the other five brigs, *Poseidon* and *Achilleus*, were already a cable off and shifting south with the freshening breeze behind them. He could see *Aris's* boat pulling hard from the shore, but he could not make out the occupants at such a great distance. He prayed that his own men were safe on the brig.

He looked back to the mountainous northern heights of Sphacteria, the still sporadic sound of firing catching his attention; Egyptians standards were waving atop the peak; jubilant troops were shouting, firing muskets as if to announce their victory; others, pursuing the fleeing Greeks, were shooting at those men still scrambling below, down the steep, rocky slope, heading for the Sikia Channel and a hasty swim across to the mainland and the fortress of Old Navarin.

From the deck of *Aris*, all her men gazed in horror at the skirmish in the water at the Landing: the final few Greeks had all been struck down, bayoneted, their throats cut, heads near severed; and then they perceived two figures swimming strongly for the brig, still anchored a hundred yards off the shore. The Greeks all along the rail shouted loud encouragement, 'Come on! Come on! Swim! SWIM!' and the two in the water kept going, a flurry of musket fire flying around them, balls splashing about them. On they came, fifty yards off, twenty-five, every Greek on *Aris* wildly screaming, yelling manically until they were hoarse, their throats sore and painful, the survival of the two swimmers in the water become the most important thought to ever possess them. Ten yards, muskets cracking from the shore, the final five and hands stretched for lines tied with loops, cast down, fingers stretching desperately for them; waiting eager grips seized failing hands, the two men pulled into reach of the net, fellow Greeks hanging from it to grab them, to haul them up and out of the water, until, coughing and vomiting saltwater, the two swimmers finally lay prone and exhausted on the deck of the brig, forty men coaxing them to take fresh water, to sit up, to spew out the last of the foul brine both had swallowed in noxious volume. Recognition was immediate, the two figures being well known to every Greek: Sakhtouri the first man and Captain Nikolaos Votsis of the brig *Athina* the second. The men of *Aris* were deeply dismayed to hear Sakhtouri's struggling and halting report of their own captain, Tsamados, shot down and killed. Indeed, Votsis himself had been reported as *"surely killed"* by a crewman of one of the already departed brigs; his own brig, *Athina*, departing upon the bad news. Votsis dragged himself from his misery on the deck, braced himself on the wheel and, coughing up more saltwater intermittently, he shouted as best he could, 'Men of *Aris*, your captain is dead, I am now your captain.' No one demurred. 'Cut the anchor cables!' The four men standing ready did not hesitate, the axes were swung, two swift strokes chopping into each and the cables parted, the brig responding immediately, beginning to drift - east into the bay. 'Let fall!' Votsis shrieked to the men aloft on the main yard; the sail was loosed and the canvas came falling down.

'Sheet home!' The seamen scrambling over the ratlines seized the sheets, hauled them aft, the wind instantly filling the mainsail.

On deck, Duncan and Jason stared, horrified, the number of Egyptians atop the spine ridge were more in number every minute. Dalby and Mason had carried the exhausted Mavrocordato below, accompanied by his secretary and his servant.

On the shore, more Egyptian musketeers had reached the Landing and were firing at the brig. Dimitris Nantes and Lazaros Pordalas, two men aloft, were hit and, unable to hold their grip, fell off the main yard, their heads splitting open on striking the deck, brain matter splattering some distance and splashing over the anxious onlookers. A few Greeks returned fire, but the enemy was so strong in number that it made not the least difference.

A mile to the north, the experienced topmen aboard *Surprise* had already let fall her tops'ls; others on deck braced the yards. The frigate was moving at last, infinitely slowly towards the south, Pat shouting for the mainsails too to be braced round to catch the weak north-westerly, such as it was in the lee of the hills of Sphacteria and Old Navarin. Directing Barton to keep her bow bearing towards distant Doganna village, on a bearing pointing just to the north-east of Neocastro, Pat reckoned *Surprise* would safely clear the Sphagia shoal before she passed abeam of the tiny Kuloneski island and thence make her turn directly south - towards the besieging Egyptian fleet, to her final destiny; for that is how things looked. How long it would take her to reach the entrance to the bay and likely the last battle she would ever fight he could not conceive - *Surprise* with little more than steerage way. Indeed, he perceived that if the weak wind - Pat thought it might be a Force two, a light breeze - were to fall away entirely then the barky would be in the gravest of difficulties, and that realisation filled him with renewed gloom, for how could they hope to escape: with no wind the massed enemy guns of the squadron at the mouth would simply pound *Surprise* to her inevitable destruction. Never, to Pat's mind, had the prospects for his men and his ship looked bleaker.

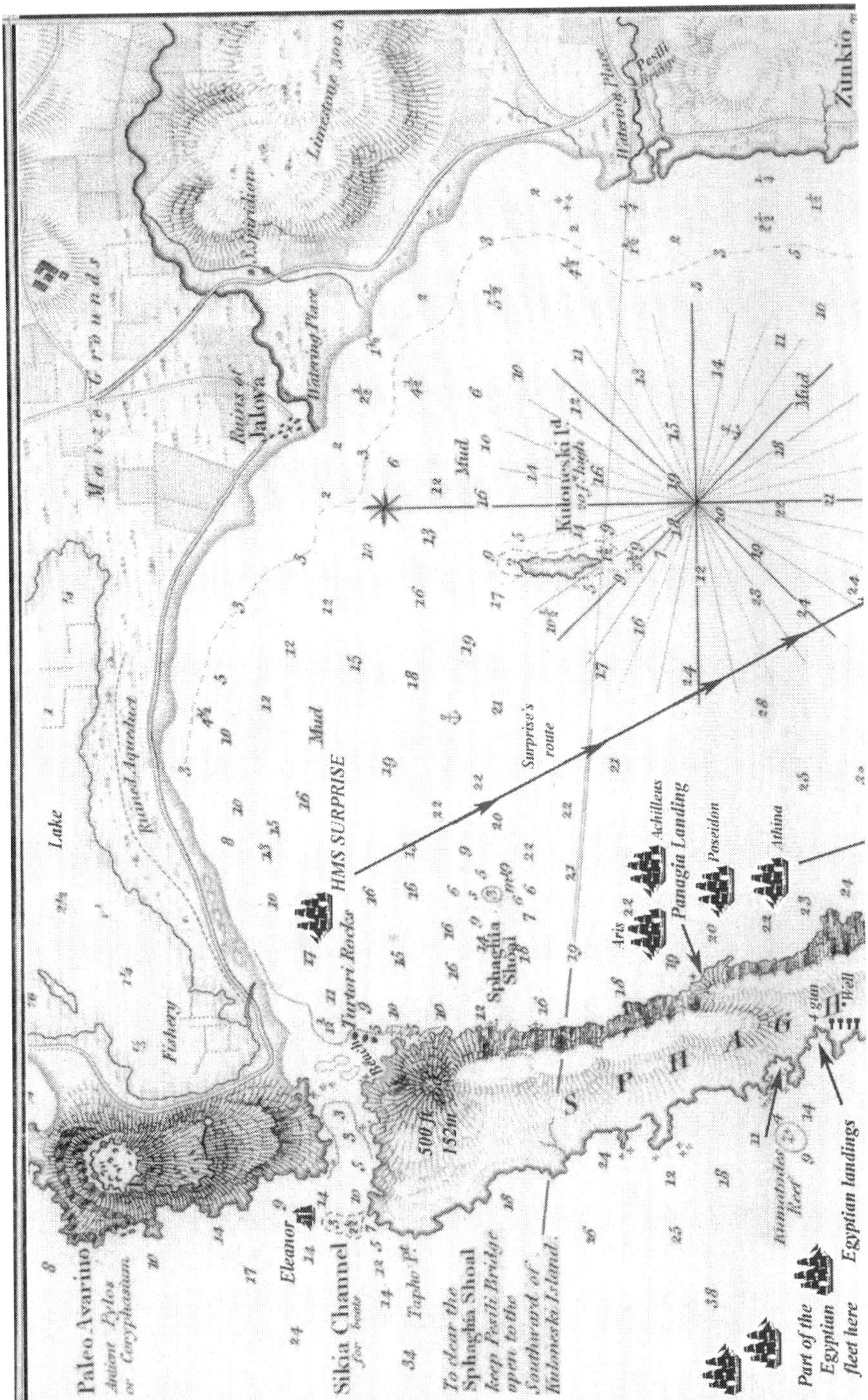
Paleo Avarino
Antient Pylos
or Coryphasium
Sikia Channel
for boats
Eleanor
To clear the
Sphagia Shoal
keep Pesili Bridge
open to the
Southward of
Kulonieski Island.
Part of the
Egyptian
fleet here
Egyptian landings
Fishery
Lake
Ruined Aqueduct
HMS SURPRISE
Turtori Rocks
Sphagia Shoal
500 ft
152m
S P H A G
Aris
Achilleus
Panagia Landing
Poseidon
Athina
Well
Surprise's
route
Mud
Kulonieski Id.
Ruins of
Jalova
Watering Place
Maize Grounds
Limestone
Pesili
Bridge
Zunkio

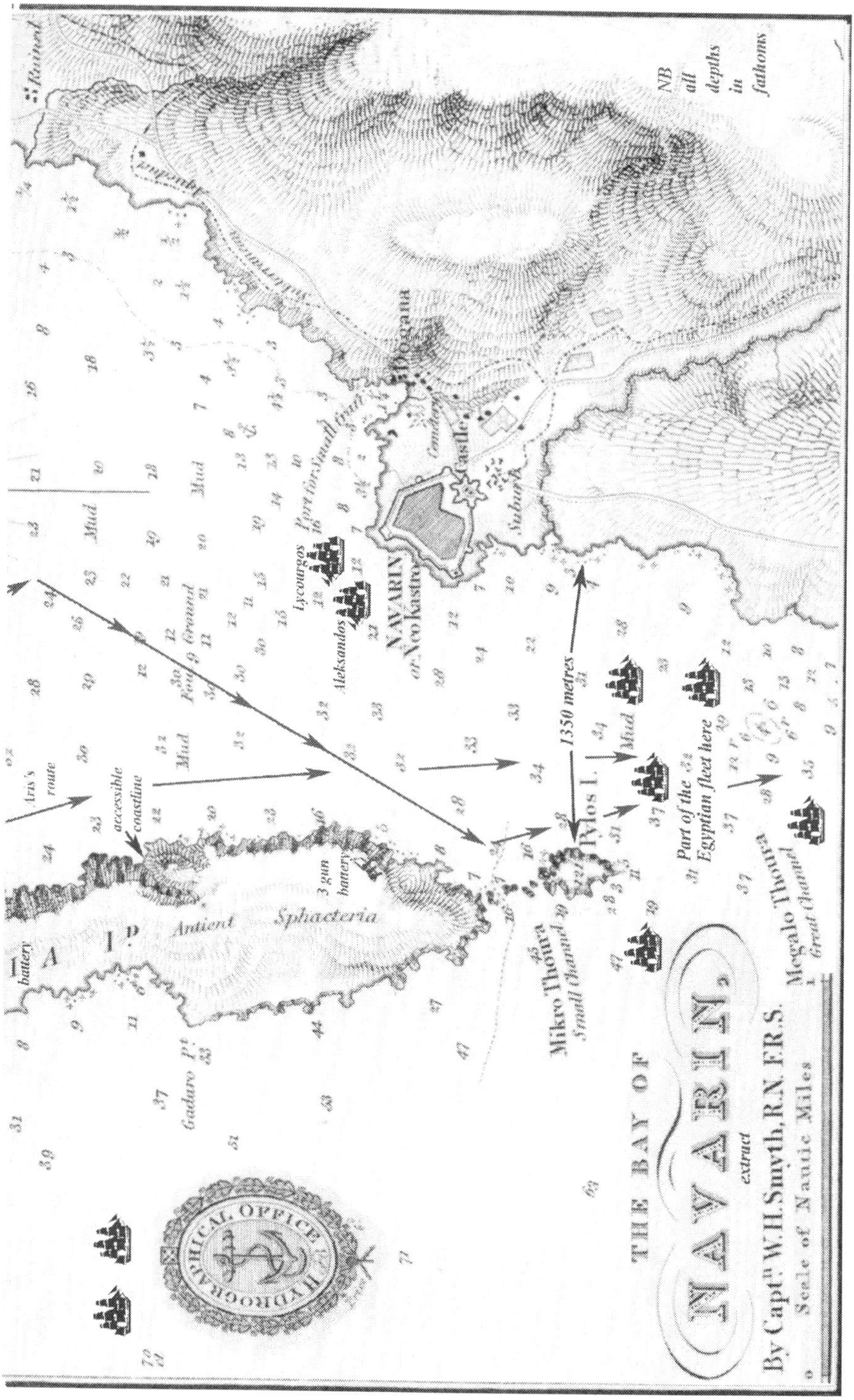
THE BAY OF
NAVARIN,
extract
By Captn. W.H.Smyth, R.N. F.R.S.
Scale of Nautic Miles
HYDROGRAPHICAL OFFICE
battery
Aris's route
accessible coastline
Gadaro Pt.
Antient Sphacteria
3 gun battery
Mud
Foul Ground
Lycourgos
Aleksandos
Port for Small Craft
NAVARIN or Neo Kastro
Dogana
Cemetery
Castle
Suburb
Ruined
1350 metres
Mikro Thoura
Small Channel
Pylos I.
Part of the Egyptian fleet here
Megalo Thoura
Great Channel
NB all depths in fathoms

Chapter Ten

Sunday 8th May 1825   14:00   aboard Aris in the Bay of Navarino

Aris at last was out of musket range and the Egyptians ceased fire, yet from the rocky island shore fleeing swimmers were still visible in the water, a handful striving to make the departing brig before they succumbed to exhaustion, others - in desperate hope and all-consuming fear - were trying to swim across the bay in its entirety to reach Neocastro, a mile to the east. Captain Votsis, who had assumed command without challenge from anyone on the brig, directed that lines should be left trailing in case any unseen survivor in the water might clutch them, *Aris* moving at a snail-like speed, little more than drifting towards the south. Along her deck a score of men stood ready to cast lines to anyone with the slightest prospect of catching them. Sadly, it was to no avail: none of the swimmers reached *Aris*, all drowning despite the placid water of the Bay. Sakhtouri, staring earnestly through the glass, reported sighting two or three more swimmers on the distant, far side of the narrows, prevailing in their efforts to reach Pylos, the water conditions generally as benevolent as they might ever be.

Votsis passed the glass to Duncan who turned to look aft in hope of seeing the status of *Surprise*, a mile to the north. That she had begun to sail was obvious to his eye, though with such a feeble wind, its customary afternoon increase being exceptionally weak, he could see it would be an hour before the frigate might reach where *Aris* was now, and by then *Aris* herself would be half-way to the narrows which were the mouth of the bay. No, unless *Aris* slackened her braces or clewed up, it was doubtful that *Surprise* would ever catch her: *Aris* would be left entirely to her own devices, her own guns. He gazed ahead: some two miles to the south the fleeing Greek brigs, *Poseidonas* and *Achilleus*, were just entering the narrows and not far ahead of them was *Athina*. It seemed to Duncan that they had - by the skin of their teeth - escaped the squadron closing to blockade the bay. Of the two Greek brigs previously anchored off Neocastro, *Lykourgos* and *Aleksandros*, he could see nothing. Looming large before the visible Greek brigs, a mile to the south, their Turk enemies included a frigate, four brigs and several corvettes.

Through the telescope Duncan could make out two corvettes closing on the fleeing *Athina*, one each side of her, getting ever nearer and seemingly intent on boarding - no difficult task in the weak wind and *Athina* likely perceived as an easy victim; and then she fired both her broadsides, the thunderous detonations clearly audible on distant *Aris's* deck. The result was unexpected: the Turk corvettes veered away, perhaps having suffered casualties; more likely their captains were minded to leave the dangerous task to their heavier sisters, the brigs and frigate. 'Bravo!' shouted Duncan, handing the glass back to Votsis, an immediate rise in morale palpable in the frightened men of *Aris* as Votsis recounted what had happened ahead.

Duncan, the glass back in his hand, stared ahead, fascinated but keen to see what reaction would develop from the Turks: *Athina* was fading into the distance, seemed to be through the blockade, but her sisters, *Achilleus* and *Poseidonas*, were imminently about to encounter it, all the Turk vessels around the two Greek brigs discharging their guns, the barrage of sound audible from a mile off, the Greek brigs - outgunned greatly and outnumbered - valiantly returning fire. The weak wind was a crushing disappointment: it had dropped to the merest of breeze, and the adverse odds were such that Captain Moulas of *Poseidonas* had seemingly hit upon an innovative idea: he had affixed barrels to the side of his brig - which puzzled Duncan. Votsis explained, 'A clever man, Moulas... the barrels are weighted, as can be seen - they hang heavy on the hull side - and so must be filled with something - likely water, for he has no tar or any other material to make fire barrels. Perhaps some of the Turks will believe he is a fireship? The trick may yet save him.'

The distance between *Aris* herself and the small battle was not great but the time between them in the weak wind was significant - an hour at least. Whatever the outcome - and it could not conceivably be favourable for the two Greek brigs presently heavily engaged - the enemy squadron would have plentiful time to regroup to meet *Aris* alone, and with the full force of all their massed guns. It was a dark and depressing thought. Then a blinding flash - quickly followed by the thunderous noise of explosion - one of the Turk brigs, that one which had been most determinedly attacking *Poseidonas* for the past twenty minutes, had vanished in an instant. 'Her powder magazine!' cried Duncan to Jason. Dalby and Mason, the two *Surprise* seamen who had returned to deck, roared exultant profanities. The effect of the catastrophic explosion of the enemy brig was immediate, all attackers sheered off from the two Greek brigs which emerged beyond the blockade relatively unscathed, this visible to the crew of *Aris* who were cheering vocally for a minute before subsiding to mute observation: cold reality had come home. On they drifted in the breeze, near nothing to propel them towards the Turk fleet, seemingly mired.

Pickering appeared on *Surprise's* quarterdeck, visibly anxious, 'The ship is cleared for action, sir.'

'Very good, Mr Pickering,' said Pat, nodding his head absently, deep in thought. 'Pray take yourself up to the crosstrees with a glass and study the Turk fleet... that is to say the number of frigates, brigs and the like near the mouth... and with particular attention to how they endeavour to deal with the Greek brigs seeking to escape... and one more thing... look carefully to the course the Greeks choose at the narrows and beyond.'

'Yes sir,' Pickering nodded and started up the rigging.

'Mr Codrington, the men are to be called to their dinner. There will be little or no time later,' said Pat. 'If we survive,' the thought he kept to himself.

Simon appeared together with Marston in that moment, both men visibly in great anxiety. 'Would you be in contemplation of leaving, Pat?'

'I dare say you may have missed - from the companionway that is - that the men are standing at their guns... and here too.' Pat waved his arm towards the carronades, three men at each.

Simon merely scowled. 'If I may enquire... what are your intentions, sir?' asked Marston with an audible degree of trepidation. Pat, taken aback by the gross queries, stared at the chaplain and pondered his reply.

'You do have a plan?' prompted Simon icily.

'Certainly I have a plan,' retorted Pat with a trifle of ire.

'I am tolerably pleased to hear it,' said Simon quietly.

The ears of all at the helm pricked up, each man studiously striving not to stare, but their glances alerted Pat to a careful answer, 'Oh, if the wind will pick up... as is customary in the afternoon, then we will have the weather gage and can choose our course for the mouth and through it. At present we barely have steerage way, but the Turk cannot enter the bay because of that... not to mention the Fort's guns. I venture it will take us two hours to reach the narrows... and a lot may happen in that time... a plentiful lot.'

'And when we reach the mouth... and the vast preponderance of the Turk fleet...' Simon's unfinished question hung in the air, everyone within earshot waiting - all else forgotten - for Pat's answer, every man praying passionately that it would be credible, encouraging.

'The fort may assist us...' said Pat, clutching for the straw he sought but which he knew, in his heart, did not exist, 'and the Turks will surely take time to come about, will likely find themselves in irons...' Blank stares from Simon and Marston, Pat added, 'and then we will take our leave.'

'You are minded this is a feasible plan?' Simon pressed.

'It is the only plan... the only way out.'

'Perhaps we should stay inside the bay... We have the protection of the fort?' offered Marston, whose courage, whilst exemplary in some circumstances - acting as surgeon being one of them - had bounds, ones which did not stretch to such momentous occasions.

Pat sighed inwardly and bit his tongue. He had thought he had seen the back of Marston's ill-considered suggestions, which seemed to recurr only in the least convenient circumstances. 'Mr

Marston...' Pat strived for cordiality, for civility with his chaplain, 'I have been in two mi... that is to say... I... I have been weighing our choices...' He sought to project a degree of reassurance in his voice, which he did not feel in the least himself, and spoke in mild voice, 'Were the Turks to enter the bay then our situation would be perilous indeed. For want of room to manouevre we would be hemmed in... bottled up inside, whilst a dozen of Turks could bombard us at their leisure. It is a perilous position to be in, no doubt, and so it is far, *far* too dangerous to stay here.'

'I see,' Marston's acknowledgement betrayed his utter incomprehension.

'No, we must use what little advantage we have with this light air. The Turk cannot come in at present, the wind being unfavourable, and so we must ready ourselves for the right moment... await the smallest increase in the wind, approach the mouth at just that instant... *to race away*... south, as fast as ever can be.' His audience appeared to be less than convinced, the words "race" and "fast" striking an incredible chord. It was no great plan, as Pat admitted to himself, and so he added, 'We *will* race away... like *Champion* in the Saint Leger... and, I collect, the Derby too in that same year.' More blank stares. 'Did you know Saint Patrick himself has won the race?' Pat laughed at his listeners gaping bemusement. 'Saint Patrick *the horse* that is.' He laughed again. 'The Saint Leger Stakes it was - only a few years back... in the year 'twenty if my memory serves me.'

'Really, brother, this is hardly the time for jest,' said Simon sharply, the realisation of the perilous prospects for escape prompting the fear settling within his thoughts. 'Would it be uncivil to ask, Pat, is it not madness to enter into the midst of such a host when there is a want of wind? Surely so?'

In reality, *Surprise* only having just passed by the Spagia Shoal and the wind having diminished to hardly a breath more than a flat calm, Pat knew in his heart that there was little hope, yet he could not admit it, for such would discourage his men, and it was not inconceivable that the wind *might* strengthen again, and in just that moment when such was needed to pass those Turk vessels which would likely be mired, held up in irons. 'Not that all such *would* be so,' he reminded himself. 'Everything will depend on timing and coincidence,' he declared, though with a degree of conviction that fell short of entirely carrying his audience, 'and, for sure, the wind. A stronger one is essential if there is to be any prospect of escape at all.'

Murphy appeared with sandwiches and a flask of coffee, handed over with no words exchanged, a mutual nod seeming to suffice for both men; Murphy cognisant of the peril they were in and the intense pressure on his master to save them all, and Pat's mind gripped with an absolute focus on planning the next few hours, on what might be done for the best possible result and the least casualties, no longer any capacity left for pleasantries or even civilities. Murphy was well aware of this and departed swiftly.

The Kuloneski islet abaft on the port quarter and Pat looked to his watch: *Surprise* had gained barely a mile in the past hour. *If only* the wind would strengthen, *if only Surprise* reached the bay mouth and the Turk fleet at that particular time it did so, *if only* the Turks were lying-to, *if only* they could not fall off and fill their sails quickly whilst *Surprise* passed by, *if only Surprise* did not lose her own sails to enemy shot in doing so, then - were all these things to come about, *every one of them* - then there was a chance, *a very small chance* of survival. Of course Pat did not care to elaborate on these possibilities to Simon or Marston, but he was sure that every other man in his crew understood them perfectly well; not that any person would speak of such, most certainly not to the surgeons, but all would be constantly weighing up every factor as *Surprise* closed on the narrows and the great firepower of the enemy fleet.

In a strained atmosphere on deck, in near silence save for a cough or a spit, on they sailed or rather drifted, for the wind showed not the least sign of strengthening, which was not what Pat had expected, because it customarily did so in the early afternoon as the land to the north and east - whence the wind originated over the Anatolian interior - warmed through the peak of the day.

'I am minded we will fly topgallants... stuns'ls too, Mr Pickering,' said Pat, 'We have need of every stitch of canvas she possesses.'

All the extra canvas hoisted, *Surprise* glided on, the additional sails making precious little difference; none at all, in fact, as Pat admitted to himself. Simon and Marston lingered at the rail on the quarterdeck, gazing south, both men aware that's Pat's attentions were closed to them.

'Will he succeed with this... this desperate scheme, colleague?' asked Marston nervously.

'Oh I have not the least doubt that he will... *we* will,' replied Simon, his hesitant voice betraying his real belief. 'We have been in greater pickles in the past,' though in that instant he could not recall any, certainly none which presented a more dire prospect, 'and O'Connor has always prevailed.'

'Deck there!' hailed Pickering. 'Three Greek brigs are engaged!' The sound of firing, two miles distant, reached the ears of all on *Surprise*, gun flashes visible, grey smoke clouds exploding to obscure the view, lingering in rising, drifting swathes, no wind of note to disperse it. The general tension aboard increased.

All about the decks the gunners were preparing for action: plentiful wads and shot stacked adjacent to the guns and slow matches lit - the gunners were happiest with a reserve in case the flintlock flashed and fizzled out, the spark not reaching the charge.

Progress being measured in yards not miles, Pat pondered what options might be open to him in the time before reaching the narrows. The firing to the south, beyond the bay entrance had subsided, the three Greek brigs had broken free from the trap which was the bay. Pickering reported on the quarterdeck - he had descended from aloft, 'The last of the Greeks, *Aris*, is closing on the Turks, sir.'

'Did you glean anything from your observations, Mr Pickering?' asked Pat.

'Only that the three Greek brigs maintained the centre of the channel, sir... did not shift to either side.'

'Mmmm... presumably they were minded to maintain lee room?' Pat was talking to himself.

'And...' Pickering resumed with his afterthought, 'two of the brigs passed through the blockade of many Turks and then a third, yet had they encountered the Royal Navy there must be no doubt that they would have been destroyed or at least taken.'

'Why, sir, would the Turk allow passage?' Marston piped up.

'The Turk has a great fear of fireships, Mr Marston,' replied Pat, 'We saw that at the battle in the Bay of Gerontas. Every captain is aware that he is aboard a... a plentiful source of combustible materials... The ropes are all soaked in tar to preserve them - *and highly flammable it is*. The deck is caulked with pitch... and that burns tolerably well - *perish the thought!* The sails, fanned by the wind, will not last five minutes were they to catch... and were the flames to reach the powder - the ready-use cartridges or - *heaven forbid* - the magazine, well... the result is what we saw off Psara... detonation and utter annihilation... not a man will survive. No, one way or another, we must look to that fear, that justifiable fear... It is the only thing which might yet save us.'

'I'm sure you are in the right of things there,' said Simon without a trace of conviction, his vacant face revealing his fears.

'And if the wind does not freshen?' Marston again.

Pat groaned inwardly, 'Such had crossed my mind, for sure...' He stared at the chaplain, looked to Simon, glanced near imperceptibly towards his men and the master at the helm, looked forward a little ways to Pickering and Codrington. It was plain that every man hung on his next words. 'Well... do you swim, Mr Marston?' A general burst of laughter from all nearby, the helmsmen both convulsed with mirth until Barton kicked them, the officers - both smiling - swiftly reining back their own chortling. The glummest of faces only from Marston and Simon, and Pat resumed, 'To tell you the truth, Mr Marston, I am minded that we have no choice, none; it is, frankly... and I would not say this to anyone, save that you have pressed me... it is sink or swim - for the barky that is, and,' Pat raised his voice considerably, nearly shouting, 'I place my confidence... *my life*... in the hands of Saint Patrick himself... *and our shipmates*, OUR GUNNERS, THE VERY BEST OF MEN , EH? WHAT SAY YOU ALL?'

From the helm, from the waist, from a score or more of men who had been listening attentively and with great amusement since

Pat's joke and who had heard his declaration came a resounding 'HEAR HEAR!'

The wind on the port quarter and, unusually, all sails aloft, *Surprise* bore down on the narrows, 'And perhaps she will be... really so this time... sailing to her final destiny?' thought Pat, his mind racing to find something more, anything, *anything at all*, however seemingly insignificant which might yet help her to survive the imminent conflagration. 'The empty pork barrels... the empty beef ones... Mr Codrington. Take thirty men and bring them up on deck. Put men to the hoses and fill them sufficiently to hold them in place - all along the waist, the forepeak... and let us have a pair on the quarterdeck.'

'Aye aye, sir,' Codrington hastened away, mystified; how strange was that? What with shifting iron ballast off to another vessel and now hauling up empty pork barrels, he could find no answer at all.

On *Aris's* deck Duncan, pulling Jason's arm, edged towards a discussion held near the wheel between Votsis, Sakhtouri and three seniors, the remaining officers of *Aris*. 'What's afoot?' murmured Duncan to Jason.

'They are debating whether to exit the mouth as close as close can be to the eastern shore, which is shallower and which may present some doubt and possibly a degree of difficulty for the Turk captains... at least hesitancy in pursuit... or whether to stay in the centre of the channel; the water is deeper there... and bear directly at - and hopefully through - the Turk ships... though the significance of either choice is beyond me, I confess,' said Jason resignedly.

'The wind,' pronounced Duncan without hesitation, 'the weak wind giving us so little motion, were we close on the lee shore over there we would have little prospect of manoeuvre - we cudnae make short boards - and would likely be pinned at their mercy until our destruction... nae, the centre of the channel it must be, come what may... at least we have the north wind to help us and they dinnae, and that advantage, precious little it is, may yet set things in our favour.'

Dogana harbour a half-mile directly ahead and Pat decided that *Surprise* would make two short boards before reaching the entrance to the bay and the Turk blockade. 'Bring her about, Mr Pickering, towards the tip of the island.'

Surprise came round slowly, the crew having no difficulty in bracing the yards for her new course, sailing now on a broad reach, the wind three points abaft the starboard beam: just one final mile to go to reach the narrows. Pat looked about him once more, a dozen of empty barrels had been evenly distributed about the foc'sle, at the waist and on the quarterdeck, all of which would be perfectly visible to any Turk officer with or without a glass. 'Perhaps, when the shot is flying and the smoke obscures all detail, they will believe that they are tar barrels,' Pat hoped, 'and they may shy away.' It was a feeble hope, he admitted, but he had precious little else available to help him. A little more than a half-mile on the bow and no more than a half-hour ahead, *Aris* would plainly be in dire difficulties in very little time: she would be surrounded by Turks and bombarded from all sides. Pat could not conceive how she could possibly long survive; the first two Turks were approaching her already; much closer and they could not conceivably miss - even were they the worst gunners in the world, which the Turks generally were, Pat did concede - but they would certainly inflict grave damage upon her, and in short order indeed. His thoughts shifted to Duncan, to Jason, to his men; he hoped they were all aboard *Aris*; if not... if they had remained on the island then they surely would by now be dead. A surge of distress surged though him and he fought to dismiss the thought.

Surprise was barely drifting at a mere one knot - so the line indicated - and Pat gazed to the south to see what more, if anything, he might see of the Turk fleet. Just at that moment his eye caught, from atop the southern extremity of Sphacteria, a quarter-mile fine on the starboard bow, three puffs of gunsmoke. 'The damned battery! The Egyptians have taken it and are firing upon us!' His mind raced, his eyes caught the splash of the shot, all fallen short off the port bow. The officers and men of *Surprise* had seen it too, anxious glances directed towards Pat. 'Hold firm, Patrick O'Connor,' he said to himself quietly, 'Hold firm to your course.'

He wanted to make as much westing as possible before coming about one final time to hold the wind on her port quarter as she exited the narrows; it would give her what precious little room there was to preserve manouevrability and a last chance to keep a trifle of wind on all the sails - which would not be possible if she changed course too soon and put the wind directly aft; 'No, that would not best serve her; keep going and damn the Egyptian gunners,' he murmured to himself.

Slowly *Aris* drifted south, the distance to her likely destruction diminishing near imperceptibly, time shifting very slowly. The crew had all gathered about their officers, all circling the priest who had been saved from Sphacteria. From below deck one crewman had emerged with an icon of Holy Mary which was passed round to every man to kiss as the priest conducted an impromptu service, every man placing all his worldly money on the icon and murmuring a few words as he held it, an ambience of setback, of rising despair prevalent amongst them. The service concluded with every man staring vacantly, in private thought, a deflation of mood seemingly settling upon them all, until one man disappeared below deck to emerge within moments with a lighted candle, plainly distressed and shouting, 'We have lost our captain!' An echoed murmur of dismay rang round the crew, the man holding the candle seemingly drawing conviction from the faces of the downcast. He shouted again, 'We have lost our captain... brave Tsamados... what is the point of living without him?' A rising surge of concern and alarm became evident to everyone, the Surprises - near the companionway steps - stared, puzzled, Jason translating with the tint of alarm in his own voice. The seaman with the candle became more distressed, shouting louder, his friends now pleading with him. 'I shall see you all in the next world!' he cried and lunged towards the steps to the lower deck.

'He is running for the powder,' shrieked Votsis, Jason translating a second later, the man nearing the companionway. Just at that moment Dalby stuck out a leg and tripped him, the candle flying towards the scuppers. Dalby and Mason promptly sat on him and seized him until Votsis and the man's shipmates could reach him. Five minutes and he calmed sufficiently to be released and closely escorted to his gun, his shipmates not taking their eyes from him, talking to him, calming him with words of reassurance, of small comfort.

'Dalby...' said Duncan, '...dinnae get any thoughts like that when we're back aboard the barky! Well done, laddie.'

Mavrocordato's black servant hastened below to report the event to his master who had elected to sit in the cabin, a pistol at hand, determined that he would not be captured.

'Nae wind worth tuppence,' declared Duncan gloomily to his shipmates. The battery on the south-east side of Sphacteria, since captured by the Egyptians, began to fire, *Aris* a sitting target, barely moving. Powerless to reply, *Aris* continued to drift inexorably into the middle of the narrows, all her sails aloft, four Turk vessels tacking at a snail's pace ever closer to her in the light air, bow chasers firing from a frigate and a corvette to starboard of her, the same a few hundred yards - no more - off her port bow and all striving to turn to open their broadsides upon her.

'FIRE!' screamed Votsis, and the Greek gunners touched their slow matches to flash the powder in the gun pans; bright flames, thunderous explosions and huge dense clouds of stinking sulphorous smoke erupted from *Aris's* eight starboard guns, the shot flying accurately to strike the frigate hard along her upper hull, swathes of debris visibly flying in all directions, several holes appearing in her sails, none clewed up with the wind so weak, near non-existent. No time to applaud, the gunners swabbed barrels, rammed in fresh charges, wads, and shot; all thrust in and rammed home as fast as could be; the crews heaved their guns back out, quickly leaping aside before their own gun roared again; FIRE! The guns jumped back as if violently thrown, as they were by the violent recoil - the process starting all over.

Duncan and the Surprises stared about them, desperately keen to do something useful, anything to assist, but nothing of opportunity was seemingly open to them; the Greek gunners were all, thus far, unscathed, but then the frigate's twenty-four pound heavy shot came whistling in, high, ripping holes in *Aris's* sails, all of which had been left hanging in hopeful wait for the wind.

FIRE! The portside guns of *Aris* detonated simultaneously, the brig heeling slightly, a great cloud of gunsmoke hanging in the still air. On their way, well aimed, flying low to smash into the nearing corvette, significant damage visibly inflicted upon the lighter vessel.

Shot continued to fly all about *Surprise* and in greater proximity, though fortunately without any strikes, until she closed the rocks on the southern point of the island, the Mikro Thoura channel a mere hundred yards ahead and Pylos Island fine on the port bow, when the Egyptian gunners were not able to depress their guns any further and the barrage ceased. Dalby rang one bell of the first dog watch as furious firing exploded again to the south: it was *Aris*, trying to breach the blockade. 'May Saint Patrick help her,' murmured Pat under his breath. He looked all about him as innocently as could be, contemplated the still exceptionally weak wind, the lack of any tension on the braces, the canvas plainly under no press of load; he looked to his men, saw nothing except steadfast commitment, a self-confidence within them; not to say he did not have that himself, for he had it aplenty, but at that moment the odds against his ship and his men surviving had never, in all his life at sea, been greater. Pat gazed again through his glass at *Aris* off the port beam and now a half-dozen of enemies closing around her, the sound of the firing, much closer, very audible, profoundly disturbing and a grim foretaste of what *Surprise* could imminently expect to endure. 'Bring her about, Mr Pickering,' cried Pat; now was the time to set her course through the narrows, in the middle of the channel, as all the Greeks had done.

The men hauled on the braces, little of tension in the weak wind, the helmsmen similarly needing not the least exertion to haul the wheel hard over, and *Surprise,* no difficulty for her in the following wind, came round to her new course, bearing directly for the middle of the mouth of the bay. She was still moving at scarcely more than a drift, no strain on the sails or braces, and all set - come what may - for her imminent destiny, 'Sink or swim?' the thought on many a mind in that crystallising moment: *Surprise* was about to enter the lions' den and there were plenty of them within it. Men of lesser courage would have despaired; the Surprises, though fearful, did not.

"BOOM, BOOM, BOOM..." the Turk firing had begun, a far frigate opening upon *Surprise*, albeit Pat had little concern at present: a strike at such range was unlikely to trouble the ship and the strike itself was unlikely, he thought; but he stared intently at distant *Aris*, the small Greek brig obviously beginning to take a pounding. Would she survive? He could see holes in her sails. All about her were four Turks firing all they possessed, one a heavy frigate. Her guns would surely do frightful damage, and he could not dispel the thought that *Surprise* was her next target.

'Run out the guns!' cried Pat, and the decks reverberated to the rumbling vibration of the heavy truck weights as the twenty-eight long guns were hauled out through their ports. '*Surprise* will show that she too has teeth,' thought Pat, 'and exceedingly dangerous ones they are, to be sure.'

From his quarterdeck Pat could see that *Aris* was about to be consumed with dire difficulties; even in the bilious clouds of grey gunsmoke filling the narrows it was possible for the Surprises to see the brig, little more than a half-mile ahead amidst five Turk vessels closing on her. Pat racked his brain for something, *anything at all* which might assist her, for the engagement was beyond *Surprise's* guns, even were she not bow on and only her small chasers capable of aim. 'Damn it!' Pat swore in loud voice, exasperated, 'There's not a thing we can do to help.'

'Never you mind, sir,' the voice came from behind Pat, from the nearest carronade; it was Old Jelbert. 'A quarter hour, sir, no longer, and we will send a few of 'em to hell.'

'Jelbert, there you are!' a despairing Pat welcomed the diversion. 'I am concerned I might be going there myself,' he confided. 'How about you... how are you?'

'Oh no, sir... I'm going up there,' Jelbert nodded his head upwards, 'I'm going to join my son... my lad.'

Pat gagged, could say nothing; he merely stared, a long and painfully reflective minute passing before he spoke again, 'You take care today... old shipmate... take plenty of care... you hear me? Will I send you to the magazine?'

'Sir, I am a gunner... I like to think I was a fine gunner... on the old *Tenedos*... and here is my place... here, at the guns. I will *never* let you down, sir... oh no; have no fears o' that.'

'I never doubted that for a minute... for never a minute,' Pat mumbled, greatly set back. He had foreseen all kinds of outcomes for the hour ahead, a daunting plenty of possibilities, mostly of the losing kind, of severe damage, many casualties for sure; and his spirits had been sinking for the past hour, but from the words with Old Jelbert he took heart, clung to a firming conviction that, whilst the battle and its likely toll would be severe, never would he have better men all about him.

Surprise barely drifted on, the weak breeze giving her little more than steerage way, a total and utter silence prevailing across all her decks and guns, the sole sound being early shot from the Turks, inaccurate thus far. 'Long may that last,' thought Pat.

The Sphacteria battery had been left astern, *Surprise* was in the narrows and under fire from the combined Egyptian and Turk fleet blocking the exit from the bay. Scores of warships of several sizes loomed large ahead of her: corvettes, brigs and even frigates. The Greek brig, *Aris*, was perhaps a mere half-mile ahead and immersed within the enemy fleet, so many of them around the bay approach in such a congested and small area that only a few could use their guns against her. Even so, to Pat's experienced eye it was plain that she was being inexorably pulverised, and he was doubtful that she could endure for sufficient time to escape; before long her sails and masts would surely be so damaged that she would lose all powers of movement whatever the wind chose to do.

Pat studied the Turk ships: they were near immobile, precious little wind for any vessel, turning near impossible and certainly a slow progress, particularly so with the weak north-easterly breeze affording no opportunity for the Turks to come closer into the narrows between the fort of Neocastro and the southern rocks of the island. How could he make use of that? He wracked his brain: *Surprise* would benefit from the wind astern - up to a point, but if and when she cleared any opposition - and "if" was a very big word sometimes - then the Turks would doubtless turn to pursue her - and in overwhelming strength. How could the barky possibly escape from them? What did *Surprise* - a relatively modest frigate in these times of modern forty-fours - have to discourage them? Plainly the simplistic deception of barrels on the deck might deter boarding - *might* - but the firepower available to the combined Egyptian and Turk fleet would enable it to pulverise her from a distance. Not that they were renowned gunners, and as long as *Surprise* preserved her masts and sails then perhaps there was a chance she could get away, but not without wind, and such was the dire state of the present weather. Fully four hours to sunset, thought Pat: it was a lifetime; indeed, it probably would be his remaining lifetime, such was the chilling thought that came to mind.

'Bring her about, Mr Prosser,' said Pat in a controlled voice, 'South-west.'

'Aye aye, sir,' murmured the master. 'Helm hard over, lads! Hard a port!' Men raced to the braces, the yards were heaved round, the wind now near directly astern, not that *Surprise* lost anything of her paltry speed: she still moved at a tired snail's pace, her starboard guns now ranging on the armada off her starboard bow, precious little off her shallower port side save for a brace of schooners.

Simon and Marston hastened below, greatly dismayed, for their future looked likely to be as bloody as anything they had experienced before. Codrington and Pickering descended to the gun deck.

Aris was under attack from all sides, shot and grape whistling across the deck, the heavy iron balls smashing with dreadful damage done at such short range into her hull. Numerous holes began to appear in her sails, her rigging was torn and ripped in several places. Duncan had great admiration for the Greek sailors, hastening through the hurricane of fire to do what they could to reaffix any rope which might conceivably hazard the brig, knotting broken ropes of all purposes, and all the while she returned fire, her sixteen guns blazing away furiously. 'Fire!' Here and there Dalby and Mason helped to heave out a reloaded gun, Dalby's great strength gratefully acknowledged by hard-pressed gunners with a grim nod, no words could he understand. 'Fire!' The meaning was clear, no translation needed. Duncan remained near the helm with Votsis and Sakhtouri, an exceedingly frightened Jason translating for him. The brig being a relatively smaller vessel than *Surprise* it was not difficult to follow the situation on board, the damage sustained and the efforts of the gunners particularly. The Greeks did not waver: men worked tirelessly up and down from below with more charges, more shot, more wads; others ran the guns out, sponged, reloaded, leaped back before the crashing explosion, the face of every man become black as coal from the frequency of the discharges. 'Fire!'

The range for every vessel firing was close and the guns of *Aris* had systematically pulverised the closest corvette which had lost much of its gunwale; its sails had been shredded, its mast shot away and tumbled, the hull holed in a half-dozen places with gaping ragged splinters projecting within and over everything on her side. Duncan believed she must be holed below the waterline and imagined that the loss of life must be very severe. *Aris* fired once again, and the corvette captain ordered his vessel to sheer off.

Strangely, the other attackers appeared to be influenced by the corvette shifting away; perhaps a general order had been given to all as they too began to increase their distance from *Aris*. Duncan had marvelled at the determination of *Aris*'s men to keep up their fire at such a tremendous rate; their aim too had been shockingly devastating - at least as far as the first corvette which, he noticed, was plainly sinking, her men taking to her remaining boat, the other smashed to splinters in the fight. A degree of caution had overtaken the other Turks, the gap opening to nearer a quarter mile from the previous hundred and even fifty yards in the case of the second corvette. Not that *Aris* could escape, for there was little wind; the near perfect calm had endured for four long hours, the motion of every vessel measured in yards, sails limp, nothing of the familiar slap of wave and roll of hull. Yet now, Duncan observed, there was a distinct feeling that the wind was picking up a little, freshening; it was no more than a light breeze, but certainly there was a flutter in the limp sails of the brig, and *Aris* had gained a little momentum, southbound, but still exceedingly slow. He wondered how long the relative lull might last.

Aris had been fighting for two hours when the Turk frigates returned, taking advantage of the improving wind, one on each side of her, firing as they crept ever closer, their movement still infinitely slow. The Turk gunners were poor, Duncan had long concluded, because much of their shot missed the Greek brig entirely, so much so that he believed it had been as much of a danger to their own ships, so close had they been to *Aris* before shifting away; but now she was the meat in the sandwich, the two frigates sustaining a slow but consistent barrage, shot and shrapnel flying the short distance to strike the Greek brig. The sails of *Aris* were shredded, her bulwarks heavily battered and broken. The *Aris* gunners, barefooted, were burning their feet as they stepped on hot fragments of shrapnel on their deck, the engagement so close, the metal cooling only slowly. Half an hour of intensive bombardment from the two Turk frigates and they began to close upon a severely damaged *Aris*. Her own fire had slackened, her men were exhausted and her powder and shot reserves were shrinking. Still no wind of sufficient strength to make an escape or perhaps to get close inshore where the water depth, or relative lack of it, might deter the frigates, *Aris* could not shift beyond the crawl of the past hour.

The two frigates were sure that *Aris* was done for - her fire had slackened considerably - and closer they came with a perceptible drift, two hundred yards only. Those few of *Aris's* guns remaining active were much slower in firing but were still inflicting considerable destruction at such close range. Closer, on came the two Turk frigates, a hundred yards off and inexorably converging, no prospect this time of shying away.

Captain Votsis - the Turk intention of boarding his brig plain to all aboard - bawled his order to two men staring at him for his directions, 'Stand by in the powder room... get ready... on my command... fire the powder and blow this vessel to Kingdom Come!' A shocked Jason translated this for Duncan, but he had already gleaned the drift of Votsis's intentions and nothing could he suggest for the better.

The nearer Turk frigate had closed to fity yards of *Aris*, desultory firing continuing from both vessels, and then came an ominous quietening as both sides' gunners ceased fire: the moment of final decision, boarding and hand to hand fighting was upon them all. Thirty yards separation, the frigate now towering over her smaller opponent, twenty yards, the convergence become a near silent drift, eerie - no longer the close roar of guns about them - all of *Aris's* men taking up their personal arms, all readying themselves for the boarding and bloody close combat. Ten yards; Votsis, near his wheel, screamed loud to reach the length of his deck, 'Prepare for the blast... the powder will be exploded!'

The men on the close Turk frigate were clearly visible, excited figures all along her deck clutching pistols and yatagan swords, readying themselves to jump across to *Aris*. The bowsprit of the larger frigate - so near - projected over *Aris*'s stern.

'Brothers!' screamed Votsis again, 'Get ready to be blown into the air!'

On the Turk frigate this was heard by dozens of men all along her decks, many of them in the open gun ports being Greek slaves. The word of Votsis's intentions spread like wildfire, swiftly reaching the Turk captain. 'Hold back!' his panicked order was bellowed instantly and the frigate hauled off, the gap slowly widening, five yards, ten, fifteen, a momentary respite gained for *Aris* and her men.

The separation opened further, the second Turk frigate similarly turning to creep away, the distance growing, the guns of both resuming fire, as did *Aris*, her men a little reinvigorated as certain death had receded, at least for the moment.

'Fire!' bellowed the Greeks all along *Aris's* deck.

'Fire!' screamed the Turk captain of the nearer frigate, and the bombardment resumed in full force. Just at that moment a fortuitous ball from *Aris* struck the Turk frigate's fore course yard, tearing it from the mast and bringing it crashing down over the deck, the frigate immediately ceasing fire.

'Hurrah!' bellowed the Greeks, reinvigorated once more; their attention turned to the second Turk frigate off the other side which had kept firing but appeared to be shifting away, very slowly, no vessel able to do more than crawl in the feeble breeze.

Surprise inched ever closer to the enemy, *Aris* just visible in the mêlée and plainly still under severe attack. The guns were all run out, the men standing ready, the drift of a slow match from near the aftmost carronades caught Pat's nose, a so greatly familiar scent and one that customarily pressaged death. He felt particularly gloomy, the odds so greatly adverse - it seemed akin to Nelson and *Victory* attacking at Trafalgar alone - and he shivered despite the heat, feeling the general rise in tension, apprehension rife on every face all about him; but - he was gratified to see - he saw no fear, and for that he was profoundly grateful; rather there was a confidence borne of experience, of past victories within his men and a belief that *Surprise* would endure, would come through. He certainly hoped so with all his heart, for he dreaded another return to Falmouth akin to the first one, so many of his men lost, so many more wounded. Yet what could he do to prevent that? He continued to wrack his brain, searching for the slightest thing, but nothing would come.

'Ready with the ensign, Barton?'

'Yes sir,' the reply was assured, unwavering; indeed Pat felt heartened by it.

'Very well, let us show our colours.'

Closer and closer, a quarter mile only of separation, *Surprise's* starboard bow on a bearing for the nearest Turk ships, and directly ahead the firing against *Aris* continued, a steady and unrelenting "BOOM... BOOM.. BOOM", gun flashes momentary and repetitive, a glimpse of bright orange flames and no more, voluminous clouds of grey smoke hovering, lingering, no time to disperse before the next gun fired, the risen smoke casting shadows over the Turk ships. 'God help her, she must be being smashed to pieces,' said Pat in a low voice, and then - no officers available to him on the quarterdeck - to Clumsy Dalby, 'The drum, if you please.'

Dalby bashed away with great strength; it was a pure convention, but every gun was already prepared, loaded, run out and waiting. 'Towards the *Aris*... the smoke,' said Pat in a loud voice to the helmsmen, a tiny adjustment made on the wheel. He stepped forward and leaned over the waist rail to shout towards the bow, 'The bow guns will prepare to open fire!' Cognisant of his lamentable lack of officers, Pat determined to make a final and fast inspection along the gun deck; he hastened down the companionway steps, swiftly paced back to where his cabin normally was, four guns projecting through the hull, the dividing partitions all removed, his deck cloth - a chequered black and white pattern - and all his furniture carried below. He nodded to his men, strived for a smile to all attending, every one gazing at him as if in search of confidence, of reassurance that all would come out well. He paused, made the briefest of complimentary remark about their readiness - which seemed to please the gunners - and slowly, deliberately, as slow as he could restrain himself, he about turned and, with a measured pace, stepped forward along the gun deck, gazing at the faces of men there who he had known for long years. They were truly his family aboard ship, every one a veteran, almost all having served aboard *Tenedos* before *Surprise*, and in the measured sense of readiness that every man exhibited, despite the general sense of approaching and likely disastrous conflict - which he saw in many eyes - he felt a tiny shred more reassured, a rising feeling within him that, perhaps, they would endure, might survive, and as he approached the final forward gun he had the warming feeling that his men were wholly with him, would stand beside him until the end. He stepped up the companionway steps after turning to make a final, brief wave to his men, came up near the foc'sle to greet the bow gunners. Not wishing to break his men's concentration, he nodded encouragingly, patted the gun captains' shoulders and hastened away, along the waist, gazing at the prodigious numbers in the squadrons of the combined Turk and Egyptian fleets, a solitary *Aris* minute and subsumed within dense, bilious clouds of white gunsmoke.

Returning to the quarterdeck, his men at the helm and serving at the carronades seemed pleased to see him, nods and grunted greetings extended from many of them.

From the lighter enemy vessels, schooners and some of those smaller brigs which had effected a turn to fall off the wind, their sides near facing *Surprise*, their guns opened a steady barrage, much of which was inaccurate, cold guns firing short, low, to splash shot into the water, ricochets bounding up and away, some of them over *Surprise's* hull, a few brushing past canvas sails under no pressure, an odd hole or two appearing in the main and fore courses, left to hang rather than being clewed up for preservation; for if *Surprise* were to survive she would badly need their motive power and before too long.

The range perfectly suited to both the long guns and the carronades Pat lifted his arm, his whole body tensing. He stepped forward to lean over the waist rail, stared the length of the gun deck. No roll or swell to be concerned about, he lifted his arm, his hat in his hand, and brought it down in a fast sweep and roared with all his voice, 'FIRE!'

'FIRE!' screamed his lieutenants, watching and waiting. There was no rippling broadside, rather a deafening simultaneous explosion as the fourteen starboard long guns and the three carronades on the quarterdeck roared as one. The frigate shook from truck to keelson, her masts quivering, the sails shaken violently, the ears of every man aboard assaulted. Haste took over, every man rushing to prepare his gun, swabbing, charge rammed home, wad in, rammed once more, shot pushed in firm, grape canisters in next, 'STAND ASIDE!' the scream from seventeen gun captains, and then the roar again, the boom, the flash, followed by the noxious discharge of stinking powder, burnt particles momentarily filling the whole of the decks, men coughing even as they strived to reload without the least pause before hauling once more on the ropes of the long guns and pushing the stubby carronades back to their firing positions. The carronades boomed out again, still a respectable simultaneous detonation, the long guns a second or two behind. Pat briefly stared all about him, then looked off, across to the obvious target to see what damage might have been inflicted. A schooner had been struck hard, her mast was down, a hole presumably inflicted in her hull - for she tilted to the side from where *Surprise* had fired; that she was turning away or endeavouring to do so was plain, her principal sail in the water, control compromised; not that there was much of that anyway in the weak wind, but that was one down, 'and plenty more to go,' thought Pat with a grim smile of satisfaction.

Irregular and inaccurate Turk shot was coming in, fired from two brigs and a corvette which had filled the immediate range of *Surprise's* starboard battery, the damaged schooner slipping away behind one of the brigs. Shot whistled overhead, a loud sharp "CLACK" as the mast was struck a glancing strike, no damage visible that Pat could see, though two holes were visible in the main topsail. He stepped forward and stared down from the waist rail to look at the long guns on the gun deck, no let up there, no losses yet, every man industriously applying himself with determination, the proven professionalism of his men very evident, the lack of officers proving no setback even though Pickering and Codrington moved all about them shouting encouragement. The port side gunners, still not engaged, helped pass shot to their starboard comrades, a train of fresh charges coming up from below, canister and grape too to be laid ready for the expected order. Pat looked at their target once more: the near brig was certainly taking a hammering; he could see several sections of her hammock netting and the gunwale below that broken away, and further below were visible impact strikes on the hull along the firing line: several shots must have impacted upon her guns and crews; indeed, her return fire in the last minute had become no more than desultory; she was a fading force, and for that he felt the tiniest tremor of jubilation. The second brig appeared to be hanging back, as did the lighter corvette. His own men were doing their job, doing it very well, with consumate skill and dedication, and for that a tremor of gratitude washed through him in that moment.

Surprise continued her onward progress; indeed, it looked to Pat as if she had made up a little distance on *Aris*, for although he could no longer see her in the dense gunsmoke, he could hear the greater proximity of the firing all about her. *Surprise* herself was shifting into deadly danger, no longer facing a schooner or corvette or two, nor indeed a brig, but ahead, perhaps four hundred yards - two cables - was the undoubted flagship of the Turk squadron if not the fleet, a 44 gun frigate - a formidable opponent and, Pat could not help but notice, very well turned out. In that instant she was, fortunately, stern on to *Surprise*, had presumably been following the engagement with *Aris*, and thus she was not capable of firing on the barky, but that must be expected to change within a very short time. In the meantime, *Surprise* continued to direct her own guns at the weakening brig, the return fire from the brig much diminished and her bow swinging away from the wind, to the west, as if by so doing she might limp away and escape from the deadly, destructive smashing that *Surprise* was inflicting upon her.

'That will never do, my friend,' murmured Pat. He rushed back to the waist rail and screamed, 'Grape, GRAPE! Every gun, NOW!' The gun captains glimpsed his frantically waving arm, heard his order reiterated in another scream and nodded their comprehension; the loaders were shouted at, and - after the wads - into the still steaming muzzles went grapeshot. The brig had turned away and presented her stern gallery; death, imminent death was nigh upon her. Pat looked at the vulnerable stern, he imagined what the result would be; no, he knew what it would be, he had seen it once before, the memory so horrific that he worked tirelessly to keep it out from his mind whenever his thoughts drifted that way. Wresting another turn in his distressed mind, he hesitated for a half-second and he bit so hard on his lower lip that he drew blood. 'May Saint Patrick preserve them... FIRE!' he shrieked, sweeping his arm down, his hand clutching his hat. 'FIRE!' screamed Codrington and Pickering. 'FIRE!' screamed every gun captain, and once more *Surprise's* long guns' ferocious bark was synchronised, fourteen guns flamed and roared concurrently to fling their destructive grapeshot at the brig's stern. The result was catastrophic: a hail obliterated her stern gallery, not a shred of it left save for hanging splinters, thousands of small projectiles flying the length of her gun deck to inflict scores of casualties upon the men serving her guns. The higher-aimed guns of *Surprise* had also swept her quarterdeck clean, not a man was left standing there. Pat swallowed hard, 'Oh my dear God,' escaped his lips; he struggled to dispel the shocking image in his mind of what his guns had inflicted and the hell that it must be inside the brig, what it would now be like for the Turk crew; he saw it clearly in his head - the bloodiest of charnel house. He averted his gaze, waved his congratulations to his gunners, turned back to his own quarterdeck and looked forward to the bow. In the action against the schooner and then the brig, *Surprise* had closed up on the bulk of the enemy fleet which now lay before her in simply frightening numbers, disparate firing from several sources directed at her, shot coming in. He still could not see *Aris*, for the smoke lay over everything ahead in a low blanket, precious little wind to blow it away, but the firing was where he thought she must still be: loud explosions, vigorous flashes, plentiful gunsmoke, a hell for *Aris*. He wondered how the men aboard were surviving, how they possibly could survive, the odds so great against them. He feared for his own men - for his close friend, Duncan, particularly; not that the prospects for *Surprise* looked any brighter; it was a the chilling realisation.

Amidst the daunting, the overwhelming numbers that were the combined Turk and Egyptian fleet all around her, *Surprise* was fighting for her life; the fundamental lack of proficiency of the enemy gunners would never have been tolerated within the Royal Navy, for much of what they fired - and that was at a much slower rate than the Surprises managed, not that it counted for much with the absolute numbers of ships and guns engaged - either fell short, wide or flew high. The audible barrage was greater than the physical one, a terrifying, deafening and continuous roll of thunder accompanied by the shrill whistling of shot and grape flying all around the men of *Surprise*, all diligently still serving their guns. Now and then came a thundering, smashing strike as a Turk ball struck the hull, the sound and vibration reverberating all through the ship.

Below, thus far the surgeons had not experienced the calamitous, blood-soaked disaster that they had feared; for grave apprehension had gripped them for several hours, both Simon and Marston dreading the desperate cries, wails and screams of their anticipated stream of casualties, one such as they had dealt with in the Samos battles, the likes of which they never wished to see again; and, thus far, their dreams, their desperately pleaded supplications had been answered. However, there was a constant flow of more minor injuries: unpleasant flesh wounds from splinters and metal grape particules lodged in arms or legs, but nothing life-threatening, and they marvelled silently at their good fortune and that of their crewmen.

One particular Turk brig had closed on *Surprise* in the thick smoke, but the barky's guns - red hot, recoiling with the most violent kick and greatly overheating, for they could not be rested - were still firing a furious three shots in five minutes, the lesser-engaged port side gunners exchanging with the starbowlins to maintain the devastating destruction *Surprise* was meting out. This did not deter the closing brig; on she came despite all the attention of *Surprise's* gunners upon her, all the frigate's guns still roaring furiously, throwing a spray of metal death and human destruction, killing scores of Turk crewmen as the range diminished. The Turk captain pressed on, seeing his own guns ripping into *Surprise*, smashing into her bulwarks, splintering the boats hung amidships, flinging gun port doors away, shot breaking through to strike guns, grape flailing down gunners.

On *Surprise's* quarterdeck, the situation looked as grim as ever it could be: *Surprise* could not long endure where she was; another hour or even a half-hour of this and she would be burning and likely sinking. In that moment, Old Jelbert shouted to Pat, 'Sir, 'tis surely time to fire my new shot?'

Pat nodded, shouted to three men to help Jelbert. The four men hastened down the steps into the hull, returning within three minutes, each carrying two cylinders. The three carronades on the starboard side were each loaded with powder, a wad and then a cylinder. That one of the Turk brigs which had closed to only a hundred yards away was now the most urgent of targets.

'Ready sir!' shouted Jelbert.

Pat nodded, 'Fire!' The three carronades cracked, flung their novel cylinder shots away, every eye on the *Surprise* quarterdeck staring, hopeful, uncertain. What would they do? Would they strike? Would they succeed?

A hundred yards of separation and the projectiles in the air: one flew between the Turk's masts to disappear, a second struck the lower hull, no penetration apparent, the cylinder disappearing - presumably into the water. The third struck the upper bulwark, breaking through onto the deck, ricocheting into some obstruction, invisible to the Surprises, a sense of deflation, of failure gripping them all; Pat shook his head, disappointed, his mind returning to the desperate difficulty *Surprise* was in, more shots flying overhead from the close Turk brig, and then there was a flash of orange light, a sharp "CRACK" noise and an explosion aboard the Turk brig, swiftly followed by a roaring fire upon her deck, a fire the size of a modest bonfire: the cylinder had exploded! Greek Fire it was which was aiding them! Pat gazed through his glass; he saw consternation erupting on the brig's quarterdeck, flames shooting up the obstructing main mast that the cylinder had struck, her mainsail aflame. All along *Surprise's* side her men gazed out through their gun ports for the brief second before the gun captain pulled on his lanyard to fire his gun. A momentary pause as the scene was taken in, and then the three carronades fired once more, the three cylinders flying away, two of them to smash upon the upper deck of the brig, fiery explosions the result within seconds, and all the Turk crew plainly in panic, everything clearly visible from *Surprise*. Two more fires began to rage, the foresails also gripped with flame, the brig's guns all falling silent. The Surprises could not believe their eyes; there was a momentary pause before a rolling chorus of cheers rang out from them. Her own gunners, no longer any need to fire upon the Turk brig - for she was plainly done for - stared and gratefully drew breath. It was doubtful that the Turk would long survive, for the fire had gained hold, her men were leaping into the sea, her sails were aflame, holes appearing, the canvas crisping.

But now the next Turk brig came into range of *Surprise's* port side guns, thus far relatively much less engaged, the gunners retaining more energy than their shipmates who had borne the burden thus far. Old Jelbert and his comrades switched to the three carronades on the port side of the quarterdeck, loaded the new weapon, the incendiary cylinders, and fired without delay. The approaching Turk brig was splattered with two of the novel canisters, flame erupting as before, an immediate hiatus in firing from the brig before her turn away, very slowly, flame rising up her mainmast to grip the course, roaring away quickly to consume the canvas. Pat and his men had never seen the likes of the new weapon, were dumbstruck, gazed in disbelief: Greek Fire, after an absence of centuries!

Aris, a half-mile south of *Surprise*, was smashed, could barely manouevre; her sails were holed, pierced and torn in many places and could not help her away from sure and eventual destruction at the guns of the surrounding enemy multitude even though the wind had freshened; for all the other Egyptian ships had left the west coast of Sphacteria, the invasion concluded, and had begun to converge on the action. They were closing slowly all about *Aris* in the greater expanse of sea south of the narrows: thirty-five ships Duncan counted with rising despair. Despite and miraculously only the two men having been killed as they departed Panagia Landing, he was mindful that there was still perhaps a half-hour of daylight remaining; it was plentiful enough time for the Turks to complete the destruction of the Greek brig; all hope of escape had consequently long been expunged and Duncan had resigned himself to the role of a fascinated observer until death - which now seemed inevitable - came upon him and all the men of *Aris*. Jason, who was customarily on the lower deck when in action, had gone below to see what he could do to help the wounded men - miraculously there were only six of them thus far, Sakhtouri being one of them - for Jason did not care to admit that he had withdrawn somewhat into his own state of shock.

Duncan stared aft, gazed north, firing continuing beyond the smoke of gunfire, beyond a score of Ottoman vessels of all sizes, the light beginning to diminish as the sun descended to the western horizon. Traditionally, the Turks did not much care to perpetuate any battle as dusk approached, and he began to feel the tiniest inkling of hope once more, to pray for the slim prospect of survival. The following battle still raging to the north had certainly diverted Turk interest from the shattered brig; indeed, the damage and destruction wrought upon her was such that the observer might conclude that she was finished, her sinking inevitable. It was getting dark as *Aris* slowly slipped away, the previous early evening flurry of wind was subsiding once more. The great clouds of gunsmoke had settled like a blanket, no wind sufficient to dissipate it; *Aris* was sailing into darkness; the Turks had lost all interest in her.

On *Surprise*, Pat was despairing. The feared Turk frigate was turning; from the short range of three hundred yards Pat knew without the least doubt that her heavy 24- or 36-pound guns would wreak havoc on *Surprise*; the present weak wind, the tortoise-like speed of his ship could never give him the slightest scope to deploy any tactical notion that might come to him; the combatants would simply be locked in a slugging match and of that there could be only one winner: it would never be *Surprise*, even were she to best the heavy frigate, for her compatriots would benefit from the destruction that would be wreaked, inevitably, on his own ship in the meantime: there was no means to avoid it, no wind of sufficient strength to shift away, to flee; no, abject destruction of his ship and his men stared him directly in the face and chilled his heart.

'Sir...' the distraction was Old Jelbert once again, 'We have three more rounds left. If it pleases yer 'onour, we will bring 'em up to use agin the frigate.'

Pat gasped; here was his last throw presented to him, and not the least alternative did he possess. He turned to his old gunner of *Tenedos* days; he looked at a man whose only son had been entrusted to him; he stared into the smoke-ringed eyes of a man who bore him not the least ill will for the loss of that precious son, who had pressed him to provide a place in the crew in Falmouth, replacements for lost men - including his own son - and Pat's heart turned within him, the feeling so profound; the goodwill of this ordinary man from Falmouth had so moved him that he could not speak a single word, such was wholly beyond him. All around the guns continued to roar, shot whistled above his head, the "thud, thud" of ball striking wood - the wood of *his* ship - resonated in his ears; doubtless impacts were registering on the fragile bodies of his men at the same time. He stared at Old Jelbert and simply nodded, dumbstruck.

Jelbert summoned his two mates and hastened away. The Turk frigate had warmed her guns, her shot was flying in, the maintop yard was struck, broken, snapped, a cascade of canvas and rope falling all about the deck; the main tops'l's contribution was lost and *Surprise's* limited prospects of escape much diminished.

Jelbert returned with his mates, the three carronades facing the forty-four swiftly loaded with his special rounds. *Surprise* was at her lowest ebb ever: in the waist the fallen canvas of the maintop had stalled the guns below. Her limited motion now largely depended on the foremast, the fore course and tops'l; the loss of the maintop had allowed more wind to the foretop, and *Surprise* was champing to go on, to continue. The wind - Pat noticed - had strengthened again. For the first time all day it offered some prospect, formerly lacking, to drive the ship under a modicum of control, of direction, but now the maintop was destroyed; Pat despaired. The Turk frigate was closing, a mere cable off *Surprise*; her heavier guns would not take long - even with the lamentable prowess of her gunners - to pulverise his ship to a swift destruction. Pat's heart sank and his mind despaired.

Behind him the first carronade cracked with its customary high-pitched detonation, the orange flames roaring out, smoke billowing away to drift forward. He turned his head: it was *Surprise's* last throw. The shell, for he now thought of it as such, smashed against the high waist bulwark of the Turk forty-four, detonated on impact, showered the deck with a fiery, oleaginous flame which engulfed everything within five yards either side. In rapid succession the second and the third shells struck home; at such short range they could not conceivably miss, and the frigate erupted into flame, flickering tongues roaring up from the bottom of her sails, flying up her rigging, her yards rapidly consumed, her sails scorching, blackening, crisping, great holes appearing, and on her deck was panic. It was already too late to launch her boats, for they too were aflame; her men were leaping into the sea, the frigate rendered wholly beyond command and burning. Pat was aghast, nothing like it had he ever seen before in any engagement. The firing all around *Surprise* seemed diminished; he looked all about him: every vessel that he could see through the thick smog of gunsmoke appeared to be moving away as best they might from this titan of destruction - as the entire Turk and Egyptian fleet apparently now appeared to perceive *Surprise*. Never in his life had he seen suchlike. He leaned back momentarily against the rail: what had happened? The day was fast fading, the last few hours had flashed by in a contrasting combination of inordinately slow movement of his ship whilst time itself had seemingly vanished; so much so that the sun was visibly sinking rapidly in the western sky and Pat could not quite believe his eyes. An ambience of stunned disbelief now infested his ship: on the gun deck the firing was desultory, all targets were shifting away, had moved away, turning in the strengthening wind, no vessel - large or small - offering any worthwhile target any longer. He shook violently and uncontrollably with the onset of abject relief, wholly unconstrained: his ship, his men were saved, and by a novel weapon, yet a weapon which had endured only in folklore for centuries: Greek Fire; yet could he really believe it himself, even now? He had seen it, marvelled at it with his own eyes. It had saved the day, saved his ship and his men. Old Jelbert himself had saved them with an idea which Pat had not originally entertained himself until persuaded. Blessed Jelbert had saved them all. Pat wiped his eyes, his face, a bloody streak smeared everywhere by the back of his hand. He turned to speak with Jelbert, to offer his heartfelt congratulations and thanks, but, sadly, the day had not finished with Patrick O'Connor. He stared aft from the helm to the aftmost carronade, to where Jelbert had supervised the loading and firing of the last shells. The veteran was propped, sitting back against the stern rail; he had been struck down in the final minutes of the battle and was in obvious pain, blood all over his chest.

Pat's heart sank to new depths in that crushing instant; his blood raced through all his body; his thoughts flooded his head with searing distress. He shouted, 'Dalby! Fetch Doctor Ferguson... RUN!' Dalby vanished. Pat hastened across to Jelbert, unmoving but still breathing, more than a trickle of blood flowing from his mouth; he was still conscious, a weak facial acknowledgement as his captain knelt beside him, a barely perceptible nod. Pat put his hand on his shipmate's shoulder, no movement at all from Jelbert save for the weakest twitch of recognition. He tried to speak but such was beyond him, another gurgle of blood spat out. Pat lowered his head, put his ear to Jelbert's lips. 'Prop me up, sir...' a bloody cough, a spatter of red all over Pat's face - to which he gave no mind. Jelbert tried again, the quietest of whisper with difficulty, 'I would see the sunset for the last time...' another painful cough, more blood expelled in a gushing flood. With his own hands, Pat - as gently as he could - his hands under Jelbert's arms, pulled him up a few inches only, sat him a very little higher such that he could stare through the gap in the shattered bulwark where the Turk shot had smashed through to leave the hole: the killing blow for Old Jelbert; the violent rending of wood, the massive momentum of the splinters piercing his chest and lungs. The distant sun - visible through the damage - was low on the horizon, setting red, fiery, burning radiantly, and so much the appropriate ending for a day which Pat had not expected to endure himself, a day of intense battle which he had not expected *Surprise* to survive. Pat did not see anything of the blazing panorama; his eyes, unwavering, were fixed upon Jelbert, Pat's face unmoving, deep distress consuming him.

Simon appeared in great haste, rushing with a manic intensity to the stern rail; he crouched, staring for just a fraction of a second at Pat's blood-spattered face, at his red-sodden clothes, his face a stark picture of heartbreaking pain and utter despair. Immediately Simon switched his attentions to his patient, and recoiled, shocked, his own spirit violently stricken in that so sickening instant. Jelbert was immobile, his eyes staring vacantly, the smallest trace of a smile frozen on his face, unmoving, his eyes wide, unseeing; Mathew Jelbert had departed this life to find his beloved son in the next.

Chapter Eleven

Monday 9th May 1825   12:00   Calamata Port

During the darkness up to midnight, *Surprise* had trailed *Aris* sailing south, the brig two miles ahead and the gap constantly diminishing until Cerigo was rounded at 1 a.m. when *Surprise* finally hauled alongside, a heartwarming greeting from the four Surprises aboard her declared by all waving frantically, neither vessel heaving-to and *Aris* declaring her destination as Calamata, the port still resisting Ibrahim's approach and capture. The Greek brig, as could be seen even in the moonlight, was in a truly sorry state, long lengths of hull scarred, smashed, holed and even missing entirely at the rail; her sails were little more than rags, her rigging a precariously fragile lash-up of hasty repairs, somehow resisting complete disintegration, its endurance afforded only by the relative lack of any strain upon it in the weak wind and benign sea state, a tranquility so rare and so beneficial for the wounded and injured below, a score aboard *Surprise* suffering. Thankfully, only Old Jelbert and two other men had been killed. The bodies of both of the latter had been slipped overboard in the heat of the battle, to be cleared away from their guns, as was the tradition. Another half-dozen men were seriously wounded, but Simon believed that their wounds were not life-threatening. To Pat's mind it was an astonishing butcher's bill: so few casualties, and that during an engagement which - for much of it - he had had no doubt would see the destruction and sinking of his ship with the likely loss of all their lives. Even now he could not quite grasp the reality of their miraculous escape, for he considered that it was truly beyond rational explanation: an entire Ottoman fleet before and all about his ship, brigs and frigates aplenty, their firepower a hundredfold greater than *Surprise's*; how could it possibly be that they had survived? His thoughts returned every time to the contribution of Old Jelbert, his suggestion back on the outward voyage from Falmouth of a new kind of weapon seeming merely a wild dream, so Pat had thought, a fantasy. No one had used Greek Fire for more than a thousand years; how was an old gunner from Falmouth to recreate such? But the idea had matured in his head until the diversion to Sicily for sulphur; afterwards he had seen Jelbert - at the galley - soldering together his precious canisters - invested with the gunner's great care and attention, with diligent application, with creativity and with a deal of imagination; but Pat had paid little attention to all that beyond an encouraging nod to the veteran gunner; and then, the battle seemingly lost and *Surprise* and all her men condemned to hell and death, Jelbert had offered his life saver. Not that Pat had known that or even would have believed it, but by then the game was already up, the battle lost, the lives of all his men hanging by a precarious thread and all hope - as was clear to Pat - truly extinguished; hence there was nothing to be lost by trying out Jelbert's dream, indulging the fantasy that Pat had believed it to be, but not entirely so. Pat had never thought it would work in the fashion that Jelbert had described; he had believed the best result may have been some form of alarming effect on the enemy officers, something akin to a fear of the unknown, a strange projectile perhaps pressaging another fireship attack. He reckoned that even if it did not work, as he expected would be the case, there was nothing in that desperate minute to lose, but - before his unbelieving eyes - it *had* worked and it *had* saved *Surprise* and all her men from the destruction so imminently before them. Pat still could not quite believe it; in fact, he thought it was nothing less than a miracle. As soon as he was able he had asked his men to carry Jelbert's body below, where it remained in the coach, a service and burial at sea intended. That would have to await another day, Simon and Marston busy with the casualties.

Noon, and *Surprise* was anchoring a quarter-mile out from the port, *Aris* closer in. Local boats had been to- and fro-ing between the quay and the brig since immediately after her anchors had been dropped. Pat stared through his glass: *Eleanor* was also there, tied alongside. It pleased him greatly; he had - the reminder of it was bitter - lost several more of his men and he felt driven to be reunited with as many of the rest of them as possible. He drank deeply of his hot coffee and stared at all before him, at *Aris* -

marvelling at the massive damage she had suffered and yet survived; he gazed at *Eleanor* - thankfully she was undamaged.

He felt very fragile himself, greatly physically tired, for of rest in the night he had enjoyed none, as was usually the case after a battle, the revisiting of which he could never put out of his thoughts for days and weeks afterwards, when his mind raced with "what if?" alternative scenarios. Three of his men had been killed, a dozen more wounded. He had stepped down on two occasions in the night to visit the wounded, to speak with the surgeons, where he had found an ambience of control, of quietude and prevailing competence presented to him, for which he was profoundly grateful and which contrasted so greatly with his inspections below after the Samos battle when many more of his men had died, when dozens more had been wounded, many of them greatly more severely.

His coffee exhausted and having not the least appetite, nothing eaten for breakfast, Pat determined to go ashore, to find and speak with Duncan, Jason and his men, to converse with Mavrocordato, to discuss the gold delivered. He assumed it had been, *Eleanor* tied at the quay. He returned to his cabin at slow pace to gather his coat and hat, passed the body of Jelbert laid upon a blanket on the deck of the coach; he broke step, a jarring realisation striking hard, hesitated for a lingering, thoughtful moment, 'How I shall tell Mower of Jelbert's death, I do not know.' The lieutenant had been particularly fond of the old man, bonds of friendship having been forged during Mower's recovery from his many wounds, a mutual affinity found despite the differences in rank and standing, Jelbert always endeavouring to help the lieutenant, perhaps seeing Mower as a substitute for his son. 'It will be heartbreaking news,' he sighed and the light left his face.

On the lower deck Pat nodded to Barton, and the sole undamaged boat was lowered into the water, Pickering in command. Pat hastily joining his boatmen who pulled rapidly for the quay on his mute nod, no man caring to disturb their captain, self-evidently wholly absorbed in his thoughts. The pull to the quay took fifteen minutes, Pat oblivious to them all, the sun appearing directly overhead through the low cloud, the previously dull grey day brightening - a very minor uplift which Pat did notice and for which he was grateful.

On reaching the quay, Pat was pleased to see his own four men from *Aris*, mingling with those of the brig's men who had come ashore, their own casualties having being fetched by a schooner which had been sent out to carry them, *Aris* herself having no useable boats, both significantly damaged - near destroyed - in the battle. 'Duncan! There you are!' exclaimed Pat, seizing and shaking his friend's hand, 'Mr Jason,' he turned swiftly, 'How glorious it is to see you!' He proffered his hand too to Dalby and Mason, both of whom seemed particularly pleased to be greeted so.

Pat looked about, the men of *Eleanor* were close by. Seeing Mower, he averted his eyes, cast around to give himself a moment to think, his rather vacant gaze seizing on Mavrocordato. He approached the prince, caught his eye and handshakes were exchanged with the utmost cordiality. 'Captain O'Connor, how pleased I am to see you again. I hope that you did not suffer a great many of casualties in escaping the bay; it was the most dreadful experience... for Captain Votsis... for the men of his... the vessel, *Aris*... dreadful indeed. How we endured is a miracle, nothing less; I have never experienced the like and... I pray I never will again. How did you fare? How are you, sir?'

Pat welcomed the diversion, for he dreaded speaking with Mower, had not the heart to mention the death of Old Jelbert. 'I am tolerably well, sir, thank you; as are my men. As you say, it was the damndest thing... getting out of that place, though we lost three men killed and a dozen wounded. Thankfully it was so few... I confess I had thought we were lost, so many of the Turks all about us. It was, sir, a miracle... nothing less, of that I have not the least doubt... and I am mightily pleased to see that you survived... your Highness, vastly pleased.'

'Thank you, Captain O'Connor, thank you,' declared Mavrocordato, genuinely pleased to hear Pat's words, even more pleased that he had survived himself, for the hours before the sunset had been terrifying for every man aboard *Aris*, survival far beyond the expectations of even the greatest of optimist. Pat was one such, but of hope he too had had none before the sunset had approached. 'Would you and your officers do me the great kindness of dining with me, Captain?' asked the prince graciously.

'Most kind, sir,' Pat found himself nodding. It reminded him that he was hungry, ravenously so in that moment of acute deflation from the terror and concentration of the prior twenty-four hours.

They repaired to a homely eatery on the quayside, the patron impressed by his visitors and flattered that Prince Mavrocordato had deigned to visit his modest enterprise; he hoped he would pay the bill at the end. The food was plain, but it mattered not a jot to any man there, for none present but the *Eleanors* had believed they would survive the night. Plentiful wine was consumed as three hours passed by in a general ambience of relief, of gratitude to be alive, a winding down to something which, whilst far from normality, was a grounding, a reassurance that they were indeed alive, could enjoy the very simple pleasures of wine, companionship and conversation about much of nothing, no one caring to return to the hours of their terror. The deep gloom of the night and of the morning was slipping away just a very little, from Pat's shoulders in particular. Food and wine was sent out to Pat's boat crew, to Dalby and Mason, all of whom sat on benches, chairs and walls outside, a loud hubbub of exchanges wafting inside from them as the wine was consumed in great quantity.

Later, the patron brought the coffee in the largest of pot with many tiny cups; it was black, thick, strong - incredibly strong and much to the liking of *Surprise's* officers; minds wandered back to the present, to the purpose of *Surprise's* presence, her mission. The prince had been too diplomatic to raise the subject, had himself been content to celebrate being alive - the relief so profound; in fact, it was overwhelming, for death had hovered over them for many an hour. The coffee restoring some modicum of focus, the prince sparked the subject with his question, one seemingly innocuous but hardly so, not that such registered in the tired minds around the table. 'Captain, it is, of course, most deeply pleasing, more so than I could ever possibly describe, to see you here, in Greece once again... with your magnificent ship... with your esteemed men, friends of Greece for ever, I have no doubt... but was there...

perhaps... any particular reason to find yourself in the bay and, if I may ask, coincident with my own presence in that place?'

'Sir?' Pat was a little shaken to make a return to such a serious subject; he knew very well that Duncan had previously become something of a confidant of Mavrocordato and so glanced towards his friend.

Duncan intervened with nothing more said, 'Your Highness; our tender, *Eleanor*, is here before us, having embarked a particular cargo for your... your interests - will I say?'

Mavrocordato stared, said nothing, a rising feeling that here was something of substance, something of importance for him about to be revealed. He nodded, turned to his secretary, Grasset, before he spoke. 'Monsieur Grasset,' he turned back to the table, 'Gentlemen... with your good grace... for the briefest of moment, would you excuse me, I must step outside.' He rose from his chair with a bow to all seated, all now staring at him in astonishment, and he stepped around the table to the door and so to outside.

Pat stood up, beckoned to Duncan, then to Mower, the three men following the prince out the door, to Mavrocordato standing outside in the still bright sunshine. 'Sir... your Highness,' said Pat, 'I regret I have said nothing of this matter until now.... the events... yesterday, last night... I confess it was... it was never foremost in my mind, so tolerably distressing it has been... until... until just now, and the pleasure of your company... the past few hours has been a pleasure indeed after... after yesterday...'

Mavrocordato interjected, 'Captain O'Connor, my friend, I am wholly of your way of thinking. It has been the worst day of my life, without any doubt; indeed, I believe it is entirely conceivable that without your own presence... and that of your men, your ship... last night, then it might well have been the end of my life...'

'Sir, of course we did nothing...'

'No, Captain O'Connor, I will not have that. There were two ships flying Greek flags last night. I know, I was there, and yours was one of them. The Turk in the very least had two targets upon which to share his attentions, and had there been but one - the solitary vessel of my compatriots - then I doubt I would be here this day. My men heard ships behind them... in the darkness, exploding, being destroyed. Why, I believe, Captain O'Connor, that you and your men saved my life and those of my fellow countrymen; of that I have not the least doubt. I am here today, I am enjoying life and your company thanks be to you and your comrades. Thank you, Captain O'Connor, and please accept my profound thanks to all your men.'

Pat was much moved, for he had harboured no such thoughts of his own ship's significance; momentarily he could find no words.

Duncan intervened, 'Your Highness, that is most kind of ye to say such things, and we thank ye for your most courteous words, aye, thankee, sir... most gracious of ye.'

Mavrocordato seized his moment, 'Why were you there, Captain O'Connor, if I may press you to say? I know of the coin press, of course... from Captain Macleod, but that is surely not the reason you came to Neocastro?'

Pat, grateful for Duncan's interjection, had recovered, 'Sir, we were bringing... we have brought a cargo for you, for your cause...'

The prince was staring, his curiosity piqued; despite that he held his tongue. Duncan eventually spoke up, 'Gold, sir. Gold it is.'

'Ahhh,' Mavrocordato's mind whirred for a long minute before he spoke again, 'I am, of course, informed through... through certain circles that a measure, a generous measure of assistance was... was intended, yes indeed; but that it was entrusted to your goodself, Captain O'Connor, I did not know... and, where is this... this gold?' His last word was only whispered, the prince cautious that all on the quay might be listening in.

'Why, sir, it is here with *Eleanor*, offloaded from *Surprise* in the bay; it is here with the metal merchants and their press - no, we have the press aboard *Surprise*... the gold is here.'

Mower, acutely uncomfortable, could control himself no longer and intervened, 'It was unloaded here on the quay, sir, yesterday; the merchants insisting so... but... it is no longer here... it's gone, sir... with Perkis and Peddler... they have gone.'

'And where have they gone to, Mr Mower?' Pat barked, instinctively possessing a rising and acutely disquieting feeling that something was amiss. He stared inquisitively at his lieutenant.

'Well, sir, I don't know. They were gone this morning when we came ashore once more to see if they needed our assistance, the pigs... the ballast... *the gold* - was it so? ... being so greatly heavy.'

Silence, no word from anyone, shock; how could this be? Pat's feeble measure of comfort thus far recovered in the day was swept away in a fleeting instant; he choked, coughed. 'Where the hell could those two rogues be?'

'The lack of money is the root of all evil,' declared Pickering, though not loud.

Mavrocordato it was that spoke next and with remarkable restraint, 'Captain O'Connor, Lieutenant... Mower is it? I will ask my people to find out where they are, where they might have gone. Captain Macleod, you appear to have particular knowledge of this assistance for the Hellenic Republic... How much, pray tell, was the gold valued?'

Duncan swallowed, looked to Pat who nodded, 'Five hundred thousand pounds, sir.'

For the first time in the lamentable turn of events, the prince looked shocked and he said nothing immediately, a few seconds passing before he frowned, nodded his understanding and sprang to life, casting off the soporific influences of the dinner, the wine, the relaxation, all brutally swept away. He rushed back into the eatery and shouted loud, 'Grasset!' His secretary sprang up and hurried out to his master who had stepped outside once more.

Pat, Duncan and Mower simply stared. The prince hailed every man on the quay in the loudest of voice - in Greek which none of the Surprises could understand, though the urgency and the gist of the meaning was plain as men hastened away up and down the quay, rushing in great haste, every man shouting to all he passed, the urgent message swiftly passing to man after man until, as far as the eye could see, every person was rushing, bawling, making the most unholy commotion. The prince had seemingly lost interest in the now bewildered Surprises, and he continued to bark out orders to an arriving stream of fresh men.

Pat turned to Mower, summoning the courage left to him after the most distressing twenty-four hours in hell, 'Mr Mower...' he put his hand on Mower's shoulder, the lieutenant plainly dismayed, shocked, 'James... I regret to tell you that... that Old Jelbert is dea.... has been killed.'

For Mower the shock was simply too great; coming after the realisation that he had handed over half a million pounds to two crooks, the news that his father figure aboard the barky was dead was devastating, 'Oh my dear God...' He faltered, his legs having not yet recovered their former strength of the time before his wounds. He wobbled, and Duncan seized him. A moment or two more and Mower had regained his physical equilibrium, but of words he could find none, the effect upon him so disturbing.

They returned to the tavern, Pat ordering more coffee, and sat for another hour, waiting for any news of Perkis and Peddler being found, everyone silent in black despondency, Mower in particular looking dreadful. Jason and Reeve, who who had gone to liaise with Mavrocordato and the search parties, returned. Pat stared at Jason who simply shook his head. Outside, shouting continued all down the quay.

'Come, all of us... back to the barky,' declared Pat at last. The prince had disappeared with Grasset. Calling for Dalby and Mason, for Barton and the boat crew, Pat and all his men clambered back into the boat to return to *Surprise*, an atmosphere of frustration and rising anger overtaking everyone as the men pulled for the ship, twenty more minutes passing until they climbed aboard, plentiful anger and stunned disbelief raging in Pat's mind.

Pat stomped below to the lower deck immediately to see his wounded men, an unhappy Mower in train. All the casualties were comfortable, well bandaged, exceedingly well dosed with laudanum, and just a few murmurs escaped from those who were turning in their difficulties to find a little more comfort. Pat sized this up as he passed slowly from bow to stern, speaking a little and very quietly to those men still awake and receptive. Fifteen more minutes and he emerged up on the gun deck, somewhat the more relaxed for the visit to men in lesser health than himself. He settled in the great cabin, shouting for Murphy, the steward hastening in immediately. 'Brandy, Murphy, if you will,' said Pat abruptly, 'and... my compliments to Doctor Ferguson and Mr Macleod, and would they care to take a whet with me?'

'Yes sorr,' murmured Murphy, recognising his captain's angst and hastening away.

Pat had already drunk his first full tumbler of brandy when his friends appeared, both seeing his discomfort immediately. Pat filled their glasses but said nothing. It was for Duncan to explain the dismaying turn of events to a curious Simon, the story so incredible that he simply sat in silence absorbing the tale of the crime of the century, taking an occasional sip of the brandy, which he did not greatly care for, but he did not wish to appear to be unsociable or unsympathetic.

At the end of the amazing story, Simon took a rather larger drink from his glass, a half-minute passing whilst deep in thought, his companions staring at him. 'I thought I knew that man... Peddler... We grew up together since we both could barely walk, back home in dear Tobermory... I can scarcely believe it... If ever I would trust my last penny to anyone... it would have been that man. Why, as children we shared everything, spent our every spare hour together, played on the beach, hunted for crabs... and he, of all people, has betrayed me. Well I never... Who would have thought it?'

Pat could find no words, the personal betrayal obviously hitting Simon hard. His own vitriolic words about Peddler he did not care to utter whilst there might be any doubt about what had happened.

'Pat, could there be the slightest doubt in this matter? Perhaps Perkis and Peddler are accommodated elsewhere in the town, the... the gold securely safeguarded...' Simon knew the answer before he finished his desperate alternative.

'I regret not, old friend. The town is a small place for a foreigner... for one with a treasure such as the gold. No, it is sure that Mavrocordato's men would have found them... They are gone, the gold is gone, stolen. I regret your trust in Peddler was ill-placed.'

Simon's face was glum. He reverted to silence, his friends similarly finding nothing to add, several minutes passing, all of them nursing their brandies; and then, without any words offered, Simon stood up from the table; he looked to the door, his thoughts racing. 'Murphy! Murphy there!' he shouted. The steward, his ear to the door as usual, rushed in. 'Murphy, be so good as to give my compliments to Mr Sampays, and would he care to come to the cabin.' Murphy stood stock still, confused; never in all the years serving with Pat and Simon had the surgeon asked him to summon anyone to the cabin. He looked to Pat, who ignored him whilst disconsolately still contemplating his brandy.

'Murphy, ye rogue, did ye know what Doctor Ferguson said?' barked Duncan.

'Yes sorr... compliments to Mr Sampays... and would he care to come to the cabin... d'reckly sorr.' He hastened away.

Pat, his attention caught, spoke at last, 'Simon, why did you send for the bosun, for all love...eh?'

Simon stood up, 'Will you excuse me for just a moment, Pat... Duncan?' and he left the cabin with a fixed gaze, unblinking, nothing more said and leaving both his friends confused. He encountered Murphy returning with Sampays as he exited the coach, and he took them both in train, ushering them down to the lower deck with harsh words, then on to the orlop, urgency in both his step and his voice, on further and eventually to the hold.

In the cabin, Pat and Duncan remained mystified. His curiosity getting the better of him after a few minutes, Pat stood up. 'This is a right stinking kettle of fish, Duncan.'

'Aye, for sure it has hit Simon hard, nae doubt of that. The damn rogue... Peddler, running away with all the money, nae care for his auld friend. I confess I never liked Perkis... a shifty swine, aye, indeed.'

'Damnable blackguards... damn them to hell! I am going to see what the devil is going on.' At that instant Simon returned, Murphy grunting with displeasure behind him and accompanied by the bosun, the two men sharing the heavy load of a ballast pig, the bosun also, with difficulty, tenuously clutching a chisel. They could hold the weight of the pig no longer and let it slip to the deck with a resonating heavy crash, men rushing from the gun deck to see what disaster had happened, the cabin filling with Mower, Pickering, Codrington, Barton, Prosser and seven curious hands extending themselves permission to enter.

'What the hell is this!' shouted an angry Pat, for his nerves could stand no more.

Simon nodded to Sampays, and the bosun offered his explanation, 'It was the pigs, sir... in Falmouth... that is to say, I wasn't 'appy with their stowage...' Blank stares all round, Pat struggling to believe, to understand what he had just heard, and Sampays resumed. 'Well, we was down a strake or two at the bow, sir... I was complaining about it to one or two of the 'ands...' Sampays swallowed hard, 'and Doctor Ferguson was listening... I said them pigs under the companionway was dam... awful 'eavy, sir... seemed much 'eavier than most others... an' Doctor Ferguson... he said to shift some of 'em to the back o' the ship... that is shift 'em aft like.. an' put lighter ones back in their place. Well... we did, sir... an' the matter was all a-tanto, the bow no longer down at all, ne'er an inch in it... sir.'

'Mr Sampays, why then am I staring at one of these accursed ingots of ballast, pray tell?' demanded Pat, nothing more than the vaguest, the most unsettling and hazy drift towards something he could not quite settle on but registering within his tired mind, and realising that, perhaps, it was wise to rein in his fast-rising temper, for such was extremely unpleasant - if rare - to behold.

'Well, 'ere be one o' them there two dozen pigs we shifted aft, sir... one o' them 'eavy sods... ingots - excuse me, sir.'

Pat simply stared, the brandy fogging his thoughts, his energy evaporating like his dwindling patience; Duncan it was who had grasped the substance of the matter. He seized the chisel that Sampays still clutched, grabbed the hammer tucked into Murphy's belt, stooped down to the deck and smashed hard upon the pig ballast with a loud clang that resonated throughout much of the ship as the chisel skidded to score a deep, deep scratch near the whole length of the ingot. Every man in the cabin, yet more arriving in haste, all craned down to see what was happening, a dozen men bunching behind a still crouching Duncan.

Pat stared down himself as a loud collective gasp issued from the assembly; he could not believe his eyes, 'RED HELL AND BLOODY DEATH!' The scratch shone bright, glistened yellow.

Tuesday 10th May 1825   12:00

Surprise heaved-to ten miles south of Calamata, the customary northerly *Meltemi* strengthening a little from the inconsequential breeze of the morning, the braces slackened and the sails flapping uselessly, edges whipping in the gusts, the frigate rolling very gently on the mildest of swell. The ambience aboard the frigate was deeply muted; all morning every man had gone about his business with few words said, the departure from Calamata one of strangely mixed feelings. Mavrocordato and his entourage as well as the men of *Aris* had all offered the warmest of farewells, the prince also being exceedingly grateful with his words after his recovery from stupefying astonishment, the gold having been carried ashore by *Eleanor* from *Surprise*.

Pat took his sighting in a sky of unbroken bright blue, not a cloud in sight in any direction; the fierce heat of the day was relieved by pleasing wind breaths, no more than that. His sextant taken back to the cabin, Pat stepped in a measured slow pace, deep in thought, out through the coach to the gun deck and looked all about him. All his men were standing there before him, save for the wounded, every man expectant; not wholly silent but the chatter was muted, respectful. All his men were attired in their best slops, washed and pressed as best as could be done aboard the frigate, and the Wesleyans amongst them had adorned themselves with their purple scarves, as was customary for funerals.

Michael Marston stood ready behind his makeshift pulpit, a stack of sea chests over which was draped an old sailcloth. Alongside him, on both sides, were all Pat's officers: Macleod, Pickering, Codrington, Mower, Jason; only Simon was absent, still below attending his patients. All the warrant officers stood there, few that they were, at the front of his men: Prosser, Sampays and Tizard.

Pat stepped alongside his chaplain, the two exchanging a few whispered words. Murphy caught Pat's eye and disappeared in haste down the companionway steps. Pat stared for a few minutes at the familiar sea of faces, at men many of whom he had known for twenty years, men who had served with him aboard *Tenedos* long before *Surprise*. He nodded near indiscernibly to his officers, to his warrant officers, coughed to clear his throat. A noisy disturbance at the companionway and Murphy re-emerged with Simon, both men hastening to stand to the side of the other officers. Pat's eyes wandered, up, up beyond the masts, yards and sails, his thoughts as far-ranging as his eyes, the subject of the gathering a farewell to a man who had declared that up was where he was going; up, and with a determined purpose. 'Would that he might indeed be reunited with his son,' thought Pat. He looked down towards the open gun port, to Old Jelbert's body on the deck, shrouded in sailcloth and wrapped within a hammock, two heavy shot at his feet. Lacking much of a familiarity with the scriptures, he searched for the words with which to begin. His personal distress was very evident: his eyes were reddened where they were not black, for no man had succeeded in cleaning off the engrained powder and smoke from the great guns of two days ago with what precious little time and resources were to be found aboard ship.

A discreet cough and Michael Marston nodded to him. Pat could still find no words, and so he simply nodded an acquiescence to the chaplain, which was entirely understood. Marston began to speak, his voice steady, unwavering, 'We are here to bid farewell to one of our dearest comrades... a man who all of us truly treasured, a dear friend and comrade... Mathew Jelbert was a man to whom any one of us could turn to... a man whose ear was always receptive to any request, great or small. I myself recall him from my own early days... I was aboard *Tenedos*, in the South Atlantic. I was suffering greatly... a storm of such ferocity that I was utterly incapable of movement for its several days. During that time...' Marston halted, a particularly loud blowing of Mower's nose was intended to disguise the plentiful flow of tears as he wiped his eyes. The chaplain resumed, 'During that time, Mathew Jelbert devoted all his time to care for me... until I had recovered. I will never forget him.'

'Hear hear,' echoed softly throughout the ensemble.

Marston continued, 'In more recent times, our dear departed friend has been helping another of our comrades, Mr Mower here, who was gravely injured last year in our battle to save Samos from the Turk invaders. As with myself, so with Mr Mower... the unstinting generosity of Mathew Jelbert was without any limit.'

'Hear hear,' again from the men.

'Before we bury our dear friend today, Mr Mower has asked if he may say a few words.'

A loud chorus of approval echoed from all the men, and Mower, who was himself extremely popular, hastily stuffed his handkerchief into his pocket and stepped across to the makeshift pulpit. He clutched a small piece of paper. 'I will always be grateful to Mathew Jelbert... When I was recovering... yet so weak and fearing for my place aboard the barky... he encouraged me to never give up... I never did so... and I will always remember him for that, for his kindly attentions... I will miss him...' Another general groundswell of concurrence came back from the men, Mower wiping his sleeve across his face. 'No words of mine can better say my feelings today than those of an ancient poet, Catallus. I would like to read his words today... before we make our final farewell to my dear friend... Mathew Jelbert.' Before continuing, Mower had no choice but to make recourse to his handkerchief, his profuse tears plain to all. Every man remaining absolutely mute, he gathered his strength, looked to his shipmates, ignored the unceasing tears, and with conviction and steel he began to speak,

> 'Through many nations and many seas have I come;
> To carry out these wretched funeral rites, brother;
> That at last I may give you this final gift in death,
> And that I might speak in vain to silent ashes,
> Since fortune has borne you, yourself, away from me.
> Oh, poor brother... snatched unfairly away from me;
> Now, though, even these, which from antiquity and
> in the custom of our parents, have been handed down,
> a gift of sadness in the rites;
> Accept them, flowing with many brotherly tears;
> And for eternity, my brother, hail and farewell.'

GLOSSARY, for pressed shipmates

Bargeman...............weevil (usually in the bread and biscuit)
Blunties ....Old Scots term for stupid fellows
Boggies....................Irish country folk
Bombard..................Mediterranean two-masted vessel, ketch
Bower......................bow anchor
Boxty.......................traditional Irish potato pancake
Breeks......................Scots term for trousers or breeches
Bumbo.....................'pirates' drink; rum, water, sugar, and nutmeg
Burgoo.....................oatmeal porridge
Captains' Thins........Carr's water crackers, a "refined ship's biscuit"
Caudle.....................thickened, sweetened alcoholic drink like eggnog
Clegs........................Scots term for large, biting flies
Crubeens..................boiled pig's feet
Dreich......................Old Scots for cold, wet, miserable weather
Drookit....................Scots term for drenched
Etesian.....................strong, dry, summer, Aegean north winds
Felucca.....................small sailing boat, one or two sails of lateen rig
Fencibles..................the Sea Fencibles, a naval 'home guard' militia
Flat...........................a person interested only in themself
Flux..........................inflammatory dysentery
Frumenty.................a pudding made with boiled wheat, eggs and milk
Gomerel...................a stupid or foolish person
The Groyne..............La Coruña in north-west Spain
Hallion.....................a scoundrel
Hoy..........................small (e.g. London-Margate passengers) vessel
Jollies.......................Royal Marines
Kedgeree..................a dish of flaked fish, rice and eggs
Kentledge.................56lb ingots of pig iron for ship's ballast
Laudanum...............a liquid opiate, used for medicinal purposes
Lobscouse................beef stew, north German in origin
Marchpane..............marzipan
Marshalsea..............19th century London debtors' prison
Mauk.......................Scottish for maggot
Meltemi ....Greek and Turkish name for the Etesian
Millers.....................shipboard rats
Mistico....................similar to the Felucca sailing vessel
Nibby......................ship's biscuit
Puling......................whining in self pity
Scrovies ....worthless, pressed men
Solomongundy........a stew of leftover meats
Snotties....................midshipmen
Stingo......................strong ale
Treacle-dowdy........a covered pudding of treacle and fruit

Trubs......................truffles
Yellow jack...............Yellow fever (or flag signifying outbreak)

I hope that you have enjoyed reading this book in my series *"The continuing voyages of HMS Surprise"*.

You can find out more about my books by visiting my website: **https://alanlawrenceauthor.wordpress.com/**

Alan Lawrence